◆━━━━━━━━━━━━━◆

Rise of the TaiGethen

◆━━━━━━━━━━━━━◆

ELVES
BOOK 2

Rise of the TaiGethen

ELVES
BOOK 2

James Barclay

GOLLANCZ

LONDON

The right of James Barclay to be identified as the author
of this work has been asserted by him in accordance with
the Copyright, Designs and Patents Act 1988.

First published in Great Britain in 2012 by
Gollancz
An imprint of the Orion Publishing Group
Orion House, 5 Upper St Martin's Lane, London WC2H 9EA
An Hachette UK Company

A CIP catalogue record for this book is available
from the British Library

ISBN 978 0 575 08520 6 (Cased)
ISBN 978 0 575 08521 3 (Trade Paperback)

1 3 5 7 9 10 8 6 4 2

Typeset at The Spartan Press Ltd,
Lymington, Hants

Printed and bound at CPI Group (UK) Ltd
Croydon CRO 4YY

The Orion Publishing Group's policy is to use papers that
are natural, renewable and recyclable products and made
from wood grown in sustainable forests. The logging and
manufacturing processes are expected to conform to the
environmental regulations of the country of origin.

www.jamesbarclay.com
www.orionbooks.co.uk

For Oliver, who completes our family

Prologue

For a hundred and twenty years, the forest bled unchecked.
Serrin of the ClawBound

They stood together on the cliffs surrounding the Ultan and stared out across the rainforest. Helpless anger set Auum's teeth to grind and his body to shiver. The scale of the desecration was so vast it was hard to comprehend.

In the early years following the human invasion, when the elves were desperately weak and scattered throughout the rainforest, their enemy had been ruthless in their exploitation of the resources they had come to steal. The damage was appalling, perhaps irreversible. Next to Auum, Serrin was trembling and his panther was nuzzling him, trying to comfort him.

'Why do you put yourself through this?' asked Auum.

'Because you must understand what you allowed to happen. It is my duty to make you see.'

The rainforest had been obliterated for a full two miles from the borders of Ysundeneth. Magic had been used to clear the undergrowth. The devastation to the west had only been halted by swamp and cliff, but then the humans had turned south and used the River Ix instead.

Roads followed the river for over seventy miles and barges pushed yet further up, carrying slave gangs into the heart of the forest to log wherever the banks offered a landing point. The river was choked with the trunks of great old trees outside the lumber mills of Ysundeneth, which worked day and night.

Ships departed every day, taking Beeth's precious wood north to Balaia, returning packed with more tools to commit yet greater atrocities at a yet greater pace. Auum knew it was the same outside Calaius' second and third cities. The forest was under attack across the northern coast. And where the trees still stood, the most valuable plants and flowers were harvested before the axes began to fall.

Where the elves had always farmed the forest the humans destroyed it without a shrug, for reasons which held a horrible logic. An elf must necessarily look forward hundreds of years and would always desire to look upon the beauty of the canopy. A human, whose life was over in a blink, required no such foresight.

Humans saw the vastness of the canopy and an endless supply of timber. They failed to realise the ramifications of harvesting so much of it and apparently cared less. Elves knew that the balance, once critically undone, was gone for ever. It had not happened yet, but that time would come. Not this year, not the next, nor in the next decade. But it would come.

And so Serrin of the ClawBound had brought Auum to see what he knew in his heart but did not want to admit.

'We are helpless to stop them,' said Auum. 'We are so few, and the cost our enslaved pay for our resistance is so great.'

'So you will sit by and watch the humans destroy our world. You. Arch of the TaiGethen. Sworn to defend your country, your people and your *faith*.'

Auum sighed. Serrin had been running the rainforest with panthers and the other ClawBound for a hundred years, and it had taken a huge toll on his pure elven side. His reasoning seemed affected; his vocabulary was diminished, and his faith was linked far more closely to Tual and Beeth than it was to Yniss.

'You know it's not that simple. My responsibility is the survival of the elven race. I have to look ahead, beyond the present and the crimes I am forced to witness. We can't defeat man, not yet. We have to build our strength in combat and magic. I hate it, but it's reality.

'Of course we could delay man's rape of our forest. But for every man we kill, an innocent elf dies in agony in Ysundeneth. I am responsible for those lives, just as I am for those elves who remain free.'

Serrin regarded him evenly and shrugged. 'When the cities are empty of slaves, who will they visit their revenge upon?'

'Look beyond your hunting grounds,' said Auum sharply. 'When the cities are empty of slaves, there will be too few elves to rebuild our people. We need them and the Katurans or we will die out.'

'The Ynissul are immortal.'

Auum faced Serrin and the sadness that swept him was akin to grief. 'You do not believe that the Ynissul can hope to survive alone.

You were a Silent Priest, an adept of the harmony, a lover of every elven thread.'

'Look at our forest,' said Serrin. 'Look at the pace of desecration. The humans will kill us one way or another. There will come a day when your words will no longer hold the ClawBound at bay. I hope you will be ready to stand by us when that day comes.'

Auum watched Serrin and his panther move smoothly away to the narrow paths down to the forest floor. Night was falling and Auum watched as it covered the enormity of man's crimes. He remained, and prayed to Yniss for guidance, until the sun kissed the land once again and recoiled at the horror it touched.

Chapter 1

After a hundred and fifty years, the bleeding had to be staunched.
                                            Serrin of the ClawBound

Auum dropped to a crouch, a curt hand gesture bidding his Tais do likewise. Down here in the leaf litter, dense scrub and brush, the echoes of animals high in the rainforest canopy were muted. Alien sounds met the ear unsullied.

Auum turned back towards the temple at Aryndeneth. The sound he'd heard had been distant and none of the five who faced him had registered it. They were all promising adepts and soon to be placed in active TaiGethen cells for the first time. All were on course to be cell leaders in a decade, maybe two.

Auum studied their faces while they awaited his words, their eyes shining with the honour he bestowed on them with his presence as their teacher. Their admiration embarrassed him but they listened well. Their camouflage had been painted on their faces in the correct manner; in deference to Yniss, father of them all, to Beeth, god of root and branch and to the rituals of the TaiGethen warrior.

None of them displayed fear. Auum knew why: because they were with him. With Auum, who had faced the Garonin and survived. Auum, who had found Takaar and fought by his side to free the elves of Ysundeneth. Auum, the Arch of the TaiGethen. Immortal.

'But not invincible,' he murmured. They should be as scared as he was. 'What do you hear?'

Each of them strained to detect the sound their tutor had already heard. He knew what they would be doing: filtering out the sounds of Tual's creatures as best they could. His students must also ignore the breeze, the fall of leaves and the sound of rainwater dripping to the forest floor. The sounds that remained gave Auum reason to shudder.

'It is too big to be a bird,' said Elyss, the best of them. She was heading for greatness. 'And there are many of them.'

'How many?' asked Auum.

Elyss cocked her head once more. 'Twenty.'

'Twenty-two,' corrected Auum. He turned to the others. 'Excellent. Do you concur?'

Three of the TaiGethen students nodded.

'I am shamed that I can hear nothing of this,' said Malaar, letting his gaze drop.

Auum smiled. 'There is no shame. But there will be combat. Elyss can hear mages on their wings of shade. They are coming to Aryndeneth, and we might just get there before them. Five-pace spread, attack on sight. Tais, we move.'

With every pace Auum could feel the enemy closing, as if they were walking up the length of his back. The pace of the TaiGethen was matched only by the panther under the canopy. Above them, though, where the dense vegetation and the grasping vines and roots were mere myth and rumour, the humans' speed was unhindered.

High in the upper reaches of the canopy, bird calls charted waypoints in the enemy's progress. Hawk eagle cries pierced the clear sky. Toucan bills clacked out a staccato message of threat and fell silent when the shadows fell across their steepling perches.

In the mid-level, the melodic calls of gibbons took on a desperate quality as they tried to reaffirm their territory against the approach of a new and terrifying invader. Everywhere, bird, beast and lizard shrilled, growled or chittered. Each sound was a call to hide or flee.

Auum looked to his right. Elyss flitted through the dense undergrowth. Her footfalls were light, the passage of her body barely disturbing bush or branch, her breathing measured and calm. And when the mages passed overhead, with the TaiGethen still a hundred paces short of the temple apron, Auum saw her react, glance skywards and increase her pace.

She felt it all. She was tuned to all that surrounded her and her mind was open to the forest, each message received through her ears, her feet and soaking into her skin. Elyss was the future. More and more like her were being born. They were the TaiGethen of tomorrow.

'They are ahead of us,' said Auum, his voice carrying to his people and no further. 'But they must still descend through the canopy.'

'We must call to warn the temple guard,' said Tiiraj from Auum's left.

'They should need no warning and the humans must not know of our approach.' Auum reached down to his belt. 'Jaqrui pouches open. Choose your targets carefully.'

Auum slid between the balsa and fig trees that guarded the approach to Aryndeneth, the Earth Home. Growing tightly together, bound by vine and liana and by ivy which trailed to snag at clothes and grab at careless feet, they were impenetrable to any man without a blade.

Fifty paces out, Auum could see the walls of the domed temple glinting in the last of the sunlight before the clouds closed overhead and the rains came again. Gold and green and covered with creepers and climbers, the temple walls were a sight to gladden the heart of any elf fortunate enough to lay eyes upon them. Sanctuary.

Auum and his Tais would break from the rainforest at the right-hand edge of the temple apron. With every pace they closed, Auum could see and hear more. Figures were running from left to right, towards the temple. Other figures darted into cover positions: the Al-Arynaar. Auum felt a small measure of comfort on seeing them; his work training the temple guard had not been in vain.

Twenty paces out, the rainforest shook with explosions and was lashed with sheets of blue fire. Debris flew into the canopy. Splinters of stone and wood sliced into trunk, branch and leaf, whining and whistling through the air towards Auum and his Tais. Auum threw himself prone behind the bole of a balsa tree as the lethal hail scoured Beeth's root and branch around him.

As quickly as it had begun it was gone and an eerie quiet descended, punctuated only by the cries of wounded animals and the screams of terrified elves within the temple. Auum moved smoothly back to his feet, noting the sound of his five Tai rising with him.

'Focus your anger,' he whispered.

The TaiGethen moved soundlessly onto the temple apron. Men crowded it. Men with swords were running towards the sealed temple doors, which still held but bore the scars of the first wave of spells. Others flanked them, driving towards the Al-Arynaar. Behind the human warriors, mages strode across the stone apron, defiling the sacred ground of Yniss with every footfall.

Above the back of the temple, Auum saw more mages descend on the village that nestled in its shadow. Each pair carried a warrior between them. He drew a sharp breath. An arrow flew from the left of the temple, taking a mage in the throat. Immediately, three others turned and opened their hands. Deep blue orbs shot with white and red threads flashed away.

Auum saw the Al-Arynaar nock another arrow and shoot at the nearest of the orbs. The shaft vaporised halfway towards its target and, in the next breath, the orbs struck the archer, the corner of the temple and the forest adjoining it alike before flame exploded from them, turning wood, flesh and bone to ash.

More spells sprang from the open palms and outstretched fingers of mages. Fire crashed into the doors of the temple, making the timbers groan. Flames caught hold. The TaiGethen could feel Yniss roar his fury through the tremors in the ground.

Auum attacked.

His feet whispered across the apron. His Tais were with him, spreading across the stone to strike. Auum chose a jaqrui from his pouch, cocking his arm and throwing on the run. The crescent blade whipped away, holes along its length catching the air and singing its mourning wail. Mages turned their heads, just as he needed them to. His target saw his death coming the instant before it struck him on the bridge of his nose and sliced into both eyes.

Five more jaqruis flew, striking unarmoured bodies, carving into hands and arms raised to protect faces, and thudding deep into guts and chests. Human blood spattered across the stone. Human voices were raised in alarm. Warriors turned to run back to their magical charges.

Auum sprinted across the open space. Four mages were down. Eight remained, facing their assailants. Auum identified four actively casting. The others were lost to panic and posed no imminent danger. To Auum's right, Elyss had drawn a blade. She powered into a pair of casting mages. Her sword took the ear from one and drove on down into his shoulder, as her elbow jabbed up into the throat of the other.

Auum took two more paces and leapt, his left leg straight, right leg cocked beneath him. His foot smashed into the head of his target, poleaxing him. Still airborne, he drew both blades from their back-mounted scabbards, drew his left leg back and hacked down to his left and right, feeling both blades bite into flesh.

Auum landed amidst the humans. Malaar landed on one knee next to him, spinning and stabbing into an enemy's groin, then surged to his feet and slashed one blade through the neck of a second, then buried the other in the gut of a third.

Auum nodded his approval and turned to face the warriors. He cursed. Flames were rising from the village behind the temple. Screams echoed beneath the canopy. The warriors were hacking open the temple doors. The spells had cracked the timbers, melted the hinges and lock, and now men were trying to do the rest.

'Elyss!' called Auum. 'My right. Tais, head around the temple. Clear the village.'

Auum ran towards the doors, seeing the six warriors drag them wide enough to get inside while the flames ate at the ruined timbers. Elyss was at his right shoulder. Auum slipped through the doors, his nose catching the sick stench of magic and fire, and into the cool darkness of the temple.

Beneath the great dome, the statue of Yniss knelt by the harmonic pool as it had done for over a thousand years. The waters still ran from beneath Yniss' outstretched hand, their sound melodic and beautiful. But it was eclipsed by the harsh shouts of men and the desecrating slap of their boots on the blessed stone. The warriors had split up to run around both sides of the pool, heading for the passage-way that led through the temple to the rear doors and out into the village.

Auum could see priests and Ynissul adepts in the shadows, helpless and frightened, trapped between the men coming around the pool towards them and those behind them in the village. Auum ran for the edge of the pool. He planted his left foot and leapt into the air, tucking and turning his body in a forward roll, blades held away from him. He unwound in flight and landed soundlessly between the two groups of warriors, a blade held out towards each trio.

'You will travel no further,' he hissed.

At least one of them understood him. His response was a laugh.

'One elf cannot stop us,' he said in passable common elvish.

The men ran on. Auum stepped up towards the passage to meet them as Elyss flew through the air feet first and thumped into the left-hand group, bringing two down and sending the third stumbling into the wall.

'One?' said Auum. 'A TaiGethen is never alone.'

Auum left Elyss to her work, hefted his blades and waited. The remaining three men came on, fuelled by the sight of their comrades dying. Their desire to reach their friends made them careless. A blade swung out waist-high. Auum ducked beneath it, coming up in its wake and stabbing the warrior through the centre of his gut, leaving the blade where it stuck, buried to its hilt.

The man stumbled back. Auum moved into the half-pace of space and reversed his other blade into the back of the second warrior's neck. The third turned, belatedly tracking Auum's movement. Auum swung round. His right fist whipped out, smashing the warrior's nose. The human brought his blade to ready, blood pouring over his mouth, his eyes betraying his surprise and pain.

For a heartbeat Auum considered letting him be the one to live and carry the story back to his masters.

'But it should be one who can fly,' he said.

Auum swayed outside a clumsy strike and calmly slid his blade into the warrior's chest, then turned from the falling body and retrieved his second blade. He cleaned both on the clothes of the dead and sheathed them. Elyss had finished her three and was moving up the passageway. Auum ran after her, gesturing priests and adepts aside.

'Stay under cover. Wait for my word that it is safe.'

Auum and Elyss ran for the rear doors, passing chambers, scripture rooms and sleeping cells, most with elves hiding within them. They were still ten yards from the doors when they burst open, a flood of workers, civilians, adepts . . . of ordinary elves spilling in, climbing over each other to escape the enemy at their backs.

The air chilled and Auum cursed.

'Clear!' he yelled. He shoved Elyss hard, sending her tumbling into a contemplation chamber and diving after her. A gale of harrowing cold howled down the passageway. Elven screams were cut off as if a door had been slammed shut against them.

Auum shivered and rolled onto his back. Ice rimed the door of the chamber and lay thick on the floor and ceiling of the passageway. It climbed the walls to create a frozen blue tunnel. Detonations outside shook the temple, where more screams filled the air. Inside the temple, the silence told its own story.

Auum pushed himself to his feet and ran out, slithering on the ice-bound floor. He dropped to a crouch, scrabbling with hand and foot to make headway towards the doors and the village. Elyss followed more slowly. Ahead of him, the passage was clogged with the bodies of defenceless Ynissul elves frozen in the attitudes of their slaughter. Hands outstretched for help, mouths open in screams of brief agony.

Beyond them, mages stood framed in the doorway. They were

casting. Auum tried to increase his pace but the ice on the floor gave him precious little purchase. He snatched a jaqrui from his belt and threw it backhanded. The blade whispered away, thudding into a mage's legs. He cried out and fell. The three others opened their palms to cast, and Auum commended his soul to Yniss.

A shadow passed across the doors; the castings were never released. A figure whipped in from the left. One mage was decapitated, his head bouncing and sliding across the ice of the temple floor. The head came to rest at Auum's feet, its eyes staring into his, its final confusion fading away.

Auum spat on the face and lifted his gaze to the doors. The elf who stood there had a wildness about his expression that he would never lose. Nor would he lose the haunted look in his eyes. Swords were dripping blood in his hands, and at his feet human mages were bleeding and dying.

'You took your time,' said Auum. 'Perhaps a little more practice is required.'

The elf ignored him, muttered to himself and knelt at the body of a still-breathing mage.

'You will take the tale of your failure to your masters,' he said. 'But only after you have told me what I desire to know.'

Auum shook his head and began to walk towards the door. He felt Elyss come to his side. Together, they moved past the elf and into the burning village.

'Is that . . . ?' asked Elyss.

'Yes,' said Auum. 'It is Takaar. Or what's left of him.'

Auum led Elyss into the fresh rainfall to witness the carnage the human magic had created.

Chapter 2

The journey from Silent Priest to ClawBound is short in distance but infinite in solace for the soul. A ClawBound will always remember. That is the price he must pay for the joy of genuine union with the most glorious of Tual's creatures.

From *ClawBound and Silent*, by Lysael, High Priest of Yniss

Auum indulged in a moment of pride. His TaiGethen students had reacted like veterans. They had killed without error and saved the lives of dozens of innocents. They moved through the village now, readying the dead for removal to the Hallows of Reclamation. They offered comfort to the injured and grieving and administered balms to wounds where they could.

Fires still burned in a few houses. The magical flame was difficult to extinguish but with Gyal's tears falling they would spread no further. Auum walked back into the temple. The ice had melted quickly, leaving the stones wet and slick. Every chamber held priests at prayer and he could hear plainsong coming from within the dome. It was a dirge for the dead and a chant for the vengeance of Shorth to be visited upon the souls of the enemy.

Back in the dome, Auum walked around the pool and past the priests and adepts kneeling at its edges to sing. A lone figure was standing at the burned, sundered doors of the temple. Auum joined her and followed her gaze as it travelled over the bloodstained apron, still littered with the bodies of human mages.

'I am sorry we were not here to save more of your people, Onelle,' said Auum.

Onelle gave a dry, mirthless laugh and placed a hand on Auum's arm.

'Without you, many more would be dead and the plight of all elves would be that much worse.'

Auum looked at Onelle and saw the haunting knowledge in her

eyes. She was an Ynissul who had suffered so much and in whom so much faith and trust was placed. She was the first and most advanced practitioner of the Il-Aryn, One Earth, the name given to the fledgling elvish magic. It had aged even her and she was Ynissul, immortal. Grey dominated her hair, which had thinned, giving her a taut and severe look when she brushed it back from her face.

Onelle's face was deeply lined and her eyes, still green and rich with the health of her soul, were edged with darkness by the weight of a task which kept her from proper rest. But her mind was strong and her desire to learn and to impart that learning had grown in the hundred and fifty years since her escape from Ysundeneth and the awakening of the power within her.

'How many did we lose?' asked Auum.

Onelle took a shuddering breath. 'We have counted fourteen adepts. More are gravely wounded. I suppose we should consider ourselves lucky that our orientation class is in the field. Those twenty-eight were saved by their absence.'

Onelle let her head drop. Auum knew she was crying but he needed to know more.

'What is left of the development and practitioner classes?'

Onelle shook her head. 'Gone. And worse, we knew this would happen.'

'What?'

'We knew they would find us if we tested our powers. They can smell the use of the Il-Aryn. They can track it like a panther tracks a deer in the depths of night. We'd been so careful until now.'

'You can't blame yourself. You have no choice but to test.'

Onelle stared up at Auum and the smile she forced through her tears broke his heart. 'And we found ourselves so terribly wanting, didn't we?'

'I don't understand.'

'We were trying to generate a shield against magical attack,' said Onelle. 'I was so confident. We had worked so hard. And then they came and cast a single spell and our shield crumbled. They all died.'

'Who?' asked Auum.

'The practitioner class. All of them but me. Along with all of the development class, who were watching and learning and were caught in the blast. So much work, so much time and it was all for nothing. All wasted. I'm so sorry.'

'No effort you make is ever wasted,' said Auum, though a dead weight sat in his chest at her words. 'We can rebuild.'

'Those still trapped in Ysundeneth don't have the time. We all know that.'

'They are in no danger if they cause no trouble.'

'They're slaves!' Onelle's voice rang harshly from the temple walls. 'We swore to free them.'

'And we will. Yniss will guide us. Don't lose your faith.'

'Auum, you don't understand.' Onelle was laughing through her tears. It was a bitter sound. 'We have been learning how to harness the Il-Aryn for almost a hundred and fifty years, ever since the soul of Ix was awakened in some of us. And in all that time we are nowhere. Don't you see?

'All ten of the practitioner class were building the same casting. One human mage blew it apart, and killed them all in a heartbeat. We have no power, no knowledge, which can possibly stand against human magic. It will be centuries before we can stand with you and defend you from their fire and their ice and all the evil they can bring to bear.

'By then, the elves will be lost. Gone or dying out. What is happening at Katura is a symptom of a disease that will sweep us all away. Humans will rule Calaius.'

Auum bridled. Onelle's words had laid bare the scale of the gulf between human and elven magic and ripped the veil of hope from his eyes. But despite that he would not turn meekly from his task.

'No human will rule my country,' he said. 'Katura has slipped into a malaise born of a yearning for things long gone. It is you and I and those we lead who must secure the future of our people. You cannot fall prey to despair. There is always something that can be done. Accelerate your learning. I will accelerate the training of my students.

'What can I do to help you?'

Onelle wiped at her eyes. 'I'm sorry. It is hard. All that effort, and they snuffed us out so easily. All our confidence and belief in our ability is exposed as a sham.'

'I can promise you that TaiGethen will once again stand at Aryndeneth as sentinels against desecration. The Al-Arynaar will stand with us. No elf will die at this temple again.'

Onelle nodded. 'At least those of us still alive will sleep better tonight. But there are so few of us now. We must find more adepts. More potential we can explore.'

Auum watched Onelle begin to think again and with those thoughts came hope. 'Then we will find more, and we will send them to you.'

'How do you do it?' asked Onelle.

'Do what?'

'Keep your spirit so strong and your soul free of doubt.'

Auum frowned and for a moment could not frame an answer. 'Because I have never questioned my faith or the virtue of my mission. This is our land, our rainforest. I will not rest until all our people are free and man's stench has been scoured from every corner. Calaius was given to us by Yniss. No human can take it from us.'

A movement in the canopy at the far edge of the apron caught his eye. It was nothing but a shadow against the light, invisible to all but the sharpest of rainforest predators. He began to run, his last words to Onelle spoken over his shoulder.

'Believe and we cannot fail. Tend to your people.'

Auum's heart was beating hard in his chest. It had been the merest glint of an eye but he knew who it was, what it was, he had seen.

'Stop!' called Auum. 'Speak to me. Tell me what you felt. Please. You are ClawBound but you are still an elf. Stop!'

But the shadow was gone. Elf and panther had melted away into the canopy.

'Serrin!' called Auum. 'It's you, isn't it? Please help me. I am Auum. Remember me.'

Auum stood at the edge of the apron, his emotions choking his thoughts and a brief hope of contact quickly extinguished. He stared into the forest, hoping against all reason to see Serrin walking towards him.

'Damn,' he said. He frowned. 'What were you doing here?'

Auum turned back towards the temple. Elyss and Tiiraj were trotting towards him.

'Where are the others?'

'Malaar is working with the priests, preparing the dead for reclamation. Wirann and Gyneev are tending the wounded. A lot of burns. We don't have enough balm.'

'The priests will provide. How many of the injured will survive?' asked Auum.

'How far can a TaiGethen jump?' responded Tiiraj. 'Olmaat survived burns that should kill any elf. It depends less on the wound, more on the spirit and the will.'

'That is not an answer. How many have burns that should kill them? How many should live because their wounds are superficial?'

Tiiraj jerked his head back towards the temple. 'I think you should come and make that determination for yourself.'

Auum shrugged and gestured for them to precede him, and they trotted into the cool of the temple. The stone flags surrounding the harmonic pool were covered with wounded adepts and priests. The stink of charred flesh was in the air and the dome echoed mournfully with moans of pain.

Auum walked slowly around the dome, kneeling by each victim to speak words of comfort or join the prayers when the priests' ministrations could not save their patients.

At the end of his circuit, Auum understood why Tiiraj had been so uncertain. He had seen those with hideous wounds across their faces, clothes burned into their bodies and hands scorched almost to the bone whose eyes shone with a fury and an energy that would drive their survival. And he had seen those with relatively light injuries but for whom the shock of the attack threatened to steal their souls away to Shorth's embrace.

'Tais,' he said, 'let us leave these fine elves to their recovery. Yniss bless you all and return you to health and your studies. We will pray for you and will be honoured to stand with you on the day we take back our land from men and free our people.'

Auum led his students outside, signalling Onelle to join them.

'I need to know about Takaar,' he said.

Onelle's expression was answer enough. Auum felt a little strength leave him.

'If he's proving a negative influence, I can organise to move him.'

Onelle sighed. 'No, no, I don't want that. We need his insights, however they are delivered.'

'And is he casting?'

'Not at the moment. He doesn't have the concentration. Too many people in his head, I think.'

'All right,' said Auum, feeling a familiar conflict of emotions concerning Takaar. 'Keep me up to date when you can. Don't let him unsettle the adepts.'

'Unsettle them? You should see them. They love him. The tales he weaves and the understanding he gives them about the earth's energies spellbind them, if you can excuse the pun.'

'And is he still making his . . . visits?'

'More and more regularly at the moment. I suppose it's no surprise given his mental state.'

Auum cursed. 'Why must he do this?'

Onelle shrugged and Auum understood her frustration. 'He always says he receives vital information, but the fact is they're friends and they like to talk.'

'How can anyone be friends with a human?' asked Malaar.

'I don't know,' said Onelle. 'Though I suppose if there was a man you could trust, it would probably be him.'

'It cannot be right,' said Auum. 'Whether or not he means to, he will betray our secrets. Looking around, I wonder if he already has.'

Onelle made to speak but stalled as the deep-throated roars of panthers split the air. They were joined by the hard, ululating, guttural cries of elves. The sound was angry, demanding vengeance and action. Auum shuddered, listening to the calls and responses echoing across the vastness of the rainforest. Eventually they fell to a silence that gave every one of Tual's creatures pause before taking up cries of their own.

Onelle was shivering. Never before had the Calaian rainforest heard such a chorus.

'What is it?' she asked.

'ClawBound,' said Auum. 'Calling themselves to muster.'

'Why?' asked Elyss.

Auum shook his head. 'I don't know but I fear their actions will be precipitate. Serrin was here. He saw the desecration.'

'You think they'll exact revenge?' said Tiiraj.

'They are the ClawBound. And humans have attacked the temple of Yniss.'

'But—' began Elyss.

'I know,' said Auum. 'But those threats are of no concern to the ClawBound. They consider those enslaved in our cities to be capable of defending themselves. This is an attack on the centre of our faith. And they will avenge it.'

Auum could see that his students either didn't understand him or didn't believe him.

'Study Lysael's texts,' said Onelle. 'Better still, talk to her when you are next in Katura, if she's still there. It may only be a hundred and thirty years since the first ClawBound pairing was forged, but the minds of the Bound elves are already so far beyond what we understand that you cannot apply your notions of sense and intelligence to them.'

'Nevertheless, we must try and stop them,' said Auum.

'How?' asked Tiiraj. 'We can't track them. How do we know where they'll go?'

'A good question.' Auum spread his hands. 'Anyone care to volunteer an answer?'

Elyss responded first. 'They'll want to make a statement. Something that'll be seen quickly by the humans and make them sit up and take notice.'

'Good,' said Auum. 'Malaar?'

'Something of high value, then. Pelt hunters or rare plant gatherers?'

'No,' said Auum. 'Men's money has no meaning to the Claw-Bound. Think. Wirann?'

'A high-density operation, then. Something close to Ysundeneth.'

Auum nodded. 'Right. Why Ysundeneth?'

'It is their power base,' said Wirann. 'It's home to Ystormun.'

'Good,' said Auum. 'Gyneev, if you were ClawBound where would you attack?'

'Logging on the River Ix,' said Gyneev without hesitation. 'It's heavily guarded, there are high numbers of slaves and guards, and it's the greatest desecration of the rainforest.'

Auum knelt, Onelle and his students following his lead.

'Tais, we pray.' Auum placed one palm on the stone and the other he held to the sky. 'Yniss, hear me. Beeth, hear me. Bless the ground on which the TaiGethen must run. Show us our path and guide us as we seek to stall the hand of your servants, the ClawBound.

'Shorth, hear me. Let those sent to your embrace this day by the malign hand of man feel the grace of their passing and the welcome of our ancients. Let those men who stand before you feel the full force of your fury.

'Ix, hear me. Guide Onelle's hand. Bless her work and swell her spirit as she rebuilds the order of the Il-Aryn. Open their eyes to the control of their power. Speed them to strength so they may stand by us to throw down the evil of man.

'I, Auum, ask this.'

Auum rose after a moment's silent contemplation. Onelle stayed in prayer a while longer. When she stood, tears were in her eyes once more.

'Ix cannot deliver me more adepts. Only Yniss can do that.'

Auum nodded. 'I hear you, Onelle. Elyss, Malaar, you will travel with me. Tiiraj, you will lead Wirann and Gyneev. Guard the temple. Don't leave here until I return.

'Tais, we move.'

Chapter 3

Anyone who wondered why the elves did not seek to attack Ysundeneth sooner was not present the moment Ystormun killed our beloved Katyett.

From *A Charting of Decline*, by Pelyn, Arch of the Al-Arynaar, Governor of Katura

There had come a time, and he couldn't remember when, when he made a game out of it. It was the only way to manage the pain. Manage . . . no, that was the wrong word. Endure, that was it. The game was to identify exactly which organ, muscle or bone hurt the most on his occasional journey to the temple of Shorth in Ysundeneth.

It began with taking a breath. That was difficult. Something to do with the fragility of his chest muscles, apparently. The problem was they were locked solid, so his ribcage wouldn't rise and each breath was like a pathetic gasp. That pain never won the day though, it was too regular, too easy to forget.

While he was climbing the stairs in a more tortuous fashion than ever before, he compiled a shortlist to consider on the long, long shamble from the stairs to the panoramic chamber at the far end of the corridor.

His head, now there was a new entrant. Ystormun had done something to stop deterioration in his brain function. He had no idea whether it had worked or not but his head was pounding away as if his brain was trying to get out through the top of his skull. His left hip was a candidate too, the result of his last attempt on his own life.

He'd thrown himself down these very stairs and broken every bone in his left leg and a few others besides. Most had been readily healed with spell and splint but his left hip was a total mess. Shattered and cracked, he was told, beyond what magic could heal, and it made every pace agony, with fire racing down to his foot and sheeting across his lower back.

It didn't help that his muscle atrophy appeared to be accelerating. He would have welcomed it but for the fact that it made Ystormun cross and liable to experiment in other painful ways to halt the decay.

Today, he couldn't put the arthritis in his hands and wrists on the shortlist because his stomach was so blindingly painful. He hadn't eaten solid food in almost twenty years, since his digestive system developed problems with anything larger than a pea. But this morning he'd woken in a puddle of diarrhoea and with cramps twisting his guts. A spell had calmed the cramps but had left the sort of pain he associated with a sword thrust through the stomach when the blade was being turned in the wound.

He reached the top of the stairs and rested against the wall while he assessed the walk he still had to make. His guards, Ystormun called them helpers though they offered little help and were clearly there to stop him attempting suicide again, waited behind and to the side of him.

'No contest, really,' he said to none of them, his voice hoarse over his dry throat and drier lips. 'Today it's the guts.'

'We're already late,' said one of his helpers. He couldn't remember the man's name. He didn't remember all that much these days. 'The master does not like to be kept waiting.'

'Well you know where he can stick it. *Master*. Pathetic sycophants, the lot of you.'

He moved on up the corridor, ensuring his movements were as laboured and slow as he could possibly manage. The sighs and muttered curses of his helpers gave him some tiny mote of satisfaction. There was little enough he controlled these days. Briefly, he considered soiling his clothes. He had regained control of his bowels since this morning but they didn't know that. He decided against it. The look on their faces would almost be worth it, but the cleaning up wasn't. It was a weapon to be used sparingly.

He liked to imagine the sun moving across the sky, albeit buried behind banks of rain-bearing cloud much of the time, while he made his agonising progress to his meetings with Ystormun. In the early years these meetings had happened every day. Not any more. And he was thankful to whichever elven god might be listening for that.

It wasn't that Ystormun had tired of the experiment itself – and

how he prayed for the day that he did. No, it was more that Calaius'
ruler had become more of an overseer, having delegated the day-
to-day drudgery of keeping his subject alive to junior mages. It was
unfortunate that the juniors were so diligent in their work. He
shouldn't have been surprised. Ystormun didn't handle disappointment terribly well.

One of his minders opened the door to the panorama room and its
glorious views across eastern Ysundeneth and into the ruined rainforest beyond the River Ix. The sun was bright for the moment,
bathing the long airy room with glorious light. It was a fresh and
bright scene quite at odds with the room's single occupant.

Ystormun was sitting in a high-backed black leather chair behind a
huge polished wooden desk. Paperweights held piles of documents in
place and the remains of a meal were scattered across three plates in
front of Calaius' lord and master. Ystormun didn't have a great deal
of flesh and his skin was stretched so tightly over his frame that every
bone of his face and hands was visible. He was a walking skeleton
wearing the loose light-weave robes favoured by those seeking relief
from the relentless humidity. It was a matter of debate which one of
them looked worse.

'Your stench precedes you, Garan,' said Ystormun. 'Sit.'

Ystormun wafted a hand at a deep and comfortable chair to his
left. Garan ignored it and sat in a straight-backed wooden chair to
the right, one he had half a chance of getting back out of following
this meeting.

'And yours surrounds you like a mobile cesspit,' said Garan. 'My
stench is your fault. What's your excuse?'

Ystormun's dark eyes flashed but he managed a thin smile.

'How old are you now?' Ystormun rasped, his voice echoing in the
largely empty space of the room.

'A hundred and seventy-six,' said Garan, and the numbers sounded
unreal as they always did.

'And in all that time you have failed to bait me as you desire.'

'There is always hope. More than that, there is satisfaction in
trying. Who else could sit here and tell you that you look worse than
a forty-day-old corpse strung up on the Ultan bridge and that you
smell worse than panther shit, and expect to live?'

'Even you have a limit to your leash, Garan.'

'And I am *so* enjoying finding out where that limit lies. The thought of exceeding it is what sweeps me to the bliss of dreams every night.'

Ystormun snorted and shuffled briefly through a sheaf of papers, plucking one from a fat leather file.

'To business. Your eyesight. Improved? Keener?'

'I can almost see right through your skin to that shrivelled black organ you probably still call your heart. Does that help?'

Ystormun growled, and the guttural sound was more suited to the rainforest than the room. Garan felt a frisson of fear and felt suitably alive as a result.

'Your kidneys returned to full function ten days ago. Have you had any negative reaction to the treatment?'

'Yes,' said Garan. 'I am still alive.'

Ystormun tensed and the sinews in his jaws and neck stood taut under his yellow, brown-spotted skin.

'Your stomach,' he said, speaking slowly and with a deliberate measure designed to convey menace but raising nothing but hope in Garan. 'Three days of a new treatment. Has the swelling reduced and your capacity to retain nourishment increased?'

Garan met Ystormun's stare without flinching, without the terror so obvious in the mage lord's lieutenants.

'My stomach remains agonising and as such is my brightest hope for death despite your inhuman meddling with my body. Your experiment is, and has always been, an abject failure.'

Ystormun was quick, and his height, when he chose to use it, was intimidating. His hands slapped onto the desk top and he loomed high over Garan, whose shrivelled form hunched reflexively, though his eyes never deviated from the mage lord's. In his peripheral vision he could see the desk crackling and smouldering beneath Ystormun's hands. *Almost. Almost.*

'Nothing I touch is ever a failure.' Ystormun's voice ground out like rock grating on rock. 'And it is time you understood that even if you expired right now you still represent a triumph.'

Garan's jaw dropped and he was aware of a line of drool dribbling from the corner of his mouth.

'Look at me,' he whispered then raised his voice as loud as he could muster. '*Look at me!* My skin splits if I sneeze too hard. Every joint is so swollen with arthritis that I can't get out of bed unaided and I can't walk more than a dozen paces without rest. Every time I breathe, the pain takes that breath away. If I fall, I break twenty bones. My whole body, my whole life, is a sheet of agony. I have not recognised myself in a mirror for fifty years. I am dead but you keep my heart beating. How is that a triumph, you bastard?'

A glimmer of long-forgotten humanity crossed Ystormun's features. The crackling ceased and the mage lord moved his hands, revealing the blackened imprints on the desk.

'Because I have given you life beyond your wildest dreams. I have given you the chance to see and hear and touch and taste when you should have been nothing but bleached bones scattered across the land. I have made your name one that will resonate through the history of man.'

'And my family will always carry the shame that I was Ystormun's plaything. I do not want to be named in history. All I ever wanted was to do my tour, return to those I love and die in my wife's arms when my time came. You denied me my rights and you still do. I spit on the ground your feet touch.'

Ystormun's touch of humanity faded and his ancient cold eyes bored into Garan's face.

'You think yourself unfortunate because I have never tired of you. I am tempted to remove your tongue. Believe me, I can make your life far more unpleasant than you already believe it to be. Dwell on this if you must: you are an unfinished experiment and I cannot let you die before you are complete.

'You have the organs of a man approaching his latter years. Your heart would beat well in the body of a man of thirty. And every day my mages get closer to solving the problem of your musculature, skin and bones. You, Garan, could be the first human immortal and yet you choose to whine about your longevity.'

'Were you ever a human?' asked Garan. 'Or did the deal you made to keep your heart slithering along also remove such notions as honour, shame and free will?'

Ystormun sniffed, managing to make the sound both dismissive and disgusting.

'You don't want to know any more about the deal I made than you already do,' said the mage lord, and Garan was damned if the skeletal figure didn't shudder beneath his robes.

'At least yours was a matter of choice,' said Garan.

Ystormun walked around the desk to stand above Garan.

'Yes, it was. And I have no time for honour or free will. There is only conquest and domination.' Ystormun leaned right down until

Garan's eyes were full of the mage lord's leathery face and his nose full of the trademark musty odour. 'And you are part of my inevitable rise to power in Balaia.'

'Got me a new sword, have you? I can't wait to see the fear on your enemies' faces when they see me limping towards them.'

Ystormun growled again. 'Something in this festering land gives the elves their long life and I will seed that in you if it takes me another hundred and fifty years. So you will live, Garan, and you will see the new breed of humans born. Those I can imbue with long life, great speed and huge strength. Unstoppable. Loyal. Willing.'

At last Garan had the truth behind the torture of the last hundred and thirty years. He tried to hold back a laugh.

'You're trying to create an elf from my body so you can build an army of *me* and take on the power of Triverne? You really are a fucking idiot, aren't you?'

Ystormun's eyes darkened and his hands crackled with power.

'You could have stood with me at the head of my dominion,' said Ystormun. 'But your every insulting word is logged and noted and you will be cast aside when I am done with you.'

'My death cannot come too soon.'

'Death? I don't think so, Garan. That would be reward, not a punishment.' Ystormun stalked across to the windows and stared out towards the rainforest. 'This meeting is over. Your next treatment will be somewhat uncomfortable but might give you more strength in your legs. It will be that or paralysis.'

Garan felt cold. Ystormun was nothing if not a man of his word. Still, there was always a chance he could be provoked enough to lash out.

'I look forward to pulling myself along by my arms to see you,' said Garan.

'Sometimes I think my work to maintain your brain function was wasted,' said Ystormun. 'You see so much less than you should.'

'So sure?' Garan raised a shaking hand and pointed a crooked arthritic finger at Ystormun. 'I can see you're fidgeting. You're nervous, but not of me. I can hear your finger bones clacking together.'

Ystormun stared at him and Garan saw the exhaustion in his eyes; quite something in orbs always so sunken and black-rimmed.

'That'll be down to too much interference from your brethren; too much long-distance debate, right?' said Garan.

He needed to lie down. Ystormun's sheer presence was draining enough. But this was one of those rare occasions when the mage lord was clearly uncomfortable about something. Garan was not going to let a mere hundred and seventy years of age get in the way of an attempt to make the skeleton squirm a little.

Ystormun's stare intensified. Garan felt the temperature on his face rise.

'Oh dear,' said Garan. 'And it didn't go so well for you, did it? What was it this time?'

'I am not in the habit of talking to you about such matters.'

'Well, I might as well go, then.'

Garan began to think about pushing himself out of the chair. It was not a prospect he relished. He feared his legs had seized up and his head felt light. Too much thinking did that to him these days.

'Did it ever occur to you that, as the only other man who was here from the start, I might have something useful to add?' asked Garan, hoping to delay the moment a little further.

There was a flicker across Ystormun's features, gone the next blink.

'I admit no weakness,' he said. 'Only the ignorance of others.'

'Ah,' said Garan, satisfied at last. 'It's the old "delicate balance" thing again, is it?'

Ystormun appeared to relax, just by a hair. 'There are those in Triverne who do not accept the threat still posed by the TaiGethen.'

'Ah. And those sails on the horizon. That's more muscle, I suppose, to hasten their demise.'

Ystormun shook his head. 'Workers.'

'Bullshit.' Garan found himself experiencing a wholly uncomfortable emotion. Sympathy. 'This place already works. It is efficient. What's going on?'

'Politics,' said Ystormun.

'More bullshit,' said Garan, sensing an opening like never before. 'I'm proud of what we achieved here. I hate you for keeping me alive, but at least I can see the fruits of my labour. If you must keep my heart beating, use me, confide in me. After all, what can I do?'

'Other than talk to your pet elf?'

Garan sank back in his chair. Pains thrashed through his body and tortured his mind. One secret, everyone was allowed one secret.

'You are pouting like a girl,' said Ystormun. 'After so long, you surely knew that nothing escapes me here.'

'He leaves no trace,' said Garan.

'As a warrior, no. But as a mage, his imprint is loud and lingering. What did you just say?'

'You heard.' Garan pushed himself to his feet, swaying and retching at the pain ricocheting through his body. 'I'm going. I'm tired.'

Garan's head was thumping. He felt violated, exposed.

'Tell your pet to keep his minions in check. They are walking a narrow path and I am all that holds back the tide.'

'You make it sound like you are doing them a favour,' said Garan.

'Just tell him.'

'No. He has other things he must hear.'

'Don't push me, Garan.'

Garan laughed. 'Or what? Save your threats for someone you can scare.'

Chapter 4

You are wrong to think of it as a sudden change. I suspect they had been evolving for hundreds of years. Perhaps from the moment we set foot on Calaius. The arrival of man was a catalyst, there is no doubt about that, but it would be a mistake to think the bonding would not otherwise have occurred. Fascinating, aren't they? But take care around them. Their minds are no longer elven. I fear they will grow ever more unpredictable.

From *ClawBound and Silent*, by Lysael, High Priest of Yniss

Serrin, for he still thought of himself as Serrin though it was a name from another life, only remembered in dreams, crouched next to his Claw. He felt the warmth of her body beneath her sleek black coat. He felt the movement of her chest with every breath. He shared everything he saw with her and she shared every scent that entered her nose with him.

Their minds were one and it was a state of joy that should never have been threatened. The fact that his joy had been dimmed by reminders of his past added extra bite to his fury. For his Claw it was something far simpler: an invasion of hunting grounds that had to be challenged.

They had heard the harsh sounds of man and the forced destruction of the rainforest by elves well before they could see or smell anything. Five other ClawBound pairs were with them, each watching from deep enough in the canopy that man's simple senses could not detect them.

What they could see and smell was a defilement greater than any of them could have foreseen: an organised clearance of the canopy, leaving the rainforest gasping its last over huge areas that would take decades to regrow. The River Ix was clogged with barges, nets and logs ready for transport north to Ysundeneth. Men were driving their slaves to hack the life from the gift Yniss had bestowed upon the elves.

Serrin had counted around a hundred elves, plus twenty men and mages. His Claw growled deep in her throat, her eyes playing over the scene and her nose sampling the air. Serrin caught the foul stench of man and felt the simplicity of her desire. Her head moved to the elven slaves, whose every axe blow was accompanied by prayers for forgiveness. *Pack. Protect.*

She focused on the humans. Her body tensed and her hackles rose. *Prey.*

Serrin stroked her flank and rested a hand on the top of her head. Rain began to fall. It was heavy and the darkness of the cloud cover suggested it would be prolonged.

Soon, he pulsed.

'I hate this.' Jeral stared up at the sky, revealed now that the trees had been cleared back from the river bank in a growing swathe cut into the forest. He shouldn't have bothered. Though it was daytime, the mass of black cloud had obscured any hint of sunshine or warmth, leaving the world grey and dismal. 'I just fucking hate this.'

'Well, that's good to hear. Again. Because having counted almost as far as ten since you last opened your fat mouth to moan, I thought you'd changed your mind, I really did.'

Jeral glanced to his left. He couldn't see Nuin's face. The mage was staring at the logging operation, his features hidden by the deep hood of his cloak. His hoarse voice was just audible over the sound of rain hammering on the deck of their barge, spattering off Jeral's bald head and the leather of his high-collared coat.

'Well, you don't have to be scared, do you? One whiff of them and you can just fly off.'

Nuin turned to him, his features still hidden but this time by the gloom of the day. Jeral could just about see his mouth move and the dark gleam of his eyes.

'You really think I'd abandon you?'

'I would,' said Jeral.

'You worry too much.'

'Really?'

Jeral gestured beyond the stern of the barge. They were anchored midstream, flanked on either side by similar barges. A net was strung between the vessels, holding back the growing mass of logs harvested from the forest. This stretch of the River Ix had been chosen for its particularly sluggish flow but, even so, the mass of wood floating in the water worried Jeral.

On land a working party of a hundred and five Sharps felled timber as slowly as the whips and threats of their guards allowed. The Sharps never spoke. Their eyes, though, spoke enough. A crime was being perpetrated here and they were complicit in it. Jeral didn't get it. Big forest, countless trees; a few hundred less was like taking a single drip from the Southern Ocean, and he was bored to tears by their endless bloody praying.

'Yes, really,' said Nuin. 'Three days, no sightings. They don't know we're here.'

'They don't know we're here *yet*.'

'You're such a pessimist.'

'And you're just an idiot. By your reckoning, the longer we stay here, the more likely it is they'll never find us. Me, I believe the opposite. That's why I fucking hate it here. Not because of the rain, but because anytime, *anytime*, they could appear and slaughter us all.'

'But they don't, do they?' said Nuin. 'They just watch. It's been like that for decades. Since—'

'I am well aware of Ystormun's interesting reprisal rules, thank you. But you feel something's changed, don't you?'

Nuin shook his head. 'Frankly, no. It'll be like every other time. They'll show up, posture a bit and we'll pack up and move on when the Sharps get too twitchy. It's a big forest and it's a very, very long river.'

The rain thrashed across the deck of the barge. Jeral stared at the Sharps again and for a moment he was in sympathy with their mournful expressions. The sounds of axes hammering at the base of another trunk fell into rhythm with his heartbeat, or so it seemed. It was mesmeric. Then an order was barked out by one of his men, followed by a shout of warning.

With attendant cracking, splintering, rustling and rushing, the great tree fell, toppling to land with its crown in the water. The thump of the trunk hitting the ground reverberated across the river, spray flew up in a shroud and ripples rocked the barges at anchor. A team of Sharps moved to divest the tree of unwanted greenery. The sound of multiple small axes striking wood filled the air.

One more down. One more towards the moment they could leave.

Jeral shuddered. Even then their safety was hardly guaranteed. It was a long slow trip to the logging station built to the south of Ysundeneth, at least two days on the river – and all the while prey to the TaiGethen should they choose to break their decades-long abstinence from slaughter.

'Never mind prey, think I might just pray,' muttered Jeral.

'What was that?'

'Nothing, my magical friend. Just a hilarious play on words designed to kill the merest fraction of time.' Jeral stared into the sodden gloom of the rainforest. 'I just fucking hate this.'

The sky darkened further. The rain intensified. Jeral closed his eyes while the water slapped onto his skull and poured down his face. He shook his head, wondering if it could really get any worse. He opened his eyes again to see Nuin's pained expression. He found it lifted his mood just a tiny bit.

'Guess how close I got to ten, that time,' said Nuin.

'Amaze me,' said Jeral and found himself smiling.

A shadow flashed across his vision and Nuin was gone. Jeral stumbled back a couple of paces, registering the panther's roar. Nuin had been carried right into the middle of the deck. The panther was on top of him. Jeral saw its claws rake and its jaws bite down hard. Blood spurted from Nuin's neck.

Jeral shouted to distract the animal, drawing his sword and advancing across the deck though he knew he was too late. The panther turned its head towards him, bared its fangs and sprang away. Jeral tracked its movement, watching it skip across the treacherous log jam and back to the river bank.

Jeral looked back at Nuin. 'Why you?'

The river bank was cluttered with humans and elves. All easier, closer targets, none of whom seemed to know what had just happened. And Nuin had just been, well, executed for want of a better word.

Jeral looked back towards the panther. The animal had stopped at the edge of the forest not fifty yards away, where the trees met the river on the border of the cleared land. An elf stood there, at least Jeral assumed he was an elf.

His face was painted half white. The other half was covered in piercings and tattoos. His ears and nose were pierced, his teeth filed to points as were his fingernails. His body, naked but for a loincloth, was densely stitched with tattoos.

Jeral, rain beating on his head and leathers, shivered. The elf opened his mouth and uttered a guttural cry. It was taken up across the forest surrounding the clearing and the roars of panthers joined it. As one, the Sharps downed tools and gathered together, kneeling in prayer.

Jeral went cold. He began to run, vaulting over the rail and onto the treacherous logs, which rolled and sank beneath his feet, heading for the river bank. That panther had taken Nuin out because he was a mage, and because he'd been separated from the others. It was a ridiculous notion but he could find no other explanation.

'It's an attack! Guard the mages. Get to barge one now!'

Tall, white-painted and tattooed elves melted out of the forest. Each had a panther by his side. At a single call, they began to run. Fast. Impossibly fast, to Jeral's eyes. He watched them break, elves and panthers streaking towards their targets.

'It can't be,' he breathed. 'It can't be.'

Jeral's feet hit the river bank.

'Barge one. Run!' he yelled, sprinting along the shore towards the muster point. 'Get the mages behind you.'

His message wasn't getting through above the tumult of the downpour. No one else could see it: the panthers and elves were working together. It was like they could read each other's minds. Jeral ran past the barge towards a knot of soldiers surrounding two mages. They were standing still.

'Move! Back away,' he ordered. 'To me.'

A panther roared and attacked from the right. It leapt at the head of one warrior, bearing him back into the knot of men. Three went down, three still stood, disoriented. Two of them were mages. A second panther was coming from the left flanked by two elves.

'Cast something, damn you,' Jeral roared.

The first elf stepped in and lashed his hand across the face of one mage, tearing four gashes in his cheek, ripping his nose to shreds and skewering an eye. The mage screamed and raised his hands. The elf dragged his fingers clear, moments before the second panther tore the mage's throat out.

Jeral shuddered and slowed. He was only ten paces from them and he was already far too late. The three on the ground were already dead. A second elf grabbed the surviving mage by the sides of his head. As the mage wailed, begging for mercy, the elf tipped his head back and buried his teeth in the exposed neck. Blood fountained into the dark sky.

Jeral cried out, he couldn't help it. He cast around for more survivors. He saw a mage and warrior running towards the forest, chased by an elf and panther pair. He had to watch, couldn't drag his eyes away, as the panther pounced on the warrior, jaws grabbing the base of his skull and front paws thudding into his shoulders. The elf ran on another pace and leapt into the air. He cycled his legs, reached out with one long arm and lashed his needle-sharp nails down the back of his victim's neck. The mage fell face first into the mud, twitching momentarily, and it was over.

Jeral turned again, a full circle this time. His breathing was ragged and he couldn't keep the heat from his face or the thundering from his chest. He gasped in air. The rain was getting lighter. The ground was covered in bodies, drenched with blood mixed with water and mud, and the last of his men had been slaughtered.

There was nowhere to run.

Jeral backed away towards the river. Maybe if he jumped in . . .

Elves and panthers watched him dispassionately. All but one pair disappeared back into the forest, ignoring the elves they had presumably come to save. One pair remained. They walked towards him. The elf, his teeth and fingers glistening with fresh blood, had one hand on the panther's head. The animal was growling deep in its throat.

Jeral felt water swirling around his feet and heard the splashes of his boots in the shallows. He stopped; it was pointless to attempt an escape.

'Please,' he said in elvish. He dropped his sword. 'Please let me live.'

Jeral had never thought of himself as a coward but the notion that he might attack this solitary pair to avenge his command never entered his head. The elf stared at him and closed to within a pace. Jeral's nostrils were filled with the scents of blood and beast. He knew he was trembling. It took all of his courage to hang on to his bowels.

The elf reached out a hand, slowly and deliberately, gripping Jeral's lower jaw. His fingernails cut Jeral's cheeks and the pressure he exerted grew painfully intense. He pushed his face into Jeral's. Jeral could feel his raw power and the enormity of his hatred.

'We are ClawBound,' he said, his voice hoarse and quiet. 'Fear us.'

The elf relaxed his grip and released Jeral, letting his fingernails scratch deep into Jeral's cheeks. Jeral felt the blood begin to gather and bead.

'We will come. We will destroy you,' he said, finding a modicum of bravado if his life was to be spared.

The elf cocked his head. 'You are mistaken.'

They walked away back into the forest, which Jeral continued to watch long after they had disappeared. One last time, he let his gaze travel over the scene of slaughter. He tried not to focus on the dead. A hundred yards from him, the Sharps were still praying. Not one of them had moved.

Jeral shook his head. He felt sick. He turned back to the river, its barges and its nets full of logs waiting to float downstream. He wondered, bleakly, how hard it would be to steer a barge alone.

Chapter 5

They are either examples of elven perfection and purity, or are symptomatic of our descent to inevitable extinction. They could very well be both.

Auum, Arch of the TaiGethen

Auum lifted the human's head from the mud by his hair. He examined the wounds and let it drop. He wiped his hands on his thighs and stood up.

'Five,' he said. 'Malaar?'

Malaar straightened from the body he'd been examining. He nodded.

'One more,' he said. 'But that's all.'

'Six ClawBound pairs,' said Auum, walking towards him. 'And look what they did. This was no battle, it was butchery. Follow their tracks back into the forest, see if there's a single direction or if they split.'

'Or we could ask them.'

Malaar indicated the elven working party. Auum didn't know whether to feel pity or contempt for them. Three hours and more must have passed since the ClawBound attack and the liberated elves still sat by their axes and the desecration they had been forced to wreak on the rainforest. They were watching the TaiGethen with a wariness that was close to suspicion.

'I'll speak to them,' said Auum. 'Follow the tracks. Tell me what you find.'

'Auum!'

Auum turned. Elyss was staring down at the ground on the river bank. The hulks of barges sat in the water, ugly and with nets still bulging with stolen timber. Auum trotted over to her across the blood-soaked churned mud surrounding the multiple mutilated corpses.

'What have you got?'

Elyss crouched and indicated a line of impressions in the silt leading north along the bank. After three hours, rain and river had erased most of the tracks but the story they told was clear enough.

'They let one go,' said Elyss. 'He can't be far away.'

'Serrin, what have you done?'

'We can still catch him. Stop word getting back to Ysundeneth.'

Auum looked at the three barges stretched across the fast-flowing river. Two had rowing boats strapped to their sterns. One did not.

'He's a lot further away than you think.'

'We have to stop him. Don't we?' asked Elyss.

'It won't stop what's coming,' said Auum. He stared into the forest, his sense of frustration growing. 'Our efforts would be better spent stopping the ClawBound repeating this. Though, Yniss knows, part of me has no desire to hold them back.'

Auum stood up, his gaze falling on the elves gathered near the eaves of the forest. Their prayers of lament had been like a murmur through the forest, leading the TaiGethen to this scene of carnage. They had not turned from their prayers in the time Auum and his people had been picking over the site.

Auum walked to them, for the first time listening to the words of the chant. He frowned. It was a lament for the lost. The ClawBound would not have so much as scratched an elf, so who was lost? Auum glanced over his shoulder at the flies clouding over the bodies now the rain had ceased. Surely not for their captors?

One elf, an Apposan by his broad back and muscular arms, was leading the service. Auum knelt by him, laying a hand on his shoulder and pressing the other to the mud.

'Yniss blesses you and saves you for greater tasks than being the slave of man. You need not mourn them, no matter what they may have become to you.'

The Apposan turned his head but he would not look Auum in the face, keeping his eyes a little to the left and focused down at the TaiGethen's shoulder level.

'Humans defile the rainforest even in death,' he said. 'Their blood will poison our river. We do not mourn them. We mourn those this attack has condemned.'

'Is it really so certain?'

'Ten elves will die for every man lying here.'

'*Ten?*' Auum heard Elyss gasp behind him. 'I am truly sorry we were too late to stop them.'

The Apposan nodded. Silence had fallen across the clearing. Auum lifted his head with a hand placed gently under his chin.

'You can look at me,' he said softly. 'I am no human. I am Auum, Arch of the TaiGethen. And you are free, all of you.'

The elf shook his head. He had a powerful frame but his face held the stress of his captivity and the wrinkles on his face and thinning dark hair gave him age beyond his years.

'I am Koel. I speak for this gang and we are not free. We will never be free.'

Auum pushed back so that he could see Koel's eyes. A hundred and fifty years of captivity had beaten his will down to nothing but there was still something there that man could not kill.

'You're going back,' said Auum quietly. 'Aren't you?'

Koel nodded and dropped his gaze to the ground once again.

'You can't!' Elyss stepped up, her voice shockingly loud in the quiet before the rains came again. 'You're free. You can join the fight. Liberate your comrades!'

Koel looked back at Auum. 'There have to be some left alive to liberate.'

'How many will they kill?'

'They kill ten for every one of us that escapes. Elves dragged from the pens and strung up in the Park of Penitence. Our people are eviscerated and left to die with the lizards, rats and birds feasting on them. The old, the sick and the weak go first. Those of us who can't see them can smell them. So no one tries to escape. We must not.'

'Then what are you doing?' asked Auum, flicking a hand gesture at Elyss to stop another outburst. 'How are you fighting to liberate yourselves?'

Koel shrugged. 'We're waiting for you, the TaiGethen. Only you can save us.'

Auum had never felt so humbled. He let his head drop while he composed himself, then stood so he could take in the whole slave gang.

'Your honour and your strength take mine from me. You are the reason that the TaiGethen work every day to rid Calaius of man. No elf may rest until mankind is gone. Your task is to stay alive. Ours is to free you. You have the respect of the TaiGethen. You have my promise that we will fight to free you until the day Shorth takes us for other tasks.

'But today we have an opportunity. Malaar, Elyss, a fire and hot food. Raid the barges or hunt for meat for our brethren. Koel, walk with me. Talk to me.'

So Koel spoke as they walked. And Auum listened.

All we had in the early days was hope. We hoped that the humans would grow bored or careless. We hoped the TaiGethen would free us. Especially as the penalties for resistance were so severe. Ystormun. That bastard. We waited for him to die because it was so obvious that without him the whole operation would fall apart. But he didn't die. He just became ever more skeletal. More evil. I don't know what he is but he is not human. I'd tell you to kill him, for that would solve everything, but he is untouchable. He is too powerful, even for the TaiGethen.

The humans are quite clever in some ways, though they had elven help. Cascargs. Someone to tell thread from thread. Even though they had us all cornered, the ones they hadn't already slaughtered, they still searched every building again, unearthed every hiding place.

They separated out the thread elves they didn't want, the Ixii, Gyalans, Orrans, Cefans . . . and they murdered them. We managed to shelter a few but it was pitiful really. We were so helpless.

I remember so much screaming and crying. You know I don't know how long it all took? I know we were all hungry and thirsty and herded here and there like pigs. They were dividing us up, you know? That was the clever part. Deciding what jobs we would do. Because that determined where we would live . . . exist.

I detest every cell that makes up their bodies; I wish the torment of Shorth upon them. But I can do nothing but respect their organisation and their attempts to divide us, flawed though they are. Funny really. They didn't realise what a great job we'd done of dividing ourselves already, did they?

We built our own prisons then, each group. They'd mixed the threads to stop blocks forming and they made sure no group so much as saw another, let alone spoke. First we had to clear the ground. We know some were placed in the old Salt quarter, some in the Warren. Some were lucky and stayed up at the Grans. We had to clear the old boatyards, because they were closest to the river jetties and to the barges heading upstream to the logging areas.

Makes sense, there's no denying that. We never see the rest of the city these days, unless we're being herded to the Park of Penitence for an execution. That's the Park of Tual to you, I suppose. At least they manage that properly. They picked the most hideous of the ancient kills of course. One of yours, I think. The old Ynissul sentence of Ketjak. Once they've staked out and eviscerated the poor victim, they take bets on which species begins to eat the entrails first and how long the unfortunate survives when the feasting starts.

It's so quiet. Sometimes there are ten thousand of us and all you can hear above the rain are the victim's screams and the taunts of a few humans. You'd think our silence was out of respect, but those who speak lose their tongues so you can understand a certain reluctance to speak, no?

Still, we have other methods of communication. The humans have never worked out the hand or head signals. Nor do they seem to notice the marks we make in the dirt or on the pens. We don't know how much the other groups pick up but we've gained the odd bit of information that way. Appos knows, we have enough time.

I don't know how much good communicating has done us. We know we all have the same conditions . . . latrine block, single dormitory, open-air kitchen and bamboo fence. One way in and one way out and all the fencing laced with wards that either shout or explode.

Anyway . . .

We live in the old boatyards because we work the trees, Appos, Beeth and Yniss forgive us. There are groups who work the timber for transport; build whatever it is Ystormun wants; farm the fields; work on the docks . . . you name it. Any manual labour. Ours is logging.

And there is one group that services the humans. Sometimes one or other of our group is taken. We used to think they were killed but we realise the truth now. Iad or ula, man's tastes are as depraved as they are godless.

We live in filth because they won't give us enough water to wash, only to drink. We are hungry because the food they give us is insufficient and of the poorest quality. We sleep on sacking and dirt. We cannot even all sleep inside because the space is so limited. Our young ones are sick from the day they are born – we would not procreate but for the fact that Ystormun punishes us if too few are born into his workforce. We can only hold to the belief we will be freed.

That belief is being challenged. More men are arriving every day and often they are not soldiers or mages but workers. They will take our tasks eventually and then we will be superfluous. Ystormun does not want the elves to survive. We are only slaves until we are of no use, until there are enough invaders here to take our place. No one knows how long that will take.

Ystormun has only made one mistake as far as I can see, beyond not sweeping the forest to find and kill all who escaped the cities before they were closed. He thought that mixing the threads would weaken us, stop power blocs forming and lessen the chances of an uprising. For a decade, he was probably right. Not now. He has done more to strengthen the harmony between the threads than Takaar did in a millennium. Funny, isn't it? We gather strength from each other, we pray together and we suffer together.

And we wait. We wait for you, we pray for you. You will come, won't you?

Auum listened to it all as if he were walking in a dream. Only at the last did Koel's desperation leak through. The two of them had walked a way into the canopy, and Auum indicated they should return to the clearing.

'How many logging gangs are there?' asked Auum.

'Thirty. We are destroying the forest much faster than it can regrow. Beeth screams his pain. Appos roars his fury.'

'But not at you. At man.'

Koel shrugged. 'We could refuse to raise our axes.'

'No, you couldn't,' said Auum. 'I see that now. Gather your people. Let me speak to them before you go.'

Back at the clearing, the gang was making ready while food was being prepared. Barges had sail canvas ready to fill. The smells of roasting meat floated on the light breeze. Koel called his people to him, and Auum watched them come: Apposans, Beethans and Orrans for the most part but two he recognised as Ixii. Their exhaustion was plain in every pace they took and in every stumble on the uneven ground. All of them wore the same expression, one which told of an inescapable fate approached with courage. Auum's heart swelled with pride.

'It is for you that I do what I do each day,' said Auum. 'The strength of the elven race lies in our spirit and our faith. In a hundred and fifty years they have not broken your spirit. And in that same time you have learned to love elves of every thread.

'I am proud that I have met you and spoken to you. And I shall speak of each one of you in my prayers. I shall use your strength and your determination to inspire all free elves I meet. Your story will be told throughout the rainforest.

'But even as my spirit soars with the dream of freeing you, I must urge you to remain strong. Do not lose faith, even in the years that might pass before you are freed. We know we can beat them blade on blade but we have no answer to their magic. Until we do, we cannot hope to rid Calaius of man.

'Speak, any who will.'

For a time there was an awkward silence but then a hand went up. Others followed. Auum picked one at random. He was a Tuali, sunken-eyed and pale with a fever.

'What was it that attacked the masters?'

Every other raised hand was lowered. Auum gave a rueful smile. In their captivity they had missed the evolution of a whole new breed of elf.

'You knew them as Silent Priests, though even then they were seen rarely enough. Now, they call themselves the ClawBound. They have reverted to nature and run with panthers.

'Today's attack followed a human raid on Aryndeneth. Many good elves were killed, elves who had been training to help free you. But the ClawBound do not take orders from the TaiGethen. They exist to cleanse the forest, to return it to its pure state.

'To them, humans are a disease, a fungus that must be eradicated from the canopy. And while they would never harm an elf themselves, they are deaf to the consequences of their actions. They understand what we are trying to do, and why we are waiting until we have sufficient strength, but man crossed a line when they attacked the great temple of Yniss and we could not stop the Claw-Bound.'

A mutter ran through the gang. The sentiment was plain, but Auum could not understand much of what was said. Koel helped him out.

'Too many of the humans now know some elvish, so we've developed something else. We've had plenty of time to, after all.'

Auum smiled. 'The will to win is greater than the desire to surrender. What are they worried about?'

Koel shrugged. 'They want to know if the ClawBound will strike again.'

Auum sighed. 'I have no reason to think they will stop now.'

Hearing his words, a collective gasp went up from the gang. Koel's voice was hollow.

'You have to stop them. We told you what will happen. Two hundred elves will die as a result of this attack alone. The humans do not care if we all die; they will simply accelerate the influx of human workers. All the ClawBound will achieve is to bring more humans to Calaius. Don't let them waste all we have lived and suffered in hope for. We want to die free.'

Auum shook his head. 'I cannot believe they would slaughter their entire slave workforce merely to replace it with humans. It makes no sense. It goes against all reason.'

'You don't know them,' said Koel. 'We do. Our lives mean nothing to them. The moment we fall sick or are deemed too old to work, we are taken away to die in the cells beneath the temple of Shorth. We are no more than animals to them. And they would kill us all if they thought it would draw you into a fight to the death.'

Auum closed his eyes briefly in silent prayer before looking to his left where Malaar stood waiting.

'Where did they go?' asked Auum.

'The tracks are separate but all head north and seem to converge on the same point. They never move in a pack unless on the hunt.'

'Yniss bless our limbs, may they be swift and sure.' Auum turned to Koel. 'Do you have other gangs further upstream?'

'No. We are the northernmost on the Ix.'

'Then they are tracking gatherers. Koel, have your people eat their fill then go with the blessing and prayers of the TaiGethen. Catch up with the human the ClawBound let escape. Take the logs too. Perhaps bringing them will speak for you. I swear that I will stop the ClawBound, and if I fail, I will break into your compound and rescue you myself.'

'Appos bless you, Auum, all of you,' said Koel. He made a circling gesture with one index finger and his gang began running for the barges. 'Somehow, we'll let the others know, and urge them to keep the faith.'

'Do that,' said Auum. He drew Koel into an embrace. 'Man will die. You will be free. But eat first, please.'

Koel smiled. 'We'll eat on the move.'

Auum watched Koel climb onto the lead barge and order the sail raised. The flotilla was soon sailing, the nets holding Beeth's hewn trees strung between them, the cargo rumbling and splashing as it began its journey downstream to Ysundeneth.

Elyss came to Auum's side. Malaar extinguished the cook fires.

'Those are bold promises, my Arch Auum.'

'And I will keep them,' said Auum. 'Tai, we move.'

Chapter 6

The elven strength of will is simple to exploit. They do not seem to realise that their extraordinary determination to survive until that mythical day when they are liberated is exactly what I desire from them.

Diaries of Ystormun, Lord of Calaius

Serrin rested beneath the beauty of the canopy, hearing Gyal's tears pattering against the broad leaves above his head before finding their way to the ground to bless the undergrowth and all the creatures living there. With his brothers and sisters gathering around him, he led their prayers. The Bound elves knelt in a circle around the great bole of a banyan tree, their panthers by them, guarding them.

When prayers were complete, Serrin sat with his back to the tree and savoured the taste of human blood on his lips and fingernails. It was the taste of the first blow struck against man in a hundred years. It was a breaking of the shackles imposed by the TaiGethen.

Serrin grunted his pleasure. Above his head, a broad leaf collected water, directing it onto the ground in a steady stream. Serrin moved his head and drank the water, its sweetness diluting the salty taste of blood on his tongue. His panther sat by him, sampling the air. Her whiskers twitched and sought alien movements in it, her nose held high.

Serrin breathed in the scents she detected. The freshness of the rain was everywhere, covering those thousands of Tual's denizens sheltering nearby. The richness of the earth and the sweetness of sap and nectar were stained with the stench of man.

Serrin stroked his Claw's head. *They are hiding behind their magic. Wait, joy of my mind, and they will tire. Their bodies will sate your hunger soon enough.*

The panther relaxed and lay down on the soaked ground, grumbling in her throat. Serrin scratched her beneath her chin and then settled back himself. *The sleep of the ClawBound is cleansing and replenishing. Tual keeps us free from harm while Yniss wraps us in his embrace. We are the children of the rainforest and we are the keepers of Beeth's realm. We are the righteous. We are the just—*

Serrin awoke. His Claw was standing, her body tense, flanks rippling. She sniffed the air and Serrin experienced a flood of odours. Most were pure, blessed by Beeth or Tual, but one was sick and acrid: their prey had stopped, either to rest or to steal. Serrin rose fluidly to his feet. In the shadows around him, five ClawBound pairs moved with him. Serrin inclined his head; time to hunt.

Serrin's Claw moved ahead by thirty or forty paces. Her whiskers filtered the air as she determined the distance and location of the intruders. Six of them. Two stank of metal and muscle and fear. The other four carried that unique complex odour, part poison, part beguiling. It meant mages, dangerous but weak of body. Serrin clicked his tongue and gave an avian whistle.

Tread slow, strike silent.

Auum ran. Malaar and Elyss followed in his boot prints. His eyes were everywhere. The rainforest had no time for the careless. He ducked low branches, hurdled dense scrub, pounded up shallow streams and whispered between the packed trees and vines that choked the space all around him. One slip in this race and they would fail. Auum dedicated his soul to Yniss for the thousandth time.

Ahead and to their left the ClawBound were closing on their victims. Rain suddenly plummeted around them, an extraordinary downpour, blotting out every other sound.

'Bless you, Gyal,' he whispered.

He glanced over his shoulder. His Tai were with him, concentration pinching their faces. They were good, these two. Sure of foot and trusting in their instincts. Auum trusted them. It was the greatest compliment he could pay them.

About thirty paces away, through the gloom of rain and shadow, Auum saw the dull sheen of metal. A glimpse was enough, caught in the dim light as the raindrops struck it. A blade, presumably meant for comfort and convenience, which had become a careless marker attracting a hunter's eyes.

The merest hint of movement to his left stilled his own. He turned his head very slowly, his eyes meeting those of a panther. The animal's gaze penetrated his soul. She growled at him, focused her attention on her prey and bolted.

'Run!' shouted Auum.

All pretence at quiet was gone. Auum sprinted headlong through the forest. His blade hacked at liana to clear his path, his feet kissed the sodden ground, every step like a clap of thunder to his ears. Elyss was just beyond him on his right, her speed prodigious. Malaar was just behind him, his breathing measured and his movement fluid.

Ahead, the humans were moving, panicking. The rainforest had exploded with sound all around them and yet they could see nothing. Their eyes, poor enough in the daylight, were hopeless in the gloom. So they stood, and the mages began to construct their magic.

'Elyss, Malaar, get amongst them. Weapons sheathed.'

The two TaiGethen cruised past Auum. To his left, panthers roared and Bound elves shrieked and hollered, sending Tual's denizens scampering in panic in all directions. Auum re-sheathed his blade, ducked his head and powered through the undergrowth, desperate to stop the Claws ripping the throats from men and so spilling the blood of innocent elves.

A sleek black panther ran by his side, eyes fixed on her target. Her teeth were bared, her body tensed to spring. Auum could see the humans clearly now. They stood in a circle among a tangle of vines, not knowing which way to look. The warriors, each flanked by two mages, were shackled by their fear while their charges were lost in concentration, trying desperately to cast before it was too late.

'Serrin!' yelled Auum. 'Draw back. Please.'

But they would not hear him. A mage cast. Flame lashed into the forest to the right. Tree trunks were scorched black, branches and leaves were turned to fire and ash. Creatures screamed and Claw-Bound pairs cried their fury. The panther by Auum leapt.

Auum dived headlong, bursting through the veil of liana in front of the terrified group of men. He could feel the panther next to him, smell her raw scent. One of the mages opened his eyes to cast and screamed instead, seeing what approached. Right before his eyes, Auum and the panther collided.

The beast's weight spun the TaiGethen out of control. Auum crashed flank on into the mage and the warrior standing by him, knocking them to the ground. The panther's claws missed the mage by a hair and she yowled in fury. Her shoulder struck the ground and she ploughed into the mud, scrambling back to her feet in an instant.

Chaos fell on the tiny circle of Calaian rainforest. Auum rolled across the bodies of the humans he'd just saved, hands and feet pushing away while he called for them to put up their blades. Elyss flew straight over his head, cannoning into two mages and knocking both to the ground. Malaar turned a forward roll in the air, landing in front of Auum, trying to shield him from man and ClawBound alike while he got to his feet.

He saw paws swipe at enemies and heard a human cry of pain. The white-painted faces of Bound elves loomed into his vision, lips drawn back over sharpened teeth and snarls issuing from throats. The pairs crowded in, seeking clear targets as the TaiGethen cell tried to cover every angle and simultaneously protect themselves from the humans, who would have no idea who was attacking them and who, confusingly, was defending them.

Malaar and Elyss pushed the humans back, shouting for quiet, calm and stillness. Whether the humans understood the words or not was doubtful, but at last some of them were beginning to grasp the situation. A mage barked something at the warriors and both put up their swords.

Auum bounced to his feet and deliberately faced the ClawBound, who circled them, menacing and furious. He tried to meet Serrin's eyes, and when the tall, tattooed former Silent Priest stopped in front of him he wondered if he and his Tai were about to die alongside the humans: Serrin's eyes were barely elven at all.

'Do not do this, Serrin,' said Auum, holding out his hands to placate his erstwhile mentor. 'All this will do is kill more elves.'

Auum was aware of the Claws positioning themselves for an attack. The Bound elves with Serrin stood back to let their leader decide the fate of them all. Serrin let his eyes travel over both man and TaiGethen, settling once again on Auum. The yellow irises inside bloodshot whites surrounded pupils which bored into him. Auum could feel the contempt radiating from him.

'Serrin, please. I know I cannot stop you from killing these strangers, but I would be forced to try.'

Serrin growled, and Auum shuddered at the sound. His life and those of his Tai rested on how much of his old mentor had survived the last hundred and thirty years. Serrin clicked his tongue and motioned with a hand, and the Claws surrounding him gathered to spring. Elyss gasped. Malaar's hands moved reflexively.

'Don't touch your weapons,' hissed Auum. 'Serrin, hear me.'

Serrin was studying him the way a predator studies new prey, weighing up risk and reward. The Bound elf's fingers were latticed together, the long sharp nails itching absently at the backs of his hands.

'Serrin, you know me. I am Auum. I am not trying to protect men. I am trying to save elves.'

Serrin hissed out a breath.

'I need you to leave these enemies with me. They will steal nothing and they will never set foot in the rainforest again. This I swear, as I stand before you and Yniss. Call off your Claws. The deaths of these vermin are not worth the retribution we will suffer within the walls of Ysundeneth.'

When at last he spoke, Serrin's voice was rasping and quiet.

'Too late. ' He licked his lips. 'Others run unchecked.'

Auum's throat was dry. Around them, the rain fell harder still. Perhaps Serrin smiled, or perhaps it was the ghost of a memory.

'Wherever men defile, we cleanse,' said Serrin. The Bound elves in the abruptly tight space began to hum a single flat note.

'Yniss preserve us,' whispered Malaar. 'There must be forty groups of men and slaves in the forest at any one time.'

'At least,' said Elyss.

'Serrin, please, listen to me,' said Auum.

The humans were growing nervous behind him, detecting the desperation that had crept into the voices of their unexpected saviours. Serrin stared at Auum for an eternity before he inclined his head.

'Thank you.' Auum took a breath. He had one shot at this. 'I respect your tasks as set before you by Yniss. I love you for your diligence, and for the understanding and forbearance you have shown across the long years. You know my desire to see every human dead or fleeing north across the Sea of Gyaam.

'But for every man you kill today, ten elves will die in the slave cities. Your actions cannot be justified under Yniss. Not until we are strong enough to liberate them all.'

Serrin merely shrugged.

'That day is eternally distant,' he said. 'We will wait no longer.'

'And those elves you abandoned on the riverside today. What of them?'

Serrin looked nonplussed.

'They are free.'

'They are not.' Auum knew his tone was pleading but there was nothing else left. 'I thought the same. But they have to go back.'

Another shrug. 'They are weak.'

'No!' Panthers growled and the Bound elves' flat humming ceased. Serrin's eyes widened. 'They are strong, stronger than you or I, and worthy of saving. If they do not return, they sentence hundreds to death. And so they are returning to face death themselves to save their fellows, while your slaughter of twenty humans today means two hundred elves will die. That is the measure of their sacrifice. And now you will render it pointless.'

'They had a choice.'

Auum's anger overcame his caution and he advanced on Serrin.

'A choice? Whether to let those they love live or die? Yniss preserve me, that is not a choice.' Auum gulped a breath. 'Damn you, Serrin, you know I am right. You waited and watched for so long. Why act now?'

'Because we cannot free them. But we can free our forest.'

'Damn the forest! These are *elves* not the branches of trees. Our people, with their souls in torment. We swore to free them. Have you no compassion? No mercy?'

Serrin frowned. Then he shrugged for a third time.

'No.'

The bulk of a panther thumped into Auum's hip, flinging him sideways and out of the ClawBound's way. He raised his arms in front of his face, turning his head just in time to avoid collision with the broad trunk of a banyan, and fetched up in a heap with the panther sprawled across him but already moving away. Auum scrambled to his feet. He was just four paces from the humans but it might as well have been four hundred.

Serrin strode forward and stabbed the fingers of his right hand through the nearest mage's neck. One of the warriors reacted fast. He was up, blade in hand, his mouth open to shout an order. It never came. A leaping panther locked its jaws around his skull.

The Bound elves moved in behind Serrin. One moved to block Malaar and Elyss. The other two launched horribly effective attacks. A mage screamed as sharpened teeth sank into his shoulder and he was borne to the ground. The lash of a claw silenced his cries. Another tried to cast but nails slashing into his face and eyes blinded him and ripped through his flesh.

Panthers howled bloodlust. Auum heard a skull crush under the

pressure of immensely powerful jaws, and then the delirious shrieks of
Bound elves admiring their handiwork. They licked blood-drenched
fingers and palms and smeared the dark red of human life across their
faces.

'Stop! Stop!' screamed Auum.

It was frenzied, more akin to a pack of animals descending on
helpless prey than the precise attack of an elven elite. Beyond the brief
orgy of bloodletting, Malaar and Elyss stared on open-mouthed.
Auum seized Serrin by the shoulders and pulled him back.

'Stop! Serrin, for the love of Tual, for the sake of your soul before
Shorth, stop!'

Serrin spun round and bared his teeth. Blood streamed from his
mouth and was smeared across his chin. His expression was blank,
his eyes showing no recognition of Auum. The TaiGethen pushed
him away, heedless of the risk he might be taking.

'The Serrin I knew would never stoop so low. This slaughter is not
elven. We are all equal in the eyes of Shorth.'

Serrin growled.

'The Auum I knew would never hide in the rainforest while his
people were enslaved by man. Perhaps you are the one who is no
longer elven.' He placed a bloody hand on his chest above his heart.
'Perhaps, in here, you no longer have the will to fight.'

Even the panthers fell silent at his words. Auum's eyes never left
Serrin's. Neither of them would blink. Auum considered their
proximity, their relative speed of hand and he calculated the time it
would take them both to draw sword or dagger. It was too close to
know for certain.

Another time.

'Call the TaiGethen to muster at Aryndeneth.' Auum tapped his
head. 'You do remember how to do that, don't you?'

For a century and a half, the call of the ClawBound had summoned
the TaiGethen to muster in the gravest of times. Without them, Auum
did not know how long it would take to gather his people together or
if he even could. Serrin stared at him a moment before inclining his
head.

'It will be done.'

Auum ran from the scene of slaughter, his Tai at his back.

Chapter 7

When I first visited Garan, he thought I was there to kill him. He was wrong. I was there to kill Ystormun and had climbed into the wrong room. It was an error which saved my life in more than one respect.

Takaar, First Arch of the Il-Aryn

Takaar scaled the wall and climbed through the small window left deliberately ajar for him. Night was full, clouds were gathering to disgorge new rain and the city was pitch black but for the torchlight illuminating the entrances to key buildings. He could smell the filthy conditions of the elven slaves even more clearly than the stench of man.

His eyes pierced the night, giving him a clean view of the bedroom he entered. It was large. One door led to a washroom, another to a landing where guards and helpers stood. Within the room, a plain single bed and a large threadbare armchair stood in the centre of a wooden floor covered in thick rugs. Tapestries hung on the walls to keep out the draughts, but the room was otherwise without furnishing or decoration, barring a pewter chamber pot and a mug of water at the bedside.

The man in the bed watched him drop lightly to the ground, his eyes shining wet. Takaar heard a gravelly clearing of the throat and a dry chuckle.

'I wondered how long it would take you to get here,' said Garan, his voice a rasping whisper that Takaar could barely hear. 'I'm sorry about what happened.'

Takaar sat, as he always did, somewhere Garan could see him without having to raise his head.

'Really? Is that why you forgot to warn me last time I was here?'

Garan sighed. 'You have a rather exaggerated view of my influence and knowledge.'

'You are not yet deaf.'

'Pardon?'

'Nor are you a comedian.'

'Spare me one thing in my ridiculously endless life.'

Takaar smiled. 'Friendship with an elf?'

'I guess that'll have to do.'

Takaar knew that Garan could barely make him out, the natural human inability to see in the dark combined with Garan's poor eyesight. In some ways it was a shame they could only meet during darkness. To Garan, Takaar was little more than a silhouette.

'So? No need to be shy,' said Takaar. 'Tell me which new part of your body has stopped working or else dropped off entirely.'

Garan's eyes closed for a few moments before he spoke. 'Sadly, I am slightly recovered. A couple of days ago one of Ystormun's researchers tried a new technique for cleansing my kidneys and it appears to have worked.'

'I'm sorry to hear that.'

'Bullshit. If I died who on earth would you talk to?'

'No, I meant it. But you're right of course.' After all these years, he still couldn't reconcile his feelings towards this human. 'And don't deny you love being a paradox.'

'I want to be dead,' whispered Garan.

Takaar felt a squeeze on his heart. 'Then let me kill you. Such a gift, to send you to Shorth's embrace.'

'I can't let you. After all, then who would you have to talk to?'

'Now who's talking bullshit?'

Garan was silent for a while and Takaar wondered if he'd fallen asleep. But his eyes opened presently and when he spoke again, his rasping voice was softer.

'Why are you really here, Takaar? Not to chastise me for the attack on your people, I'm sure.'

Garan gasped and Takaar tensed, but he knew better than to mop his brow or clutch a hand.

'I thought you said you were improving?'

'They haven't quite sorted out my gut yet. Still dissolving in its own acid, or so it feels. So. Why are you here?'

'I'm sure your mages have been able to detect the Il-Aryn and its principal location for decades. So this attack is . . . a change in strategy, isn't it? It's provocative. I expect humans across the rainforest are already dead as a result. And none of your temple attackers survived.'

'Oh? I thought you always let one go to spread the fear.'

'I changed my mind.' Takaar shrugged. 'I was going to, but I didn't hear what I needed to.'

'Which was?'

'An answer to the question I just asked you. And I'm happy to kill you too, whether you answer it or not. Just say the word.'

'I see I'm not the only one who's not a comedian.' Garan was wheezing. 'Damn. Need to turn over. No muscle to speak of in the chest you see, so eventually my lungs slide together. Or that's how it feels. Quite painful.'

'I can imagine,' said Takaar.

'Don't be ridiculous. And don't even think about helping me or I'll call the guards.'

Ah, another test for your oh so fragile emotions.

'Leave me,' hissed Takaar.

I don't think so. This promises to be such fun.

Garan began to move and Takaar's eyes brimmed on the instant. He couldn't take his eyes from Garan's face, twisted in agony. His features, so aged and wrinkled, his flesh so thin and loose that he was utterly unrecognisable as the man who had escorted Takaar, bearing the body of his beloved Katyett, from the city a hundred and fifty years ago. Only his eyes, which retained their cynicism and surprising intelligence, gave the man within away.

Garan grunted and began to roll, having worked one arm beneath his body. He was a featherweight but his muscle was so withered that moving himself when he was prone was a true physical trial. His features contorted, hiding his already screwed shut eyes completely. Small whimpers escaped his lips and his body moved with agonising slowness. His right arm juddered and shook as he forced it straight. Drool ran from the corner of his mouth and Takaar heard tendons crack.

No, no. Don't close your eyes. You swore you wouldn't do that.

'I have to help him.'

You could end his pain but he won't let you, and you are so crucified by your respect for a human that you acquiesce to that. Or is it that your hatred for him is so intense that you drink the pain of your enemy like the sweetest of honeys?

Garan fell onto his back, an exhalation of relief ending in a violent coughing fit that sprayed a fine mist of blood into the air and left him clutching at his stomach. There was a thud on the door. Takaar froze. He saw the handle move ever so slightly downwards.

'Garan, do you need assistance?'

Garan's response was another fusillade of coughs.

'Garan!'

The handle moved further and the door opened a crack. Takaar readied to flee.

'I'm fine,' croaked Garan. 'Never felt better. Now bugger off and let me sleep in peace.'

The door closed on a muttered insult. Takaar smiled.

'So what happens now? Will your lungs sink through your back and into the mattress?'

Garan choked back a laugh. His voice dropped back to a whisper.

'Listen to me, Takaar. We don't have long before someone comes in to check I haven't suffocated myself with my blanket.' Garan's eyes bored into Takaar's face, searching for his features in the darkness. 'Change at home will bring changes here. Unless we are fortunate indeed, there is going to be a hideous struggle for magical dominance, so bad that those stationed here will be glad they are.

'There are more styles of magic than you have seen. Four schools dominate and the ethics controlling them mix poorly. Ystormun and his ilk represent a school of magic that deals in things best left untouched. You and your kind deal in a far purer magic which Ystormun has been under pressure to repress ever since it flared all those years ago. Now he is tasked with destroying it.'

'And you're playing into his hands.'

Takaar felt slapped. 'How?'

'Because those you assume are the natural practitioners of elvish magic are not.'

'The Ynissul are the natural masters of the elves and the only thread to demonstrate any feeling for the Il-Aryn.'

Garan closed his eyes and brought trembling hands to his face.

'And you call yourself the father of the harmony? Your prejudice is entrenched as firmly as Sildaan's. Did it never occur to you to wonder why Ystormun wanted to exterminate the Ixii and the Gyalans? The *Ixii*? Didn't that give you the smallest clue?'

Takaar opened his mouth to reply but closed it sharply against a rising nausea.

Oh for shame. A hundred and fifty years passed and so much of it wasted on the wrong elves. How does it feel to know you have failed again, through your own blindness? I'd be running for the forest to hide again if I were you.

'You've known this all the time?'

'Of course.'

'But—'

'Don't be naive, Takaar. We're friends. Friends of the most curious kind, to be sure, but friends nonetheless. But when have you or I ever passed each other useful information, eh? Never forget that I believe in our occupation. Or I did.'

The last was almost inaudible.

'And now?'

'This occupation is no longer to the benefit of Triverne. It is merely a resource base that will tip the balance in the magical struggle to come. Ystormun and his dark magic must be driven out before he becomes unstoppable. The future of both Calaius and Balaia depend on it. You understand what I'm saying?'

Takaar nodded, mumbled his assent.

'There's something else,' said Garan.

The bedroom door slapped open, lantern light flooded in. Takaar leapt straight upwards, his fingers snagging on the timber roof supports high above the bed. He swung his legs up and his body swivelled, planting him astride a central beam. He flattened his body along it, one eye peering down through the dust he had dislodged, which spiralled towards the ground.

Ystormun swept into the room flanked by four of his cabal of mages and two guards. Garan watched him come and, though any other man might quail, he rolled his eyes and sighed dramatically.

'He's been here. I can smell the mana on him. Give him to me.'

'Naturally,' said Garan. 'He's hiding under my blanket.'

One of the mages moved to pull the blanket back. Ystormun stopped him with a hiss.

'Idiot,' he snapped. 'Don't waste my time, Garan. Where is he?'

Garan, lying prone, shrugged extravagantly. 'There are so many places to hide in this room.'

Ystormun glared at Garan. He snapped his fingers and gestured towards the door to the washroom. A mage scurried off to check.

'You are testing my patience,' said the mage lord.

'It is the only pleasure remaining to me,' said Garan.

Takaar was calm. Seven enemies in all. He could kill six before they touched him, three of those before they even knew he was there. But Ystormun was an unknown factor. There was an aura of invulnerability about him mixed up with the reek of magical power that enveloped him. And something else too: something seething and malevolent that ran through his veins and every cell of his being.

Takaar waited and watched. He needed Ystormun to move directly beneath him. Dropping on him like a constrictor from a tree was his best and only chance. But as if he could sense Takaar's intent, Garan stared upwards for a heartbeat and gave an almost imperceptible shake of the head.

'Last chance,' said Ystormun.

'Or what?' rasped Garan. 'You'll torture me for the truth? Have me executed? There is nothing you can do to me that I do not crave, nothing you have not already done that I fear. Even a demon-addled skeleton like you should realise he left through the window some time ago. Now get lost, Ystormun, and let me sleep. I'm an old man in case you hadn't noticed.'

Takaar felt the air chill and saw the mages shrivel in anticipation of Ystormun's response. But the mage lord merely nodded. Takaar's heart began to thrash in his chest. Ystormun was going to leave. Alive.

You don't have the guts. You never did.

Wrong.

Takaar dropped head first from the rafters, arms outstretched. A guard stood below him. Takaar caught the man's head in his hands, twisting his neck while his body slammed into the victim's back. The guard crumpled. Takaar turned a forward roll and was on his feet, twin blades in his hands.

Takaar slashed the first through a mage's midriff and the second through the neck of a guard still trying to draw his sword from its scabbard. Takaar ran forward, turned a roll over Garan's bed, thumped to the floor the other side and cracked a roundhouse kick into the second mage's temple.

Takaar kept his momentum into the turn, ducked a flailing fist and sliced up through the guard's face. The final mage was casting. Takaar dropped his left-hand blade, reached into the jaqrui pouch at his waist and threw the crescent blade. The keen edge buried itself above the mage's nose.

Takaar stretched out his right arm, the blade he held touched Ystormun's neck.

'Your turn.'

Takaar pushed hard. The blade would not penetrate Ystormun's flesh. He pulled back and hacked at it. The blade bounced, not even unbalancing the mage lord, whose fleshless face modelled a parody of a smile.

'Very impressive, Takaar of the TaiGethen, but as you can see I am made of sterner stuff.' Ystormun pushed Takaar's blade aside. 'Now, what to do with you, I wonder. I'm disappointed in you, Garan. Didn't you warn him about me?'

'I tried to.'

Ystormun was deceptively quick of hand. He loomed over Takaar and grabbed him by the throat, pulling him close. Takaar gagged. There was a reek to the man that was unlike any other he had experienced. The odour of power clad in the darkest of nights. It was as if his soul was a channel for an extraordinary malevolence.

Takaar reached up to try and dislodge Ystormun's fingers but instead the grip on his neck tightened, the mage lord's nails drawing blood. Ystormun studied him as though he could see right through his flesh to the mind and soul that lay within.

'In many ways it would be a pity to kill you. Such conflicts within a creature so primitive would be a pleasure to examine at length, after all. But you are dangerous alive. You have . . . ability. The question is whether your martyrdom would make you more dangerous still?'

Ystormun glanced down at Garan.

'I know what your answer would be, but I know better than to trust anything you say.'

'I'm hurt,' said Garan. 'But I urge you to keep Takaar alive. Yes, he is my friend, and friendship is a rare beast between our races, but your idea of his influence and popularity is exaggerated. Dead, his memory will gain power. Alive, he does himself more damage every day.'

He really knows you well, doesn't he?

Takaar swallowed as hard as he could. Ystormun's grip had not slackened. He weighed up what to say and concluded that silence was his best choice. Ystormun's eyes bored into him once more.

'I see. I am aware my men all died in the attack, but what of your . . . adepts, Takaar?'

'Your magic was stronger than ours but not every adept was at the temple,' said Takaar in the clipped human tongue Garan had taught him. 'You may consider your action a victory but the full price for it is yet to be exacted.'

Any hint of humour or humanity disappeared from Ystormun's face.

'Any reprisals on behalf of your warrior force, such as still exists, will be met with vengeance you can only shudder to consider,' he said.

Takaar tried to shake his head but Ystormun's grip made it an impossible gesture.

'You don't understand. You attacked Aryndeneth. The temple at the heart of our faith. Now the ClawBound are cleansing the forest. No human may step beneath the canopy again and hope to live.'

Ystormun hissed a fetid breath over Takaar's face and dragged him from his feet. Takaar began to choke, his hands scrabbling use-lessly at Ystormun's fingers.

'They will cease or you will all perish. We have only let you live so long as you do not harm us. Do not think we fear you. Not now, not after so long. Especially not now we are so strong.'

Abruptly, Takaar was released. He dropped to a crouch, massaging his throat and gulping in a painful breath. He caught Garan's eye and the human could do nothing but shake his head in resignation.

'So the decision is made. You will live for now and you will carry a message to your ClawBound, whoever they are. Their reprisals will end immediately. If they do not, I will fire the forest and everything in it. You have three days to bring me their response.

'Remember who rules this accursed continent, Takaar. I will suffer no further loss at the hands of elves.'

Takaar stood slowly and faced Ystormun.

'Guarantee that Garan will be free from harm and I will deliver your message,' he said.

Spoken like a true coward.

Ystormun laughed. It was a hollow sound, quite without soul.

'Oh I am happy to guarantee that. In fact, my temporary loss of interest in Garan the experiment has been quite reversed and he can look forward to a long, long life to come.' Ystormun leaned forward. 'Go.'

Chapter 8

I once told Auum that we'd got it all wrong. There is so much in the rainforest to kill an ignorant human, I said, that we should welcome them in and just let the forest do its work. Let Beeth and Tual carry out sentence. He didn't smile. Sometimes I wonder if it's because for a heartbeat he actually took me seriously.

From *A Charting of Decline*, by Pelyn, Arch of the Al-Arynaar,
Governor of Katura

Koel signalled the elf at the helm to move the barge into the deep water midstream. He breathed in the purity of the River Ix and the rainforest. He relished their fleeting freedom. To the north, the dark sky was further smudged by the smoke of Ysundeneth's industry. In a day they would be behind the fences once more.

Koel had found himself praying for much of the time. His meeting with Auum had touched him deeply, bringing him comfort, strength and despair in equal measure. The temptation of freedom was so strong, but not one of them was prepared to desert their loved ones still trapped in the city. Though they aided the plans of man, Koel was intensely proud of his people. And pride, for an elf, was in short supply.

'Koel.'

Koel tore his eyes from the smoke billowing up into the sky. Liun was standing forward towards the bow, and had been taking soundings. She was a strong stubborn Beethan – weren't they all – but he had grown to respect her obduracy and he trusted her to be his second on the logging team more than he did one of his own Apposan thread.

'Are we bottoming out?'

Liun shrugged. 'The depth is fine. If I know this river at all there's a fathom beneath the keel for the next twenty miles. I'd love that to be our biggest problem.'

Liun said no more, merely pointed to the starboard bank ahead of her. Koel could see nothing but the forest crowding the river's edge. Branches leaned out from bowed trunks, leaves kissing the water. On closer inspection, though, Koel could see a bubbling and frothing, the water boiling beneath the broad leaves of an evergreen.

'Piranha,' he whispered and he hurried across to the rail. Before he got there, he saw the remnants of their feast. 'Yniss preserve us.'

A disembodied head was bobbing on the surface. Much of the flesh was gone and when it rolled in the water under the weight of attack, it revealed a torn ear. It was a human head. Remnants of bloodied clothing were trapped within a net of small branches. A larger mass bobbing under an overhang of the bank revealed itself to be a limbless torso. Other scraps could be seen among the frenzy that would ultimately leave no trace at all.

Koel sucked at his bottom lip and looked into the forest beyond the water's edge. Elves knelt there, praying. He counted seven and there would be more. He knew them. They were a search team, scouting for new logging sites and clearing any settlements they found. It was the harshest of the slave duties; no one wanted to come upon one of their own and end their freedom.

Koel rubbed his hands over his face.

'Launch a boat!' he called. 'Pick them up, any who will come with us.'

He turned away, catching Liun's eye.

'Why?' she asked. 'We will just transport them more quickly to their own executions.'

Koel spread his hands and shook his head.

'Because we have to stand as one. And die as one if we must.'

Auum's mind was clouded. He ran knowing he risked injury to himself and those who followed him. He ran hard down stream beds, through the grabbing, clawing undergrowth and across abandoned hamlets and villages lost to the voracious growth of the rainforest.

The haunting cry of the ClawBound calling the TaiGethen to muster still echoed in his mind. It had split the forest, reaching into the highest boughs of the canopy and penetrating the deepest valleys and most distant caves. Auum had stopped running only when fatigue forced him to rest.

'Tai, we pray,' said Auum.

They knelt facing each other. Rain drummed on leaf and tree. Mud on the ground moved under the weight of water draining through it. The dark of the night was complete, cloud blotting out any hint of light from the heavens. Gyal was crying in the darkness, and the gods were listening.

'Yniss hear me, your servant Auum. We seek your blessing for the task set before us. We seek your guidance. We are few and we are alone. Cover us with your embrace as we strive to free the enslaved and rid our country of the evil of man. Deliver our souls to Shorth should we fall. Secure us from harm, guide our blades and our limbs.

'We do your work. Hear us.'

Auum kept his head bowed for a few moments, aware that Malaar and Elyss were staring at him. He did not look up when he spoke to them.

'You want to question me. Disagree with me. Perhaps rebuke me. But you think you do not have the authority. Fear has no place within our calling. It does not matter who I am. What matters is that I am TaiGethen and if you believe I am in error, you must challenge my decisions. I already know that you think I am taking the wrong path. Speak. My respect for you can only grow as I hear your words.'

'You are the Arch,' began Malaar.

'I am elven first, Ynissul second and TaiGethen third. None of us is infallible.' Auum raised his head and found he could give an encouraging smile. 'Go on, before I tell you what you are thinking.'

It was Elyss who spoke, her words gushing out like water bursting from a dam.

'Your anger has stopped you thinking clearly. Your fury at the ClawBound and your guilt over Koel's likely fate is leading you to sacrifice all of our lives. You have schooled us in the virtue of patience for so long and yet now it seems that is all gone, washed away in a desire to prove yourself to a Bound elf. Don't let this setback take us from our plan. We have time. The humans do not.'

Auum raised his eyebrows. 'It should have been obvious to us, for a long time, that this thinking is just plain wrong. Serrin has learned as much and so must we. Individual humans certainly have little time, but we aren't fighting one generation. They are endless. And with every year we get weaker while they grow stronger.

'They are not going to get bored and they are not going to become careless. Ystormun is as strong as he is untouchable. His revenge for the ClawBound action will be merciless. The only way to hurt him is to prove we can take our people back from under his nose.'

'That was always our plan,' said Malaar. 'But we have no magic to aid us.'

Auum nodded. 'But what choice do we have? You know how many humans the ClawBound plan to kill and what that means for the slaves of Ysundeneth, or perhaps those of Tolt Anoor or Deneth Barine. Knowing that can you, with Yniss as your witness, turn your back?

'I cannot.'

Elyss and Malaar looked at each other. Their expressions were unsure and their camouflage, streaked by sweat and rain, gave their faces a mournful aspect. Auum understood their doubts. Throughout their run towards Aryndeneth he had asked himself the same questions.

Elyss was going to try just one more time. 'We are not ready to mount such an offensive. We are not strong enough to attack them.'

'If there is one thing the attack on Aryndeneth has taught us it is that the humans will never let us be ready. And our people will start dying again in mere days. You and I know that we have no choice.'

'You and I know that most of us will not return, if we do this,' said Elyss.

'We should eat,' said Auum. He sniffed the soaking air. 'Guarana pods west, acai berries too. Malanga roots are all over the place here, boniata too. Gather what you can quickly. We can't rest for long.'

The night darkened still further and the rain fell in an unrelenting surge that set the ground running with a thick and treacherous sludge. It was as if Gyal was already mourning what was to come and was pouring out her heart across the vastness of the forest.

Yet, even through the thunderous downpour, rain and echoes bouncing all around them, Auum fancied he could hear men's screams. Fractured sounds, filtering through the deepest valleys and falling like dust from the steepest slopes. Screams of terror as unseen assailants delivered death before melting away, leaving their kills to be reclaimed by Tual's denizens.

A new beast strode through the undergrowth. It moved with grace, it wore the forest like a mantle and it was utterly without mercy. The ClawBound had come of age.

*

Ystormun placed the plump cushion on the table in front of him and waited. His heart raced and he could feel the pulse in his neck thudding like a muscle tick. Although he knew it was time, he still wished that there was some warning before the actual connection, a build-up of pressure or a rising intensity of sound. Anything rather than—

Ystormun's body jackknifed where he sat and his forehead slammed into the cushion placed on his desktop. He gasped for a breath and forced it into his lungs while the echoing clamour of voices in his head resolved into a coherent stream. He considered lifting his head and sitting upright but instead turned his head to the right so he could lie in a modicum of comfort and look through the panoramic windows.

The pressure in Ystormun's head faded as did the pain from his impact with the cushion and the desk beneath it. He felt cold and began to shiver with the force of the wills joined with his own in the imagined halls of communion. The atmosphere reeked of disappointment and cynicism. This was not going to be an easy debate.

'My lords,' said Ystormun. 'Your contact is welcome.'

The lords of Triverne were ancient and steeped in magic and its lore. Their power had gone unchallenged for decades, but now they were under increasing pressure to open their circle to change, and to include representatives from the other three schools of magic. They were a circle of six, including Ystormun, and their names ran like a threatening mantra for parents trying to scare disobedient children. If only they knew the half of it.

Pamun, Arumun, Belphamun, Weyamun, Giriamun, Ystormun.

'We care little for your platitudes and much for news of progress.' Pamun's cold voice cut across Ystormun's mind like the slap of thunder against bare rock. 'Detail your achievements.'

'Our experiments on tracking the use of elven magic are complete. And the destruction of much of their magical strength has taken place,' said Ystormun.

' "Much"?' asked the dry mind that was Weyamun. 'Your reports are that inaccurate?'

'We have had no reports at all,' said Ystormun. 'I tire of reminding you that this is not Balaia.'

'Meaning?' demanded Weyamun.

'No members of our strike teams survived to give me accurate numbers.'

'Yet you are certain of at least partial success,' said Arumun, his tone dripping with contempt. 'How so?'

'My sources are none of your concern,' said Ystormun sharply. 'Trust that I am correct and that there is currently no magical strength to threaten us.'

There followed the silence he had grown to hate. When Ystormun had left Balaia he had been the strongest of them. Now he was looked upon as a mere digit on the hand of the greater body that was the other five. He had been gone for far too long.

'We feel resistance,' said Giriamun. 'We sense the next logical step is not forthcoming. We have heard nothing to suggest that a change in the ultimate plan is necessary. What we glean from you is all obfuscation and delay. That cannot continue.'

'Any of you is welcome to travel here to advise me in person.'

'You are the appointed representative of the cadre on Calaius,' said Pamun immediately.

Ystormun laughed and felt the righteous anger flowing across the Southern Ocean to drown his mirth. Despite the pain he felt, Ystormun spoke with as much force as he could muster, hoping to send some small part of that pain back.

'I will continue here as long as I deem it necessary. I am here not because I am the junior partner but because I am the most capable among us. I will decide when and if the remainder are to be hunted down, and I will decide how it is to be done.'

'Your isolation can be made permanent,' snapped Belphamun.

'Calm yourself,' said Pamun. 'Ystormun. We are a collective. None of us acts in isolation. You must hear us.'

'I hear you far too often and with excessive volume. Before you think to instruct me, do any of you deny that this facility works? Deny that the products and resources I export to you have made you wealthy beyond your most fevered dreams and have allowed you to increase our standing army to an unheard-of level in peacetime Balaia. Do you deny that continuing our mission here will further increase our strength, wealth and influence?'

'We deny none of these statements,' said Belphamun. 'Your problem, Ystormun, is your ignorance of the changing situation here. You are correct that our standing army is large, but you control more than a third of it at any one time. Those soldiers and mages are required here.'

'The rotation must continue,' replied Ystormun. 'The security of this facility depends on it.'

'Then amend the situation so your security can be maintained using hundreds, not thousands, of souls.'

'It is not that simple.'

'It is that simple!' Pamun's voice blared across the divide and every muscle in Ystormun's body spasmed. 'Seek them out and destroy them. They are so few and you are so many. Stop hiding inside your palace and do what you were sent to do.'

Ystormun was exhausted. The stamina required to maintain Communion over such a vast distance against minds as strong as the five lords' was considerable. He fought to remain calm. He had to win this argument with reason.

'One does not simply dispatch a force into the rainforest. It could swallow Balaia whole. I am already working to uncover their most secret hiding place, but to march before I have confirmed my information is foolhardy. Add to that the issue of the enemy. They are few but their skill is legendary and we have no idea how many of them now have the run of the rainforest.

'I will not burn the forest indiscriminately to drive them out, because that robs us of resources. I will operate this task to a time-scale dictated by the situation on the ground here. There is, my lords, no other way to proceed.'

'You are afraid,' said Giriamun.

'I am cautious,' said Ystormun. 'And I am right to be. Our current understanding with the enemy means I can work against them without striking out at them, and in the meantime I can continue to harvest the forest unmolested.'

'Your time is up,' said Belphamun. 'We are under threat. Our enemies know the size of our commitment in Calaius and will soon believe themselves strong enough to challenge us. You will receive no more military support and indeed you must prepare for the recall of the bulk of your army.'

'You still don't understand,' said Ystormun. 'If I embark on an undirected attack there might be no army to be recalled. Our enemies remain the masters of the forest, and there is a balance between us. Recruit more men for yourselves. Don't threaten this facility with precipitate action.'

'Your stubbornness will prove costly,' said Pamun.

And abruptly the contact was broken. Ystormun waited, with his head still on the cushion, until the shivers had subsided and the ache in his head died away. When he finally lifted his head, its left-hand side and the cushion were soaked with sweat. An aide stood before the desk, his face to the floor.

'This had better be good news.'

The aide shook his head. 'There have been more attacks.'

Ystormun sighed. 'Not now. Not *now*.'

Auum led Elyss and Malaar into Aryndeneth an hour after dawn. The temple doors stood open and the stone apron at the front was busy with workers and TaiGethen who had already responded to the ClawBound call.

'Elyss, get me numbers and information on who else is coming. Malaar, brief them on what we've witnessed and what the Claw-Bound intend. Say nothing of my decision. I'm going to find Takaar.'

Auum trotted into the cool air beneath the dome. He knelt in prayer before the statue of Yniss before hurrying into the depths of the temple. The low hum of voices, one louder than the rest, travelled to him on the still air. They were coming from a chapel close to the block of individual prayer cells and visiting priests' rooms.

Auum stood at the door for a moment, watching Onelle talking with a group he recognised as the orientation class; they had been lucky enough to be in the forest when the humans attacked. The voices hushed when he walked in, the adepts bunching reflexively and moving half a pace backwards. Onelle smiled at him. Auum embraced her, kissing her eyes and forehead.

'I must look quite a sight,' he said.

There was nervous laughter.

'You need to reapply your camouflage,' said Onelle, her expression sober. 'You didn't stop them, did you?'

Auum shook his head. 'They are starting their own war and their actions force us to save those who cannot save themselves. I need Takaar. Where is he?'

Onelle hesitated and Auum felt his anger flare. 'He's . . . visiting. Or I assume he is. He's been gone for two days.'

'Damn his Ynissul heart!' Auum clapped his hands to his face. The adepts flinched as one.

Onelle took his arm and walked him back into the passage and then through the rear doors to the village.

'It doesn't matter whose side you're on, no one is very comfortable in front of an angry TaiGethen.'

'They may need to get used to it,' said Auum. 'Why did he go now? Surely even he, or his other self, could see the risk the ClawBound posed. And his reaction is to run off to talk to a human? Perhaps he is not fit to school the Il-Aryn.'

Onelle had kept him walking and they had passed through the village and into the forest, heading towards a shrine to Tual that nestled near a Hallows of Reclamation.

'Take a breath, Auum. What's happening? We're still in shock after the attack, and the rites of reclamation for the dead have only just been completed. I'll have nightmares about those victims' faces for ever, and worse about those whose deaths left no trace at all.

'What am I trying to say? We heard the ClawBound call the muster. The TaiGethen are arriving here and people are scared. *I'm* scared. The forest feels strange and we can sense changes in the lines of power. You've decided to attack the humans, haven't you? When I have no one to help you.'

Auum took Onelle's shoulders and gave her what he hoped was a calming smile.

'I'm sorry, Onelle. It's all moving faster than a taipan strike, I know. Listen: the ClawBound aren't just taking revenge, they're starting a cleansing . . . which means hundreds of elves in the slave cities are going to die unless we can save them. Serrin will no longer hear reason and he as much as challenged my courage and authority.' Auum sighed. 'He's forced our hand. We have to attack Ysundeneth, and to save as many as we can.'

Onelle's glorious oval eyes widened in her age-worn face. She gestured about her. 'But we . . . I mean, I can't—'

'I'm sorry, Onelle. We have to get into Ysundeneth before news of the attacks gets to Ystormun. We're already too late to stop some of the deaths. And now it grows worse because, without Takaar, we have no one to guide us past the wards. No one but you.'

Auum could see her shrinking from the prospect. But it wasn't fear of humans or conflict that drove her emotions when she shook her head.

'I can't go back there, Auum. Not after what happened. Not after what they did to us. Some of the elves who persecuted the Ynissul are still alive in there. Others are living in Katura. Why do you suppose I came here? It wasn't just to learn magic.'

Auum looked at Onelle anew. She was shivering with the rawness of memories which were a hundred and fifty years old.

'Then why do you teach, if not to arm us for the fight against mankind? I have learned to forgive those of other threads who attacked my Ynissul brothers and sisters. If we are to prosper under Yniss when the humans are gone, we must all forgive each other.'

'It's easy for you, Auum. No one kicked down your door and raped you while your husband was beaten and forced to watch. No one shouted in your face that the Ynissul would pay when they saw mixed-thread offspring drop from their wombs.

'I teach magic so that humans like the ones who murdered my husband in the rainforest might die in flames as he did. But I cannot go back there. I'll never go back.'

'Onelle you must—'

'There is nothing I *must* do. Not even for you, Arch of the Tai-Gethen. Give me another fifty years and I will school new Il-Aryn for you. But that is all I will do. If you want to get into Ysundeneth, you'll have to find Takaar.'

Her eyes were brimful with bitterness. Auum held her gaze a moment longer before nodding curtly and walking away around the outside of the temple and back to the apron. He had to respect Onelle's decision, but it was clear that her isolation here among the Ynissul had deprived her of the opportunity to heal her mental scars.

In front of the temple, Elyss and Malaar were addressing the assembled TaiGethen. Auum counted seven cells and did not hide his disappointment at the low numbers. He joined his Tai, nodding for Malaar to continue speaking.

'. . . we are certain of little but that the ClawBound will continue cleansing the rainforest, and that means more and more innocent elves will die. Auum.'

Auum stepped forward. 'How many other cells are on the way?'

'Four from the south and eastern patrol zones. None as yet from further afield, like Tolt Anoor or Deneth Barine. That's to be expected.' Elyss shrugged her shoulders. 'The call only went out at dusk yesterday.'

Auum nodded curtly. 'Others will come, but for now we few will have to suffice. Leave word of our destination with Onelle. Tais, we must ask Yniss to preserve our souls and protect our bodies for the greater tasks to come. We need the silence of Tual and the cover of Beeth. We need the luck of Ix and the strength of Appos. We must liberate the slaves of Ysundeneth and we must find Takaar before we get there. Cover every northern approach to the temple on the way out.

'That bastard is going to help us get into Ysundeneth, human-lover or not. Tais we move.'

Chapter 9

Yniss blessed the blackened earth and from it sprang the glory of the forest. Beeth's eyes were the widest in wonder and so Yniss bestowed upon Beeth the honour of being guardian of all root and branch. Beeth breathed in his new life, reached down and caressed the canopy. 'You are long-lived,' said Yniss. 'But no tree is immortal. So shall it be for your children.'

The Aryn Hiil

The city of Katura nestled in the palm of Yniss. It was without question the most beautiful place in the rainforest. Towards the southern perimeter of the forest, from which it was three days' run before the glory of the canopy gave way to the baking-hot plains, it was set within a spectacular landscape of cliffs, lakes, valleys and mountains.

The elves called it the playground of Tual, and for centuries it had been a reserve where Tual's denizens could run unchallenged. No two-legged hunters confused the chain of life and death here. No vegetation was used for food, shelter or fire. Untouched, glorious, virgin rainforest; until man came and elves were not safe even in their own temples.

Rainforest lore said that all Tual's creatures spilled from the palm of Yniss and so it was the right place, the only place, for the battered elven race to find sanctuary – back at the heart of life. A place where they could tend to their wounds, gather their strength and learn to live again. If anywhere could provide a balm for the soul, it was here.

The palm of Yniss was a great horseshoe-shaped basin nestling at the base of sheer cliffs backed by tree-covered mountains. Waterfalls roared and ran over the edge of the cliffs in five places, gathering into a food-rich lake whose northern outflow was a distant tributary to the River Ix. Both lake and river were named Carenthan, like the mountain range behind them, while the falls were called Katura.

A vast plain of grass and low trees grew on the sheltered lands bordering the lake and along the banks of the river. It was a perfect place to settle, farm and glory in life, and had it not been forbidden elves would have settled there many generations ago.

But the palm had not just been chosen for its beauty and mythology. It was a hidden land, surrounded by mists and low cloud that periodically swept off the mountains and down the thousand-foot cliffs. To stand on the cliffs and look down on the plain was the culmination of a journey up cleft, over mountain peak and through deep forest where the panthers were still masters of the land.

The only way to reach it was along the base of the sharp-sided valley through which the Carenthan River flowed. The river was wide and the paths alongside it were narrow and treacherous, climbing steadily towards the plain. The sides of the valley were part crag, part balsa woodland, rife with vines and ivies and largely impenetrable.

To walk the valleys, find new paths and glimpse fresh views of the vastness of the forest, where the sun seemed to engender new life wherever it kissed the green leaves, was a joy for any who made the effort. So Methian forced his aching, ageing body up the final incline and joined Boltha at the top.

Two old elves, one Gyalan, one Apposan, gazed across the miles of unbroken forest canopy and down on the city that nestled in the palm of Yniss. Smoke smudged the sky, and even this far distant the echoes of elven prayers were carried on the prevailing wind, along with the clang of hammer on metal and the rasp of saw against wood.

Boltha spat on the ground.

'We are a stain on perfection,' he said. 'A slime that is oozing its way into the bedrock and corrupting the very place that should have inspired us back to greatness. We do not deserve saving.'

Methian tore his eyes from the ungainly sprawl of the city. Katura had become the elves' greatest shame. Work which had begun with such energy had become lack-lustre and lazy. There was not a single building they could be proud of. And within the city limits, enmity grew by the day.

'How long since you set foot in there?'

Boltha's watery eyes squinted back at Methian. His close sight was poor, indeed he feared it was fading altogether.

'More than fifteen years. Ever since we took the Apposans to the

Haliath Vale. We couldn't bear to stay another moment. No wonder you retired.'

'I didn't retire,' said Methian, and he could not keep the bitterness from his voice. 'It is an enduring sadness that I was made unwelcome by the very people I was sworn to help.'

'You can't blame yourself. Edulis is a drug that removes reason, sense and any familial feeling. She dismissed you because she no longer knew you.'

Methian sighed. 'I could have stopped her becoming an addict. I should have seen her falling.'

'Addicts are clever right up until the moment they lose their minds. She's still alive, is she?'

'Dead addicts don't make any money. Dead governors don't pass handy new laws. The suppliers are careful. After all, the birth rates are so low now that they have a practically stagnant population. They can't afford to start killing them.'

Boltha barked out a laugh. 'We should torch the place.'

'I hear you, old friend, but not everyone there has sunk so low. Some still work and there are many people still praying for redemption in Katura.'

'Which god will hear them?' Boltha's tone was harsh. 'It's a cesspit, nothing more.'

'And you did nothing to help when you took your thread away.'

Methian hadn't meant it quite the way it came out and he saw Boltha's face pinch in sudden anger.

'We did nothing that Auum didn't do when he took the Ynissul from Katura almost before a tree was felled to build the damn place.'

'He had to,' snapped Methian. 'He had to develop the new TaiGethen and provide adepts for the Il-Aryn, and the Ynissul birth rate is so low that every new Ynissul child is cause for a celebration as if the gods were walking the forest once more. What excuse did you have? You whose hands helped to build what you now despise.'

'We relied on the Al-Arynaar. Your leader's spectacular failure is the seed of all that Katura has become. I only removed my thread when the reports began to say innocent elves were being forced into addiction. And what riches are the harvesters and dealers making for themselves, I wonder?'

'Land,' said Methian. 'What else? Pelyn was given the power to grant each elf land in the forest and on the plain. Much of it is in the hands of the Tuali and Beethan drug gangs now. They are strong. They own Katura.'

Boltha raised his eyebrows. 'Really? Has anyone told Auum?'

'Auum hasn't been here in over fifty years. No TaiGethen come here.' Methian sighed. 'I'm sorry. I do not mean to bait you.'

Boltha smiled. 'You and I will always clash, as our threads dictate. So why did you invite me on this hike with you? Not to recreate our journeys of past years, I'm sure.'

'No, indeed,' said Methian. 'Come, let's sit. I've got some rather good spirit and some bread, tapir and dried fruit too.'

'I knew I could rely on you,' said Boltha.

The old Apposan, still strong of arm, chopped some scrub and vines away from a fallen log and the two old friends sat. Methian reached into his backpack and passed Boltha a clay jug stoppered with a wood plug.

'Sip it,' he said. 'Strong stuff.'

Boltha took a swallow. He breathed in slowly and Methian smiled as he imagined the liquid burning its way down his throat.

'Where does *that* come from?' said Boltha. 'Tastes a bit like yams.'

'Yes, but we've distilled it with guarana. Makes you drunk but you don't want to sleep. Helps with the headache next day, too.'

Boltha took another sip and passed the jug back to Methian.

'At least you haven't wasted your whole life.'

Methian sniffed the jug before wetting his lips with the spirit and then letting a long trickle run down his throat.

'I'm old, Boltha,' he said once he'd stoppered the jug and fished in his pack for the bread and meat. 'But I've only just begun feeling it. I was a warrior of the Al-Arynaar for over three hundred years and I am as proud of that as I am of being Gyalan.

'I've seen the very best of the elven spirit and believed that we were genuinely entering a golden age of harmony and progress. But the last years have been relentless decline and conflict and I find I cannot accept that as the epitaph of my life in service.'

'Why do you think I took my leave? Katura is a cancer.'

'Yes!' said Methian, and he felt the spirit coursing round his blood energising him. 'And it must be excised.'

'So talk to your erstwhile leader, if she ever returns to lucidity. How many Al-Arynaar still wear the cloak?'

'Who knows? We probably have fewer warriors than the Tai-Gethen for the first time in elven history. Not even enough to police a city of twenty thousand.'

'And growing fewer every day . . .' said Boltha.

'It has to stop, and though there is desire in the city to see it cleaned up, there is no strength.'

Boltha held up his hands. 'I know where this is going.'

'You are strong,' said Methian, leaning forward and offering him dried mango which Boltha took and ate. 'Your thread is pure. You are the thread of the axe. Others fear you, even the Tuali. Come back. Help me cleanse the city. Help me return Katura to purity. To harmony.'

'The only way to do that is to burn the place to the ground.'

Methian shrugged. 'If that's what it takes.'

'Why should I risk my people for those who cared so little for us?'

'Because if you do not it will render everything we did when Ysundeneth fell a waste. It will render your faith a sham. And I know you, Boltha. You believe in the harmony. Help me and we can start again, to make Katura great before we die.' Methian smiled as rain began to fall. 'And Gyal knows neither of us has terribly long left.'

A primeval, guttural sound grew from the north. It echoed among the trees and fed up the valleys. Even beyond Katura, panthers took up the cry. Methian shuddered.

'What is that?'

'It's the ClawBound. They're calling the TaiGethen to muster.'

'Are you sure?'

Boltha nodded and pushed himself to his feet. 'I need to get back to Haliath.'

'I understand,' said Methian. 'Think on what I've said. Help me. Help us all.'

The calls faded away.

'Do you have a plan for this rebellion of yours, or whatever you call it?'

'I know where we have to strike, if that's what you mean.'

'And do your enemies know you're plotting against them?'

Methian chuckled. 'I'm an old Gyalan. I don't even carry a weapon any more. No one suspects me of anything barring being a grumpy old loudmouth.'

'Well we can all agree on that.' Boltha took Methian's shoulders.

'These are dangerous people you're facing. Don't assume you are not seen as a threat. Will the Al-Arynaar back you?'

'I have to hope so.'

'Good enough. Then come back with me – you'll be safe with the Apposans until it's time to strike.'

'You're with me?'

'I can hardly let some arthritic old Gyalan get all the glory, now can I? Anyway, I don't think I have much option.'

'Why?'

Boltha gestured north.

'I can only think of one reason for the ClawBound to call the TaiGethen to muster and that scares me. We need Katura to be strong, to be the sanctuary it was designed to be. If it isn't, I fear for us. I fear we will not survive.'

Ystormun looked sick. Sicker. It was normally hard to tell, but today there was a greyness to his skin that left him looking closer to death than Sildaan had ever seen him; and she saw him every day. Such was her misfortune. Like Garan, she fervently wished for death each night when she was allowed to rest. And like Garan, Ystormun seemed to take perverse delight in keeping her alive.

Sildaan stood before the great wooden desk, awaiting questions from her human lord and master. She had resisted admitting that's what he had become to her, but she could not escape it. She was an Ynissul who dreamed of a return to ultimate power over the elves, one who could reach out and touch it yet was an impossible distance from ever achieving it.

Punishment indeed, and Llyron should have been standing here to suffer with her, yet the former high priestess of Shorth would never do so. She had found her way to death and that had made Sildaan's task all the harder.

So Sildaan took the brunt of his evil. She looked to her left and out into the Calaian night sky. The lantern light playing on the windows showed her a reflection of herself, and she shrank inwardly at the sight of her thinning hair, gaunt face, sunken eyes and bloodless lips. Her ears, so delicate, were bent at the tips like an elf a thousand years her elder. She still remembered the strength of her arms and the power in her heart and mind. Proud Ynissul, now laid so low. Such was the price of her god casting her aside. Sildaan could not contain the whimper that escaped her lips. She turned away from the window.

In front of her, Ystormun dragged in a shuddering breath. He was in pain. His hands shook and there was sweat on his brow. Veins pulsed at his temples. He opened his eyes. Sildaan gasped. They were white. No pupil whatsoever. Yet he could see her and the man who stood by her. He examined them while he weighed up his first words. Something moved beneath the milky whiteness and Sildaan thought she might be sick.

'Times move ever faster,' said Ystormun. 'So there are things I must know.'

Ystormun's voice was altered, discordant as if he was speaking with multiple tongues, all of which moved in fractionally different ways to form the same words.

'What must you know, Lord Ystormun?' asked the man, who was profoundly lucky to be alive and standing in his presence.

'Ah. Jeral. Reprieved by the mercy of an animal, were you not? I would ask how is it that with the strength of mages and warriors you had under your command you were unable to defeat weaponless elves and their feline pets. But I am sure I would hear useless talk of speed and stealth and the forest shadows. Instead, I will ask you about the only point of interest in your entire report.'

Ystormun wafted a hand at a single roll of paper.

'It is an honest report.'

'Yes, detailing incompetence, slack management and ignorance of the first rule of handling Sharps in the field. Always keep a mage in the air. Now tell me, Jeral, your report mentions that the elves and their panthers worked in harmony. "Like they were of one mind" were your exact words. Explain.'

'Thank you, lord, for the opportunity.'

'It won't necessarily save your life.'

Jeral's words caught in his throat. He stammered and coughed.

'The attack was fast and it was impossible to defend against because each elf worked with a panther and they needed no words to effect their plan. I saw their leader, I think he was their leader, look into the eyes of his animal once and, beyond that, they attacked our mages as one before turning their attention to the warriors.

'They were just animals but they knew exactly who to take out first. You cannot train that into a beast. And I know we have spells that achieve much the same thing, but the elves have no magic like this. I was standing beside Nuin and he didn't sense any magic being used. That was right before he had his throat ripped out by a panther while I was left wholly untouched.'

'A shame,' said Ystormun. 'But something worthy of further investigation. Sildaan, you're looking well. You bear your responsibilities with more grace every day.'

'Only by accident,' said Sildaan.

Ystormun began to chuckle, but it became a hacking cough and his expression hardened.

'Do you recognise this skill in your people?'

'There was no such link the last time I was in the rainforest.'

'So Jeral is lying. I'm uncomfortable with liars.'

Jeral whimpered a desperate 'No.'

'I can't say that with any certainty,' said Sildaan quickly, feeling a bizarre kinship with Jeral. 'But I can postulate.'

Ystormun picked up the roll of paper and shook it open.

'Yes, please do. The ClawBound, Jeral called them. What are they?'

'There have always been stories about elves forging closer and closer ties to Tual's denizens. Elves whom no snake would bite, no insect sting, no predator hunt. It has long been held that the Silent Priests were actively seeking a true bond to every creature in the rainforest to greater understand the workings of Tual and, through him, of Yniss.

'I have read Jeral's report and there is no doubt that the elves he describes, though much changed, are Silent Priests. It is possible that they have spent their time working with panthers but I can give you no explanation how they might have forged a mental link with these beasts. I can only tell you that it is possible, because Yniss and Tual have the power to bestow such gifts.'

'Your faith can explain anything it chooses, Sildaan, and you know I have little time for religion. The question is, would you reckon your life on it being possible?'

Sildaan did not have to think. 'Yes.'

Ystormun nodded. 'We thought as much. Very well. Jeral you are dismissed. Get some rest. You and your cohorts will have need of it.'

Jeral left the room with ungracious haste and Sildaan felt abandoned. Ystormun sank further into his chair, muttered and closed his eyes. He shook violently and words in a human language Sildaan had never heard before forced themselves from his lips. His entire body tensed and then relaxed. He opened his eyes and Sildaan saw they were his more usual dark colour, with bloodshot whites.

'What are they doing, these ClawBound?' he asked.

'They are cleansing the forest,' said Sildaan. 'The Silent Priests always promised they would.'

'So I have already been told. And they will not stop?'

Sildaan smiled. 'No. Not until all humans within its boundaries are dead. You can consider the forest closed to you.'

'Now that is a shame,' said Ystormun. 'Because at this time, this pivotal, crucial time, I cannot afford that.'

Sildaan quailed under his gaze, which was utterly bleak and murderous. 'Please. Do not make the innocents suffer. This does not break any unspoken agreement you have with the TaiGethen. This is a calling of elves acting alone, I'm certain of it.'

'You think me so stupid,' said Ystormun. 'Certainly stupid enough to slaughter my workforce in retaliation. I concede I was tempted. Eviscerating Sharps is always tempting, but not this time. This time even I have orders. We may not be ready but our hands have been forced by events in my country as well as the actions of your kin.

'And so we shall take the rainforest and in doing so shall end the resistance – the existence, I should say – of the elven race. Do you want to watch the extinction of your race? I can offer you a prime seat.'

'You cannot possibly believe you can defeat the TaiGethen in their own forest. Human blood will run in our rivers and you will never find our hidden city. Not even I know where it is.'

'It's called Katura and I am sure you know exactly where it is, Sildaan, but don't worry, I won't torture you in an attempt to find out. I don't need to. I have someone who will lead us straight there.'

Sildaan had to steady herself against the side of the desk.

'No elf would betray our people in such a way.'

'No? Well, I suppose you are well placed to make such a judgement. And as it happens, you still retain your exalted position as betrayer-in-chief. This elf has no knowledge of the damage he is going to do his people. And the really pleasing thing is that he is one of your most fervent, most spectacularly faithful, people. He is possessed of talents not even he can fathom and is determined to use anything he can to the benefit of the elves.

'Unfortunately he doesn't realise that the focus of mana within his body is stronger than the scent of blood in the River Ix. He reeks of it, exudes it and can do nothing to hide it. And we, my dear Sildaan, could use it to follow him through the very bowels of the earth.

'You really ought to come along and watch the show.'

Chapter 10

The rainforest is so utterly vast it is truly difficult for the mind to comprehend. Fly with mages, stand on the highest peak, sail the longest river, and you will achieve some small perspective. The way to truly understand is to walk for day upon unending day in a single direction and after the fiftieth, sixtieth or seventieth day know that you could be only halfway to the other side. Know that you are equally distant from its borders in any other direction. Know that the TaiGethen have trodden every inch of this land and have identified every place in which to kill their enemies. Know that there are an infinite number of such places.

Reminiscences of an Old Soldier, by Garan,

sword master of Ysundeneth (retired)

Takaar had run to the eaves of the forest, there to curse his misfortune.

Misfortune? Remember a TaiGethen is never alone.

'I am no longer TaiGethen and that blade would not enter his neck. Do not ask me why.'

I have no need. Your cowardice rears its head at the most spectacular moments and reduces your strength to that of a dung fly. Oh, the elves must hear of this latest betrayal.

'You cannot goad me as you once did. And even then I was too strong for you. Did I step from that cliff edge? I did not. You lost this battle decade upon decade ago and still it hurts that you cannot control me.'

I have no desire to control you. Only to see you crawling on your belly like your beloved snakes with the eyes of every true elf upon you, knowing the truth about their erstwhile hero.

'They already know the truth!' Takaar's voice set creatures scurrying deeper into the undergrowth. 'And they have forgiven me, taken

me to their hearts once more and allowed me to work to make them
stronger, able to stand proud as men are driven from Calaius.'

*Taken you to their hearts, have they? Is that why you run off to
Garan the moment something goes wrong? Keener to hear the words
of man than of elf when the world darkens?*

'Garan gives more than he takes and this time he has unlocked a
secret and opened my eyes. I knew he would turn against Ystormun.
I knew he would see man's invasion for the sacrilege it is.'

'What has Garan unlocked, exactly?'

Takaar spun as he rose, his twin swords whispering from their
sheaths. He counted five, but more were circling him, unseen.

Yniss preserve you, how careless.

Takaar smiled and sheathed his blades.

'I was expecting you.'

Auum's expression was bleak. 'Really? And you always welcome
your friends with your blades, do you?'

'Your approach was quiet, I'll admit and I was—'

'Engaged in another conversation. Quite vocally, considering his
proximity.'

Takaar heard the whisper of laughter from among the TaiGethen,
who were emerging into his small clearing in some numbers. Fifteen
of them now.

Don't let him goad you. He's goading you, isn't he?

'No one is goading me.'

'I beg your pardon?' said Auum, walking closer.

'I was not addressing you,' said Takaar sharply.

'Clearly,' said Auum. 'You and I need to talk. In private. Just the
three of us.'

Takaar searched Auum's face for the humour he was sure would
be there, but for some reason it was absent. He felt a moment's
confusion.

*Idiot. And I thought you'd be used to people insulting you, laugh-
ing behind your back, that sort of thing.*

'I do not like your tone,' hissed Takaar.

Finally.

Auum walked closer. Takaar could smell the camouflage paint.
He turned his head slightly and couldn't stop his hands wringing
together.

'I do not much care whether you like it or not,' Auum replied. 'I care that soon Ysundeneth will once again be full of the corpses of innocent elves and their blood will be on the hands of man.'

Takaar chuckled. 'It's good that I'm here, isn't it?'

'It is never good that you are anywhere near things that matter. Walk with me.'

Auum made a gesture towards his TaiGethen, who scattered into the new growth that had sprung up in the wake of the wholesale logging near Ysundeneth and the Ultan bridge. Only Auum's cell remained, and he indicated they stay in place before stalking off into the deeper undergrowth to the south.

Do you think he'll come back if you just stand here?

'Why would I do that? I am the bearer of all that is important. He needs me.'

Pathetic. You're like some snivelling servant, so anxious to please your master. Even for you, this is a new low.

Takaar followed Auum. 'The elves must survive, all else is secondary.'

You mean all else is secondary to justifying your existence to an elf who once idolised you. At least test him. Prove yourself his better in the one thing he holds most dear. That is the minimum if you are to retain any self-worth.

'I have no need of such proof.'

No? Do you even remember being one of them?

'Show yourself and I'll prove I could still be one.'

I'd laugh, but you killed our sense of humour about a hundred and sixty years ago.

'Why are you plaguing me?'

Because you always seek me out when you need answers.

'Enough.'

Takaar moved quickly, following Auum's footsteps. Thirty paces into the thick of the undergrowth, where the lower level of the canopy swooped towards the ground, Auum had stopped and was facing him. There was a look of disappointment mixed with contempt on his face. He knew what was in Takaar's mind.

'Don't do this,' said Auum. 'Do not even attempt it. You know, I always found it admirable that even in your madness and solitude, you still practised the art to its highest degree. When I found you, your skills were unparalleled. But now? You do not train and your mind is fogged with thoughts of magic. You are no longer quick enough to test me.'

Takaar said nothing but Auum's words wormed deep into his heart. He dropped quickly and swept out a foot. He found clear air. Auum landed hard, dropping a knee onto Takaar's chest, swiping his arms aside with impressive speed and putting a dagger to his throat.

'I don't have time for this,' said Auum. 'I need a way into the city and unfortunately that means I need your help.'

Auum moved his knee and stood back. Takaar got to his feet. His mind was darting here and there; his tormentor was ridiculing his combat skills and the magic within him was unsettled, barely under control. He felt a weight in his mind and a powerful sense of injustice. He gripped Auum's shoulders.

'What lies inside me is so hard to control. You see. And now I can see a path. We have been blind, you know. Blind to what is in front of us. There is no time to lose. Perhaps then I can release my pain.'

Look at Auum. I'm not the only one who has no idea what you're talking about.

'Shut up, shut up, I cannot focus. Auum, my clear moments are so few, but I was clear when Garan spoke to me and I know what he told me. But with every day I get greyer. In my head. We must fight back while there is still time. Do you not see?'

Congratulations. Not a word of sense. Not a single one.

'I need you to know I am behind you. Every day I am trying to unpick the mysteries of my gift so I can pass it to those who can use it better than I. To try to build a new strength in elves that will allow us to defend ourselves for generations to come.'

Better.

'I have to find our new practitioners. I can't wait here. None of them are here, are they? So stop delaying me and let me go.'

Oh dear.

Takaar fell silent. He couldn't remember a thing he had just said. Auum prised his hands from his shoulders and Takaar felt the crushing strength in the TaiGethen's fingers before he was released.

'There is nothing I want more than for you to go, but I have two problems. I think you are unfit to teach the Il-Aryn, but Onelle seems to trust you. And I think you are unfit to help me get into Ysundeneth, but I have no choice but to trust you.'

Sharp, this Auum, isn't he?

'I don't—'

'Be silent and listen,' said Auum. 'If I had my way, you would not be allowed in the same chamber as anyone who might wield the

Il-Aryn. You are a menace, you consort with humans and from one heartbeat to the next you do not know what you will think, do or say. That is how I see you, Takaar.'

'But right now you are going to come with me and my people and help us liberate elves from Ysundeneth because if you do not, there will be more blood on your hands. Am I making sense?'

Takaar shook his head. 'If you go in there, you will all die.'

'If we don't, hundreds of innocents will die, the ClawBound have seen to that.'

'But you can hear nothing, can you?' asked Takaar.

'What do you . . .'

Auum's expression cleared and he turned towards Ysundeneth. Takaar could feel him willing the forest to silence, tuning out the ambient sounds, straining his hearing towards the city. He stood there for an age, completely still, and Takaar could find it inside him to admire the elf's focus. Auum breathed in, uncertain.

'Why is it so silent?' he whispered.

'Because there is to be no death within the walls,' said Takaar. 'The humans are reserving that for the rainforest.'

'Meaning?'

'Your precious ClawBound have not started a wave of revenge with their actions, they have started a war.'

Auum stared at Takaar with fresh interest and Takaar nodded solemnly and challenged his tormentor to say something. Anything. That voice was silent.

'This had better not be one of your games,' said Auum.

Takaar shrugged. 'You do not need to believe me. Ystormun gave me an ultimatum. I have since spoken to the ClawBound and they will not treat with him. And so the humans will come to finish the job the Ynissul unwittingly invited them into do.'

Auum's stare did not waver but his eyes widened.

'You spoke to Ystormun.'

'I tried to kill Ystormun.'

And failed.

'And failed,' said Auum. 'Why? Magic not strong enough? Arm not quick enough?'

'Contempt does not become one who has not faced this enemy alone.'

You almost sound impressive. A pity you will never get another chance to.

'So enlighten me. You were in a position to threaten our greatest enemy and yet . . . what?'

'He is protected by more than mere magic. My blade would not even nick his skin.'

Auum turned away. 'Then perhaps you should keep your blades keener.'

'Do not presume to judge me. I, who have presided over the deaths of so many, am the only one who can judge me.' Takaar slapped the heel of a palm to his forehead. 'And in here, *in here*, I hold the keys to our survival. You can wait until dawn to see the humans march from their city. I must begin my search for those who might, if you can thwart the humans just a little, return us to greatness.'

Auum was back at him, jabbing a finger into his chest. Takaar didn't want to, but he whimpered at each impact.

'And there is the root of my problem with you. Always seeking the ultimate glory. Always needing to be a head higher than the rest of us, desperate to feel the adoration that you once felt on Hausolis. Always keeping something back to retain one trembling hand on power.

'The elves cannot afford to indulge your self-interest. We cannot afford your bloated ego, lusting after times long gone. So go, Takaar. Lose yourself in whatever quest it is you are so compelled to undertake. Chasing more practitioners, is it?' Auum waved a hand and then pointed back towards Ysundeneth. 'If the humans are coming then it is not magic in fifty or a hundred years' time that we need. It is strength and honour and speed and warriors in the next handful of days.'

A blade was at Takaar's throat and in truth he hadn't seen Auum draw it.

'Steel will win this war, if war it is. Man thinks his magic dominates all. But this is my forest. And it is a lonely place in which to die.'

Takaar backed away, and he knew he was shaking and could not control it. He pointed a finger at Auum but it carried no conviction.

'Garan has already given me one great gift and he will give me another. He has said as much. So dismiss me at your own risk, Auum. I am Takaar. I am still the future.'

The blade was back in its scabbard but Auum was no less intimidating.

'No, Takaar, you are yesterday's elf, not tomorrow's. Take any who love you and leave the rainforest. Find another place to peddle your insanity. The elves have no time or use for magic.'

Takaar opened his mouth to speak but there were no words.

Like I said: sharp, this Auum, isn't he? Laid you bare with a handful of words.

Tears were flooding down Takaar's cheeks. He wanted to bellow at Auum that he was wrong. That he had to embrace magic in any form they could because it was as natural as the breath in their lungs and the blood in their veins. But Auum was a warrior. He was TaiGethen. And there was nothing he had to understand that he did not already know.

You're going to run, aren't you? Scamper away like a deer with a panther bite in its rump. Another failure. Another act of the most supreme cowardice.

'You are right and you are wrong, as I will show you.'

'Are you talking to me?'

Takaar shrugged. 'I'll let you decide.'

And Takaar ran.

Koel nursed the barge around the final bends of the River Ix. The river ran below the level of the city, through a rock cleft thirty feet deep, before emerging to join the sea just beyond the river jetties and lumber mills. The flow was fast here, the cleft narrow and treacherous, affected by tides and rainfall like no other stretch of the river. It was a place where the piranha waited under overhangs; a place where elf and animal perished should they take a single careless step and fall into the current. If the river didn't get them, the piranha would.

Behind Koel, the other two barges made slower progress, with the nets keeping the sodden lumber in place stretched between them, their crews busy fending the vessels away from the rock walls. They had passed the Senserii Approach, which led across the river and into the temple of Shorth, and had been seen by guards, who would ensure they met with a difficult welcome at the mill quay.

Ahead of them, out of sight for a little longer, was the Ultan bridge. Koel breathed the night air, fresh and beautiful, unsullied by the filth of the city. The sky was clear. Gyal rested and her cloud and rain rested with her. He could almost imagine himself free but for the stench of the city, so strong in his memory.

'Koel.'

Koel stiffened. There should be no one with him at the tiller. He turned. There, on the aft rail, stood Auum. Koel took in his painted face and sensed the determination in him as he stepped lightly onto the deck. None of the others had looked up from their work, he was so silent.

'Where did you come from?' asked Koel. Auum's eyes glanced up. Koel followed his gaze up the cliff. 'What are you doing here? I thought—'

'We have come to it already,' said Auum.

Koel shook his head. 'To . . . ?'

'I need you to be as ready as you can be for what is to come.'

'You're going to attack?' Koel couldn't grasp what had changed in so short a time. 'Now?'

'No,' said Auum. 'The humans are going to invade the rainforest. That is where the confrontation will happen and, whatever the outcome, you have to find a way to make all enslaved elves ready to fight.'

'We can prepare,' said Koel, and he could not stop the smile edging onto his face. 'We have dreamed of little else.'

Auum regarded him for a moment. 'I expected you to demand we free you. After all, much of man's strength will be departing the city.'

'Aye, but if you do not have the magic to divine wards and traps, it doesn't matter how many men are guarding us. You'll still all be killed. Better you take them on in the forest. It's the chance you've dreamed of, isn't it? Defeat them there and you can free us at your leisure. We've waited a hundred and fifty years. We can wait a little longer.'

Auum said nothing.

'I understand, Auum. Don't feel conflicted by your decision. To fight them in the forest is the right way.'

Auum nodded his thanks. 'We will not necessarily win this fight. We will be tens against thousands. Should we win, I will need your people to help sweep the remnants of the human filth from the streets. Should we be defeated, you must kill every man you can when they come for you.

'Make no mistake: this invasion is designed to rid Calaius of elves. First in the forest and then in the cities.'

Koel sighed. 'The ClawBound have done this.'

'They have not helped,' conceded Auum. 'But perhaps this gives us a better chance.'

'Win for us,' said Koel. 'I will lead prayers for you each day.'

Auum squeezed Koel's upper arms.

'Our blood will come at the highest price.'

'We will be ready,' said Koel.

Auum nodded. Koel watched him jump back onto the rail and then onto the cliff face, clinging like a lizard before climbing quickly out of sight.

'Liun,' called Koel. 'We have new work to do.'

Auum was concealed in the bamboo shroud that grew along the sheer bank of the Ix as it approached the Ultan bridge. It was dawn. The bridge guards were uncharacteristically alert, and from within the walls every shout, every clang of metal or movement of a thousand steel-toed shoes spoke of an army preparing to march.

No matter that they probably outnumbered the TaiGethen by a hundred to one; no matter that they had magic to ram home their overwhelming numerical superiority, they would be walking into the jaws of hell. And with the grace of Shorth, Auum would make them pay for every desecrating step they took.

He knew they were coming when a phalanx of mages flew over the bridge and out across the narrow strip of grassland that bordered the ruined rainforest. He counted thirty of them, spreading out to ensure safe passage for the army. They'd flown directly over him and he could see them hovering over at least two TaiGethen cells, placed there to help Auum assess the army as it came past them.

Auum concentrated on the bridge once more. The ground was beginning to vibrate with the approach of Ystormun's men and over the next two hours they crossed the bridge. Warriors and mages marched to the borders of the forest before turning onto the logging paths that ran alongside the banks of the Ix. Elven slaves among them could be seen carrying heavy packs of equipment, weapons and clothing.

Simultaneously, a fleet of lumber barges was sailing up the river, each packed with soldiers, mages and supplies. Auum bit his lip. He'd expected them to split their forces, but hadn't thought each part would be of such size. He estimated there were three thousand on foot with a further thousand on board the barges.

Unless the humans had left Ysundeneth largely unguarded, Auum had seriously misjudged the scale of the occupation. What Auum most feared now was that similar armies would also be leaving Tolt

Anoor and Deneth Barine, either to join forces or move against the forest on separate fronts.

It begged the question of why this move had not been made before, when the elves were weaker. This could not be solely a reaction to the actions of the ClawBound, though surely they were a factor. Something had changed; something else had forced their hands.

Auum watched the tail of the army disappear around the first bend in the river. More guard mages flew above them. Auum rubbed a hand over his face. The decisions the TaiGethen made now would govern the fate of all elves. He moved off to join his Tais, his mind racing.

If every cell answered the muster, fifty-four TaiGethen faced four thousand men from Ysundeneth alone. The only chance they had was to track and attack, strike and fade away. Wherever their enemy went, the TaiGethen would hound them, bleed them and teach them what it really meant to be an enemy of Yniss.

Chapter 11

Was it truly guilt that began to forge a change in the ClawBound psyche? I remain unconvinced. Fear is a key driver among Tual's denizens. Far more likely then that the ClawBound, faced with the destruction of their habitat, simply changed their tactics in response, and that the tiny elven element within them mis-interpreted that change as a desire to assuage their guilt.

From *ClawBound and Silent*, by Lysael, High Priestess of Yniss

The TaiGethen tracked and watched for five days, examining the enemy for weaknesses. There had been occasional glimpses of mages through breaks in the canopy and reported by scouts in the high branches, but Auum did not consider them a threat.

During the day squads of mages and warriors flanked the main column, providing early warning of any attack. Scouts moved ahead of the army, seeking the best path through the eaves of the forest when the river bank became impassable. Auum ignored them all.

But he could not ignore the heavily-guarded detachment of elves that moved three hours ahead of the column, marking the route, digging latrines and preparing areas for cook fires by clearing the undergrowth between the trees and collecting wood. There were more than a hundred elves in the party, accompanied by twenty-two mages and some fifty soldiers.

When they halted to prepare a site, the mages prepared multiple castings. Some were aimed at the ground and had to be wards while others were cast on the guards positioned around the site. Auum was unconcerned by any of them; he had no intention of walking in through the front door.

'Elyss, what do you see?' he asked.

'The warriors are comfortable with their tasks,' she said immediately. 'They are elite soldiers, lightly armoured and with short blades. They've trained for combat here. We must respect them. They are not like the ones who attacked the temple.'

'Excellent,' said Auum. 'Malaar, tell me about the mages.'

'Half of them cast while the other half rest. Onelle has told us that using magic drains energy. So the more they are forced to cast or maintain their castings the more vulnerable they are. They do not cast solely defensive and offensive spells. Some are clearly for illness and injury. However I don't understand why a single casting is made across the whole elven work party.' Malaar smiled. 'I look forward to asking them what it is.'

'Good. Pass your information on and then meet me at the first jump point.'

All around the perimeter of the human campsite, TaiGethen climbed the great banyan trees. Five cells swarmed up the trunks, their fingers digging into the bark when there was no branch to hand and their feet pushed flat against the broad boles, propelling them up quickly and quietly. Auum raced Ulysan, a powerful TaiGethen with a long reach whose toes found the merest dent in the bark seemingly at will and whose fingers grabbed the strongest branches or penetrated the perfect knotholes.

They ascended two hundred feet, feeling the breeze begin to play on their faces and the heat of the sun beating down into the upper canopy. Ulysan was twenty feet above him when he sniffed the air and stilled. Auum followed his gaze. Through the leaf and branch cover he could see a mage tracking across the sky. He was circling above the campsite and working his way further outwards with each pass.

Auum gave the piercing cry of the howler monkey and was answered by calls both real and imitated from miles around. They had climbed high enough. He could see Ulysan smiling.

'We'd better not dawdle. Sounds to me like you've just found yourself a mate and three challengers for her.'

Auum looked inwards and downwards, seeking his launch and landing boughs. The banyans themselves were well spread, and between them rainforest pine, balsa and palms grew, all reaching lesser heights than the banyans at maturity. Auum worked his way back down to a branch as thick as his torso and there he waited. Ulysan joined him. Shortly afterwards, so did Elyss and Malaar.

'Lost your cell, Ulysan?' asked Elyss, a glint in her eye.

'I note it is a long way down should you lose your grip,' said Ulysan.

'Focus,' said Auum. 'We are a Tai of four and are the stronger for it.'

One by one, Auum heard four calls rise above the ambient noise of Tual's creatures. Reptile, bird, insect and mammal sounds were repeated over and over. Auum responded with the call of the kinkajou and knew that his Tais were on the move.

Auum led, moving along the branch until it narrowed enough to bow under his weight. His feet were atop it, his hands clasping it, his body leaning forward. He felt the thrill as he gained momentum and his heart beat harder as he saw his target.

Mouthing a prayer to Yniss, he rocked forward, took his feet from the branch and swung hard beneath it. Auum waited until his body was horizontal then let go. He tucked, turned a backward roll, straightened once more and thumped onto his target branch on the next banyan. Auum came to a crouch, gripped the branch to still his momentum and ran to the trunk of the tree.

He didn't pause. No good could come of watching the others jump. He had descended fifty feet. Still he had no sight of the ground, but he knew he was positioned directly over the perimeter of the camp. One more jump to go. Auum moved around the trunk, climbed up to a suitable branch a few feet above his head and began to move out along it.

He moved slowly, studying the terrain, looking for any chinks in the canopy which were large enough for him to see the ground. The branch began to dip under his weight. Ahead, a palm grew up through the lower branches of the banyan he was in. Perfect. He turned. Elyss, Malaar and Ulysan were all waiting on the trunk. His young Tai warriors were buzzing with the excitement of the jump and brimful of their trust in Yniss. He remembered how that felt.

Auum indicated the target of the next jump. His Tai nodded their understanding. Auum moved further out. This was a far simpler jump, into the crown of a tree, which would leave him a mere sixty feet above the enemy.

He took two quick paces forward, used the banyan branch as a springboard and leapt out. Auum brought his legs into a tuck, ducked his head briefly to his chest against the beat of leaf and twig then stretched his body out. He shot through the upper branches of the palm and dropped right into the centre of the crown, stilling his momentum instantly.

Auum backed to the edge of the crown and beckoned Elyss on. He watched her with a smile on his face. Her step was light, her jump was perfect and she whispered onto the palm. Auum caught her arm and the two stood together, balanced to catch Malaar and Ulysan, both of whom landed without error.

Below them, Auum could see warriors patrolling around the working party. The resting mage team were sitting with their backs to trees, or lying stretched out on cleared ground, using their cloaks against the damp. Auum waited until he heard the calls that signalled each cell was ready.

'Strike hard,' he said. 'Keep moving and target casting mages first. Don't chase the extra kill. Tais, we strike.'

The kinkajou call sounded a second and last time. Auum grabbed the tip of a palm branch and stepped off the crown of the tree. He fell fast, his descent slowed at the critical point by the tension of the branch. Ten feet from the ground, he let go. Below him, a warrior began to look up, aware at the very last moment that he was under attack.

Auum landed, legs around the man's neck. His hands came down and clamped around the soldier's head. He twisted hard, breaking his neck. The man collapsed but Auum was already moving again, his weight forward, turning a roll as he hit the ground. He came up in a crouch, Elyss and Malaar landing by him. Faleen's cell dropped just in front of him and headed towards the perimeter guards.

Men were screaming orders at each other. Warriors inside the perimeter grouped and ran towards the resting mages. Auum sprinted left, his Tai with him. He couldn't see Ulysan. Behind them a man screamed, and Auum felt blood spray across the back of his head.

'Get among the mages,' he shouted.

Elyss and Malaar split left and right. Ahead, warriors had heard him and were turning. Four of them, with short blades in hand and bucklers on their forearms, faced him without fear. Three others tracked the movement of his Tai. Auum drew a blade with his right hand and snatched a jaqrui from his belt with his left. He threw the crescent blade as he advanced, seeing his target deflect it high and away with his buckler.

Auum grabbed his second blade and attacked, tracing its tip in the leaf litter as he came. The enemy stood in close formation, bucklers in front of their chests and necks, their short blades held low. Auum feinted a move right and saw the rightmost warrior tense just as he jammed his right foot into the earth and leapt left and forward, left-hand blade carving down into the space below him.

He felt its edge bite into shoulder flesh and heard the howl of pain. Auum was turning out, his back to the enemy for a brief moment. He drove into the turn with his right blade, landing as it struck square on the buckler of a second warrior. Auum was facing them once more.

Both flanking warriors rushed in, blades coming at him at chest height. Auum blocked them with his swords and kicked out straight, catching the wounded soldier in the gut. The man fell back. His sword had tumbled from his grip and blood surged from the wound in his shoulder.

Auum moved on, his arms still outstretched, holding the enemy blades at bay. A buckler thudded into his side and Auum twisted as he fell, turning the weight of the blow into a tumble to the left. A blade bit the ground just behind him; Auum bounced to his feet and snapped a right-footed kick around in front of him. His heel cracked into an attacker's arm, breaking it at the elbow.

Auum dived right, rolling around his shoulders and back on his feet in a moment. Two warriors disabled. Elyss jabbed a blade into the gut of a third guarding the mages and ran forward towards those readying a casting. Malaar was caught up fencing with two more. He was not going to break through fast enough.

'Uly—'

The barrel-chested Tai soared over Auum's head and landed right in front of Auum's two remaining attackers. Auum ran to his left. Ulysan aimed a roundhouse kick at the head of one, smashing his arm and buckler up into his temple as he tried to defend himself. The second struck down at Ulysan's open flank. Auum's blade came down, severing his arm at the wrist. He screamed and looked round in time to catch Auum's second strike in his mouth and through the back of his neck.

Ulysan needed no invitation. He ran after Elyss, straight at the mages, and blood misted the air. Those that were not downed in the next few moments split and ran.

'See them away!' shouted Auum.

He swung about. Faleen's body was at right angles to her attacker, her leg straight out and high, pinning him to a banyan with her foot in his throat. He was eviscerated by Wirann's blade. Acclan led his Tai against a knot of six soldiers defending a group of mages who didn't see Illast's Tai advancing on them from the rear.

Acclan threw a jaqrui. It thudded home into a warrior's thigh. He did not break stride, instead leading a charge directly towards Acclan's cell. With their bucklers held before them as battering rams and their blades cocked to stab out straight, the humans raced into battle.

'Evade!' Acclan yelled.

He leapt straight up, grabbing a trailing vine to hasten his rise above their attackers' heads. To his left, Tiiraj threw himself to the side and was on his way up almost as soon as he hit the ground. But to his right, Gyneev had not reacted fast enough. He was caught by a flailing arm as he moved, a buckler catching him on the side of the head and knocking him senseless against a palm trunk.

Auum roared a panther's warning call and sprinted to his defence. He was just ten paces away. Acclan landed behind the group, turning towards his fallen Tai. Tiiraj dragged her blade through one man's leg and charged at the mages. Illast's cell raced in. Auum looked up as he ran, seeing Tiiraj fly into the attack. In turn, Auum threw a jaqrui at the warrior nearest Gyneev, distracting him for a critical moment.

Mages cast.

Illast and his Tai were picked up and hurled backwards into the forest by the blast. Auum jumped into the space before Gyneev, fielding a blow on one blade. Warriors came at him from either side. Acclan came too but he alone would not be enough to make a difference.

'Acclan. Mages,' ordered Auum.

Three warriors were on top of Auum already. He cracked a low kick into the knee of one and blocked the downward strike of another with his left blade. This stabbed out, slicing the same man's side and drawing blood. But the third dodged around him and plunged his blade to the hilt into Gyneev's back as the young TaiGethen struggled to regain his feet.

Auum's fury was unbound. 'Coward!'

He landed a kick in the man's chest, sending him sprawling back. Auum swung right and lashed a blade into the wounded warrior's face. The third aimed a blow but never landed it. Malaar's foot connected with the base of his neck, killing him instantly.

Auum turned on Gyneev's murderer. The man was backing away, suddenly alone in a sea of TaiGethen with blood on his hands. Behind him, Acclan and Tiiraj slaughtered the mages that had not turned to run. He saw Faleen race past towards Illast and his fallen cell, ready to defend them from the warriors still loose in the forest. Auum paced forward.

'No TaiGethen kills a worthy foe with a blow to the back,' he said.

His left blade whipped out, slicing the soldier's face open from forehead to chin.

'No TaiGethen disrespects an adversary who has honour.'

His right blade crashed down on the man's buckler, ruining his forearm.

'No TaiGethen will henceforth see a worthy foe in man, nor can any of you achieve honour.'

Auum's blades switched in front of him and the man's sword arm was severed at the shoulder and his throat cut – but not fatally. The soldier was shaking with pain, shock and terror. His death was in his eyes. Not yet.

'I am Auum. I am Arch of the TaiGethen. And if you survive the journey back to your army, tell them this: not one of them will emerge from this forest alive. You are travelling to the gates of a place you would term hell, and we will torment each of your souls on its way.

'You cannot defeat us, you can only fear us and fall before us. We are the elves. The forest is ours.'

Auum swivelled and planted a straight kick into the warrior's face, smashing his nose across one cheek.

'Run. And may Tual's denizens feast on your blood and flesh before your death takes you screaming to Shorth.'

The warrior stumbled away, his heaving cries already beginning to reverberate through the forest.

'Auum, it is done,' said Ulysan. 'The rest are scattering back towards the main column.'

Auum turned. The fight was won, but at too high a cost. Gyneev was dead. Acclan and his Tai would be injured at best. The elven work party was bunched together a hundred paces away, their axes and shovels abandoned where they had dropped them to run to relative safety.

'Ulysan, find Faleen and report on Acclan. Illast, your Tai has fallen. Prepare his body and we will pray for him when we are safe.

Elyss, report back to me with injuries. We need to tend to those we can. This is just the beginning.'

The ground was scattered with bodies. Auum counted thirteen mages and twenty warriors whose bodies would be left for Tual's denizens to reclaim for the glory of the forest. Auum moved among them. He signalled a Tai to him; Hassek of Faleen's cell.

'Take anything of use from the bodies.'

Auum walked towards the elven work party. Malaar and Wirann were ahead of him. The liberated elves shrank away, putting up their hands to warn the TaiGethen away. Auum frowned and picked up his pace.

'What's wrong?' he asked.

'They're frightened,' said Wirann. 'Telling us we must not touch them.'

'It's all right,' Malaar was saying. 'We're here to help you.'

But they continued to back off. Most were standing now, shouting that it was a trap and they would all die.

'No one can hurt you now,' said Auum, sheathing his swords. 'Calm yourselves. You're free. There is no trap but the one we have sprung ourselves. You are slaves no more.'

Malaar was laughing. Wirann's smile was sympathetic and warm. After so long in captivity, who could blame them for believing every word their captors told them? One of the elves stumbled over an exposed root and fell onto his rump. Wirann reached out to grab his arm.

Auum felt a dread chill spread all over him. Something Malaar had said, something about a single casting on the elves.

'Wirann!' he screamed. 'No!'

Wirann touched the elf's arm and the forest turned to blue fire.

Chapter 12

I was always taught that being able to face your enemy is the prime requisite in choosing whether or not to fight him. The trouble is that when fighting the TaiGethen in the rainforest, you don't get to face them and you don't get to choose whether to fight or not. It's best just to make sure you have a comfortable place to fall when you die.

Reminiscences of an Old Soldier, by Garan,
sword master of Ysundeneth (retired)

Heat and roaring and screaming and burning.

Auum rolled onto his back and opened his eyes. He was surrounded by blue tinged with yellow and blown through with thickening smoke. Magical fire gorging on precious trees and . . .

'Malaar!'

Auum tried to sit up. Pain slammed along the length of his right leg and up into his back. His left shoulder was dislocated. His left arm hung limp and pain grated across his neck and up into his skull making him nauseous. Smoke brought tears to his eyes and fogged his vision, but he could see enough. His right ankle was twisted, lodged in a root.

Auum tried to clear his head. A few details filtered in. The explosion had rushed towards him, engulfing Malaar and Wirann. Auum had dived for the cover of a palm tree trunk but hadn't quite made it. His leap had been spun out of control by the force of the blast.

The roaring in his ears was losing intensity and he could hear the screams more clearly now. From his position, he could see the seat of the explosion and TaiGethen rushing in to see if there were any survivors. The screams told him they were witnessing something awful.

The fire was spreading around the clearing. The trees all around them were ablaze and weakened branches were beginning to fall. The palm tree against which Auum rested was burning on the opposite side. There was fire on the ground all around him where he lay in partial shelter.

Auum put his right hand on the trunk and pushed up with his left leg, letting his right foot drag out from beneath the root as he stood. His whole body was alive with pain and he could feel blood running down his face. The fire surrounded him, the heat growing by the moment. His people were scattered and scared. He needed to move.

He pushed away from the tree, adjusting his balance to mitigate his two key injuries. There was a vibration running through the ground – heavy feet, running hard. Auum cast about him, but the smoke and flame obscured anything beyond twenty yards or so. He was breathing hard, clinging on to consciousness. The air was thick and poisonous and he was struggling to manage the waves of pain sweeping over him.

'Auum!'

Auum looked to his left. Relief was a balm on his agony.

'Ulysan.' The powerful TaiGethen came to his side. 'Help me get this shoulder back in.'

'No time,' said Ulysan. 'The humans are coming back to finish what they started. Now we know why they ran so readily.'

'I have to be able to fight,' said Auum.

'You're joking,' said Ulysan. 'You're half dead. Come on. Let me support you.'

'I will not leave as an invalid. Help me. We have to get our people away from here. You can't organise it with me hanging off your shoulder.'

Ulysan sighed and shook his head. Ordinarily, Auum would have laughed; he knew exactly what his Tai was thinking. Auum, his right hand resting on the tree trunk and with flame licking ever closer, smoke thickening fast, lifted his left arm, feeling the shoulder ball grating against the socket and his muscles protesting.

Ulysan took the arm in both his hands, continuing the lift as slowly as he dared, his eyes continuously flicking across to the spot where the enemy would emerge, or from which new spells would come. When his arm moved past the perpendicular, Ulysan took Auum's wrist and bent his forearm around the back of his head and towards his right shoulder.

Auum breathed slowly, feeling the joint move into position. With a distinct thud through his ribs, the ball popped back into the socket.

Ulysan released his arm and Auum moved it back down to his side. There was an intense ache across the top of his back and down the arm but at least it now worked. He made a fist and grimaced. It would have to do. He put his right arm around Ulysan's neck.

'Let's go,' he said.

Auum's injured ankle would take no weight whatsoever. The TaiGethen pair moved as fast as they could towards the remains of the elven working party. Despite the risk of fire and smoke, the surviving TaiGethen were all gathered there.

'Form up!' ordered Auum. 'Away into the trees. We cannot—'

Elyss was kneeling on the ground, heedless of the smouldering leaf litter all around her. When he spoke, she turned round and the expression on her face stalled his next words. He and Ulysan moved towards her. She was shivering. Tears flooded down her face, smearing the ash dust that clung there. She was holding something in her hands.

'It's all that's left,' she said, her voice cracked and raw. 'How could they do this? Even for them this is . . .'

Elyss opened her hands and Auum could see they were burned. The belt clasp of Malaar's jaqrui pouch, fused to the melted remains of the throwing crescents, was sitting in her palms. Auum let his eyes track over the ground, across an area that was scorched black.

Nothing remained. Not a bone remained of a working party of a hundred elves. The force of the spell had obliterated them completely, along with anything else in its radius. The earth was rock hard and had been pitted into a shallow crater studded with irregular black scorch marks.

That Malaar's jaqruis were recognisable was a surprise in itself but it hardly mattered. Both he and Wirann were gone; wiped from the rainforest as if they had never existed. It made awful sense of all the screams. How could even a soul hope to survive such a conflagration?

Auum reached down with his left hand and half-pulled Elyss to her feet. The surviving TaiGethen were gathered, Illast and his cell among them, bruised but unbroken.

'TaiGethen,' he said softly and every eye turned to him. 'You can all feel through your boots what is coming. Every one of you is carrying an injury. And you are looking at an atrocity that eclipses all others. I know you wish to fight for the memory of those who have fallen but we do not have the strength, not right now.

'We will head for Aryndeneth to rest and heal. If the humans are heading there, we must be ready. Go now. Acclan will bear Gyneev. Ulysan will remain with my cell and we shall grieve our fallen when we pray.

'Tais, we move.'

Bitter cold flushed through the forest at their backs. The last fires were extinguished. Ice fell from the trees. Boughs blackened by fire shattered and fell, shot through by the chill.

'Run!' yelled Auum.

The TaiGethen fled the scene of slaughter. Auum pushed Ulysan away and let himself drop into an untidy heap on the ground

'Go, Ulysan. See to Aryndeneth.'

Ulysan looked past Auum at the onrushing frost. He nodded and ran. Auum turned onto his back and saw the cloud of ice carried on an unnatural gale of wind stampede about four feet over his head. He prayed his Tais were fast enough. The vibration in the ground told him that the enemy had slowed to move in behind their spells.

The air was clearing of smoke now and a cold rain fell from the trees, any leaves which had survived the fire had been blackened by frost up into the mid-canopy. Beeth would be urging Gyal to bring fresh rain, but it would not save these ruined trees. Auum lay where he had fallen, waiting.

From his position, feet first towards the enemy, he saw five warriors moving slowly into the cleared space, three mages in close attendance. No doubt there were many others but he dare not move his head. Not yet. The men came forward, swords held ready and bucklers still strapped firmly to forearms. Voices echoed in an arc in front of Auum and there was harsh laughter.

Auum tensed, feeling the strained sinews and muscles in both shoulder and ankle. Mercifully nothing was broken, though his ankle and right leg were useless to him. Nonetheless he wondered how many he could take before they finished him. Two warriors were walking towards him. He could tell by their approach that they assumed him dead, but they were still wary.

Auum's eyes were closed to tiny slits and he let his body relax. One warrior kicked his right boot. Pain flooded Auum, too much to deny. He cried out and kicked hard with his left foot, feeling his toes connect with the warrior's groin. Auum sat straight up as the man doubled over, grabbing his light mail shirt and pulling him down and left, and used the momentum to carry him to his knees. Fresh pain crashed through his lower body from his right ankle. Auum ignored it. He grabbed a blade with his right hand and chopped it into the warrior's neck.

Auum pushed the body aside and bounced up onto his left foot, forced to leave the right one trailing. His stance was awkward, leaving him feeling clumsy. He smashed an elbow into the face of the second warrior and threw a jaqrui at the nearest mage, seeing it deflected by a buckler thrust out instinctively and fly up into his target's face.

Auum hopped to the right, his left foot kicking down briefly but tellingly on the second warrior's throat before he landed on solid ground. The remaining three rushed him. Behind them, two mages began to prepare castings and he could hear others racing in from the left and right. The attacking men slowed, seeing him crippled. They spaced out, intending to give him no chance.

Auum focused on the central figure. Clean-shaven and fresh-faced, he was a young man of little experience if the way his grip shifted on his sword was any guide. Auum watched him come in, striding quickly, confident in his chances against an injured elf.

Auum snatched a jaqrui from his belt and hurled it at neck height. The young man ducked. Auum flexed his left leg and jumped high, kicking out straight as he rose, catching the soldier on the top of his head and sending him sprawling backwards. The other two were running at him. He threw his blade at one, missing, and dragged out his other as he landed.

Auum turned to his left. He had little time. In his peripheral vision the mages had completed their preparations and Auum asked Yniss to preserve his soul. Auum dived headlong, his sword thrust out ahead of him, hoping he might evade whatever spells were coming.

His blade skewered the soldier in the gut. Auum's body thumped into his as it fell and the two of them tumbled in a heap. The dying man landed on top of Auum's injured leg. Auum screamed and tried to shove him off, scrabbling back and fighting a rising nausea. A mage appeared above him, his palm open to reveal blue fire growing within. The mage reached down towards Auum's face.

A keening sound split the noise of the skirmish and the mage jerked, blood bursting from his mouth and flooding down his neck. He fell to the side, plucking at the jaqrui lodged just beneath his ear. TaiGethen hurdled Auum's body as men called out frantically. Auum saw Ulysan poleaxe a warrior with a massive punch to the chin and Elyss ram a blade under his ribs.

A spell was cast. Brief flame shot out and Illast leapt, turned in the air above the flame and kissed back down to the ground, his blades already coming across his face in their killing strikes. Auum could hear swords clash further away. He heard more jaqrui sing through the air and a man howled briefly in agony. Running footsteps dwindled away into the forest and the last human voices faded away.

The dying human was pulled from atop Auum and his neck broken. Ulysan reached down a hand and Auum took it gratefully.

'This is becoming a habit,' he said. 'Faleen's after the others.'

'I thought I told you all to run,' said Auum.

Ulysan smiled and rubbed an ear theatrically. 'Did you? Damned explosion must have left me half deaf because I'd never knowingly defy one of your orders.'

'May Yniss keep your hearing muted, Ulysan,' said Auum. 'Come on, let's get out of here.'

The assault on Serrin's sense of smell fed directly from his Claw and it was truly vile. He was travelling with eight pairs, tracking the human army and dreaming of their blood on his lips.

But this stink had driven all other thought from his mind. The air was laden with a multitude of scents: burned wood, ash, seared flesh and boiling sap just a few among them. Dominant, though, were the twin odours of magic, which hung heavy on the ground caught in the leaf litter and undergrowth, and elven blood, a great deal of which had been spilled.

Serrin walked into a blackened clearing and knew that much of the guilt rested with him. His Claw sampled the ground, finding a charred, fused crater smothered in the remnants of magic and the ashes of elves. Scattered across an area a quarter of a mile on a side, were the bodies of men. Some appeared to have thawed from frozen and all bore the wounds of jaqrui, elven blade or TaiGethen open-hand strike.

Serrin paused, his hand on his Claw's head. She had moved from the crater and was nosing at a bloodstain on the ground. She breathed it in deep and Serrin experienced a pain of loss he thought never to feel again.

Auum.

His Claw could not be sure if he had perished here and been borne away by his Tais, but he had certainly fought and bled here, and one set of tracks leading away spoke of an elf with serious injuries. Serrin stared at the ground, looking for signs that Auum had moved away unaided, but the tracks were confused. Ten sets of prints criss-crossed the ground, led away, ran back and disappeared into the undergrowth, all of them heading for Aryndeneth, a day's run to the east.

Serrin, or at least that part of him which glimmered with the memory of a Silent Priest, prayed to Yniss that Auum's soul had been preserved, whether alive or dead. For those caught in the magical fire and the ensuing inferno, there could be no such hope.

The ClawBound were all assembled in the clearing. Each pair maintained physical contact while the shock of what they saw ebbed away to fuel their desire for blood. They all looked at Serrin, awaiting his signal to close on the tail of the human army and begin to seek their vengeance.

And so they would, but not like this. Serrin let his eyes travel the devastation once more and allowed the guilt to follow. He should have foreseen this reaction. He should have realised Ystormun would prefer to strike back at free elves rather than rip the hearts from his useful slaves in revenge. He should have listened to Auum. He should have stopped his cleansing. They were not strong enough to repel this invasion.

Serrin crouched on the ground and tears welled up in his eyes. He touched the earth and felt its pain. He sampled the air and smelled the death of the rainforest all around him. He listened and heard the desperate cries of Tual's denizens, unable to comprehend the horror being visited upon them.

And all because the ClawBound had become more animal than elf.

'Yniss forgive me,' whispered Serrin. 'We have fallen too far.'

Chapter 13

*Yniss walked the glory of the forest and marvelled at the colours
and the sounds and the scents. He looked above him and saw the
purity of the sky above and knew his tasks were not yet done.
Yniss laid a hand to his right and it rested upon the head of Gyal,
the most beautiful, the most effervescent and the most expressive
of his kin. And Gyal's tears began to fall, and where they struck
the ground, life surged and blossomed. 'I could give this gift to no
other,' said Yniss.*

The Aryn Hiil

Auum awoke. The forest was peaceful and the temple was cool. He
was lying in a priest's chamber. The bed was comfortable. He lay
quietly, listening to the ambient sounds outside and the movement of
elves within Aryndeneth. Memories started to filter into his mind.
The run from the fight was vague. And he didn't remember getting
here at all, certainly not into this chamber.

Auum sat up. Pain jabbed at his leg and his shoulder throbbed. He
dragged the thin blanket from his body and looked down. He was
wearing a clean loincloth. His ankle was strapped, the dressing was
clean. His shoulder showed a mass of bruising but it was a couple of
days old at least. His stomach was tender to the touch and when he
stopped to think for a moment, his whole body ached.

Auum swung his legs out of the bed and stood on his left foot,
using a bedpost for support and hopping towards the door. He
swayed when the blood rushed from his head, sitting back down
heavily until the nausea passed. He looked around the room and
chuckled. Someone knew him well: a walking stick had been left by
the open door. He levered himself up and made for it as a figure
appeared in the doorway. The beautiful face and warm, welcoming
eyes were wonderfully familiar and totally unexpected.

'Good to see you up and about,' said Lysael, holding out the walking stick.

'Thank you,' said Auum.

He took the stick and tested his weight on it. It looked old. It was carved from dark pine and had a pommel moulded to a polished ball by the caress of countless hands. Auum's fingers closed on it, feeling a roughness at his fingertips which was all that remained of the carvings of birds and trees that had once adorned the pommel but were now confined to the neck.

'Come with me,' said Lysael. 'Onelle and the TaiGethen are outside. It's the Feast of Renewal today. Are you hungry?'

Auum paused in mid-stride. 'That's not possible. The feast is three days away.'

Lysael laughed. 'There are some things that I'm good at, as High Priestess of Yniss. One of them is knowing the dates of all my god's festivals. Trust me on this.'

Auum's heart began beating faster.

'I can't have been unconscious that long,' he whispered.

Lysael didn't respond. The pair of them walked beneath the temple dome. Auum's stick gave a hollow clack against the stone which echoed into the ceiling high above. With each step he tested his injured ankle a little more. The strapping was effective, stalling any lateral movement, but whether he used heel or toe he could feel the weakness and tenderness in the joint, musculature and ligaments.

The smell of cooking fires was wafting into the dome. Auum's stomach growled and he began salivating. Tapir, jao deer and hare were on the spit. Vegetable and herb stews were steaming away. Fruit soups added a glorious sweetness to the mix and the scent of fresh-baked bread completed the image of the feast. Auum hurried on as best he could, and out into bright sunlight. Gyal had blessed this feast day; it looked as if the rain would hold off for some hours.

The apron was busy, not least with TaiGethen warriors seated on cushions surrounding a host of plates of food. The cook fires were all away to the right at the edge of the stone. Temple workers buzzed and flitted around them carrying ingredients, cutting meat and serving.

Auum moved towards his people, counting them as he came. Forty-four had joined the feast. Including him, he had fifteen cells at his disposal, leaving only three cells out in the field. Merrat and Grafyrre's cells were both tracking the Ysundeneth army, and the fact that he couldn't see Corsaar probably meant the veteran cell leader was collecting information about other human forces in the forest.

Ulysan saw Auum approach and stood, motioning them all to do the same. The TaiGethen held their cups out to Auum and bowed their heads in the traditional greeting, awaiting his permission to sup.

'Gyal fills our rivers and the forest provides our roots. The skills Yniss bestowed on the elves brings the joy of taste to our mouths and freedom for our minds. Drink, lest Ix steal your spirit.'

'For Auum. For the Arch. For the TaiGethen. For the forest.'

The salute given, they drank and retook their seats. Auum sat with Lysael in a space made between Ulysan and Onelle. He chose water rather than spirits and filled his plate with jao dressed with fruit soup. It looked lovely but he couldn't eat, not just yet.

'What happened, Ulysan?'

Ulysan set down his cup and wiped his mouth with the back of his hand.

'You finally lost consciousness as we reached the temple, though in truth you were incoherent for the last half of the run here. We thought you'd simply lost more blood than we'd thought but we couldn't find any wound deep enough. It was Onelle who actually saved your life.'

Onelle was blushing before his gaze was upon her.

'I am for ever indebted to you.'

'Don't be so stupid,' said Onelle. 'After all, if I said that after every time a TaiGethen saved my life, I'd still be catching up now. You do killing; I do fixing. All for the same god.'

'Using the Il-Aryn?'

Onelle smiled and gave a small shrug. 'It is a pity to ignore a skill when it can genuinely help. And you needed help, Auum. The impact that dislocated your shoulder broke a rib, and that rib pierced you inside. You were slowly bleeding to death. I could stem that bleeding and straighten the rib.

'The Il-Aryn saved your life.'

Auum didn't know why but the knowledge made him intensely uncomfortable. He scratched at his ribcage up by his shoulder as if doing so could dislodge the magic Onelle had used.

'Thank you,' he said.

'Are you sure?' asked Onelle.

'Yniss blessed you with an ability that has allowed you to prolong my work here on Calaius.'

'That doesn't answer my question,' said Onelle. 'But don't let it worry you. You'll get used to the idea one day. You all will.'

Auum inclined his head and returned his attention to Ulysan while Lysael and Onelle fell into a conversation of their own. He gestured for Ulysan to speak.

'I'm sorry, Auum. There didn't seem to be another choice.'

'I will address it in my prayers,' said Auum. 'What of the enemy?'

Ulysan searched Auum's face for blame but he didn't find any.

'They continue to advance along the river. They are ignoring this temple, and make no search for Loshaaren or the Ynissul. There is a certainty in their route and I fear they know something.'

Auum saw his train of thought and it was bleak indeed.

'They cannot know the way, can they?'

'All reason says not, and Onelle will tell you that no mage could possibly have the range to fly over Katura Falls . . .'

'Yet they've surely received some information. Why else would they ignore Aryndeneth?'

'We have found no other answer that makes sense.'

'Katura is in no state to defend herself against such an army,' said Auum.

'Katura's people are in no state to feed and clothe themselves, let alone fight,' said Lysael. 'How long since you've been there?'

Auum shrugged. 'Fifty years at least. There seemed no reason to go back once the last of the Ynissul had been persuaded to leave. Pelyn was in control, growing the Al-Arynaar. I know things have been more difficult of late but—'

'You have neglected them for far too long,' said Lysael. 'Nothing is left of the place and the people you remember, not even hope.'

'I cannot be everywhere,' said Auum quietly. 'I must trust others. I trusted Pelyn. Was I mistaken?'

Lysael let her gaze drop to her plate. 'When we are alone and our prayers are not answered, we may all fall prey to temptation.'

'Where are the watchers? Why did no one tell me?'

'Because there are those within Katura who have no wish for the TaiGethen to know what is going on,' said Lysael.

She couldn't look at him and that scared Auum more than anything else he had seen or heard since the humans had invaded the rainforest.

'But you could have,' said Auum gently, placing a hand on her shoulder. 'You and I speak whenever we are here or Loshaaren. We have no secrets.'

When Lysael turned her face back to him there were tears running down her cheeks. Auum was aware that conversation around the feast had quietened.

'I have failed in my duties.' Lysael's voice was a cracked whisper. 'The temple to Ynissul lies dormant. No priest resides there now. I have not been back for almost ten years.'

'Why not?' asked Auum, unsure how to feel about her revelation.

'Because the last time I was there, I feared for my life.'

Silence bled out from the TaiGethen and enveloped the cooks and servants. Auum swallowed hard. He took his hand from Lysael's shoulder lest his fury caused his fingers to tighten. Here, on the apron of the elves' most sacred place, where Yniss gazed down unfailingly and his embrace kept all from harm, his high priestess had been forced to reveal such a fear.

Auum dared a glance around his Tais. All they awaited was his word.

'Were you threatened?' asked Auum. 'Did an elf actually threaten your life?'

Lysael stared at Auum, her lips pressed together against a sob. Then she nodded.

Uproar exploded among the TaiGethen. All of them were on their feet yelling for justice and revenge. Only Auum remained seated. He held out his hands and the TaiGethen fell silent.

'Keep your anger for man,' he said. 'Direct your fire at those who would rape our forest and see us exterminated. Trust me. No criminal will escape justice. A particular state of pain and torment awaits those who dared look into the eyes of our beloved Lysael and thought to end her life.

'Now return to the feast. Do not dishonour our ceremony. Rest well. Tomorrow, we move.'

Jeral watched Hynd while the mage communed with Ystormun. Hynd was pale and shaking. Sweat covered his brow and his lips were ragged and bleeding where his teeth tore at them. His eyes moved erratically behind closed lids, and when he appeared close to losing his balance, Jeral reached out a hand to steady him where he sat cross-legged near the river's edge.

Dusk was approaching. It was the time of day Jeral feared most. Before the campfires, torches and lanterns lent a facade of security to the perimeter, and well after the time that any of them could see into the eaves of the forest to any degree.

Jeral itched at the deep scratches the ClawBound elf had given him around his throat and lower jaw. They would scar. Jeral was certain that had been the intent. He shuddered every time the memory of that face appeared in his mind, so very close to his. He could still feel the elf's breath on his face, smelling of blood. He could still hear the words too, and he did fear them.

Dusk was the ClawBound's time, and the only question he had no answer to was why they hadn't attacked the army after so many days. They were so vulnerable in the forest despite the wards the mages laid every night. Almost four thousand men were strung out over miles of logged river bank. Organised into soldier and mage units, each was connected to the units on either side, and each was responsible for the safety of all three and also for a team of Sharps, who were tethered before being ignored for the night.

Guards stood at the perimeter with shielded lanterns throwing light as far into the forest as possible. More guards patrolled the entire length of the camp. Groups of mages were positioned between the camp and the perimeter, acting as quick-response teams. It all sounded great, but Jeral knew that should an attack come they would still pay dearly for every elf they killed.

Jeral glanced out over the river at the barges floating at anchor in midstream.

'Lucky bastards.'

Hynd sighed. Jeral looked back at him, once again glad that he wasn't one of Ystormun's mages. Hynd's body sagged and he blew out his cheeks. His eyes opened and he squinted at Jeral, who had squatted right in front of him, holding his shoulders.

'Are you . . . ?' Jeral began.

Hynd's face was grey and sick-looking even in the half-light.

'Oh God,' he mumbled.

Hynd turned his head and vomited. The puke poured across Jeral's arm and spattered on the ground, and the acrid reek brought tears to Jeral's eyes.

'Fantastic.'

'Sorry,' said Hynd, spitting out the remnants.

'Here.' Jeral passed him his water skin. 'Don't dribble your sick into it either. I don't want to taste your vomit next time I'm thirsty.'

'Thanks.' Hynd took a long swallow, flushed his mouth and spat once more. 'Bloody hell, he's a bastard.'

'Oh, you've noticed, have you? Well done.'

Jeral walked to the river's edge and washed his arm. He sniffed the sleeve of his light leather coat and wrinkled his nose. It wasn't the kind of odour that was going to fade in a hurry.

'No. I mean, yes,' said Hynd. 'I mean, I've got to report to the generals.'

The army commanders were spread throughout the column. They'd spent one night in their ridiculous tent and by morning some wags had painted a target on it in mud. Others had marked the path to the doors with arrows. It had been an effective piece of vandalism.

'Loreb is a few units downstream. I think Pindock and Killith are up near the head. Take your pick: the drunk, the coward or the total fuckwit.'

Hynd shook his head and lowered his voice. 'I don't think our boys need to hear that, Captain Jeral.'

'Anyone who decides to march the bulk of the army through this continent-sized mantrap deserves nothing but my scorn and the scorn of us all. Just ask your boss.'

'You had a better idea, did you?'

Jeral gave a short laugh. 'Yeah. Build. More. Barges.'

'But think of the time that would take,' said Hynd.

'Think of the people who won't be dead if we did,' said Jeral. 'Think of the final condition of those who actually make it to this mythical place, wherever the hell it is.'

'Ystormun wants to send a message to the Sharps. Marching through their land is the best way to do it.'

'No. Ystormun wants to wipe them out. There's no point making a statement if the goal is to leave no one alive to take it on board. Waiting fifty days and using those massive stockpiles of timber to build troop transports would send a much better message. One that reads: we're coming to slaughter the fucking lot of you and there's nothing you can do about it. The way we're going about it now, the message is: help yourself to rich human pickings because this column is totally indefensible.'

Hynd flapped his hands dismissively and stood up.

'We are where we are,' he said. 'And I have a message to take to the people who are actually in charge.'

'Oh yeah,' said Jeral. 'What did he say anyway?'

Hynd smiled. 'Well, among all the things I can tell you, there is one you'll really enjoy. He said we aren't making enough progress. We have to march faster and longer each day.'

Jeral felt his mouth hang open. 'You have absolutely got to be joking.'

'I never joke, Captain; you know that.'

Out in the forest, downstream somewhere, a man screamed. The sound carried clear above the hubbub of the camp. Alarm wards were triggered, sending sheets of light out into the forest. A heartbeat of silence along the column was broken by a concerted move to make ready for action. Weapons were drawn, mages began to prepare.

Jeral shot to his feet and ran down the river bank with Hynd right behind him.

'Stand your ground!' he yelled. 'Stand!'

Jeral flew down the lines. The wards were going off in an arc about a hundred yards downstream and fifty yards into the forest, right in the middle of his section of the line.

'Stay out of the forest. Remember your training.'

Jeral cursed under his breath and scratched at his face. He could feel his fear growing and the memories taunting him. Light flickered through the trees and sound wards blared out their flat tones, setting sleeping birds to flight and driving animals deeper into burrows or higher into the trees.

Jeral wished the wards were quieter. He wanted to know if they were up against TaiGethen or ClawBound. He ducked into the forest as a spell was cast ahead of him. A cold wave surged away into the trees, ice rattling against wood with a sound like breaking glass.

He could hear orders being barked. Someone was still screaming. And finally he heard the roar of a panther. Jeral's legs wobbled and he stumbled. His stomach churned, his face felt hot and his hand sweated on his sword hilt. He could see lanterns and guard fires just ahead, shot through with the shadows of men and ClawBound.

Jeral pounded on, driving himself forward, refusing to give in to the fear. He raced around a banyan trunk and was struck by two hundred pounds of solid muscle. The wind was knocked from him and he was hurled back to sprawl through the leaf litter, fetching up face down in a slew of muddy sludge.

Jeral rolled over quickly, getting his sword in front of him, but all he could see was Hynd standing stock still, his back to a tree, staring towards the river. Jeral surged to his feet, gasping a breath into a bruised chest. The panther had not broken stride and was streaking towards the water's edge. Jeral could see elves too, and other panthers, all taking the attack to the main column.

The screaming behind him hadn't stopped. Guards ran past, chasing the ClawBound. The sound of the last alarm ward died away and Jeral looked to the screaming. Bodies lay around a fire. One man still stood, a mage by his clothes. He was rigid, his hands clenched by his sides.

Down towards the river, orders were hollered out. Jeral heard men come to ready. He heard the roar of many panthers and realised he didn't have a choice. Not really.

'Shit,' he muttered. 'Hynd, see to him.'

Jeral turned and ran back towards the river, where he saw it all. ClawBound pairs exploded from the forest, hammering into his men. Panthers leapt. Jaws and claws ripped and raked, sowing confusion and panic. He saw a mage spin about and fall into the river, his face torn open. A warrior sliced the empty air with his sword as a panther leapt above it and clamped jaws about his skull, bearing him down.

But the elves weren't with them. They were attacking to the left and right of the targeted units. This was no random attack to scare and kill. This had a defined purpose.

'Target the elves! Stop them!'

Jeral leapt over a root, ran through some brush and burst from the forest. The body of a mage slapped into the ground in front of him. The panther snapped its jaws through his neck and turned to roar at Jeral.

Jeral slashed at it with his sword, simultaneously trying to slither backwards. His blade clipped an ear, slicing off the tip, and the panther howled, unaccustomed to a fight, and leapt away. Jeral tracked its path straight to an elf who had broken from the fighting to clamp a hand over his own ear.

In the midst of the fight, Jeral stared open-mouthed, just for a few moments. Swords flashed all around them. Men and ClawBound engaged in ferocious fighting. The army was closing in on both sides, and in the midst of it all the elf knelt by his panther and covered her wound with his hand. The pair of them touched heads then turned to stare straight at him. Then they moved, fast.

'Oh no.' Jeral cast about him. He was surrounded by fighting but there was no one close enough to help. 'To me! I have incoming!'

Jeral couldn't back away except into the forest, which offered nothing but a lonely death. The ClawBound pair streaked towards him. To his left, a mage cast. The invisible mana cone caught up two elves and hurled them back into the forest. The next instant, a panther roared as if in mortal pain. She pounced on the mage, her claws slashing great rents in his chest and her jaws ripping flesh from his shoulder.

The ClawBound pair was on him. Jeral held his sword in front of him, determined not to die a whimpering coward. But they did not attack. They moved apart and slowed, forcing him back. The elf barked like a wild dog and the elves and panthers pushed away in their attacking arc, forming a defensive line into which enslaved Sharps ran.

'Cast!' shouted Jeral. 'One of you ca—'

The elf in front of him stepped in and cracked a punch against his chin. Jeral didn't even see it coming until he was falling. He hit the ground and all he could hear was running feet. Belatedly a spell howled away, and he heard the death cry of a single elf and the agonised roars of panthers.

Jeral tried to get up. His head was swimming. Rough hands helped him back to his feet and someone pushed his sword into his hands. Men were running into the forest and Jeral went with them, groggy at first but then with increasing sureness. He ran towards the guard fires, coming to a stop by Hynd and calling to his men to end the pursuit. They were already chasing shadows.

'Hynd,' he said.

Hynd was with the stricken mage, who was still standing in the same position, staring at the forest. Men were filtering back past them. Some saw the mage and their eyes widened as they hurried past. Hynd gestured Jeral to him.

Jeral could see the blood before he saw the wounds, and when he looked at the poor mage could feel nothing but pity for him. Around the fire, the quickly slaughtered guards and other mages lay mercifully blind. Jeral understood the violence of their deaths, but he could not comprehend the cruelty that had been visited upon the sole survivor.

Jeral thought he recognised him as Pirian but could easily have been mistaken. The cuts, inflicted by panther and elf, began on his forehead. A long wound ran from temple to temple, described with clinical precision. Blood ran down into his eyebrows and over his face. His nose had been sliced along its length and the cut continued down and through his top lip.

Pirian's cheeks each carried four ragged tears that ran from the sides of his nose all the way to his ears, both of which had been bitten half away. And finally, his neck had been sliced from the tip of his chin all the way to the top of his shirt. No single cut was deep enough to be fatal but every single one was designed to scar. Jeral touched his own facial wounds and blessed his relative good fortune.

Pirian himself was lost to shock. His eyes were seeking an end to his nightmare and his face was shrouded in his blood. But while his face and mind were wrecked, the rest of his body was wholly undamaged.

'Can we move him?' asked Jeral. 'Have you tried?'

'He's totally rigid. I think we'll have to carry him,' said Hynd, his voice quiet. 'Why have they done this? Why not just kill him?'

Jeral sighed, and another small door into the elven psyche opened for him. His fear and respect for them grew in equal measure.

'It's a message,' he said. 'By morning, everyone will know what has happened to him. Sooner or later, everyone will see him. The elves know we can't kill him, or leave him behind, and so every day he will be there, the most chilling reminder of what is waiting for us out here.'

'They came all this way just to do that? Deliver that message?'

'Oh no,' said Jeral. 'This was just a sideshow. They've just freed about seventy Sharps. Didn't bother killing as many of us as they could have, either. But they've weakened us nonetheless.'

'What can we do about it?'

'Build. More. Barges.'

Chapter 14

There was Ix, jumping and sparkling, laughing, capricious and mischievous. Yniss laughed and the forest echoed with his joy. Ix danced along the lines of the earth and cavorted in the rivers and streams, matching her movements to the energies Yniss had laid there. Because she loved it so, he made her its warden and her laughter echoes still among Beeth's boughs.

The Aryn Hiil

It was not until the next morning that Auum noticed something that he should have seen much sooner. He found Onelle, and after they had prayed together at the statue of Yniss, they walked towards the Hallows of Reclamation beyond the village.

'Takaar has been here, hasn't he?' asked Auum.

Onelle nodded. 'I've wanted to speak to you about it but Lysael's news rather took over, didn't it? And you needed more rest last night. I'm sorry. I shouldn't have let you be the one to bring it up.'

'You have nothing to apologise for. He's taken your orientation class, hasn't he?'

Onelle put her head in her hands.

'Auum, he was wild. He was unshaven, he stank like he'd run all the way from Ysundeneth without pause and he was weak from hunger and thirst. He should have collapsed but there was something in him, driving him on. He brought the Il-Aryn together, and he gave this extraordinary oration. It lasted for an hour, maybe more, and we all sat and listened though so much of what he said was little more than ravings; nonsensical mutterings. Half the time I wasn't sure if he was talking to us or talking to his other self. I have never seen anything like it.'

Auum nodded. It sounded like a continuation of his meanderings outside the city a few days before.

'He'd been talking to Garan,' said Auum. 'Something got so far inside him he couldn't shake it. He's descending fast, isn't he?'

'Is he? I don't know, Auum.'

'You're going to explain that, I hope,' said Auum. 'Because from where I'm standing he's a menace, pure and simple.'

Onelle sighed. 'I know you and he don't see eye to eye but I've spent a great deal of time with him during the years since his return. We've studied together, worked together and talked endlessly about the Il-Aryn and how best we can harness it for the good of us all.

'He's passionate to the point of zealousness and he's given to flights of fancy, but more than that, he's a genius. Don't scoff, Auum, because you don't know, you don't see. He believes Ix is the rising god in our pantheon and that the Il-Aryn are the bedrock of our future.'

Auum's heart missed a beat. 'I see. The days of the Ynissul are over, are they?'

Onelle stopped and Auum was surprised to see the frustration in her expression.

'No, Auum, you're missing the point. Yniss will for ever be the father of us all, but we have to evolve. Man is here with his magic and we have to be able to fight fire with fire or we will fall. Magic has been awakened within us. In some threads it will remain dormant but in others it will burst into brilliant life and we have to be able to harness it. Ix is undeniably in the ascendant and you have to face that. Embrace it. Magic will be the salvation of the elven race.'

'Really.' Auum raised his eyebrows and gestured in the direction of the River Ix. 'There are thousands of men in the forest right now and magic will not save us from them. Takaar would do much better to refine his fighting skills and join the TaiGethen. If we can repel them, then we can talk about where our future lies.'

'You cannot stop what is happening,' said Onelle. 'Why can't you see that?'

'No, I can't stop it. But our enemies can. Right now we have no magic, and so we need to fight in the way we always have.' Auum walked on a few paces. 'I need to know that he is not going to cause any more problems. The Ynissul are safe and hidden, which is something. But Takaar has taken what little magical force we do have and run off with it. What exactly was this genius raving about? And why didn't you go with him?'

Onelle managed a brief smile. 'You know very well that my travelling days are long done. I will never leave this temple.'

She stopped and Auum could see she was nervous, uncertain about what to say next.

'You began by describing a lunatic to me but you've just been painting a picture of some sort of tortured genius. I understand your loyalty, but it seems to me you're confused about whether you want to follow him or warn people away from him. So tell me what he said.'

Onelle wiped her hands on her leggings. Her beautiful oval eyes sparkled with moisture and she had to clear her throat twice before she spoke. 'I love Takaar. I love what he has brought us, though I have often struggled with his methods. When he ran in, he had no time for anything but taking our Il-Aryn adepts with him. He called them all teachers and said their role was not to be that of pioneers. He said we'd been sailing the wrong rivers and that others would provide what we lacked. He said Ix had been laughing at him, but that he had the answers now.

'After that, he began to mumble. I heard something about a gift, how time would wait for the just and something else that, I admit, was really strange.'

'Which was?'

'He was talking to his other self. I know because he was looking to his right and not at us. And he was getting angry. He said that they were after him but he wouldn't let them get him. Then he laughed at something and said that not even Shorth was fast enough.'

'Who do you think he was talking about?'

Onelle shrugged. 'I thought it was you, the TaiGethen.'

'He flatters himself.' Auum didn't feel the need to go any further. 'But why on earth did the adepts go with him? I'd have been running in the opposite direction.'

Onelle frowned as if the answer should have been obvious.

'Because he asked them to.'

'Could they really not see through him? Where's he taken them and what does he think they're going to do? There is at least one human army in this forest, after all.'

'He's looking for other threads than the Ynissul with active Il-Aryn potential. Presumably the Ixii are high on his agenda, though not one of them has shown the slightest potential so far. He didn't say where he was going, but there's really only one possibility, isn't there? He has to be going to Katura.'

As soon as Onelle began to speak, Auum felt a hollow fear open up inside him. And the moment she mentioned the home of the free elves, the true scale of the unfolding disaster was made plain to him.

'No wonder they didn't strike here,' he whispered. 'They didn't need to.'

'Auum?'

'He's been betrayed,' said Auum. 'He's going to lead them straight to Katura. We've got to stop him or he'll bring about the death of us all.'

Takaar should have been easy to track. Or rather, the tracks of those in his charge should have shouted louder than a troop of howler monkeys seeking mates.

Fifteen cells were engaged in the search, yet after two days they had found no trace whatever. Not a fading water-filled boot print; not a broken vine or scratched tree trunk. Not a dead campfire, nor a scrap of cloth or evidence of elven defecation. Takaar had to be leading them south, but even if he had taken them across to the Ix or towards the other great rivers Orra and Shorth, the Tais should have seen some evidence of it on the ground.

It was as if Takaar and the adepts had disappeared into thin air.

Auum knew that it smacked of desperation but his climb above the canopy was made with a last lingering hope of spotting stray smoke. The land rolled away north back towards Aryndeneth and Ysundeneth and smoke smudged the landscape. The greatest concentration of it was away towards the Ix where the human army was moving along the course of the river, presumably tracking the elf that he could not.

Up in the sky, human mages could be seen as specks among the great eagles and soaring birds that graced the domain of Gyal. Clouds were gathering from the east where more smoke was evident, signifying more enemies moving deep into the forest. Corsaar would put a number on their strength when he reported.

Yet to the south, where the hand of Yniss had plucked at the earth to forge valley, mountain, ridge and rise, there was nothing. Its beauty was wholly undisturbed.

'Where are you, Takaar?'

Auum's ears pricked and opened fully, sampling the familiar sound behind and to his left. He listened as it approached, not turning his head. Instead, Auum stood, his feet locked to the very highest bough, his body straight and in perfect balance while the wind picked at his clothes. He stretched his arms out to either side and breathed deep.

The whispering became the ghost of the sound of flapping wings, accelerating as it approached. Auum dropped to his haunches and a mage's legs whistled by just above his head. He saw the man on his wings of shade bank up and left and come to hover twenty yards distant from him.

'Too late for you to learn to fly, Sharp ears,' the mage said with that flat-toned accent men always gave the elvish language. 'This is freedom and I bet you would give anything to try it.'

'I prefer the glory of the forest floor,' said Auum, standing once more, his arms loose by his sides. 'You are trespassing where only Gyal may tread.'

'Well, when I see Gyal I will be sure to make reparation.'

Auum smiled. 'Only the dead may see a god.'

'Then he will have to wait a while.'

'She,' corrected Auum. 'And I will send you to her.'

Auum swept a jaqrui from his pouch and threw. The crescent mourned away, chopping into the mage's gut just above the groin. The mage coughed, clutched at the wound and doubled over as his wings guttered and blew apart like mist on a gale. He screamed as he fell, colliding with branch and leaf all the way down.

Auum descended quickly, calling to Ulysan to search for the body. He dropped the last thirty feet from the banyan's lowest branch and ran to his Tai, who was signalling his position with a pitohui trill. The mage was broken and bloodied but he still clung to life.

'It is better to keep your feet on the ground,' said Auum. 'Not so far to fall.'

The mage coughed blood. Auum could see his chest was smashed through the rips in his clothes. His hands still covered the jaqrui. Eventually, the fit subsided.

'I'll keep that in mind,' he said, voice choked with fluid and gore.

'What are you searching for?' asked Auum. 'Speak and I'll hasten your passing so you can make your reparations to Gyal, should Shorth give you that dignity.'

The mage lay in a heap, surrounded by TaiGethen who did nothing to make him more comfortable. Ulysan stood with Elyss.

Faleen and her Tai had also come to see Auum's victim. The man's eyes were dimming and he was struggling for breath.

'My passing is coming soon enough. I will tell you nothing, but I will offer some advice.'

Auum waited while the mage suffered another violent coughing fit. When he was done, it was plain it would be his last.

'Your forest is unendingly beautiful. I commend you for your choice of home. But it belongs to us now. Take your people and leave or Ystormun will see you exterminated. Nothing can stop him.'

Auum knelt by the mage.

'We know you seek Takaar and we know where you think he will lead you.' Auum saw the mage's eyes widen. 'But we will find him first, and your armies will walk in circles until we have the time to kill each and every one of them. You will never find Katura, not while one elf walks the forest.

'Take that to your gods, if you have any. May Shorth offer you small mercy. Now, I need my jaqrui back. It seems to have a particularly fine edge.'

They took two daggers from the mage's body and his lightweight cloak from his back. Nothing else was worth saving and the body was left to be reclaimed. Auum took his Tais to a waterfall and plunge pool where they bathed, ate and prayed while Gyal's tears fell.

Auum waited until all were with him before he spoke.

'Auum?'

'I cannot believe he has disappeared. Thirty or so Ynissul should have slowed him to a crawl and he was only two days ahead of us when we set out. He must be using magic to obscure his position and his tracks . . . and that will only make him easier to track by our enemies. I need a solution.'

'Do you think he knows?' asked Ulysan.

Auum scratched his forehead. 'No. He is many things but he is not a traitor. But nor will he believe us, which makes our job all the harder. Do you still speak to Sikaant?'

Ulysan shook his head. 'He's been running with Serrin for many years now and his transition is just as deep and binding.'

'We need them,' said Auum. 'How can we find them?'

'Go to the Ix. Get close to the enemy and perhaps they'll find us.'

'That's a step back, Ulysan. Takaar is not travelling north.'

'There's another reason. We need a contingency if we don't find Takaar.'

Auum shook his head. 'The day I have to consider the defence of Katura is the day we are perilously close to the end.'

Ulysan paused and reconsidered what he'd been about to say.

'In all our years I have never heard you utter the words of an end to hope.'

Auum swallowed and realised he had spoken his darkest fear.

'Sometimes it is hard to have faith when our enemies close around us and those we consider our friends work against us. If Yniss is testing us, then this is the sternest of tests. How can we prevail, Ulysan? We are fifty-one against thousands, and their weapons are powerful. If Lysael is right then there is no Al-Arynaar any more. Takaar has fled, taking any magical ability we had, and drawing our foe to Katura like a beacon. And the ClawBound are no longer fighting for the cause of the elves but for the forest and Tual.

'I do have hope, Ulysan, but it is so hard to hold on to it. Every day it leaks away like water through rotted stitching. I try to catch it again, but it always escapes my grasp.

'I'm sorry.'

Ulysan put his hands on Auum's shoulders.

'Why?' said Ulysan quietly. 'It is because we care so much that we cannot bear the thought of a life without everything we love. It just makes you one of us, Auum. And that makes me happy, because you will fight all the harder to save us. It is why we all love you . . . and why you must let us all share the burden.

'We are TaiGethen. We are one under Yniss.'

The TaiGethen murmured their assent.

Auum smiled. 'I was wrong to despair. Forgive me.'

'There is nothing to forgive,' said Ulysan. 'And there is always hope. We must invoke Beeth, Tual and Appos and use all the gifts they provide. Use the forest. Ignore nothing.'

Auum stared at Ulysan and cursed himself blind.

'And we must trust no one but the TaiGethen,' he said, not quite believing what was staring him clear in the face. 'I know where he is.'

Chapter 15

*Yniss and Tual had no love for each other. Tual challenged Yniss,
declaring himself father of the elves, father of all living things.
Yniss merely laughed and his laughter brought all creatures to
him. 'Here is your father,' said Yniss. 'He is Tual and his love will
comfort you always. I am the father of Tual. I am father of the
world.'*

The Aryn Hiil

'Where is he hiding?' Auum demanded.

He, Elyss and Ulysan had run without rest, food or prayer. The
remaining TaiGethen had split up, looking for the ClawBound
moving towards the two enemy forces.

They had confronted Onelle inside the temple dome, where she
was kneeling before the great statue of Yniss. Priests were in attendance, preparing for a service of light. Auum gestured Elyss and
Ulysan to block any attempt to stop him disturbing her prayers.

Onelle jolted visibly when she heard Auum's voice close behind
her, but she remained on one knee, with one hand placed on the
stone floor and the other open to the roof of the dome. She completed
her intonation then stood, dusting off her dress. She turned to him
and Auum could see she was shaken.

'What are you doing here, Auum? There's a war out there, so you
tell me.'

'Where is he?'

'Who?'

'Don't insult me further by pretending ignorance. You've already
lied to me enough. I trusted you, Onelle. You have no reason to lie
about this: where is Lysael?'

'She returned to Loshaaren yesterday. Her flock is growing there.
The ClawBound took seventy freed slaves there two days ago, not
long after you left to seek Takaar.'

'Then at least some of our supposed allies are still fighting for us,' said Auum. 'Unlike you, who has let us waste two days seeking an elf who never left Aryndeneth. Because he didn't, did he? We cannot find his tracks because there are no tracks to find.'

'Auum, I swear, I don't know—'

'Your words mean precious little to me right now. You know, it took me a while to work out the truth. Like an idiot, I assumed the enemy were ignoring Aryndeneth because they were tracking Takaar. But then they stopped, and I was so slow to realise why.

'Because if Takaar was not in Aryndeneth two days ago, he most certainly returned here. And do you know how I know that? Because the humans already know Aryndeneth and it is not the place they are looking for. So they are waiting for him to move on. They've cut him loose knowing he will lead them straight to Katura. He's going to betray us all.

'So, Onelle, you have one final opportunity. Where is he?'

The six priests, gathered in two groups in front of Elyss and Ulysan at the sides of the pool, were plainly getting anxious. Auum glanced to both sides then back to Onelle. Her face crumpled and her lower lip quivered.

'You must let him act, Auum. Please. He will save the elves, not betray them.'

'Elyss, Ulysan, search the temple. Open every door. Go, I'll catch you up shortly.' Auum's eyes never left Onelle's face. 'Don't waste any more of my time. Tell me.'

Onelle shook her head. 'He has to get to Katura before the humans do. We cannot risk the new Il-Aryn.'

'He isn't just risking them, he's going to get them all killed, can't you see that?'

Auum turned and ran around the pool, shoving priests aside on his way to the clutter of rooms, chapels and prayer cells.

'Don't harm him!' Onelle shouted at his back. 'His ways are the future. He will save us! We will not let you stop him.'

More voices were raised in anger. Priests and acolytes were clashing with Ulysan and Elyss. Auum heard Ulysan barking something followed by the sound of a door slapping against its hinges. Auum raced to join him.

'Anyone harbouring Takaar and the Il-Aryn is working for our enemies against the elves,' said Auum. 'Stand back.'

A senior aide of Lysael's stood square in the central passageway, others at her side, blocking the way. Auum knew her well. She was an old Ynissul who preferred to shave her head rather than admit how white her hair had become. Her face was lined with age and her eyesight was fading. How many thousands of years had she lived, only to be faced with such trials now?

'Your actions are an affront to Yniss. Step away from your path, Auum.'

'This is not of your doing, Ainaere,' said Auum. 'Lysael's generosity and trust allowed the Il-Aryn to live and train here. Her trust has been betrayed. Don't hide Takaar through a misplaced sense of loyalty.'

'The devoted are at prayer and at peace within these chambers you wish to throw open. You have no right to disturb them.'

'Then tell me where he is,' said Auum. 'I have no wish to disturb the faithful. I am Arch of the TaiGethen. I am charged with the protection of this forest and all who dwell within it. Right now Takaar threatens our survival.'

'I will not betray him, though I swear to you he is not in the temple,' said Ainaere. 'Ix has blessed him. He has powers which he can awaken in many of our people, and Ix is the daughter of Yniss, who presides over us all. What greater path is there to follow?'

'Then the priesthood acts against all reason too,' said Auum quietly. 'Stand aside, Ainaere, or I will be forced to move you out of our way. Tai.'

Elyss and Ulysan came to Auum's shoulders. Weapons remained sheathed but that scarcely lessened the threat. Ainaere stared at Auum and her fortitude had clearly not withered over the centuries. She did not move. Auum spoke again.

'We are both vassals of Yniss. My faith is unsullied by the promise of new weapons and I will not stand by and allow the questionable pursuit of magic to lead our enemies directly to Katura.' He paused. 'The humans are tracking him through his magic. Thousands of them are in the forest right now, waiting for him to show them the way. The tragedy is of course that you, like him, do not believe that, do you? Stand aside.'

'Even if I did believe you, it merely makes his mission more urgent. Trust me now,' said Ainaere. 'Turn from this path. Return to the forest. Fight as you know how. Come no further. I cannot stand aside.'

'Then I am sorry,' said Auum. 'Yniss forgive me. Tai, we move.'

Auum strode forward. In deference and respect, he did not raise his hands, choosing instead to use his shoulder to force a path between Ainaere and her entourage. One laid a hand on Auum's right arm, and Auum stopped and stared into the young Ynissul's eyes.

'Your honour, such as it is, is already secured. Much good will it do you,' he said. 'Your hand is touching my shirt. Drop it or I will remove it.'

Auum marched on, feeling the young priest's fingers relax and fall away. He moved on towards the rear doors, motioning his Tai to continue their search within the temple. He felt sick and betrayed by those who stood at the head of his faith. Only Lysael, it seemed, had not been beguiled by Takaar's words. Worse, they would not listen to any other voices.

The rear doors of the temple stood closed and bolted. Behind him, the temple's workers, priests and acolytes were emptying into the central passage, following the lone TaiGethen cell. He heard shouts designed to shame him, turn him, accusing him of acting against his god. He heard threats of retribution from Yniss, from the Il-Aryn and from the whole of the elven race.

'And for this, we are trying to save our people,' he said to his Tai when they reached him. 'He's out there, isn't he?'

Auum unbolted and threw open the doors to the temple village. He walked into the light.

'You know that, if I chose, I could pin you and your precious warriors to the walls of the temple and there slowly crush your bodies until you beg for my mercy,' said Takaar.

'Then do it,' said Auum. 'And see how fragile your following really is.'

Takaar loved nothing if not the dramatic. So it had been through-out his life, his spectacular and tragic fall from grace and his rise back to some semblance of honour. Here he was, standing in the centre of the village with his Il-Aryn followers spread around him in an arc. Temple workers were gathered in groups at the sides of the village or peered out from the half-open doors of their dwellings.

'What are you doing here, Auum? I thought we said all we needed to say at the borders of Ysundeneth.'

Auum walked further away from the temple, happy to allow those clustered behind him to come and hear what was said. Elyss and Ulysan followed him, never more than a pace behind. Ulysan had his eyes everywhere, searching for any hidden threat. Elyss' fingers rubbed at her palms and her breathing was too fast and shallow.

'Your great human friend has betrayed you, Takaar. Garan has only sent you to Katura so you can lead his warriors to the gates. You're like a firefly, showing him the way through the darkness. And your light will bring the flame and ice and horror of human magic down on our people. It will bring human steel down upon the helpless and the innocent. It will signal the end of the elven race.'

Takaar applauded. His handclap was slow and contemptuous.

'You should really save such speeches for your own people. Very impressive, Auum, but your words, as I have sadly come to expect, are full of nothing but lies and scaremongering.'

'Scaremongering?' Auum pointed towards the Ix. 'What did you tell them, Takaar? That there is no army marching along our great river? That the rainforest is not invaded? They are here, and they are following the signature of your magic. And worse, you intend to lead them exactly where they want to go.'

Takaar appeared completely lucid. There was no confusion in his eyes signifying chatter from his other self. No distraction in his gestures. Auum had come to see Takaar's tormentor as a sometime ally; if they were in agreement for once, it would make his job infinitely harder.

'No elf would deny the threat facing us,' said Takaar. 'You insult me and all those who stand with me by suggesting as much. It is *because* there is an army marching through our forest that I am tasked by Yniss to build a force of Il-Aryn capable of defending our race. And achieving that is only possible because Garan, friend to the elves, has shown me the way. He has shown me our errors because he desires our survival. He should be feted by all elves, not cursed by the TaiGethen.'

The crowd surrounding them was hanging on Takaar's every word. Shouts of assent greeted every one of his assertions; fingers were pointed at the TaiGethen in their midst. Auum did not like the fervour contaminating the atmosphere around them.

'War comes today, Takaar. Tell me, how long will it take to train an elf to be a mage strong enough to combat the might of men? Twenty years. Thirty? More?'

'We must build for the future even as we fight for our present.'

'Takaar,' said Auum. 'I know you're no traitor and that you believe you are doing the right thing. So pursue this course with my blessing, if only because it keeps you away from me. But you cannot do it by travelling to Katura to collect your new subjects.'

Takaar said nothing for a moment. He scowled deeply and waved a hand to his right.

'I will handle this,' he hissed. 'I will not reveal all of my plans unnecessarily.'

'Someone else agrees with me, do they?' asked Auum.

Takaar's gaze, when it returned to Auum, was brim with fury.

'None but your sycophants agree with you,' he spat, his voice low and hoarse. 'You and I both know that the enemy will reach Katura, it was only ever a question of when. And when they find the city they will march in unhindered, because there is no strength or will left there to fight.

'So I am travelling there to rescue those who will become the bedrock of our race in the years to come; the Ixii, Cefans, Orrans and Gyalans. I will not leave them to scatter into the forest. As for the others in Katura, they had best pray to their gods and commend their souls to Shorth, for that is the only place they will find mercy.'

Prayers for the fallen of Katura swept the crowd, and Auum found himself muttering a few words too before attempting reason one more time.'Takaar, I have heard your words, now listen to me. Return to the Verendii Tual. You know like no one else how to hide there. Take your Il-Aryn and continue their training. Go with the blessing and the protection of the TaiGethen and all who follow the pure path of Yniss. I will protect Katura and I will bring your students to you personally. I guarantee their safety.'

'I will not entrust this task to any other,' said Takaar.

Auum addressed himself to the crowd.

'And are you truly with him? Do you understand what his actions will do? Thousands will die for the sake of the lives of a handful. How can you stand behind him while he commts this crime?'

There was a murmur in the crowd. One voice rose above the rest.

'He is committing no crime. The humans are the criminals. Takaar only seeks to save the elves.'

'But he — ' began Auum, but the noise in the crowd in support of the speaker would have drowned out anything he had to say. He scanned the elves gathered around them and shook his head in weary disbelief.

Auum looked to either side and his Tais nodded they were with him.

'Takaar, I don't know how you have convinced them so utterly but I will not stand by and let you lead human steel to the throats of elves.' Auum walked forward until he was five paces from Takaar. Close enough that he could not attempt a casting. 'I am forced to place you into the custody of the TaiGethen. You will be held somewhere you can do no more harm and where, should the humans continue to follow you, you will have led them far from those I am sworn to protect. Should you or any of the Il-Aryn attempt to reach Katura, the TaiGethen will strike you down for the protection of our people.'

Though none of the hundred or so who heard him could have been surprised at his announcement, the hiss of indrawn breath was loud and the muttering was low and angry. Takaar adopted a beatific smile and opened his arms wide to encompass all.

'And would you strike these people down too? These *iads* and *ulas* who have devoted their entire lives to Yniss and have seen a path to salvation?'

Auum raised his voice to carry across the village.

'Those who would follow you to Katura are deluded and represent a threat to all elves. None of them can stand against the TaiGethen. Should they try, they announce themselves enemies of the elves and yes, we will strike them down.'

'It is as I feared, my friends,' said Takaar, speaking in the manner of the ancient orators of Hausolis. 'Those who are sworn to protect us will instead raise their hands against us. So it is fortunate that I have found the true defenders of elven faith.'

He clapped his hands together. Auum stiffened. The TaiGethen were the true defenders of the faith – could Takaar have convinced a cell to join him? Doors opened to four houses in the heart of the village and Auum prepared himself to fight rogue TaiGethen, even though every nerve in his body protested that only in a nightmare could Takaar have swayed them.

Fifteen figures issued from the houses. They were cloaked in grey, wore cloth masks over their faces and carried long double-bladed spears – *ikari*. They spread out between Takaar and the TaiGethen, forming a barrier Auum knew he had no chance of breaching.

'Senserii,' breathed Auum. 'That bastard has found the Senserii.'

Beside him, Elyss moved to a ready position. In front of them, fifteen *ikari* snapped upright and forward; the Senserii were poised to attack. Auum put out a hand.

'Elyss, no. They'll kill you,' he said.

'He finally speaks sense,' said Takaar and he chortled like a child. 'A history lesson, Elyss my love, a history lesson. Will you, Auum, or shall I?'

Auum felt his anger surge and fought to keep himself in check. He jabbed a finger at Takaar and moved to force his way between two Senserii. Their *ikaris* clashed in front of his face.

'Auum!' hissed Ulysan. 'Elyss, stand right where you are. I have seen them in action. Everything you have read about them is true.'

Auum had not moved. He did not lift his head to look at either Senserii before him.

'I know you, Gilderon,' he said quietly. 'I know all of you and I respect your skills. You know me. This need not come to blows between the elite warriors castes. We need you to aid us in the fight against men. You have heard why Takaar must not reach Katura. Let me through, I will not harm him.'

They did not speak, or even move a muscle, to suggest they had heard, understood or would accede to his request. Auum rubbed a hand over his mouth. He wanted to scream in their faces that they were wrong and that Takaar was fooling them all, but it would have been a waste of breath. Takaar was going to bring an avalanche of human steel and magic down on Katura and Auum would have to risk all the TaiGethen to try and even the odds.

'So be it,' he whispered.

Auum stepped away from the Senserii, turned and motioned his Tai to follow him. He ran around the edge of the temple before leading them back into the rainforest. At the first fast-running stream, he stopped to wash his face and scrub his hands.

'As soon as Takaar heads for Katura, the enemy will move. We will have to be ready.'

Ulysan nodded but Elyss pointed back towards Aryndeneth.

'Why didn't you go back through the temple? We should have prayed. I needed to pray there.'

Auum shook his head. 'Yniss no longer listens to prayers uttered there. Until Aryndeneth is rededicated, it is no longer our temple.'

Chapter 16

One of the enduring tragedies of the enslavement of the elves and the betrayal of Llyron, High Priest of Shorth, was the disappearance and presumed death of Juijuene, teacher of the Senserii. It was perhaps the first of many mortal blows unknowingly struck by the hand of man.

From *A Charting of Decline*, by Pelyn, Arch of the Al-Arynaar, Governor of Katura

In the vastness of the rainforest there was nowhere to hide. Auum ran as never before while his mind struggled to develop strategies and his soul to maintain the merest vestige of hope. Neither was proving simple. The calls had gone out, the TaiGethen had met together. For some, it would have been for the last time.

Two days after the stand-off at the temple, the army camped on the banks of the Ix had begun to march again and Auum had known Takaar was on the move.

The TaiGethen were split. Fifteen cells, including Auum's, would harry the Ix army while the remaining two cells under Corsaar would track and obstruct the smaller army from Deneth Barine, which it had been confirmed was approaching along the River Shorth.

Auum tried not to think about the size of the forces Ystormun had sent into the forest and the paucity of the defences. Ulysan had been right of course, the elves had to use their land to their advantage. But the only really positive news Auum had heard was Onelle's mention that the ClawBound were attacking the enemy in order to free slaves. Auum would have preferred to develop a coherent strategy with them, but that seemed an unlikely prospect.

The enemy had passed the Olbeck Rise on foot, while their twelve barges were half a day further on, soldiers and mages staying firmly on board and the vessels anchored in midstream when night fell.

It was almost dusk when Auum finally caught up with Merrat and

Grafyrre's cells about a mile north of the enemy. A steady rain was falling and looked set for the night, happily making camping uncomfortable for the invading army. The nine TaiGethen climbed into the lower boughs of a sprawling banyan and sheltered beneath its broad leaves while they talked.

'What's their attrition rate?' asked Ulysan.

'Conditions are poor,' said Merrat. 'Many of them are sleeping on the ground and we've seen plenty of infestation, bites and infections. The trouble is that the mages seem quite capable of curing most things so I don't think we can look to the smaller of Tual's creatures to do much for us.'

'All right, so let's focus on how we can damage them at rest. I don't want to risk a direct attack right now. Better to do something covert that supports the ClawBound's efforts. Can we introduce a mass infection, for instance? Something on a scale which would overwhelm the mages. Waterborne is the obvious choice, but we cannot risk poisoning the water courses.'

'They boil all their drinking water; they even fill their skins with boiled water. They're being careful, experience has taught them that much,' said Merrat. 'So there is not much joy to be had there anyway.'

'What about their food supply?' asked Elyss.

'Their diet is principally fish,' said Nyann, who with Ysset made up Merrat's cell. Nyann was a young TaiGethen, one of the newest to be fully fledged. 'The braver ones go hunting, or they did. The ClawBound returned last night's hunters to the camp perimeter in pieces. They are carrying large quantities of dried food, though. It's all loaded on the barges in crates and barrels. Which makes sense, I suppose.'

Auum thought for a moment. 'All right. Here's what we'll do: their route is bound to take them towards the Haliath Vale and straight past the Apposans on their way inland to Katura. I want all the remaining cells up there including yours, Graf. You're going to be in charge of preparing the ground and canopy for defence. Use every-thing. You know how the Apposans like a fight and the Scar is a perfect ambush site.'

Grafyrre nodded. 'And the rest of you are . . .'

Auum smiled. 'Going swimming.'

*

'Anyone cut?' asked Auum.

'We'll soon know enough,' said Merrat. 'Plenty of crocodile and piranha on the scent right here. Actually, Auum, you've chosen a particularly well-stocked passage of the Ix for this.'

It was full night. The rain had eased a fraction. Auum, Elyss and Ulysan sat with Merrat, Nyann and Ysset, smearing their bodies with a dense sticky poultice of verbena, vine leaf and crushed tubers. The preparation would mask their scent in the water and hide any cuts. It would be good for the swim downstream but would not be so effective for their return to the shore.

'Beeth has been unkind,' said Elyss. 'This stuff itches like fly larvae under the skin.'

'But at least you know it's sticking,' said Ulysan cheerfully.

'But what else is it doing?' asked Elyss, the best swimmer of the six.

'Playing havoc with your complexion,' said Ysset. 'You'll need a good infusion of lemongrass and camu to reduce the rashes on your skin afterwards.'

'How comforting,' said Elyss. 'There are few things I detest more than lemongrass. I think I'd rather take the blotches.'

Auum let them chatter. His plan had been greeted with silence followed by fervent and anxious prayers, and they were now only two hundred yards from the prow of the first barge. All twelve lay at anchor line astern in the centre of the channel.

Lights from the barges and from the multitude of fires in the enemy camps along the bank gave the nighttime a curious flickering glow. Bright pinpoints of light blinked as people walked in front of lanterns and torches. The sound of an army settling to rest carried up the river along with the smells of cooking and the unholy stink of man. The rasp of weapons on whetstones sounded like the call of a rainforest lizard, overlaying the fizz and crack of damp wood and chatter of men.

Auum smoothed the verbena paste across Elyss' forehead, up into her short-cropped hair and along the line of her nose and cheeks, leaving no speck of skin visible.

'Close your eyes,' he said. He covered her eyelids and worked the paste into the corners of her eyes. She winced. 'Sorry. All done.'

Elyss opened her eyes and smiled. 'Your turn.'

'I can't wait,' said Auum, closing his eyes and leaning forward.

Their poison of choice lay at their feet: black cap mushrooms, finely cut and warmed over a hidden flame to dry them out ready for sprinkling. Auum had no idea if human magic could defeat their harsh toxins, but the thought of causing widespread gut cramps that felt like evisceration, combined with vomiting and shitting blood, and leaking bile from ruined kidneys, however temporarily, would give the ClawBound fresh opportunities to strike and buy the TaiGethen more precious time.

By the time Elyss was finished Ulysan had placed the dried mushroom crumbs in two small leather pouches. He threw one to Merrat and the other to Auum.

'Swim with your arm in the air.'

'I've got a much better idea,' said Auum.

They swam slowly and gently, hidden behind the rainforest debris that washed continually down the Ix from the Cerathon Falls a few hundred miles to the south. Auum and Merrat perched their pouches of mushrooms atop knots of vines and branches.

Approaching the lead barge, Ulysan and Elyss slipped away into the shadows of the craft's hull. Auum abandoned his float as he reached the fourth barge. Merrat's cell was heading for the eighth and twelfth barges. Auum rested a hand on the hull, the mushroom pouch caught between his thumb and forefinger.

Lights ringed the gunwale rail, pooling weakly on the open forward deck, which was filled with soldiers attempting to sleep. Guards wandered along the rail, their eyes on the banks of the river some hundred and fifty yards to either side. They knew what lurked in the water. Not one of them trailed a lazy hand in it.

Auum worked his way towards the stern, past the mast to the cargo stays, where dozens of barrels, sacks and crates were lashed to the deck a beneath a timber rain hood. The tiller deck was behind them, three steps up and surrounded with its high rail. Four men stood there talking, looking along the length of the barge and directly across the cargo.

Auum tossed the pouch in among the nearest sacks and waited, looking upstream. He could make out Ulysan's head at the prow of the lead barge. Of Elyss there was no sign until her head broke the surface and the pair of them began moving along the length of the craft.

Gently, as if propelled by the merest breath of wind, the barge began to turn towards the bank, pivoting on the stern anchor. A single shout of alarm sent men scurrying about the deck. Orders to raise the sail echoed across the river and Auum saw men hauling on the anchor rope only to discover it untied. When the barge was at almost ninety degrees to the others, Elyss released the aft anchor as well.

Above Auum, the deck had come alive. Men ran down to the prow. The tiller deck emptied, scowling sailors marching forward, leaving one looking suspiciously down at the spot where his anchor rope disappeared into the dark water. Auum heard raucous laughter and a few cheers from within the barge, over which furious shouts and orders fought to be heard.

Auum moved quietly around to the rear of the tiller deck. The guard was still staring down, almost daring his anchor to shift, when Auum saw the merest shadow in the water, about three feet down, heading for the rope. He smiled.

Something flashed up the rope, using it to propel herself out of the water. Elyss slammed into the guard, a dagger thumping into his throat. He made a low gurgling sound, cut off when he hit the deck. Auum stared over at the fifth barge, fifteen yards away in the gloom. No one had seen her.

Auum moved silently onto the deck, keeping himself low. Elyss was kneeling over the body, her hands slick with his blood.

'I'm sorry,' she said. 'There was no other way to do it. But they'll see this, won't they?'

'Don't worry about it. Watching all those humans has given me a better idea than all this stealth nonsense. Watch for my signals.'

Elyss nodded, wiped her hands on the soldier's leggings and moved forward along the port side of the cargo. Auum retrieved the pouch and crawled over the cargo, beneath the rain hood, sniffing at the lid of each crate and barrel, seeking dried meat. He found it in four barrels, all securely lidded and three sealed. The fourth had been opened. Auum used a knife to lever the lid up and sprinkled mushroom shavings over the salted meat strips, mixing it in with a hand.

He replaced the lid; next, grain. The humans had a bizarre fondness for barley soups and stews, and it would be stored in sacks. Auum crawled back down to the deck, motioning Elyss to return to the tiller.

Another loud commotion broke out: Merrat's Tai must have begun their attack. Auum smiled and began checking the sacks. Three were open and roughly tied at the neck. Auum glanced down the length of his barge. Men were walking back down the deck – one was waving soldiers back to their mats with little success. The other three were marching with some purpose towards the tiller.

Auum's time was short. He grabbed the thin rope from the neck of a sack and tipped the mushroom into the top. He scooped it under the surface and pushed the rope back round the neck, hoping it would go unnoticed. Ahead, the trio were splitting up to walk either side of the cargo. Two were coming Auum's way; so much the better.

He looked behind him. Ulysan was now on deck with Elyss and both of them had seen the approaching danger. Good. It was impossible to ignore this opportunity to inflict more damage on the enemy . . . and as for their own escape, they'd just have to make that up as they went.

Auum pressed himself hard into the shadow of the cargo. Humans were blind and these two men wouldn't see him unless they stepped on him. He drew a dagger and held the blade close to his body, hiding the shine. The deck was only wide enough for one man. The pair didn't stop talking as they hurried on, gesturing angrily at the barge behind them and the commotion ahead of them.

They were four paces from Auum when he stood to block their path, shouting in the ancient tongue of the elves, '*Flethar kon juene bleen.*' *Make the river red.*

Auum leapt forward and flashed his dagger across the first man's face. He threw up his hands up to defend himself. Auum reversed the blade across the backs of his hands, stepped in and jabbed an elbow up into his throat. The man began to choke, his eyes widening in fear as Auum spun on his left leg and cracked his right foot into the side of his enemy's head. The move was quick. The man lost his balance and plunged into the river.

Auum did not pause. He ran at the second sailor, straight-kicked him in the stomach and shoved him hard on the shoulders as he doubled over. The man scrabbled for a hold on the ropes tying the cargo. Auum swept his dagger down, severing a finger. The man cried out and fell sideways into the water. It was only a matter of time now.

Auum paced past the cargo and on to the open deck. To his right, Ulysan was moving past the falling body of the third sailor and mirroring Auum's advance. Elyss was behind him. Ahead, the enemy were just waking to the fact they were under attack. Shouts echoed across the river. Men surged to their feet, seeking weapons and armour.

'Get in, and get out,' said Auum. 'We have business elsewhere. Tai, we strike.'

One of the humans in the water gave the long scream of a man suffering a thousand bites, while Auum sprinted into the heart of the enemy. There had to be almost a hundred soldiers on board, living in a cramped chaos that could only aid the TaiGethen. As many scrambled away as squared up to them, peering into the half-light of the gunwale lanterns.

Auum lashed a foot into the face of a soldier who was still searching for his sword, sending him spinning away towards the side of the barge, where he knocked a lantern into the river. The water had already begun to boil with piranha. Down in the water, a man was screaming to be saved, his screams alerting those on deck that to fall in was to die. Auum's smile was bleak. The risk for the TaiGethen would be just as great should any of them be cut before they returned to the water.

Ulysan flew through his peripheral vision, both feet thudding into the chest of a big soldier, who crashed backwards into another hiding in his shadow. Elyss moved in behind him, her twin blades carving cuts into her enemies' exposed bodies. Auum pivoted on his right foot and swept his left high, across his face. His heel caught his target on the chin, knocking him down, and Auum stepped forward. He drew a blade with his left hand, sliced open the man's buttocks and threw his victim over the side.

Auum rolled to his right. A blade split the deck behind him, missing his left shoulder by a whisker, then he was back on his feet, too fast to track. Two men were ahead of him. He jumped high and kicked out with first his left then his right foot. Both connected hard, his left smashing the warrior's nose across his face, his right making a mess of his target's lips and teeth.

Auum landed between them, dropped his left shoulder and shoved one overboard. Simultaneously, he kicked out with his right foot, cracking it into the knee of the second man, smashing the joint backwards. Auum moved past him, hacking a blade deep into his neck.

He moved fast to his Tai. Ulysan butted a burly soldier in the face and the man staggered back towards the starboard rail. He reached out and grabbed Ulysan's arms, his weight overbalancing the

TaiGethen. Ulysan pulled back but his heels were slipping on the blood-slick deck. Auum couldn't get there in time. Ulysan was heading for the frothing, screaming water where crocodiles were already gathering to join the feast.

He slithered closer still, desperate for a way to escape his fate, his eyes wide. The soldier's ankles struck the rail. Ulysan jerked back but the soldier's grip was too strong. Auum heard a yell as Elyss' blades hammered down one after the other, severing the soldier's arms near the elbows. He plunged into the water, blood spewing from the stumps, too shocked to even scream as the water closed over his head.

Ulysan staggered back a pace before finding his balance again. He was vulnerable. Auum moved to his left, hacking both blades into the gut of a soldier who thought he'd seen an opportunity. Ulysan nodded his thanks. Elyss moved to his other side.

'Quick,' said Auum. 'Let's take one more.'

The TaiGethen cell turned and sprinted for the tiller deck, sheathing their blades. Arrows began to fly as soon as they were clear of the enemy, skipping off the deck and whistling past them as they ducked and jumped. Beside them, the water was alive with flesh-eating creatures. Screaming bodies thrashed and blood topped the foam.

Auum reached the tiller deck, leapt on to the rail and dived out as far as he could, his body entering the water with barely a ripple. He cleared the blood frenzy and trusted to the remains of the salve to shield him. He opened his eyes. Silvery bodies flashed past to either side of him; the river seemed choked with them. He could see the great shapes of crocodiles moving fast, their tails driving them through the water at stunning speed.

Auum swam hard, breaking the surface and powering towards the bow of the fifth barge. Ahead, he could see the last of the twelve barges drifting into midstream, its anchor lines detached. He saw men gathering on the shore, pointing and hollering advice and he could see chaos on another barge, presumably the one Merrat had attacked. A third barge had managed to raise minimal sail and was moving down the line to lend aid.

His target barge was crowded with men yelling out instruction, order and support. Almost all were armed but none even considered entering the river. Archers elbowed their way to the bow and took aim at the water. Elyss was driving on past Auum, Ulysan was a few strokes behind.

Auum dived below the surface once more, just in time. An arrow fizzed into the water, its fletchings brushing his forehead. Auum looked for and found the anchor rope. He swam towards it, seeing Elyss' body flicking towards the stern of the craft, a dagger held in her teeth. He watched her angle her body and still her movement as a huge crocodile powered past her.

The beast loomed up on him, an evil black shadow in the gloomy moonlit water. Arrows criss-crossed in the water seeking targets, and one nicked the corner of the crocodile's eye, bouncing off its scales. It turned its head and changed direction so fast Auum could barely track its movement. Auum's blood chilled. He swept his legs hard, driving himself faster towards the barge, the reptile closing on him at a horrifying pace. Auum grabbed the anchor rope. He pulled himself towards it. His vision was full of dull green. He got his other hand on the anchor line, and then a foot, broke the surface and ran up the taut rope.

The crocodile surged out after him, propelled by speed and anger. Auum leapt high, past the gaping mouths and wide eyes of the soldiers crowding the deck. He twisted in the air, drawing his blades and executing a perfect back flip. The move gave him a brief view of the crocodile, anchor rope in its mouth, landing square on the deck, flattening some and scattering the rest into the water or across the deck. Timbers cracked. The beast hissed.

As he spun through the air Auum looked down, seeking clear deck. He landed four paces from the bow, his blades already slicing out and forward. Ahead, the crocodile thrashed and snapped its jaws. Men were pushing back, trying to get away from it. More fell into the river.

The crocodile rushed forward. Its huge tail thrashed left and right striking men clear off the barge and into the water. The reptile's jaws opened wide and shut with appalling force. There was a scream, a fountain of blood and a body was flung into the air. Men turned to run, only to find a TaiGethen warrior waiting for them. Elyss and Ulysan climbed over the starboard rail. Their blades worked hard. Auum moved forward, adding to the confusion at the bow. The crocodile was heading back to the water, a wailing victim in its mouth.

Auum turned and ran towards the tiller deck, his Tai with him. Panicked men parted before them. TaiGethen blades licked out, slicing deep into flesh. Nimble feet tangled clumsy human legs. Bodies sprawled across the deck or fell into the frothing water.

'Lanterns!' called Auum.

He ran to the gunwale, sheathing his blades and pushing a frightened soldier over the side. He snatched up a lantern and hurled it at the cargo. The glass shattered under the rain hood and spread burning oil across the dry crates and barrels. Elyss and Ulysan followed his lead and soon six lanterns had been broken across the cargo, flames already licking up, heat building rapidly beneath the hood.

On the tiller deck, men stood with nowhere to go. The skipper was at the tiller, keeping the barge in midstream. Two others hefted long swords.

'Elyss, tiller. Ulysan, drop kick.'

The Tai cell sprinted on. Ulysan took the left, Auum the right. Three paces from the guards, both TaiGethen leapt, legs straight, hammering into their targets' faces before either could raise his blade high enough. Auum landed astride his enemy, dropped his knees onto his chest and smashed his windpipe with a single punch. Elyss rolled by overhead, landed in front of the skipper and roundhoused a perfectly placed kick into his temple. He fell stunned against the rail and lay there until Elyss helped him over the side.

'Enough,' said Auum. 'The water's getting too dangerous now. Let's get to shore before the piranha and crocodiles begin to seek fresher meat than humans.'

The TaiGethen dived off the stern and swam hard for the shore opposite the enemy army, heading for the agreed meeting point with Merrat. Three barges were ablaze, their provisions lost, another two now carried poisoned food supplies. Two more were adrift. Auum paused at the bank to appreciate the chaos they had caused. The river was awash with blood and bones, although they had killed relatively few of their enemies. But that had not been the purpose of the night. Auum smiled.

'A good night's work,' he said.

Chapter 17

A human will never understand the essential simplicity of the forest and he will die as a result.

Auum, Arch of the TaiGethen

' "Build more barges",' said Hynd. 'That was what you said, wsn't it?'

Jeral tore his eyes from the river, the burning barges and the awful thrashing in the water. He glared at Hynd, assuming he was being ridiculed. But Hynd wasn't even looking at him. He was staring at the garish scene, his face drawn and pale in the half-light.

'Yeah.' Jeral's voice caught and he cleared his throat. 'Yeah, that was me.'

The three burning barges had not been put out yet and Jeral didn't blame anyone for not getting any closer to the river than they absolutely had to. All three still had crew and soldiers aboard. The fires were contained, at least for now, and it looked as if heavy rain was coming. They could hope to salvage the hulls if not the cargo they carried.

Jeral wasn't sure what would happen now. He'd have brought all the barges to the bank and disembarked everyone for the time being. The trouble was, no one knew where would be safest – not now.

'Did we know they could swim?' asked Hynd. His head was shaking slightly and he gestured out at the water.

'I think we all assumed they could swim, Hynd. Y'know, most of us can swim.' Jeral stood up and moved another pace further from the bank and nearer his fire. 'But there's a difference between going for a dip and volunteering to swim through infested waters to get at a load of humans you could easily have killed on land.'

'What surprises me most is that they didn't launch a land attack too,' said Hynd. 'After all, none of us were watching our backs, were we?'

Jeral shrugged. 'It's all the same message. Like we didn't know we weren't safe out here.'

'There's got to be more to it than that,' said Hynd, turning from the river at last.

'Sure there is. They're trying to wear us down, make us scared of closing our eyes to sleep, and it's working, isn't it? Now every man on those barges feels exposed and is shitting himself waiting for the next ripple to get close to their boat. Put a foot in there and you lose it, right? Can't shoot an arrow across the deck. Can't wash it with a spell either. You won't catch me on one of those things now, that's for sure. Not a fucking chance.'

Jeral looked back at the water. Burning barrels and sacks had been pushed into the water, diminishing the fires still further. There was almost total silence. The water had ceased to churn. A couple of rowing boats were scudding between barges. Men were being transferred and the occasional glow signified mages at work, tidying up wounds. But of those who had fallen into the river, there was nothing left to save.

In the forest the pickets had been strengthened, and everywhere you looked hardened soldiers were shuddering and shivering as if cold. It wasn't even raining yet.

'Seen anything of our glorious leaders?' asked Hynd.

Jeral sniffed. 'What do you think? No doubt they surrounded themselves with mages, castings and spears and crawled under the biggest rocks they could find. No, strike that. It's the middle of the night, isn't it? Loreb will be pissed and won't know anything's happened. Killith is probably organising a sing-song or something. Pindock, now he will be under a rock somewhere with shit dribbling down his legs. What we could really do with is a word from your lot. I mean, how much further is this place? It had better fucking exist, that's all I can say.'

'Takaar is on the move,' said Hynd. 'All we can do is follow him.'

'But for how long? Ten days? Forty?' Hynd shrugged and Jeral blew out his cheeks. 'Look around, Hynd. There are plenty of scared people out there. We don't know how long we're going to be marching deeper and deeper into this hideous leafy hell and we've just lost a load of our food into the bargain. How are your blisters?'

Hynd smiled. 'Being a mage has its benefits.'

'Haven't fixed mine though, have you? And I'm not the worst. We've got rot and splits deep enough to have been made by a knife.

What we need, us ordinary soldiers, is a bit of communication. This can't go on.'

'Tell Killith then,' said Hynd sharply. 'It's not up to me, is it? Anyway I don't know any more than you do.'

'Really?'

'Really. You know how this works. We follow the elf to Katura and then we kill whatever we find there.'

'And we hope to hell he doesn't just wander around in a big circle.'

'Ystormun doesn't think he will.'

Jeral spat. 'Well Ystormun isn't out here. And I think we've already had ample evidence that the elves are a bunch of sneaky bastards. I wonder how many men we'll have left when we eventually get a proper fight?'

'You worry too much.'

'Nuin said the same thing, just before a panther ripped out his throat,' said Jeral, scratching his scars. 'I mean, has it really not crossed your master's mind that Takaar might lead us astray to give the TaiGethen more opportunities to scare the crap out of us?'

'He's travelling almost due south,' said Hynd. 'He's not going in a circle. We're scouting ahead of him when we can but our stamina is finite.'

'So is the flesh on my feet. So is the army's morale – especially after tonight. We're marching into nowhere and every footstep places us nearer an enemy we can barely touch. Hardly matters how few of them there are, assuming that piece of intelligence is remotely accurate. Until we get to this city, they don't have to meet us head on, do they?'

Hynd rubbed his hands over his face. 'All right. I'll go and talk to Lockesh. So long as you stop whining.'

Jeral chuckled. 'I can promise you a lot of things but don't ask that of me. After all, what would I have left then?'

'Companionable silence.'

'I am loyal among the faithless. I am the truth among lies. I am the word among savages. I walk through history and I am the future. I am the first breath of the new born. I am the last and fatal blow for the dead. I am the Arch of the new immortals.

'I am complete.'

The last of his paint was across his chin. Takaar stood in the wet dawn of the new day and his nostrils were full of the glorious scents of Ix and her energies.

Who is it you are today?

'I am Takaar and I am the first of the Il-Aryn.'

And the camouflage . . .

'Today we fuse magic with the art of the warrior. Who better to teach this than he who walks among the gods.'

Dear Yniss preserve us, this is going to be good.

'You think me unsound of mind?'

Well, you're still talking to me.

'But for all you are ever present, you missed my walk into the light of knowledge as we all slept.'

Please go on.

'The path is clear. The learning shall be swift and the rise of the Il-Aryn assured.'

Which I presume means you're taking your leave of your poor confused followers.

'You're wrong. They believe in me.'

They believe in Onelle. They are wary of you. This little act should tip them right over the edge.

'I am the only one who can school them. The only one who can save them.'

Save them from what?

Takaar smiled and began walking back to the camp perched on the banks of the River Shorth.

'Save them from the Il-Aryn, a power that will consume them unless they can truly accept it.'

What are you talking about?

'Listen and learn.'

I hate you when you're like this.

'Then I am truly One today.'

The Senserii were loading the boats and organising a simple breakfast soup of root vegetables, guarana and bright-smelling herbs. The students were awake and most of them were out of their hammocks and gathered near the cook fire. The first one to see him started visibly, shuffling back into his friends before tugging the shirt of the nearest. The desultory conversation ceased, smothered by a sense of unease.

Oh brilliant. You've got them right in the palm of your hand now.

Takaar hissed then covered it with a smile.

'If my appearance surprises you, then you must brace yourselves for greater shocks to come. I have awoken this day and the knowledge you must possess is within me. I will bestow it upon you. The path will not be easy. Some of you may fail. But for those who succeed, your names will resonate through the millennia.'

Takaar walked towards them, his arms open and welcoming. But they did not respond with the beatific smiles he had anticipated. No matter. Instead, they bunched a little closer together and looked to the leader within their midst. He moved to the front of the group. Takaar blessed him with a nod of approval. A talented young *ula* with an odd name . . . what was it? Ah, yes, Drech.

'My Lord Takaar, I'm . . . confused. *We're* confused.'

'All will become clear, my student.'

Drech's smile was halting. 'Yes, of course. But are we now to learn the way of the TaiGethen? Your camouflage . . .'

'Ha! Yes.' Takaar clapped his hands. 'You are right to think that way because, at its heart, an understanding of magic is a combat as keen as any TaiGethen blade.'

'Surely we have already understood—'

'You have understood nothing!' spat Takaar, feeling their fear and bewilderment as food in his gut. 'You do not know why the shield failed at Aryndeneth. I do. You do not know why our magic cannot match that of the humans. I do. And I can teach you, but it will be a fight. I have won that fight—' Takaar smiled and allowed himself an expression of superiority '—but I am TaiGethen.'

Drech looked round at his peers and none of them possessed the spark of understanding. Takaar huffed and his frustration began to grow. His tormentor was chuckling. Takaar tried to ignore him.

'Surely we are travelling to become, as you explained, the teachers of the new Il-Aryn,' said Drech. 'We can already help them to an awareness of the power within them, teach them about shapes and stamina. Where does combat fit in?'

'You have opened the door but you cannot hold back the flood,' said Takaar. 'The power you have flowing through you will destroy you unless you learn to control it.'

'We do control it,' said Drech. 'We harness and direct it.'

'Really?' Takaar scratched his chin. 'Then let me educate you in your utter weakness in those areas.'

Drech's eyes widened. Takaar strode forward until he was a single pace from the young adept. He opened his arms.

'What would you have me do?' asked Drech.

'Attack me,' said Takaar. 'Use your quickest and most powerful casting. You can make flame on your hands can you not? Aim it at my face. Melt my camouflage, burn my skin.'

'I cannot—'

'Cast, or turn back to Aryndeneth now and live with your shame. I will tolerate neither disobedience nor cowardice.'

Drech met Takaar's stare and Takaar saw courage and fury there. Perfect. Drech's eyes unfocused briefly and his hands shot forward, flame wreathing and encasing them. Fire surged out, and Takaar opened his mouth. He inhaled the flame, feeling the fuel that created it surge through his veins. He changed its nature, using the core of his body, and exhaled a hurricane.

Cloaks were blown over faces, loose debris was cast into the air and the soup cauldron rocked violently on its makeshift tripod, steadied at the last moment by a Senseri. Drech was blown back into his fellows and they fell in an untidy sprawl on the soaked ground.

Takaar folded his arms and waited for the students to untangle themselves, stand and brush loose mud from their clothes. He could see that Drech was furious.

'Humiliation should not sit well with any of you,' said Takaar. 'Do not accept it and do not allow those feelings to be repeated. Learn this. An elf who can saw wood cannot call himself a carpenter. All you have done is taste the magic, and all you can do with it is make constructs of paper. Until the energies of Ix are part of your soul, twined around your bones and running in your blood, you will never be in control.

'You will not be just weak, you will be in danger from a surge of energy which could rip your mind apart. So you must learn to drink the energy, be one with it and accept it as an integral part of you, your mind and your body. It has to *be* you. Or it will consume you.'

Takaar watched them fighting whether to believe him or not. Drech, he could see, had shaken off his humiliation and was staring at Takaar with undisguised awe and desire, not for him but for the knowledge he possessed. Now that was what Takaar had expected to see in his students.

'I want to feel what you feel,' said Drech.

But Takaar could see he had not yet convinced all his fellows and Takaar wanted them all.

'I don't want anyone with me who does not believe in me. I won't stop any of you running back to Aryndeneth, to Onelle's bosom. She, unlike you, has always been at one with the Il-Aryn. And she, unlike you, will not die screaming one day because she has already contained the flood of magic in her mind. Without me, you cannot hope to contain it yourselves.

'It really is your choice. Come, learn from me and teach the new generation in your turn. Or go back home and wait to die.'

You really are a total bastard, aren't you?

'Thank you. Thank you very much.'

Chapter 18

Man's magic can cure ills, it can burn the flesh from bones and it can shout louder than a falling mountain. But it cannot confer faith, and thus men remain essentially weak.

Auum, Arch of the TaiGethen

The stew was not sitting well with Hynd. Or perhaps it was that he'd just been bawled out by Lockesh for daring to suggest the rank and file were given a little information, like how long this torture would go on. It had taken him a whole day's march to pluck up the courage to request an audience, and the early end to the march had seen his stomach do an uncomfortable flip.

Jeral had made him eat first, probably so he could taunt him about his meeting for as long as possible. And to bore him rigid with his endless litany of complaints, complaints he had never taken to his generals. Hynd had let it all roll over him while he watched the barge repairs progress.

By the time he'd been summoned, his guts were gurgling and thumping away as if he'd had a hard night drinking the worst spirits the elves could dredge out of their revolting vegetable roots. The toasting his ears had received had taken his mind off it for a while but now, on his way back to Jeral via the outlying pickets to 'clear his mind of stupidity while he checked every ward on the perimeter', he was experiencing sharp pains he put down to an upcoming bout of violent wind.

The first disabling cramp struck him while he was restructuring a badly designed alarm ward that would have triggered when anything larger than a hare crossed its threshold. He was already crouching, so when the pain defeated his balance he didn't have far to fall.

Hynd grunted and clutched his stomach. The cramp went on, grinding away at his innards, bringing bile to his throat and sweat to his face. Hynd tried to force himself back to his feet despite the pain. A few yards away the guards at the picket were tending to one of their own who was writhing on the ground.

Hynd dropped back to all fours and vomited. Green and brown sludge spattered across the leaf litter and he almost passed out. He just managed to stay conscious, rolling on to his back away from the vomit and heaving in a breath of humid, close air. He could hear someone calling out but it seemed to come from a great distance.

Hynd tried to focus, creating the shape for a healing spell. It was to no avail. Nothing would form. He couldn't concentrate. Fear washed through him, intensifying when he felt a hand on his shoulder. He opened his eyes to see one of the picket guards standing over him.

'Guts?' he asked.

Hynd managed a nod and ground out a shudder of exquisite pain. His head began to ache horribly, pounding so hard he could barely hear what the guard said next.

'. . . iver. *Hund* . . . your feet.'

The guard held out a hand to help him up. Hynd nodded and waved to the man to give him a moment to gather himself. The cramp had eased ever so slightly, until he merely felt as though he'd swallowed slivers of glass, or perhaps an entire longsword. Sideways. He reached up his hand but the guard wasn't looking at him any more.

'Are you—'

There was a vibration through the ground and a rustling of the leaf litter before the alarm ward exploded, flooding the immediate area with light and sounding a discordant alarm which sheared into Hynd's head. A panther battered into the guard taking him beyond Hynd's field of vision.

Hynd forgot his pain just for a moment and scrambled up to run back to the river. But another cramp stole his strength before he reached it and he had to lean against a tree for support. He heard a sound through the pounding in his head and opened his eyes to see a panther crouched in front of him. The animal leapt at his chest, knocking him down and pinning him to the ground. It moved to bite down on his neck but stopped, jutted its muzzle forward and sniffed his mouth.

Hynd was frozen. He had no idea what it was waiting for. His life was over and at least this would be a release from the awful pains inside. The panther growled deep in its throat, drew back and sprang away, roaring what sounded like a warning.

Hynd rolled over and dragged himself back to his feet. He could see the shapes of elves in the shadows. The light from the alarm ward was dimming and illuminated a few bodies and a single writhing man left alive, much like himself. Hynd vomited again, his muscles straining so hard he wasn't sure they'd ever relax. But they did and, using every tree and branch for support, he stumbled towards the river, aware that he was crying incoherently for help, and crying for relief from the pain.

No one ran past him towards the picket, and that was wrong. He could hear people shouting but it was coming from way off to his right, and when he burst out of the forest he was confronted by a scene befitting a sick house, not an army at rest. Everywhere he looked men were lying on the ground or kneeling, clutching their heads or stomachs. The stench of shit and vomit was overpowering and the cries of the stricken chimed with his own.

Hynd searched for Jeral, finding him bent double over the river, wiping puke from his mouth and breathing hard. He dropped to his knees by his friend.

'Jeral,' he managed.

'We've been poisoned,' said Jeral. 'Fuck it hurts.'

'I know,' gasped Hynd. 'But it's saving us too.'

Jeral looked at him. The whites of his eyes were shot through with red and his brow was covered in sweat. He lost his balance and jammed a hand into the dirt to steady himself.

'What are you . . . talking about?'

'Panther. It wouldn't touch me. Took one sniff and moved away.'

Even through his agony, Jeral managed a smile, and his eyes sparkled just for a moment.

'Don't think that was the poison, Hynd.' He gasped and retched violently, green bile dribbling from his mouth. 'Help is coming. Not everyone affected.'

Hynd whimpered at the tightening of his latest cramp. He tried to keep a count while it gripped him but couldn't even concentrate on that. He heard the sound of running feet nearby and a heavily accented voice cut across his self-pity.

'Allow us to ease your pain.'

Jeral forced himself upright, swayed and put a hand on his sword hilt.

'Hynd. Get behind me.'

Then Jeral fell.

Serrin brought the ClawBound to the sanctuary of the Mallios Caves a few hours to the south of Aryndeneth. They had not all come. Serrin had no certain idea how many pairs ran the forest but it was more than those who had been harassing the humans on their march along the River Ix.

Some had descended so far into the realm of Tual that they would not run with any other ClawBound. Others sought seclusion for their own reasons and still more had chosen to cleanse the forest at Tolt Anoor or Deneth Barine. And, of course, Serrin didn't know if the entire calling of Silent Priests had chosen the way of the ClawBound or not. Faith dictated that they should have, but some might still carry the message of Yniss in the old way.

At least all those who gathered within the cool seclusion of the caves recognised him and his right to call himself their guide. Fourteen pairs occupied much of the rough, cool floor space. No other of Tual's creatures used this place except in the direst of need. This was a refuge for the ClawBound.

Serrin sat with his panther close, as did they all. He looked around at his brothers, flaring his nostrils at Sikaant and Resserrak, with whom he had run during the years after Ysundeneth fell. Others whose former names he remembered were Ayrol, Tamoor and Venras. The others were dim memories but he knew their names would come in time.

'You are all here and so we are stronger in the eyes of Yniss and Tual,' said Serrin. 'And here we must stay until we can identify our role.'

'We cleanse,' said Resserrak. 'We purify the forest.'

'Yes,' said Serrin. 'But too many of us have forgotten the root of our faith. We are not alone in the forest. We must work with others who share our desire.'

There was a collective hiss at his words. Serrin snarled back and his panther's hackles rose.

'It is they who have brought us to this state of despair,' said Venras. 'They cannot help us.'

'They *are* helping us. Without them we cannot prevail.'

'I will not let them choose our path. They do not have the faith,' said Venras.

'They will not. But we have seen their actions against the enemy. Their poison is clever, but it poses a risk to us and even more to our Claws. We have freed over three hundred elves. Now it is time to defend what we have.'

'That is not cleansing,' grunted Resserrak.

'You would prefer desecration?' asked Sikaant, moving with his Claw to stand by Serrin.

'I do not understand,' said Venras.

'But you should,' said Serrin. 'And that is a sign that we should all consider to what level we have descended. Is it the inevitable end to our calling that we become true denizens of Tual and shake off the embrace of Yniss? I do not think so.'

'It is our natural state,' said Resserrak.

Serrin shook his head. 'No. It is your base desires alone that lead you down that path: the thrill of the hunt and the taste of an enemy's blood. But we are not animals. We are the bridge between the elves and Tual's denizens. It is a narrow way and we have strayed.'

'What would you have us do?' asked Tamoor.

'Think like an elf once more and outthink man. Tell me, if you were a human, what would you do now?'

Serrin's question was met by a blank silence. Resserrak glowered at him and his Claw was growling, tense and angry. Others responded as though they'd not understood a word he said. Or perhaps they just didn't care.

'Any who wish to return to the forest and run alone, you have my blessing in your work.'

None of them moved, not even Resserrak. Perhaps they simply did not know what to say. But there was something in the atmosphere of the cave that changed. Panthers began to move, stretch their jaws and stare deeply into one another's eyes. The hands of bound elves moved unconsciously to their Claw's heads.

One by one the pairs rose and filed past Serrin, bowing their heads in reverence. Resserrak paused and laid a hand on Serrin's chest.

'We all know where to go.'

'Tighten it further,' said Auum.

The tourniquet was tied around Elyss' thigh just above the knee. Ulysan turned the stick thrust through it and she grunted.

'Where the hell is Merrat? I need the uncaria quickly or this is going to spread.' Auum looked into the shadows of the forest and back to Elyss. 'Keep your breathing steady. Let's not pump too much of this stuff around.'

Elyss smiled though her face was pale and shone with sweat. 'It didn't hurt until you put the tourny on.'

'Liar.'

Auum dabbed at the dwindling supply of tea tree oil in the warm log pot sitting on the embers of a small fire. He turned back to Elyss' wound. The crocodile had snagged her calf with a claw and flooded it with bacteria as it had swum past her. Piranha had taken bites from the wound as she'd swum to the shore. Throughout the follow-up attack later that night on the humans succumbing to the poison, she'd said nothing of it. She had killed with customary efficiency though she must have been in acute pain.

It had not been until the following morning that she had displayed any symptoms of infection. Now, in addition to the problem with the wound itself, she was developing a fever.

'You know better,' said Auum. 'You cannot afford to stay silent.'

'Stop fussing,' said Elyss. 'We only had the one chance to attack. And look at the damage we did.'

'And I'm still laughing that they think the poison has finished its work,' said Ulysan.

'I'll celebrate with you when Elyss is on the mend,' said Auum. 'Concentrate.'

Auum smeared the tea tree oil over the wound. It was angry and red, torn at the edges where the fish had bitten, deep and dark where the crocodile's claw had stabbed her and raked backwards.

Elyss winced. 'That means it's working, right?' she said.

'And that there is something in there to fight,' said Auum. He smoothed his free hand across her forehead. 'You're getting hot.'

'I'll be fine,' said Elyss.

'Keep on thinking that.'

Auum glanced up at Ulysan. The big TaiGethen looked anxious and Auum couldn't give him any particular comfort. He placed his hand over Ulysan's.

'I'll take the tourniquet. Get the other pot ready. Merrat will be back soon.' Auum smiled down at Elyss. 'Looking forward to your soup? Uncaria is magnificently awful to drink.'

'I thought you were making a poultice.'

'As well.'

Merrat reappeared from the forest, Nyann with him. He squatted by Auum and failed to disguise his concern at what he saw.

'I'll prepare the roots and vine,' he said. 'Ysset is hunting down the vismia we need.'

'Good. Thank you.'

It took an age, or it felt like it. Merrat and Ulysan were quick, cleaning and cutting the uncaria and adding it to boiling river water, but the wait for the vital liquor to form was interminable. All the while, Auum watched Elyss fall into her fever. The tourniquet could not stop the infected blood making its way through her body. The tea tree oil was not strong enough to combat the disease at source.

'Keep your eyes open,' said Auum. 'Talk to me about something.'

Elyss' eyes fluttered. 'Like what?'

'I don't know,' said Auum, and he released the tourniquet to give her some relief from the pain. 'Not much point in that now, is there? Tell me, what is it you pray for today?'

A smile played across Elyss' lips and she licked them with a dry tongue. Auum squeezed water into the side of her mouth which she sucked in greedily.

'I pray that whatever poison runs through my body does not stop the joy of what I could feel happening yesterday.'

Auum frowned. 'And what is that?'

'It is my time, Auum.' Elyss' eyes spilled tears and she gripped his hand in hers. He could feel the heat of her fever through her palms. 'I so want to live to know the glory.'

Auum found a cool cloth and mopped her brow. She was going down so fast.

'Stay with me,' whispered Auum. 'What is the glory? See it, believe it and you will know it.'

Elyss spoke but Auum couldn't hear her. He glanced over at Merrat, who spread his arms.

'Soon, Auum. I can't rush this. Not enough is as bad as none at all.'

'I know,' said Auum. 'Come on, Elyss. Tell me again, don't be shy. Shout it out. What is the glory?'

'Wh . . . what every Ynissul *iad* . . . desires.'

Auum gasped. 'Yniss preserve you, Elyss. Merrat, tell me you're ready.'

'Almost.'

Elyss' head had fallen to one side. She was unconscious. Auum tapped her cheek lightly but there was no response.

'It has to be now, Merrat, she's slipping. Shorth is waiting.'

Merrat came over with a water skin. 'Raise her head. We'll have to do this for her.'

Elyss was limp, her fever so intense that just touching her skin was uncomfortable. The infection had gathered strength incredibly quickly and Auum prayed that she had not kept her silence for an hour too long. He had an arm under the back of her neck and with his other hand tried to open her mouth, pulling on her lower jaw.

'Ulysan, I need you,' said Auum. 'Work her throat; don't let her spit this up. Gently, Merrat.'

With as much care as he had time for, Merrat poured the decoction of uncaria into the side of her mouth, a few drops at a time. Her swallow reflex was still there and Auum relaxed his hold on her jaw to let her work the liquid down her throat with Ulysan's tender help.

'Come on, Elyss. You can do this,' said Auum. 'You're doing just fine. Soon have you up and running again. Slowly, Merrat.'

'I know what I'm doing,' said Merrat.

'Yniss bless you,' said Auum.

'You too, my friend.'

Ysset ran back into the camp. 'How is sh—'

'Start extracting the resin,' said Ulysan. 'Know how to do that?'

'Yes.'

'Good, we'll need it for the wound. The tea tree isn't enough.'

'All right,' said Merrat. 'That's all of it. I'll make another decoction for when she wakes up. Right now you'd better make her comfortable. I'll string a hammock for you.'

Auum regarded Merrat through a mist. 'She has to live. She has so much to give us.'

Merrat pushed himself to his feet. 'We cannot afford to lose one TaiGethen to a blow such as this. She's strong.'

Auum laid Elyss' head back on the soft ground and stroked the sides of her face. She was so dreadfully hot but her face was so terribly pale. Her eyes were completely still beneath their lids but her body quivered and was sheathed in sweat. Ulysan touched his shoulder and handed him a cloth, damp and cool with rainwater. Auum nodded and wiped Elyss' face and neck with it.

'Ulysan, scout the enemy. I need to know when they move and what strength they still have. Let Merrat go to Haliath Vale to join

Grafyrre when they've made the poultices and decoctions. When Elyss wakes, we'll travel there too.'

'What about you?'

'I'm not leaving her. She's TaiGethen. My cell. My place is here.'

Chapter 19

Where would I be without faith? I would be breaking bread with humans.

Auum, Arch of the TaiGethen

When Hynd awoke he saw Jeral standing over him. He looked a bit green about the gills but otherwise undamaged. Hynd frowned.

'Didn't some elf give your intestines an airing?'

Jeral laughed. 'At the time it would have been a relief. No, like the hero I am, I fell down with a cramp of quite extraordinary agony. I'm told that we were both saved because Fifth Company, who hadn't eaten from the same pots, joined the fight. We were both pretty incapacitated while it all went on around us. Don't you remember the noise and the screaming?'

'Only my own.' Hynd sobered quickly. 'So what happened?'

'Here, let me help you up and you can see for yourself.'

Hynd knew he shouldn't have been so selfish but the first thing he noticed was how well he felt. There was a small ache in his lower back across his kidneys but apart from that he felt ludicrously refreshed. Until he looked beyond his own fire and saw the debris of a vicious conflict.

Their section of the river bank had become churned mud streaked with the gore that no one had yet had the time or the stomach to clear up. The wounded were being treated just inside the forest canopy in lines three deep and twenty long at least. The dead were piled up downstream and downwind, ready to be burned. And soldiers and mages lay everywhere, exhausted and filthy.

'How many attacked us?'

'Just six,' said Jeral.

'But we killed them, right?' Jeral didn't answer. Hynd sighed. 'But there are elves among the dead.'

'Just Sharps. Some blamed them.'

'They'll have to carry their own kit now.' Hynd spat. 'Fucking idiots. We know exactly who is to blame for this.'

'But we couldn't lay a finger on them. We lost fifteen soldiers and about thirty mages yesterday, because the elves targeted any casters trying to neutralise the poison. We got lucky, you and I. We were the last men our saviour managed to heal.'

'And what about the poisoned men who didn't get help?'

'Some lived, some died.' Jeral shrugged. 'Fancy some breakfast?'

'Can't wait. But no oats this time, all right?' Hynd stretched his back. He must have lain badly; the ache was growing. 'This can't go on. They're beating us, Jeral. You're the captain of First Company. Time to speak to your general, isn't it?'

Jeral nodded. 'I was waiting for you to wake up. You're company lead mage, after all.'

'And you don't want to take the blistering on your own.'

Jeral smiled and spread his hands. 'You know how I like to share.'

'It figures. Come on then. Before Loreb starts the day's drinking.'

Jeral rubbed at his back and screwed up his face. 'They could have found us a mattress or something. I feel like I've been rabbit-punched. Let's go.'

The pair picked their way along the river bank past disconsolate groups of soldiers, mages with nothing left to give and anxious-looking groups of Sharps. Out on the river, the barges were alive with activity. Hynd could feel castings being played over the food cargo as mages tried to discern what was poisoned and what was not.

Every barge was being checked. Hynd could feel the suspicion among the men. He shared it. Soldiers were gesticulating. Someone heaved a crate over the side of a barge and a mage and a barge skipper went nose to nose over it. Shouting filtered across the water. Hynd shook his head.

'Look at that. Can't say I disagree with them. Frankly, I'm not going to eat anything I don't catch or pick myself.'

'Looks like you'll be going hungry, then,' said Jeral.

'It won't matter. We're all going to die anyway.'

Hynd spun around. The voice had come from a group of Sharps. One of them was staring at Jeral from her position, hunched on the ground. She looked dreadful – they all did – fatigued, malnourished, bruised and ragged. One of the other Sharps dug her side with an elbow and tried to hush her.

Jeral spat on the ground between his feet and pushed his sword under her chin, lifting her face a little further.

'Think your pathetic band of warriors can really bring down this army?' The Sharp shook her head. 'Want me to prove exactly how easy it is to kill an elf?'

The Sharp smiled, revealing a mouth of rotting teeth and bleeding gums. 'Make it quick because the alternative is agonising and your mages will be powerless against it. I ate the poison too, and I know what's coming next.'

Another dig in the ribs was followed by some angry words in elvish. Jeral blew out his cheeks and sheathed his sword.

'We're going to find your city and kill every last one of you inside it. If you're lucky, I'll let you watch as the light of your race goes out for the last time.'

He turned away. Hynd made to follow him.

'Is your back sore yet? Just wait until you need to piss.'

The human terminology sat uncomfortably on her tongue.

'What did you say?'

Hynd massaged at his back absently. The Sharp pointed and shrugged.

'That's how it starts. When the urine makes you scream then the poison has hold of you and by then it's almost too late.'

Hynd dropped to his haunches and grabbed the *iad*'s ragged shirt, pulling her featherweight towards him easily.

'What is it? What have they done?'

'God in the water, Hynd, you don't believe this bullshit, do you?'

Hynd felt a sweating cold encase his hands and face. There was truth in the Sharp's eyes, he could see it.

'Tell me,' he ordered. 'And the rest of you shut up or my friend will start cutting out your tongues.'

'Hynd, we don't have time for this . . .'

'There is nothing more to tell,' said the Sharp. 'All of us who ate the black mushrooms will die. You thought last night's pain was bad? You know nothing of pain. The whole forest will hear our screams and Shorth will be waiting to take us to his heart and to condemn you to torment unceasing.'

'You knew it was poisoned and yet still you ate?'

'To refuse would spark suspicion. I am proud to die for my people, for the TaiGethen. They will remember me. No one will remember you as you lie and rot.'

Hynd shoved her away and stood up, wiping his hands down his shirt as if it would cleanse him of her words.

'Why are you telling me this?'

'Because a human who dies in helpless terror is a joy to behold as I make my own way to Shorth.'

Jeral's blade jabbed in front of Hynd and into her throat. She jerked in shock and blood flooded down the blade. Her life flowed away terribly quickly. Jeral removed the blade, and as she slumped into another Sharp's lap, Hynd could have sworn she was smiling.

'Enough of that sort of chatter,' said Jeral. 'Any of the rest of you want to speak up?'

He wiped his blade on the dead elf's clothes and walked away towards Loreb's command post. Hynd hurried after him, fighting against a seething anger.

'You're judge and executioner now, are you?'

Jeral did not break stride and Hynd could hear the growing comments in support of his action coming from all around them.

'You expect me to listen to that sort of shit from a Sharp, do you?'

'She was trying to help us.'

'Really?' Jeral rounded on him. 'It sounded very much like a promise of an agonising death to me.'

'That's because you weren't listening,' snapped Hynd.

'She's just messing with your head.'

'You're so sure of that? You've got a pain in your back, haven't you? Over your kidneys? Me too. And it's not getting any better.'

Jeral's expression bled just a little anxiety. Hynd took a quick look around the First Company.

'Looks like we have a whole lot of people with back trouble here, don't you think?'

'You're seeing things. It's just tiredness.'

'What if it isn't? Want me to check you over? It won't cost you a bean.'

Jeral shrugged and rubbed at his back. 'If you must. But make it quick. Loreb'll be getting thirsty by now.'

'Turn around, then.'

Hynd laid his hands on Jeral's back and formed the shape for a seeking spell. He was tired and the shape was difficult to maintain even though it was a simple enough construct of fine mana tendrils. He probed into Jeral's back, letting the various signatures the casting touched register in his mind: veins, bones, arteries, nerves. The casting brushed a kidney.

'God on a burning pyre,' he breathed.

The sensation of sickness overwhelmed him and he had to step back. The kidney had been grey, dead and cold over almost all of its surface. A parasitic disease was swamping its function, bloating the organ and rendering it practically useless.

'What is it?' asked Jeral, anxiety in his voice now. 'And can you fix it?'

'You'd better hope so,' said Hynd. 'Lie down.'

Hynd poured everything he had into the casting while trying to ignore the knowledge of his own situation. The shape came together in a fractured form but it would be all right. All Hynd could think to do was smother the disease in a thick blanket of mana then blow it clear out of Jeral's body. He was sure there was a more delicate, targeted spell that would do the job but he didn't have time for complexity. Hit it now and hit it hard.

Hynd suppressed the worry that grew with the discomfort inside him and poured his casting into Jeral. He felt the soldier relax muscles he hadn't even known were tensed and a sigh of relief burst from his lips. It quickly turned into a stream of expletives.

'What's wrong?' asked Hynd, falling to the side, gasping in air and trying to still his tired body. 'Fixed you, didn't I?'

'Fucking pissed myself,' said Jeral.

'Oh yeah, probably should have warned you about that.'

Jeral pushed himself on to his back and sat up, his expression turning from ire to concern at the sight of Hynd.

'You all right?'

'Not sure, really. Some pain, much fatigue. That's spell casting for you.'

Hynd could feel the pain edging deeper. The disease was gaining ground rapidly. It would be affecting hundreds in the camp: almost all of the First Company and their Sharps.

'Sleep later. Fix yourself first.'

'Sorry, Captain, that was a one-cast-only job. You're fixed so you can organise help for as many of the First as you can from Loreb. I'll try and hang on while you do.'

Jeral shook his head, stood up and dragged Hynd to his feet.

'Fuck that,' he said.

Jeral dragged Hynd through the camp. Hynd didn't feel he was in immediate danger of death but he knew he didn't have the stamina to heal himself. He'd have thanked Jeral but the captain was too busy roaring for help.

'You! Get over here.' A young mage walked over. 'Don't they teach you to run in Triverne? Move! Name.'

'Selyak, Captain Jeral.'

'Selyak, get casting. Hynd, tell him what to do.'

Hynd did and the mage, tired from a night's vomiting and the fear of death at the hands of the TaiGethen, made a reasonable fist of the construct. The mana smothered his lower back, snuffing out the disease and flushing his kidneys clean. He voided his bladder, as Jeral had before him, but the warmth of urine across his crotch and down his leg felt like salvation.

'Thank you,' said Hynd. 'Now, how are you feeling? Can you do the same thing for yourself?'

'I'm not sure. Something doesn't feel right.'

'Get yourself to another mage. The whole of First Company is in danger because the poison is still active. Go. Don't die of it.'

Selyak smiled. 'I'm honoured by your care.'

'Care has nothing to do with it, youngster,' said Jeral. 'He just doesn't want to feel guilty over your sorry corpse. Now go. Help will come. And make sure you take a piss before you let anyone fix you.'

Jeral and Hynd ran towards the command post. They could see it through the mass of soldiers of the First Company, their mages and Sharps. Jeral ordered his people to look to themselves, find mages, get themselves healed. To trust him, not question him and to believe that they would die unless they did.

Hynd backed him up, shouting to any mage that could hear what was required. But he could count too. And there were nowhere near enough mages to carry out the healing. They desperately needed help from other companies. Loreb would have to listen, and quickly.

The inebriate general was leaning on a broad log looking at a map of the known routes through the forest. His inner circle surrounded him, no doubt speaking the words of the inane, the sycophant and the ingratiating. A cohort of guards and mages ringed them and within the eaves of the forest there were more wards than any one man could really want – except perhaps Pindock.

Jeral was stopped by one of Loreb's aides.

'The general is busy, Captain. You will have to wait.'

Jeral spat on the floor between his feet. 'I'll make myself

comfortable, Ishtak. But please tell the general, at your leisure and his convenience, that you will shortly be hearing the First Company dying en masse.'

Ishtak was a soldier by title only; a glorified administrator and obfuscator by trade and the epitome of the type of man Jeral detested. Ishtak narrowed his eyes suspiciously.

'Been having bad dreams again, Captain Jeral?'

Jeral smiled. 'I'll put it another way: they are all going to die. Let me talk to the general or I will break your stupid cringing neck and then talk to him anyway.'

Hynd looked back over his shoulder. The beginnings of panic could be heard in the tenor of the shouts and the bunching of multiple groups of soldiers and mages.

'You can't just march i—' began Ishtak

'When my company is about to be wiped out, I'll do what I damn well like.'

Hynd threw up his hands and marched past the bickering pair. He shouldered two of Loreb's strategists aside and spoke straight into the general's ear.

'Order mages from across the army to report to the First Company. Please. The elves' poison is about to claim hundreds more lives. Sir.'

Loreb started in surprise and turned his face to Hynd. He was unshaven, looked as if he had barely slept and his breath stank of alcohol. A large goblet was cradled in his hands. His expression darkened.

'I am unused to being disturbed while planning the next stage of our conquest.'

'I make no apology for trying to save hundreds of your men and mages from elvish attack.'

Loreb raised one finger for silence and drank deeply from his goblet. Hynd could hear Jeral's voice behind him, low and menacing.

'The one thing that raises us from the level of the savages around us is a sense of order and a proper chain of command. You will report to my aide and your concerns will be given due process.' Loreb drained his goblet. 'More wine, Ishtak.'

Hynd knew he was gaping. 'General. Please! You must listen.'

'Ishtak!'

Hynd heard the unmistakable sound of a fist meeting flesh. Jeral hurried to his side.

'Ishtak can't hear you right now, General, but you must listen to us,' said Jeral. 'We need as many fresh mages as possible to come to the First Company now. The poison is—'

'Jeral! Good. Tell me, why did we pass the temple at Aryndeneth and leave it unmolested?'

'What?' Jeral looked genuinely confused. He stared at the sneering expressions of the inner circle 'Sir, we have a critical situation here. You have orders to give.'

'I think Aryndeneth will make a fine residence for the general who claims the prize. Jeral, organise a raiding party and see to it. Clear the place. I need more wine. One of you, the flagon is over there by my sword.'

Hynd put a restraining hand on Jeral's shoulder. 'Don't do it. It isn't worth it.'

Jeral's fist unclenched and he dropped his voice to a hiss. 'Get to Pindock, go to anyone. Beg other mages. We don't have time to wait for common sense to prevail.'

'I'm on it.'

Hynd turned and ran hearing Jeral's next remarks as he went.

'Sir, I will do as you ask. But if you do not do as I ask, there will be no First Company left to secure your prize.'

Loreb stared past him at the growing noise from the head of the column.

'I see. Well, tell Ishtak to organise it. And you can reflect on your failure to foresee this incident as you make your way to the temple.'

'Welcome back,' said Auum.

'You look terrible,' Elyss replied.

Auum hadn't slept for two days. Elyss had walked so close to the embrace of Shorth. Her breath had become so faint and her heartbeat so frail. Merrat had refused to leave them and the five TaiGethen had sat around her, praying to Yniss to spare her for other tasks in the forest. Auum had prayed silently too, beseeching Yniss to let her enjoy the gift he had bestowed upon her; to let her play her part in the continuation of the Ynissul thread.

Her fever had finally broken shortly before dawn and Auum had watched her relax into healing, dreamless sleep. Even then he had refused to leave her, needing to be the one she saw when she opened her eyes.

'I'll fetch you a mirror.' Auum smiled. 'Tell me how you feel.'

'I ache. And I feel weak. Hungry though, really hungry.'

'Good,' said Auum. 'Merrat, broth and meat. Our patient is hungry.'

'Well that is good news indeed,' said Merrat.

Auum helped Elyss out of her hammock and to a sitting position with her back against a tree. Merrat brought over a steaming bowl of broth – a hare, root and herb soup infused with guarana. Auum held the bowl and gave the small wooden spoon to Elyss. She reached out a trembling arm from a shivering body and Auum shook his head.

'I'll do it,' he said quietly. 'You'll only spill it.'

'I'm sorry,' said Elyss.

'For what?'

'I've delayed us, stopped us from fighting. I—'

Auum proffered a spoonful of broth to stop her speaking.

'Quite the reverse,' he said. 'You've bought us all time and we have landed a heavy blow.'

Elyss managed a thin smile. A dribble of broth ran down her chin.

'Really?'

'Really. Hang on. Ulysan? Come over and tell Elyss what you saw yesterday morning.'

Ulysan trotted over. He knelt by Elyss, kissed her cheek and then sat down facing her.

'Good to have you back.'

'The mushrooms worked then?'

'You could say so. Hundreds of them died yesterday morning. Their mages weren't prepared and there was confusion in their command. We lost elves too, to man's revenge and to the mushrooms, but we knew that would happen. Be happy that the ClawBound have freed so many or we would have lost more.'

'Are we winning?' she asked.

Auum shrugged. 'It would be premature to think so. Perhaps after Haliath Vale we will be. But four thousand started out from Ysundeneth and only a clutch over three thousand now remain. We are tearing the heart from them and draining the courage from their souls. But we must not let our guard down. We are so few that one reverse could turn the tide.'

Auum glanced around him. All six of them were gathered to listen. He offered Elyss another sip of broth.

'Ulysan, what of the direction of our enemy?'

'They're on the move again but very slowly. Their defence has become far more solid. Mages are evident on the flanks of the army and I believe they are lacing the forest with wards as they go, determined not to be taken by surprise while they march, whereas before they only really feared the dark hours.

'Their strength of arms on the flanks is also much increased. For now, it seems, speed has been sacrificed for security. Unless they change direction, they will pass close by Haliath Vale, and at their current speed they'll reach it in five days. We've done well. Their warriors are nervous and their mages are using up their stamina casting so many extra spells.'

'We won't attack them again until they walk into the teeth of our ambush. Let's rest here today while Elyss regains her strength and move on tomorrow at dawn,' said Auum. 'Men's blood will flow at Haliath.

'Tais, we pray.'

Chapter 20

Today was a dark one. I had to formulate legislation concerning the manufacture and distribution of narcotics. Katura was built as the elven sanctuary. From where did this great evil grow?

The Diaries of Pelyn, Governor of Katura

Boltha was too old for another fight but the Apposan spirit within him would not let him step aside for the younger of his thread. It had always rankled with him that they had been forced from the Olbeck Rise to Katura by a combination of human expansion and elven harmonic pressure – or something like that.

The irrevocable descent of Katura had given him the excuse he had needed to take his people back into the forest and to the Haliath Vale, a place he had coveted for decades. A broad valley floor was threaded through with a fish-laden tributary of the River Ix. The great head of the canopy hid them from human mages' prying eyes and the richness of resources here allowed a sprawling settlement to grow up along both banks of the stream.

Far to the south, the steep-sided valley was packed densely with trees clawing at the sunlight and eventually led into the sheer landscape of the Katura approaches. To the west, the rainforest ran towards the main flow of the River Ix. To the north, the river broadened into a swamp that was impassable by river craft and was only risked by the foolish, stocked as it was with crocodiles, large constrictors and other lethal predators.

That left the east as the only viable route from the River Ix to Katura. It was very easy to miss the Vale. First you had to find the hunting trails through the forest and up the long steep slope to the crest of the Haliath valley.

If you missed them, you would walk along the sludge of rain runoff, heading gradually up a narrow cut in the forest whose sides fled away into shadow even on the brightest of days. It was a place made by Yniss to trap and slaughter enemies of the rainforest and the place which Grafyrre of the TaiGethen had made his own. It was known locally as the Scar.

Boltha and Methian had been preparing the Apposans to retake Katura, but Grafyrre's arrival and his news of the human invasion of the forest had changed all that. For days they had put themselves under the command of the twelve TaiGethen cells that had run into the Vale on that dreary morning. Boltha had tried hard not to be excited, he was very old after all, but there was something undeniably *exciting* about working with the TaiGethen and that feeling was not tempered by the thousands of enemies flooding their way.

Today, though, new excitement had gripped the entire settlement with the arrival of Auum, Merrat, Ulysan and their Tais; all three were legendary TaiGethen warriors of fame and renown who brought an aura of invincibility with them. Word of Auum's arrival brought old and young alike from their houses and ensured an expectant crowd awaiting his every gesture.

Auum, though, spent little time in the settlement, just enough to see one of his cell, Elyss, to comfortable rest. His only other concern was the Scar and the work that had been done there. Boltha almost burst with pride when he and Methian were asked to accompany the TaiGethen inspection.

The two old friends hung back behind Auum, Grafyrre, Ulysan and Merrat but the Arch motioned them into the heart of the group.

'This is your land,' he said.

Boltha met Auum's gaze.

'This is a fight for all elves,' said Boltha. 'And I will do everything in my power to see it won.'

Auum put his hands on Boltha's shoulders and kissed his forehead.

'It is for elves such as you that the TaiGethen fight. For you and for the true heroes still inside Ysundeneth. For Koel.'

Boltha gasped, his heart leapt. 'Koel lives?'

'He lives and is at the centre of the rebirth of harmony among elves. When we are finished with the humans in our forest, we will free every slave in every city on Calaius. Koel will be first. Then you and your people can go home,' Auum said.

Boltha smiled. 'I wonder how many will. Much has changed.'

'You will always be welcome in the forest and we will always protect you.'

Auum had walked down to the base of the Scar and was looking along its length. Boltha and Methian flanked him with the other TaiGethen grouped just behind them. The Scar ran in an almost dead straight line north to south, the merest easterly curve taking it off true.

The edge of the swamp was a hundred yards to their right and the approaches at their back narrowed naturally to drive travellers along the Scar.

'Graf, speak to me.' Auum began walking. 'Thoughts, plans and positions. Everything.'

Grafyrre fell in beside Boltha. The two had formed a friendship over the last few days, adopting a familial relationship that had some of Boltha's friends joking that he had adopted a new son and bodyguard combined.

'The Scar is eight miles long and the Vale runs beside it the whole way. We will allow the army to walk in unmolested for three miles. I've worked on the assumption that they will travel four abreast; it has been their chosen column width so far and the Scar allows it comfortably. This will leave them well short of the first dwellings in Haliath beyond the ridge, but those three miles will mean the whole army is inside the Scar when we can close the jaws of our trap on them.

'We are assuming they will send flanking forces up both slopes, but given they will have to stay within earshot of the main column, we have set our principal trigger points about two thirds of the way up either side. The ideal situation is that the tail of their army is only just inside the Scar when the traps are sprung.'

Grafyrre trotted on a few paces and crouched, pointing up the left-hand slope. Boltha knew what he was indicating. Auum looked on and nodded his approval.

'We have forty disguised log runs, twenty to either side of the scar. The greatest concentration is at the one-mile point, where we hope to break the back of the army and split it in two around a significant obstruction. We expect the army to do two things: exit and retaliate. And they will fracture further while they are doing so.

'The rest of the traps, snares, log swings, pits and spikes are designed to drive the enemy back down the slopes. We plan to harry the rear of the column into the swamp and I'll have a significant number of Apposans with TaiGethen waiting to show them the way. We aim to scatter them and pick them off as they attempt to climb out further up the Scar.'

Auum gestured up the slopes. 'And what happens to those who continue climbing through the traps?'

'Apposan archers will be hidden in the trees, Apposan axes on the ridges and TaiGethen as a roving defence force in case of any significant breakthrough. I'm not worried about humans breaking through to the east, the forest is so dense there that it alone will turn them back. So most of the defence will focus on the Haliath side. We'll lead out any slaves who fight free, but the fact is that many are going to be hurt or killed.

'It's not a perfect plan but we have limited numbers. I'm happy to make changes as I can, though.'

'Not necessary, Graf.' Auum punched him lightly on the shoulder. 'That's why I sent you here.'

'One other thing. Takaar passed through here just before we arrived. Seems he's making decent progress. He'll get to Katura well ahead of us.'

'We just have to pray he doesn't do too much damage before we get there.' Auum sighed. 'Right, next: I want two cells scouting the approaches to give us a half-day warning of their arrival. Give us time to tension and set snares, pits and so on. The rest need to walk the ambush site and ensure there are no holes in our defences. How many snares do you have?'

'About a thousand. Not all set by us. Boltha's hunters are highly skilled.'

'A thousand is good but we can always have more. Boltha, I need as many as you can spare to set snares wherever they can. You're using balsa and palm branches, I presume.'

'What else?' said Grafyrre.

'Good. We're ready. I'll walk the entire Scar later this afternoon. First, Boltha, Methian, with me. It's time to talk to your people.'

'They will be honoured,' said Boltha.

'My intent is not to honour them but to keep them alive,' said Auum. They began walking, retracing their steps to the hunter trail that led to Haliath Vale, the only safe passage to the settlement for four miles. 'I'm glad you're here, Methian. I've heard any number of stories about the situation in Katura. What will I find when we get there?'

'Will you get there?' asked Methian. 'Will you need to?'

'It would be foolish to assume we can stop them here. We can severely weaken them, but they will break through in significant enough numbers. And there is another army heading for Katura, taking the trail east from Deneth Barine and approaching along the Shorthian channels. So yes, I will need to go to Katura.'

Boltha saw Methian shrivel inwardly. The ancient Gyalan had invested so much in the harmony only to find himself an exile. He tried to speak twice, only to sigh as though he thought he was beginning in the wrong place. The third time he just ploughed on.

'The few of us who hold to the original reasons for founding the city are practically outcasts. Within the city the threads have divided. The power resides not with the Al-Arynaar but with those controlling the supply of edulis and other narcotics. There are those who eke out what passes for a normal life, working, farming and building, but the city has no soul. Unless it is the soul of a criminal.'

'And what of Pelyn?'

Methian's head dropped and his next words were hard spoken.

'She is lost to drugs, in thrall to the criminal element, and she has disbanded the Al-Arynaar. There is no controlling force within the city. Yet the sheer number of elves there means we cannot afford to abandon them. Boltha and I had thought to retake the city, which is why I was here, but now I hope you will lead us.'

Boltha watched Auum's reaction carefully. He had expected any number of emotions to surface, but the Arch just studied the path ahead as if he'd been expecting Methian's words. Eventually he glanced at the loyal old Al-Arynaar.

'One of them threatened Lysael's life. I'll start there.'

Boltha shuddered and walked on, following in Auum's steps and seeing that he managed to leave almost no impression on the wet ground. When the TaiGethen began to speak, Boltha jumped.

'This enemy will use magic and they do not care who it touches. They are here, in the forest, to finally destroy the elves. Their sheer numbers will overwhelm the spirit of the common elf. Grafyrre should not have involved you in this fight and your settlement will have to go cold. No fires until the humans are gone. No chants, no prayers, no hunting. No evidence that elves live here. It isn't a place for the young, the old or the elf seeking a quiet life. You cannot stay here, Boltha. Take your people into the mountains to the west until it's over.'

Boltha stopped so suddenly that Methian walked into his back. Auum sensed the pause and turned.

'You will not dismiss me, TaiGethen. And you will dismiss neither the courage nor the skill of my people.'

'I mean no dishonour,' said Auum. 'Merely to save the lives of those who are not warriors and should not feel obliged to take on that mantle.'

Boltha nodded and his anger dispersed like river mist under a deluge.

'You hide away from those you swore to save and so you misunderstand us completely.'

'Then enlighten me. What do I need to understand?'

'Elves' hearts are strong, and our desire for our people's freedom has never dimmed and will never die. That there is nothing we would not do to end the human occupation. I and all those of my thread here in the Haliath Vale would gladly die in your service to set our people free.'

For the second time, Auum kissed Boltha, this time on the eyes.

'Then I will be honoured to stand by you in the fight to come, and die with you if that is my fate.' Auum half turned but turned back almost immediately. 'I was going to speak to your people . . . but it should be you. With me at your shoulder.'

Elyss' room was dark and cool. Boltha's house was modest but of sound and sensible construction and its position on well-drained land made it comfortable and dry. Boltha was still talking to the Apposans.

Auum had ultimately left him to it, feeling himself surplus to requirements and needing to check on his Tai. Elyss was asleep when Auum moved the curtain divider and stepped in. He walked the few paces to her cot and straightened the blanket which was caught about her waist, pulling it back up to her chin.

The room was sparsely furnished with only a single chair and a small table which held a bowl and jug for washing. Auum thought to dampen a cloth before remembering Elyss no longer had a fever. So he sat on the edge of the bed and looked down at her perfect face. High and prominent cheekbones, a delicate Ynissul nose and large oval eyes which opened while he watched.

Elyss smiled and took in a long energising breath, stretching her body as she exhaled.

'I didn't hear you come in,' she said.

'That really shouldn't surprise you,' said Auum.

Elyss laughed. 'Sorry,' she said.

'For what?' Auum shrugged. 'How are you feeling?'

'Rested. Ready to go. When will they get here?'

'We've got a couple of days to perfect the trap,' said Auum. 'Graf is sending two cells out, Faleen's and Illast's, I expect, so we'll get a half-day warning of their arrival. Build up your strength. You'll need it.'

'Auum.'

'What is it?'

'Why are you really here?'

Auum leaned back a little way and blew out his cheeks. 'You're my Tai. I need to know you are well enough to fight.'

'Just "well enough to fight"?'

'Yes. Well, no. Come on, Elyss . . .'

Auum tried not to squirm but her eyes skewered him. She shuffled herself into a sitting position and took his hands. A thrill surged through him.

'I know we're short on time,' she said. 'We do not know who will survive the coming fight. I will pray, endlessly, that both of us will walk away. But if we don't then we cannot live alone or die together regretting what we did not do.'

Auum nodded. His heart was thundering and he wanted, more than anything, to hold her close enough to feel every tiny move she made and to bury himself in her scent.

'I'm at peak fertility, Auum. There is not an Ynissul that does not feel the pressure to conceive . . . but I care little for that. I care that the *ula* I choose is the right one to give my child the best chance to follow me into the TaiGethen. That *ula* must be someone I love and would lay down my life to save.

'It's you, Auum. Would you consent to be the father of my child?'

Auum was unsure if he was feeling fear or feeling faint, but the cold sensation across his body was pure euphoria. He thought he was probably grinning stupidly and he couldn't have cared less.

'It would be an honour I could not describe in words.'

'Then don't speak,' whispered Elyss.

Auum drew her towards him and their kiss entwined their souls.

Chapter 21

They think to buy my favour with edulis. Have they really no mind at all?

The Diaries of Pelyn, Governor of Katura

Jeral strode onto the apron before the temple at Aryndeneth. He was alone. There was something fundamentally thrilling about standing at the heart of your enemy's faith completely unmolested. He turned a slow circle to face the open doors once more. He began to walk towards them, drinking in the silence, the lack of threat and the feeling of victory.

'What are you *doing*?' hissed a voice from the undergrowth.

Jeral glanced over, seeing several figures tracking him.

'I'm going inside. What does it look like?'

'That place will be full of hiding places. It's suicide.'

'Hynd, there's no one here. That ought to be obvious, even to you.' Jeral stopped. 'Why don't you all come out here?'

Reluctantly, they did. Forty-seven of them: thirty-eight soldiers and eleven mages. They were all that remained of the two hundred men and forty mages of the First Company, now rather hilariously nicknamed Dead Company. Jeral stared at them and wasn't sure if they were the cursed or the fortunate. It hurt deeply, far more deeply than Jeral was prepared to admit. He and Hynd had fought to save as many as they could. But Loreb's delegation to Ishtak had meant other companies were slow to help, unaware of the urgency until Hynd got to them through Lockesh, and by that time it had been far too late. And, in the aftermath of the agonising deaths of so many fine young warriors and mages, it was the captain and first mage of the company who had taken the blame.

'Fucking typical,' muttered Jeral. 'That fucking souse has probably forgotten he sent us here by now.'

They had marched back along the river for a day and then inland for two more while the main force of the army continued towards Katura with agonising slowness. Jeral's ire had matured with every pace and his determination to survive had been honed in equal measure. And here, on the empty stones before Aryndeneth, he was beginning to feel strong.

'Your bitterness taints the sweetest of places.'

'And why not, Hynd? Why aren't you bitter? Loreb sent us here to be killed. We saw what he did, or rather didn't do, and the blood of my men is on his head.'

Jeral began to walk towards the temple. He sheathed his sword.

'What are you going to do about it?'

'First, I'm going to prove that this place is completely empty.'

'And then?'

The rest of the raiding party had joined them on the apron. Jeral motioned the soldiers to move around the temple building.

'Then I'm going to report as much to either Killith or Pindock, whichever dimwit looks the least pathetic at the time.'

Jeral and Hynd walked beneath the dome of Aryndeneth and relaxed in the calming cool, which was augmented by the sound of running water. The two men stared at the statue.

'Wow,' said Hynd. 'That's a true work of art. No wonder Loreb wants to live here, the whole place just *feels* beautiful.'

'Yeah, well, he'll live here over my rotting corpse,' said Jeral. 'At the very least, I reckon I can start our generals bickering over who gets this place.'

Hynd was frowning. 'Why would they abandon it?' he asked. 'Isn't this supposed to be their most sacred place?'

Jeral slapped him on the back. 'Ah ha, now you're starting to think. Why do you think we need to report?'

Hynd shrugged.

'Hynd, you never studied.'

'Not boring military crap, no.'

'Then let me enlighten you. As we explore we will find that this place has been left neat and tidy, telling us that they didn't run away in a panic when they heard we were coming. That's because they knew we were coming in good time, or that they guessed we would come.

'That tells me they are thinking clearly and will have taken any strength in magic or arms away with them, to wherever they think they can best use it against us.'

'You think they know where we're going?'

Jeral laughed. 'God on the bonfire, Hynd, they've *always* known. What worries me is that they know the route we'll be taking too. Last thing we need is to walk into a carefully planned ambush, don't you think?'

Jeral walked around the pool and headed off into the depths of the temple. After a few moments, Hynd trotted after him.

'Don't we already expect an ambush? I saw the way the army was forming up to move.'

'Yes, brilliantly done,' said Jeral. 'Really slow, ponderous, heavily protected marching formation ensuring the maximum time for the enemy to set up whatever ambushes they want, wherever they want. Loreb has prepared the column for an attack at any time and he's telling any Sharp who cares to look exactly how the defences will work.

'As usual, he's missed the blindingly obvious: to beat this enemy, we have to have proper reactive tactics, something to surprise them, or they'll hit and run the way they have every other time.'

'I don't understand. How does arriving here tell you that?'

'It doesn't. It confirms what I already thought,' said Jeral. He stopped to look at Hynd's blank face and shook his head. 'My dear mage, ever since we embarked on this fool's mission, the elves have out-thought us at every step, despite there being so few of them. This empty temple is just another example of that.

'We should worry that the Sharps know where we're going and how far away it is, while we have no clue how much further we have to march. Nor do we know the forest, and so we amble blindly into the shadows without knowing when or where we will emerge. Our wonderful leaders cling to the belief that all the elves are falling back to Katura and will wait there for us to come and slaughter them.

'They will not. We have to force them back to the city by beating them in the field. And we will only do that by out-thinking them. They've moved their magic from Aryndeneth, Hynd. Where to? Where will their next attack come? Will it be magical or just those fucking TaiGethen or more of those elf-cat things?'

The two of them walked out into the light and the village behind the temple, and Jeral knew he was right. The village was closed and tidy. The evacuation had been planned and executed perfectly.

'But surely that is why we have to march as we currently do? Defensively.'

'No! We should work out all their potential attack styles and have plans to combat them. Then we need to march as fast as we can because every day spent in this accursed place claims more lives, stamina and morale. And now food is running short too, isn't it? As we are, we'll be so weakened by the time we reach Katura, we might not even beat the little bastards.'

Jeral stared at Hynd and saw the light beginning to dawn.

'Well we'd better get back quickly, hadn't we?' Hynd said.

'Why?'

'Because they're about to leave the river and head inland.'

'So they are,' said Jeral. 'Into the maw of the beast.'

Hynd walked with Jeral as he crossed the outer pickets. The army had stopped for the day and was camping along a minor tributary from which dozens of glorious fish were being pulled, having been stunned by a sound-wave casting. Fires were already burning and the smells of cooking were, for a change, not tainted by suspicion.

'Still angry?' he asked.

'Still alive?' said Jeral.

'I urge caution,' said Hynd.

Jeral shrugged. He'd been thinking about what he'd say all the way back. Caution wasn't the primary feature of his planned conversation.

'Why?'

'Well, there's good news and there's bad news. The good news is that the generals are all in one place discussing tactics. Lockesh is with them too. The bad news is that they anticipate an encounter tomorrow and I don't think they'll much care about Aryndeneth right now. Maybe you should keep your counsel until we camp tomorrow night.'

'Actually this sounds like the perfect opportunity. In fact keeping quiet now might cost us more lives, especially if we don't change our tactics.'

'And you know what the right tactics are, I suppose,' said Hynd.

Jeral felt his anger flare up. 'Well I tell you something, those idiots certainly don't. What's your problem? I'm not making you come with me.'

Hynd's shoulders sagged. 'It ought to be obvious. We're friends, or I like to think we are, and I've watched you wind yourself up to a spitting fury ever since we left Aryndeneth. I'm with you, our generals are mismanaging this whole army, but getting yourself strung up on an insubordination charge isn't going to help our cause, is it?'

'Sorry, Mother, I'll promise to try to stay calm.'

Hynd sighed. 'It'll have to do, I suppose.'

'So it will.' Jeral felt his tension ease just a little. 'Look, I hear you, all right? But I need *them* to hear *me*.'

'Well, Loreb apart, I think you have a certain standing among the rank and file tacticians.'

Jeral raised an eyebrow. 'Is that a compliment?'

'Nearly.'

'Right.' Jeral looked about him. The rest of Dead Company was waiting for his word, every one of them angry, feeling isolated, betrayed and looking to him to improve their lot. 'Let's make this easy on ourselves. You lot, no violence but don't let anyone stop me joining the meeting either, all right?'

Jeral led his men along the outer picket line, not wishing to draw unwanted attention to themselves. The meeting was being held right in the centre of the camp, inside a tent erected for the purpose. It was ringed with soldiers and mages, most drawn from Pindock's personal company nicknamed the Yellow Guard. Aides were clustered outside the entrance and a table had been erected for some purpose that escaped Jeral.

Jeral motioned his men to back away and spread out while he strode ahead with Hynd at his shoulder. One of Killith's aides nudged Ishtak and Jeral gave him a broad smile. Ishtak's expression was less than welcoming. Jeral saw his lips move and his whole body tense.

'Pleased to see me, Ishtak?' said Jeral, finding the aide's evident discomfort extremely gratifying. 'Or just disappointed to see I'm still breathing?'

'That rather depends. What do you want?'

'Well, as you can see, we are surprisingly well given our latest mission. And as you know, to complete the mission I am required to deliver my report to my commanding officer. So, here I am. Show me in.'

Ishtak's smile was thin to the point of vanishing. 'I don't think so, Captain. General Loreb is meeting the army leaders to prepare our tactics for the advance tomorrow. This is not the sort of company into which I am prepared to introduce you.'

'My dear Ishtak – glad to see that bruise on your chin fading by the way – I have information which is vital to that discussion. I must have audience.'

Another aide leaned in and whispered in Ishtak's ear. Ishtak nodded and an oily smile spread across his face. He moved aside.

'Then please, Captain, do go in. The generals and principal mage will be delighted to hear more words of wisdom from the man who oversaw the poisoning of his own company.'

Jeral let his shoulder collide, hard, with Ishtak on his way into the pavilion. Inside, the smell of pipe smoke was nauseating. The generals were seated on a crude arrangement of fallen logs, a hastily drawn map on the ground in front of them. Both Pindock and Lockesh were puffing away on pipes stuffed with the most revolting of elven tobacco. Lockesh appeared bored to the point of distraction while Pindock was as nervous as Jeral would have expected.

Of Loreb and Killith he could see little. Both had their backs to him. He cleared his throat.

'My generals and honoured Lord Mage, please forgive my intrusion.'

Loreb spat out whatever spirit he had been knocking back and jerked so violently Jeral thought he might slip from his log. He managed to regain his balance and turned, standing as he did.

'I'll forgive you nothing,' he said. 'Get out.'

'No. Sir.' Every head turned to watch him. 'With respect, each of you needs to hear what I have learned. I have information that will save lives.'

'Always so dramatic, Captain Jeral,' said Pindock. 'What do you say, Killith, shall we hear him?'

'Never mind Killith,' snapped Loreb. 'Captain Jeral, you will excuse yourself or you will be escorted out under guard and brought up on charges.'

'I'm sick of your posturing, you pissed old oaf,' Jeral muttered under his breath.

'I beg your pardon?' demanded Loreb.

'I'm so sorry. Let me repeat myself more clearly.'

'Jeral!' said Hynd.

'Out!' shouted Loreb.

'No,' said Jeral. 'Sir.'

Loreb roared for the guards. Killith was shouting something incoherent and Pindock had already retreated across the pavilion.

Then Lockesh spoke, his voice reaching into every mind and prompting mouths already open with accusations to slam shut.

'Hynd,' said Lockesh. 'Saddling yourself with this troublemaker. Why?'

'Because I believe he must be heard,' said Hynd.

Jeral nodded his gratitude to Hynd. Lockesh was a tall man with heavy features and a powerful frame that would have served him well as a warrior. He stood. The generals seemed to shrivel in response. Jeral was pretty sure he'd cast some kind of spell to achieve that effect but it was hard to tell. He was a particularly skilled mage.

'Then he shall be heard.' Lockesh's eyes fixed on Hynd. 'And he had better have something civil and pertinent to say, or you will both pay for this interruption.'

'No pressure, Captain,' whispered Hynd.

Jeral shrugged. 'Aryndeneth was empty, General Loreb. The Sharps had gone long before we got there.'

'No doubt running scared,' said Killith. 'And well they should.'

'No, sir,' said Jeral. 'They knew we would mount an attack on their temple and they withdrew. They know what we're going to do long before we do it. We are being out-thought. I know how we can change, how we can take the fight to them before we get to Katura. If we don't, I fear for us. I fear we won't make it to our prize at all, let alone reach it with the strength to take it.'

Guards had entered the pavilion but Lockesh waved them back outside. The trio of generals regarded Jeral, unsure what to say. Lockesh cleared his throat.

'You have evidence?'

Jeral felt chilled by his words, as if they were working their way into his heart and cooling his blood.

'Witness every attack they have staged so far. They strike and run. And we just stand there watching our comrades die. Our only, small success was in the first attack on the forward patrol and camp builders, and that was only won by chance. Since then we have not hurt a hair on any of their heads. Hynd tells me you are expecting an encounter tomorrow and that our route is a narrow one.'

'Yes,' said Killith. 'We expect an ambush.'

'Respectfully, sir, what counter tactics are in place or are for discussion?'

'We have agreed that our current formation is our strongest defence. It is designed to fend off an ambush,' said Killith.

'You just don't get it, do you?' said Jeral.

'I've heard enough of this!' said Loreb. 'I want this man out of here and stripped of his rank.'

'Do you want to hear how we can survive?' asked Jeral, looking at Pindock before turning his gaze on Loreb. 'Or would you rather hear why I was sent to Aryndeneth?'

Loreb actually growled and, for the first time since Jeral had known him, looked dangerous – until he drank from the bottle still clutched in his right hand rather than smashing it across Jeral's head.

'I'd love to know why you were at the elvish temple,' said Lockesh.

'Reconnaissance,' snapped Loreb. 'Talk tactics, Jeral. Then you and I are going to have a quiet conversation.'

Chapter 22

Methian held an amnesty for edulis addicts wishing to find redemption. The crowd at the door was eight times larger than the room within could hold. Far more shocking was the number of Calen's thugs looking for recompense for their lost business.

The Diaries of Pelyn, Governor of Katura

Rain thundered from the heavens. It had begun at dawn and showed no sign of letting up. Auum had briefed the TaiGethen before dawn and each cell had then spoken to those Apposans under their care. The village had emptied of life and those who could not fight were hidden in the forest far from the Scar.

'Gyal blesses us today,' said Merrat.

'She makes the ground treacherous for our enemies, dulls their eyes and muffles their ears,' said Grafyrre.

Auum smiled. 'She was Katyett's favourite god.'

'Most useful god in combat,' corrected Grafyrre.

'We could do with her today,' said Auum.

'Every day,' said Merrat. 'And with fifty more like her.'

Katyett, former Arch of the TaiGethen and Merrat and Grafyrre's cell leader, had been the single greatest loss to the calling during the human invasion. And not just for her extraordinary abilities; Auum was convinced that her death removed the last plank of Takaar's bridge to sanity, leaving him the dangerous uncontrollable maverick he was today.

'I wonder how far he's got,' said Auum half to himself.

'Takaar?' Merrat shrugged. 'Well, we know he's still alive and travelling in the right direction, don't we?'

Auum recalled the fire and the fury in Takaar's eyes outside Aryndeneth. It was not a break in his spirit, as it had been on Hausolis, but the effect was the same. Takaar was running, and tens of thousands of elves were at risk as a result. At least this time there was a chance to save some of them.

The TaiGethen fell silent on approaching Grafyrre's position. Each was aware of the enormity of the task before them and how perfectly their ambush must work to give them any hope of victory.

Grafyrre was at the heart of it all, the elf who would trigger their attempt to break the enemy. Auum looked at the log construction. Four stout palm trunks were driven into the ground and braced by staked vines that doubled as the release mechanism. More than a hundred and fifty logs were stacked behind the palms, ready to roll.

The path down to the valley floor had been cleared with great care, leaving the lower branches of overhanging trees to obscure the run. A similar construct sat on the other side of the valley and a short distance north to double the intended chaos and destruction. Thirty-eight more runs were positioned along the length of the ambush, ready to inflict devastation.

'You have the signal?' asked Auum.

Grafyrre raised his eyebrows.

'I set the signal,' he said.

Auum nodded his head at the Apposans gathered above the log run.

'See them safe. Don't hesitate to call them clear if the ambush goes astray. Every death hurts us.'

'Not one will die by my careless hand,' said Grafyrre.

Auum stood.

'Fight well,' he said to them all, 'and die old, not today.'

During these early hours Auum travelled every pace of the ambush site. He spoke to every cell and every band of Apposans, and he saw anticipation and determination in them all alongside a healthy fear. Ulysan joined him as he trotted back along the base of the Scar, bringing news of the human advance. Bird calls relayed the message across the valley.

They were coming.

'How are they marching?'

'A little differently as it happens. They are protecting their mages more: they are spread more evenly along the column with fewer protecting the flanks. It's clear they expect something, but that is no surprise. The mages have done some scouting here and even humans can see the Scar is a good ambush site.'

'And when will the first of them set foot in here?'

'Two hours,' said Ulysan.

'Let's pray the rain continues to fall.'

The two TaiGethen moved off the valley floor and away from the swelling tributary that ran in its centre. Rain pounded down even more heavily in response to Auum's prayer. Water was running off the valley sides, bearing with it a sludge of mud and leaves. The ground was treacherous underfoot. The gods were bestowing what aid they could.

At the base of the valley, Auum led Ulysan up the safe path to Elyss and the band of Apposans tasked with driving the tail of the army into the swamp. Over a hundred Apposans, led by the ageing but capable Boltha and Methian, were positioned between two banks of traps which would guard their flanks when they attacked.

Auum's cell would run with them. The atmosphere was relaxed. Methian was a veteran of many conflicts in his time as an Al-Arynaar, and his words, backed by the huge character of Boltha, kept spirits high.

'We are set,' said Auum. 'Everyone is in position, every trap has been checked and every trigger point released. Remember your routes, your impact points, your escape calls and rally areas. Most of you are not warriors and I am proud to fight with you.

'But I warn you, the thrill of the fight can blind and deafen you to the reality of victory or defeat. Do not become isolated. Know where your friends are standing and what they are facing. Respond to every call and order. All battle is a risk but do not throw your life away in the desire to be a hero. Die old, not today.

'Tais, my Apposan brothers and sisters, we pray.'

They could hear the army long before they could see it. Despite the incessant downpour, the discordant, aggressive chatter from thousands of human mouths and the beat of feet carried along the Scar, as did the vibrations through the earth. Tual's creatures were running before them.

Auum felt the mood change. Methian was still speaking but now he was directing the minds of the Apposans to the coming fight. Axe blades were being sharpened, short bows strung and prayers begun that would not cease until blood was spilled.

Auum turned to Elyss.

'You take care of yourself,' he said softly. 'I will keep you in my sight.'

'You will do no such thing,' said Elyss. 'Fight as you always have. To do otherwise is to risk yourself.'

'But—'

'No,' said Elyss sharply. 'Nothing matters but defeating the humans. Nothing.'

Auum felt stung. He glanced at Ulysan, who quickly turned his head away.

In an act of bitterness and petulance that was wholly unsurprising, Jeral had been ordered to lead the army into the narrow steep-sided valley. The rain had been as hard as he'd ever known it since he'd arrived on Calaius three years before and the mulch and mud would churn horribly underfoot before two hundred men had marched in, let alone three thousand.

The valley boasted a fast-running tributary that was shallow enough to cross with ease, and the army marched five abreast, split two and three either side of the water. Jeral's plan had been adopted in its entirety. Mages and Sharps walked in single file within a twin skin of warriors. No mage walked on the flanks, and the warriors who did had standing orders to retreat if they encountered any trouble whatsoever.

'Your lot know what to do?'

'We won't let you down,' said Hynd.

'It's not just important; it'll win us the day if we are attacked. No one can deviate from their brief.'

'I get it,' said Hynd. 'Look, just because you're effectively on trial—'

'Damn right I am.' Jeral felt good about it though, really good. He grinned at Hynd. 'Best part is that, despite my advice, our trio of fools have chosen to travel in the centre of the army. At least Lockesh was listening to me.'

'Lockesh just wants to be first out the other end.'

'Yeah well, he'll have to push past me first,' said Jeral.

He looked around him. The valley sides along which the point troops were moving were dense with trees and bushes. He couldn't see them even though they were only ten yards above him, and that thought made him nervous. He had to trust that their line of sight down to the valley floor was better.

Above them, the canopy was unbroken and the few mages flying as spotters would be able to see nothing at all. They'd be more use on the ground, but Lockesh had refused to travel without mages in the air, even though they only gave the illusion of a tactical advantage.

Every pace they took brought more of the same: rain, thick green vegetation and slippery, shifting ground underfoot. But after two hours of peaceful marching, the men were beginning to relax.

'Idiots,' he breathed. 'Pass the word back, Hynd. We aren't even at the point of greatest risk yet. I want to know the moment the last man enters the jaws of the valley.'

'And then?'

'If this is an ambush, that's when the jaws will snap shut.'

Very soon afterwards, he received word that the army was now completely within the valley.

'Now we go to work,' Hynd whispered.

Above the battering of the rain, the valley sides had begun to rumble.

Grafyrre heard the destiny of the elves; he prayed the humans heard their deaths. The palm trunks had been dragged aside and the logs cascaded over each other, gathering momentum with frightening speed and thundering down the valley side, jostling and bouncing as if the wood fought to be the first to crush and break an invader.

Grafyrre held up his hands, keeping his party back. Across the valley, he knew Merrat would have released his log run as well. Timing was critical. If the elves arrived too early they would meet a similar fate to that which they wished upon the humans. Too late and their enemy might have time to regroup.

Below him, the logs forced their own route. Most barrelled straight down the intended path but others were knocked askance and rebounded from trees to either side of the cleared route, or turned on their ends and spun through the lower branches of the canopy. Grafyrre estimated the moment the enemy would see what was coming for them and visualised their reaction. He prayed he had it right.

Grafyrre dropped one arm. The Apposans came to ready, weapons free. He nodded at his Tais, Allyne and Borrune.

'Yniss guide our hands,' he whispered.

Grafyrre dropped his other hand. The TaiGethen sprang forward, leaving the Apposans in their wake. Mayhem first, bludgeoning hatred second. Grafyrre sprinted ahead with the TaiGethen, following the log avalanche.

He prayed while he ran and his strength grew. Yniss guided his footfalls and the air in his lungs broadened his senses. Life smelled sweet, looked more beautiful than ever and sounded like the death of man. The Scar was alive with the thunder of logs rushing towards the soft flesh and brittle bones of the enemy. Tual's denizens were scattering into the sky and the upper boughs of the canopy. Below them, on the valley floor, the humans would hear their doom approaching and the panic would be spreading among them like a disease carried on foul water.

Grafyrre felt his cell with him. Allyne cruised down the slope with that easy sprinting style Grafyrre had always envied. Borrune, head thrust forward and eyes wide, charged ahead. He hurdled a dip in the ground and ploughed on. Below them, the logs were battering down the low brush.

Grafyrre heard one shatter against a standing tree along with the thudding sounds of collisions and rebounds. The forest echoed to the tumult, eclipsing all else. It was a benefit he hadn't considered. If it raised his heart rate, it must be chilling the enemy to the bone.

Under his feet, the gradient lessened very slightly. The logs had left scars in the ground, catching up mud and leaf litter to further increase the weight that would strike the invaders. Grafyrre counted back from ten. *Now.* Now he could hear the cries of alarm and the drone of thousands of human voices finally seeing what was hammering down the sides of the valley towards them.

And at the last he could see them. Standing still and facing outwards. The logs tumbled over one another, bounced and spun and struck. Blue light flared up, guttered and died, and the men who had been cowering behind it were obliterated. Grafyrre exulted at the sight and charged in, bounding across still-moving logs with complete assurance.

The sheer scale of the noise in the Scar was extraordinary; thousands of logs colliding with one another as they bounced off magical shields or crashed through them, destroying whoever lay within. Grafyrre yelled orders to his Tai but he would not be heard. Beneath his feet, the muddy ground was covered with bodies and ran red with human blood.

Grafyrre turned south. Just ahead, soldiers cringed behind a shield that had not been struck. Grafyrre raced towards them, Allyne and Borrune on his flanks.

'Target the mages.'

Soldiers came at them, spreading across the base of the valley. Grafyrre ducked beneath the sweep of a long blade. He shoulder-barged the wielder aside and carried on running. More soldiers were filling the path ahead. Grafyrre pulled out a jaqrui and threw it. Here, within the magical shield, the weapon flew true and sliced deep into the wrist of a warrior raising his sword to protect his face.

Allyne joined him. Borrune had turned back to face the line they had brushed past. Grafyrre drew his swords. He crossed the few paces and hammered his right-hand blade into the injured man's skull, knocking him down. Using the momentum of the strike, Grafyrre spun on his right foot and lashed his left into another's chest.

Grafyrre's move brought him round to face more of the enemy. He dragged his right blade across the neck of a third man and chopped the left past a fourth's defence and into his side, feeling the sharp edge bite through to the spine. He glanced left. Allyne was airborne. He turned a forward roll and landed in the midst of a group of mages.

The shield above them pulsed a deep blue once, twice, three times. Allyne began the slaughter. Grafyrre called Borrune to join them. Grafyrre jabbed his elbow into the throat of the last soldier in his way and ran into the gap. At the same moment an order ran up and down the human column. Everywhere, the humans closed their eyes and threw their arms across their faces.

'Tai! Guard your eyes!'

Grafyrre dropped his blades and jammed the heels of his palms into his eyes.

Above the rumble that assaulted their ears and fed through the ground, Jeral heard his messengers relaying his orders down and up the army column.

'Hold,' he ordered again. 'Stand.'

Mages prepared. He'd tried to ensure that every single one of them understood the importance of casting what he wanted, when he wanted it. He'd given spells numbers and divided the mages into colour groups. Today he would see if there was any discipline left in the army. If there wasn't, the elves would win right here.

'Red. One!' yelled Jeral. *Shields.*

Hynd's voice echoed his own. Others took up the call. Mages

prepared, crouched and cast, and Jeral felt the multiple spells flip into place.

'Your boys had better not let me down,' said Jeral.

'Trust is a wonderful thing,' replied Hynd.

The undergrowth and lower branches of trees on both sides of the valley began to bounce and vibrate. The roar of tumbling wood grew steadily. The shattering sound of impacts and breaking timbers ricocheted over their heads. Jeral felt the mood of those around him and couldn't help but sympathise. Fear.

'Whatever comes at us,' he shouted. 'We *can* stand against it.'

Jeral could see shapes among the trees. Dark and massive ones, moving downslope at terrifying speed. Twigs, dirt and small stones rattled over the shield cover. The last of the undergrowth was pushed aside. A single tree trunk spinning end over end carried clear over his head and then the forest itself seemed to rush onto the valley floor and strike them.

'Brace!' yelled Jeral, but his voice was lost in the extraordinary din.

Dozens of felled trees, their trunks smoothed of all branches, slammed into the magical shield. Jeral stopped breathing, able only to stare. His hands came to his face and all his words about trust and strength were made flesh. Helpless and terrified, he winced as tree after tree slammed into the shield. Blue light flared each time.

Jeral felt as if he was watching the scene elsewhere. The trees made no sound when they struck the shield, only when they clashed together following the impact. Logs spun past overhead, bounced back down to crash into logs still rolling down the slopes and mostly clattered into one another. It was a wall of wood seeking to taste his blood and crush his bones.

Mages grunted with exertion. Soldiers willed them to stand firm. Jeral began to hear the screams when the tumult declined. Around him, soldiers and mages breathed out, relaxing.

'Focus,' he roared. 'Blue! Three!'

And a few moments later.

'Eyes! Eyes! Eyes!'

A blinding white light flooded the valley.

As fast as it had come, the light was gone. Grafyrre had been able to see it through the flesh and bone of his hands. He heard screaming from all around, and among those of dying men crushed under timber were those of elves, caught by a spell that had blinded them.

Grafyrre moved his hands, his eyes adjusting immediately. He dropped to a crouch to grab his blades, re-sheathing one and taking out a jaqrui. All around him, soldiers and mages were readying themselves. Allyne was already fighting. Grafyrre spun around, surprised at the speed of the human fightback. Borrune was down, lying against a pile of logs, his hands on his face. There were men about him. Borrune had not been fast enough and had taken the full force of the spell. Others were striking back.

'Allyne! To Borrune fast.'

Borrune had been seen. Grafyrre hurdled dead bodies and logs to get to him only a few paces away.

'Borrune! Guard above!' he yelled.

Grafyrre threw the jaqrui. The blade flashed over Borrune while the TaiGethen struggled to orient himself, plainly still blinded. It struck a soldier squarely, wedging in his armour and punching the air from his body. Others came on and Allyne breezed past them. He took two paces and leapt, feet first, spear-kicking a soldier poised to strike down.

Borrune was trying to scramble away, but he had no sense of direction in the din of the fight.

'To me!' Grafyrre shouted.

He hurled another jaqrui, this time seeing it harmlessly deflected high. Four men had seen the vulnerable elf and were moving in for the kill. Allyne was back on his feet and stood above Borrune, a blade in his hands which he swiped out waist-high, trying to keep the enemy back.

Grafyrre came in on his left. A huge soldier dived from the pack onto Allyne, bearing him away, and Grafyrre surged in. His blade cracked into the thigh of one enemy, sending him sprawling. Another turned to face him. The last stood by Borrune, who was on his feet at last but still saw nothing.

'Borrune, away!'

Grafyrre fenced away the blade thrust at him and jabbed in a riposte, putting his enemy down for the moment. Beyond him, Allyne killed the big human and heaved the body aside. He dived for Borrune, meaning to knock him aside from an attack, but was too slow. The soldier rammed his blade into Borrune's unprotected chest and blood erupted from the wound that pierced his heart.

'Coward!'

Grafyrre hurled himself at the soldier, who had no time to pull his sword from Borrune's body. Grafyrre's blade opened up his face on the down strike and sliced his neck on the return. The man fell.

Allyne was with Borrune; the TaiGethen was dead. Grafyrre howled his fury. A light pulsed across the remaining magical shield, green this time. Grafyrre looked out to the sides of the valley and belatedly saw the elves strewn across them, stumbling and confused, blindly trying to escape.

'Allyne! New casting. We have to get the Apposans away. Go, go!'

Grafyrre muttered a prayer for Borrune while he ran into the midst of a group of Apposans clinging to one another. Allyne was by him, still with an eye on the enemy, who had not yet moved to attack.

'Get upslope,' called Grafyrre. 'Crawl if you must, but go. Get to the high ground.'

The Apposans began to respond. Some were regaining their sight quicker than others and helped the worst affected along. They began to move back into the treeline, but they wouldn't be fast enough.

'Graf! Casting now.'

Grafyrre's heart missed a beat. He looked down the valley side to the floor less than twenty paces away.

'Get to cover!'

The air chilled. A wind began to howl. Grafyrre saw grass, leaf litter and undergrowth blacken across a wide front that fled upslope.

'Oh no. Up, Allyne, up!'

Grafyrre leapt straight up. His hands grasped the branches of a tree and he swung his legs, linking them over a higher branch. He let go with his hands and pivoted his body, arching his back and grasping the branch about which his legs were locked. The gale of ice howled below him. Grafyrre closed his eyes but there was no stopping his ears from hearing the screams.

Chapter 23

*So quickly the weak are beguiled by the promises of Calen and
Jysune. I have lost so many Cloaks I can barely police the city.
Calen was here earlier, recommending the Al-Arynaar become a
single thread force. I must stop their march but I do not know
how.*

The Diaries of Pelyn, Governor of Katura

Auum and his cell flowed down the valley side with the human
reaction to the carnage already filtering up into the canopy. They
had left the Apposans behind and Auum was glad of it. He wanted
them to come upon an enemy already on the brink of rout.

Elyss was running to his left. Auum knew he shouldn't check her
progress but he couldn't help himself. Her feet seemed as sure as
ever, her body as fluid and balanced. Auum checked her path, seeing
roots, low branches and trailing vines. He opened his mouth to warn
her and ducked reflexively. He felt the brush of leaves by his right ear
followed by Ulysan's voice.

'The TaiGethen who ignores his own path will fall to the merest
risk.'

'Who told you that?'

'You did.'

Auum knew he was right. He refocused, tuning his eyes to his
path and his ears to the situation beyond the cover of the trees and
undergrowth. They were forty yards from the base of the Scar. Then
he heard many human voices repeating the same words and had the
time to wonder why that worried him so much.

He glanced across to Ulysan to check the big TaiGethen's reaction
and in the same instant a blistering, blinding white light filled the
valley. Auum clapped his hands to his eyes and slid, feet first, on to his
front, aiming to protect his head. Elyss cried out, Ulysan was silent
and behind him the cries and calls for help told of the Apposans

descending into panic. The only voice he could hear was that of Boltha, shouting for calm and for them to stop.

Auum took his hands from his face and opened his eyes wide. The afterglow of the spell haunted his vision. The outlines of trees, no more than pale shadows, swam against whiteness fading to a bright yellow and then to a burning orange. He blinked rapidly, trying to force his vision back to something approximating true sight. Down on the valley floor, the effect must have been ten times worse.

He could hear Ulysan moving towards him and the clarity of the sound alerted him to the silence within the Scar in the wake of the light.

'We're blind,' Ulysan whispered. 'We're all blinded.'

The silence was fleeting. Human voices filtered up the valley sides. Again it was a few words, repeated along the column. Two sets of words, one following the other. Auum shivered; more spells.

Auum's vision was returning but it was poor, the way he assumed a human's was. He couldn't penetrate the shadows and the edge of every leaf seemed thick and furred. He pushed himself to his feet, his unease growing. The air inside the Scar stilled again, and then it roared. Auum knew that sound.

'Oh no.'

He began to run, fending off the shadows of branches as best he could and holding an arm in front of him to ward off the trunks of trees still indistinct against the glamour that tricked his eyes. He mimicked the alarm call of the howler monkey, an urgent echoing hoot designed to penetrate the densest of forest growth.

Ulysan tried to grab his shoulder to slow him but he threw it off, continuing his half-blind charge towards the enemy. His mind played out the massacre the gales of ice would cause. Helpless elves would be frozen in moments. The forest would be blackened and ruined, countless creatures slaughtered in hives, nests and burrows. The ambush would be left fractured, leaderless and confused. Any who survived the blasts would be prey to the swords of man.

'Auum, slow dow—'

Ulysan gasped, his shoulder thumping into a tree. His momentum spun him into Auum and the two elves tumbled to the ground. Ulysan finished atop Auum and held out his hands for calm.

'You can't kill what you can't see,' said Ulysan, rolling away and holding out a hand for Auum to grab. Both stood. 'You have to trust your cell leaders. They'll do the right thing. Merrat, Grafyrre, Faleen . . . they are great TaiGethen. Take a breath.'

Elyss trotted over to them, squinting as she came. Auum blinked. His vision was clearing faster now but the detail of the forest was still denied him.

'All those who followed the log runs will be too close to the enemy,' he said. 'Somehow we have to force them on to the defensive.'

The roar of the ice spells had died away. Auum couldn't hear fighting from anywhere along the column. The elves had been silenced. Orders flashed up and down the enemy army. The unmistakable sound of weapons being drawn and readied echoed across the Scar.

'We're out of time,' said Auum. 'Call the retreat to the outer rally points. We've got to get the survivors to safety.'

Jeral watched the spells surge away. They blistered foliage, forged spectacular ice sculptures where they splashed against the boles of trees and tore through the undergrowth, seeking out the Sharps where they lay helpless and blind. This was the critical blow and it had to be driven home.

'Swords! Two!' he bellowed. He waited for the call to return along the column. 'Away. Chase them down.'

Jeral watched his warriors moving away up the slopes of the valley to either side. In close groups of five, they hacked away standing foliage, clearing their path. Elves broke from cover, TaiGethen by their speed and camouflage paint. Jeral smiled. They weren't fighting, they were running. Animal calls were bouncing around the forest. There was movement everywhere, and all of it was heading away from the valley floor. The battle was won.

Jeral watched his soldiers chase the Sharps upslope. His view had been cleared by the passage of a hundred logs and the sport was deeply satisfying. The warriors around him were cheering, some were laughing. Hynd put a congratulatory hand on his shoulder.

The TaiGethen were moving erratically, their vision clearly still imperfect. They were slow by their standards, slipping on the mud as they climbed. Jeral's warriors were gaining slowly, each group with three ahead of the other two and all of them cheered on by those watching from the column.

Passing between two trees, three TaiGethen increased their pace and leapt high, turning rolls in the air before landing and hurrying on. Jeral barely had time to wonder why before three leading soldiers disappeared from view, their cries of alarm cut off with mortal finality. The two behind them slowed and passed to either side of the pair of trees. Neither of them passed any further. Panels of wood swung round horizontally, slapping into his men's chests and driving spikes clear through their bodies.

Cheers died in throats, laughs dried on lips. Jeral heard other screams from behind him. For the second time today he found himself staring. The TaiGethen stopped and turned, crouching to see their foe's reactions. They chittered animal and bird calls to each other before disappearing from view. Above Jeral the forest was coming back to life.

'Green! Two!' called Jeral. *ForceCones*. 'Red! One!' He cursed under his breath.

'We need to get this army moving,' said Hynd. 'We're still in charge here.'

'Agreed,' said Jeral. 'Signal the advance.'

Grafyrre heard the enemy break formation to attack up the slopes. He dropped to the ground with Allyne and they ran past the blackened, hideous statues of Apposans caught in the blast of ice. He carried on running, hurdling a stake pit and sidestepping a whip trap on his way, praying to Yniss that men would die upon them. He soon had that wish granted.

The TaiGethen pair ran beyond the second line of traps, urging the few survivors they could see to head for the rally points. Just in view of the valley floor, they paused in a patch of good cover. Grafyrre looked down at the enemy, seeing them uncertain in their advance, eyeing the ground with suspicion.

'Grafyrre.'

Allyne was pointing along the valley to the north. Kerryn's cell was crouched thirty yards away, watching some humans beginning to move back down the slope, hurrying to join the rest of the army. Orders were being carried along the column and mages were preparing new castings. Red and green lights pulsed along the broken shield line.

Grafyrre clicked out the call of a parik bird, seeking Kerryn's attention. He gestured for them to move left and down before pointing at his chosen targets within the army and bringing the points of his fingers together in a pincer. Kerryn nodded.

'Let's give our people some time to escape,' said Grafyrre. 'Beware the mages. Take them whenever you can. Tai, we move.'

Grafyrre headed downslope, angling slightly right, keeping his targets in sight. They looked like a command group. Older men with their swords still in their scabbards and surrounded by elite human warriors whose eyes scanned the forest continuously. Mages sprouted from the group too, some of whom appeared deep in concentration. Others waited to cast.

More orders rang out along the enemy column. They readied to move.

'Hit them,' said Grafyrre.

A howler monkey call carried along the valley from the northern end – Auum was signalling the retreat to rally points – but Grafyrre couldn't let it end like this. They'd barely laid a blade on the enemy. Only Beeth's great trees had done any real damage and even then not on the scale they'd planned. All his work, all his effort; Grafyrre would not let it be for nothing.

Grafyrre ran at the army, Allyne on his heels and Kerryn mirroring his attack. In five more paces he'd be beyond cover and into the mess of logs, mud and blood.

'A quick hit and away!' he called. 'I'll take the old men.'

Grafyrre stormed down to the floor of the Scar. Men were still rejoining the column, shaken by the traps that had claimed their brethren and careless in their haste. Grafyrre heard warnings shouted out. Isolated soldiers began to turn. Allyne threw a jaqrui which sliced into his target's thigh. Grafyrre leapt feet first, catching the same man on the side of his head.

Grafyrre landed, not looking behind him, bouncing back up and dragging a jaqrui from his pouch. He threw, only to see it bounce off a magical shield and fly harmlessly away back over his head. Allyne was at his shoulder. The Tai warrior hacked to his right, felling a second enemy who had been too slow to regain the column.

Grafyrre drew both blades and charged into the midst of the humans. Kerryn crashed in beside him. Grafyrre kicked out straight, his foot thudding into a human gut. His momentum brought him forward, one blade across his body to block a riposte, his other over-head, splitting the man's skull through his leather cap.

Gore spattered across the column. Men bunched together. Soldiers moved quickly towards the TaiGethen while mages backed away. Allyne took the sword hand from one and snapped a roundhouse kick into the head of another, sending him spinning into the stream and taking two more with him.

Ahead, Grafyrre could see his targets. One was white with fear, a second had a bottle in one hand and his sword in the other. The third was on his feet roaring instructions but no one was listening. Grafyrre blocked a thrust to his left flank and backhanded his free blade up into the face of his attacker. The man went down in a spray of blood.

Behind him, a mage opened his hands and cast.

'Down!' Grafyrre yelled.

He dropped and rolled, his blades out and carving at the space into which he came. He connected with the mage a heartbeat too late. A low hum hurt his ears and, behind him, he heard Kerryn scream. On his way back to his feet, Grafyrre saw her flying backwards through the air, her body smashing against a banyan and flopping, broken to the ground.

'Break off!' called Allyne.

'No,' spat Grafyrre. 'Not yet.'

Soldiers were moving around to flank and trap them. Another spell was cast. Flame roared out from the column and Grafyrre heard an elven scream. Above the chaos, howler monkey calls sounded again. This time, their import and their meaning penetrated Grafyrre's rage.

He uppercut his right-hand blade into a mage's chest, crushed the kneecap of a soldier with a reverse kick and fled the enemy.

'Get to cover,' Grafyrre shouted as he ran. 'Get to cover!'

Charging Apposans all but ran him down. He flung himself out of their path and gaped. Where had they come from? Howling obscenities and promises of death, they moved to the attack, their eyes fixed on their enemies, axes, swords and clubs held firmly in hand.

'No!' shouted Grafyrre. 'Break off, they'll—'

Spells screamed out. Fire, ice and pure magical force slammed into the Apposans. Elves shrieked as their skin was flayed from their bodies or scorched to the bone. Some, like Kerryn before them, were borne back to be crushed against the trees they so cherished. A few managed to escape, running blindly back up the slopes, heedless of their route, so careless that one, who thought himself safe, was skewered by a waiting trap.

Grafyrre ran too, his rage centred firmly on himself. Allyne had survived but Borrune and Kerryn's Tai were gone. Apposans had been slaughtered like animals and the enemy's cheers were the final humiliation. He had failed. Worse, he had led precious survivors to their deaths.

Grafyrre ran on, contemplating his words to Auum and his prayers to Yniss.

All the way down the slope, they had sounded the rally point call, and all they could do now was hope it was heeded. Auum, Elyss and Ulysan running at the head of an Apposan force of forty elves had broken cover right at the base of the Scar and thundered into the rear section of the enemy army.

Jaqruis had bounced from the magical shield but it had not protected the soldiers from close-up blade, fist, axe or foot. Their targets had been slightly isolated from the main column by two log falls that had burst through the magical protections. Bodies lay torn and twisted among the logs and the path was completely blocked, forcing soldiers who were prepared to risk it to travel upslope, through the traps.

Auum knew he was venting his fury but found he had no desire to mitigate the extra risk that posed to him. With his eye ever darting to Elyss, who fought effortlessly, he pressed his attack into the centre of the group of some two hundred soldiers and mages while the Apposans surged in at the flanks.

'Push left,' called Ulysan. 'Break through them.'

'Pushing left!' returned Boltha.

Auum saw the old Apposan duck a wild sword swing like an elf a third his age and bury his axe in the man's skull. The Apposans with him roared their approval and pushed harder. Auum looked beyond them to the main column. Soldiers were breaking away to come to the aid of their fellows. Time was short. He needed these humans broken and running *now*.

'Follow me.'

Auum moved forward again. He ran three paces, swords in hand, and jumped high. Bringing his legs up tight to his chest, he cleared the human front line and cycled his arms, feeling his swords bite into flesh. He landed behind the line, in a confusion of mages and soldiers, his feet slapping into the stream.

Auum rose from his crouch, already spinning, blades out to lace cuts into legs, torsos, arms and faces. Ulysan landed a few feet away. Elyss turned a roll over Auum's head and landed with her legs astride a mage's neck, breaking it as she twisted down to the ground.

Humans were scattering all around them. Auum thrashed a blade into the back of a mage who had turned to run; another spun towards Auum. The TaiGethen raised his blade to strike but a split appeared down the mage's face – Ulysan's work. Auum moved in the direction of the swamp and the enemy in his path turned and fled.

'Keep them moving,' called Boltha, leading his Apposans in the charge. He paused by Auum. 'Go. We'll see them into the jaws of Tual. You need to regroup your people. We'll harass the humans as long as they remain here but we can't stop them, can we? They've learned.'

'Don't risk yourselves. Get your people to safety,' said Auum.

'We'll rejoin you at Katura.'

'No. Disappear. Your people have done enough. We'll find you when it's over.'

Boltha nodded, turned and ran. Auum glanced at the enemy moving towards them. Elyss and Ulysan were by him.

'Auum?'

'Let's see who we can save.'

Chapter 24

The fight between the Tuali and Beethan gangs was a statement.
Made on market day, in the heart of our lives. Who really runs
Katura? Who can hope to stop them? The people look to me, and
I am not sure I can save them.

The Diaries of Pelyn, Governor of Katura

Auum's run along the mid-slopes of the Scar was the most desolate of
all his long years.

Apposans, those few who had survived, were scattered across the
higher slopes or had already fled back into the Haliath Vale, heading
for the rally points. Auum supposed that was good news, of a sort, as
they'd responded to the calls to fall back. But that was where the
good news ended.

Bodies littered the slopes. Burned, blackened by frost or crushed
almost beyond recognition. Spells were still playing into the forest,
preventing the collection of the dead for reclamation. Auum could
see foliage flattened by magical force where mages played their spells
in wide arcs, forestalling any fresh efforts to attack.

Among the Apposans near the centre of the column, Auum saw the
broken bodies of Kerryn and her cell. They were too far down the
slope to tend to so Auum knelt with Ulysan and Elyss and prayed for
their swift reclamation. While they did, they looked down the ruined
valley.

'What happened here?' whispered Elyss.

'They found strength,' said Ulysan.

'No. They had a plan,' said Auum.

The magical shields had repulsed enough of the weight and violence of the log falls to save hundreds of men, and the following,
blinding magical response had rendered the ambush force helpless
against the killing spells that came next.

'How can we defeat this power?' asked Elyss, her voice tremulous.

She placed a hand on her stomach and Auum covered it with one of his.

'We cannot lose hope, not now,' said Auum.

A tear spilled from Elyss' eye and splashed on Auum's hand. 'How can we not lose hope? This was the day when we were to defeat them, but instead they will march on almost unhindered while we count our dead. How many TaiGethen have we lost? My heart quails at the thought.'

'We will grieve and we will move on,' said Ulysan, standing and offering them each a hand to pull them up. 'Because we have no other choice.'

Elyss tried to smile and what burst from her lips was a desperate laugh. 'What do we do, mount another ambush? Look what happened to us. Look!'

'No. We cannot risk this again,' said Auum. 'Katura is the only place where elves live in great enough numbers to threaten the invaders.'

Elyss shook her head. 'You said if we had to go there to defend our race then the battle was already lost.'

'Then you must prove me wrong. And so must the people of Katura.' Auum trotted away towards the forward rally point while below the human army resumed its march south. 'Come on. We need to know what we have left.'

Praying for the best of news but fearing the worst, Auum led his Tai to meet the remains of the TaiGethen.

Jeral, Captain of Dead Company, felt ten feet tall and invincible. They had lost in excess of four hundred soldiers and mages in the elves' failed ambush, but there was not a man walking the valley floor who didn't realise how much worse it could have been.

He was receiving personal messages of thanks from individuals in every company. And, in the vanguard, Lockesh had taken a moment to congratulate him on his tactics and organisation while Hynd stared at him with something akin to awe.

But as the march continued into its second hour after the fight, with mages maintaining a single-skin shield and a moving guard of mana force playing over the lower slopes, a nag was growing in Jeral's mind.

'How long can we keep the protection up?' he asked.

He looked down the column towards where the generals marched.

None of them had sent so much as an aide to congratulate him. He knew he shouldn't be surprised but the worry would not dissipate.

'It's one of those balancing acts you're so fond of,' said Hynd. 'At this cripple's pace, the mages can maintain their concentration fairly easily, but stamina will become a problem in a couple of hours and we have little in reserve. By my calculations and your scout reports, that means we will still be in this valley when the castings begin to break down.'

'Advice?'

'Well, my feted captain, I think we have beaten them back far enough that they will not attack us again – today, at least. Keep the shield skin but not all along the column, and drop the mana cones altogether.'

Jeral smiled. 'And the mages will rest while the soldiers protect them.'

Hynd shrugged. 'Well it's not as if you've had a lot to do today so far.'

'Let's do it.'

'Captain Jeral.'

Jeral flinched, he couldn't help himself. Something about Lockesh's looming presence did that to a man, even one who was apparently in his favour.

'My Lord Lockesh . . . twice in one day. I am honoured.'

Lockesh moved alongside Jeral and waved Hynd back a couple of paces.

'Do not take this as any sign of weakness,' said Lockesh. 'But I have enough respect for you to warn you of the consequences of your success. Hynd, disguise our conversation.'

'Immediately, my lord.'

Jeral sighed and nodded. 'The silence from my generals has been loud indeed.'

'It is far worse than that,' said Lockesh when Hynd had completed his casting. His face was hard and cold, his eyes fixed on Jeral while he walked. 'They positioned themselves in the centre of the army believing it was the best place to survive the slaughter they assumed would be visited upon us here at the head. Now, they are stuck there, humiliated by your success and hearing words of congratulation for you from in front and behind.

'Every man in this valley knows they had nothing to do with your

plan and can claim no credit for it beyond putting you in charge and
expecting you to die.

'A slighted commander is a dangerous animal, Jeral, and the last
thing they want is an unlikely champion rising from the ranks. Loreb
has already tried to kill you twice and discredit you once. Now all
three of them detest you in equal measure. You will need your
friends. Keep them close.'

'And are you a friend, my Lord Lockesh?'

Lockesh raised his eyebrows and barked a dismissive laugh.

'Hardly, Captain. I am a man who desires to survive, and you
currently represent my best chance to achieve that. Should someone
supplant you, I will turn my back on you the same instant.'

'Well, that's honest at least.'

'I am never anything less.'

Jeral was silent for a moment and Lockesh continued to walk
beside him. The rainforest was regaining its energy. Animals and
birds were calling again. Monkeys hooted and insects rasped. The
order to reduce the weight of spell coverage had passed down the
column and Jeral motioned for an increase in speed.

'You think they'll try to kill me?' asked Jeral eventually.

Lockesh chuckled. 'It is never quite as simple as that.'

'Isn't it?'

'Certainly not.' Lockesh cleared his throat. 'Our esteemed generals
achieved their positions by basking in very public success, not by
muddying their own hands with the unpleasantness of career-
enhancing murder. At least, they have never been directly associated
with one.'

'So . . .'

Lockesh clacked his tongue and shook his head. 'Dear god on a
pyre, has Hynd not schooled you in the political machinations of
achieving senior command?'

'Probably,' said Jeral truthfully. 'But I'm just a soldier. I don't
suppose I listened.'

Hynd made a noise of complete agreement behind him.

'Then listen to me, and when you have listened consign what I
have said to memory and think on what it might mean for you,' said
Lockesh.

'I appreciate your taking the time, my lord,' said Jeral.

'It is not altruism, it is self-interest, and that should be your first
lesson, by the way. The generals are your commanding officers and

you may not question their orders, though you have come perilously close to doing that more than once. In any case, you need not worry about being placed on a charge and executed for any trumped-up reason. That would be far too obvious.

'Indeed you could argue that while we are travelling this perilous path, you are safe from any harm directed at you by Loreb. After all, you have proved yourself capable and they, like me, have a keen desire to survive, no?'

'That is what I was thinking, yes,' said Jeral.

'Hmm. Naive, sadly,' said Lockesh. 'Firstly, having seen exactly how to conduct the defence of the army against the elves, they will assume, erroneously, that it is simple to replicate. Secondly, they already consider themselves safe. I'm sure it has not escaped your attention that each keeps mages around him tasked to fly him from harm should the need arise.'

Jeral shrugged. 'Actually, it seemed quite sensible.'

'And why do you not have the same insurance on your life?'

'Because I will fight and die as a soldier. I am a leader, not a runner.'

'Exactly.' Lockesh glanced back over his shoulder. 'And that's something on which they will utterly rely.'

'So they won't kill me, they'll merely put me in positions where I am likely to be killed.'

'Now you're getting it.' Lockesh smiled for the first time. 'And should you manage to make it all the way to this mythical elven city we're seeking, then you will see how quickly an experienced general can take centre stage when victory seems assured. And how easily a figurehead such as yourself can find himself face down drinking his own blood.'

'You think all three of them are incompetent as leaders, do you?' asked Jeral.

'I'm walking at the head of the column, not in the middle,' said Lockesh.

'But leadership is what this army lacks,' said Jeral, finding himself exasperated and unsurprised in equal measure. 'Surely I make them look better by doing their bidding and succeeding, don't I?'

'It depends on your point of view. If you are a genuine career soldier risen to the rank of general, then yes, absolutely. If, however, you are a political animal choosing the army as your route to power in Triverne, or indeed greater Balaia, then above all things you must not be undermined by any under your command. And you, my dear captain, have undermined first Loreb, and then all three of them in very quick order.

'Now you are marked. Accept it. Check your food. Check your boots before you thrust your feet into them. And the moment we are out of this valley and in slightly less dangerous terrain, look behind every order Loreb gives you. None of them will be to the benefit of the army.'

'I've always said the wrong people are in charge of this army. It needs changing,' Jeral said and regretted his words instantly.

Lockesh caught and held his gaze and Jeral expected the rage he saw in the mage lord's eyes be given voice. But instead Lockesh's eyebrows lifted the merest fraction and his head inclined by the smallest degree.

'I must return to the generals before my continued presence here is noted,' said Lockesh. 'And you, Jeral, must heed my words. And your own.'

Lockesh turned aside. Jeral fought not to watch him go, keeping his eyes on his feet.

'Still got that spell going, Hynd?' he asked.

'Yes,' said Hynd, his voice small.

'Did he really just suggest what I think he did?'

Hynd's next affirmation was even smaller.

Chapter 25

Today, I told Tulan and Ephram to forsake the Cloak and wait
for the chance to strike back. It could be a long wait. I know what
I must do to keep them alive. Methian tells me I will lose my sense
but I have placed my trust in Tual. My soul is pure. I am strong
enough to resist the nectar's charms.

Final entry in the Diaries of Pelyn, Governor of Katura

Takaar stood for a moment to let his raging emotions subside. Of all
the things he had expected to see in this room, this was not it. Ten
days before, he had felt the sick rush of mass castings and had known
the TaiGethen were failing against the might of human magic. He
had known his path was the only one which could save the elves and
that he must reach Katura quickly to remove those he needed from
the enemy's path.

So he had run as only a TaiGethen can, while the Senserii brought
his young practitioners towards the agreed meeting point half a day
shy of the palm of Yniss and hidden from the suspicious eyes of
Katura.

Night had given him the anonymity he needed and his faded skills
were more than enough to see him into the hall of the Al-Arynaar
and unseen into the Governor of Katura's chambers.

All for this. To have his brief flicker of hope crushed, leaving only
emptiness and anger, disgust and betrayal behind. The stench in the
bedchamber was dreadfully familiar. Smoke still rose from the pipe
that lay discarded on a low wooden table by the bed and a small
leather bag lay next to it, the merest hint of its contents sprinkled
near the neck.

Pelyn lay on the filthy sheets. She was naked. One arm hung, elbow
locked and hand limp, over the edge of the bed. She was probably
unconscious but it was impossible to be sure with the three Tuali *ulas*

obscuring Takaar's view. Two watched the third abusing her body, which moved slackly in response to his thrusts.

All three had their backs to him and he crossed the floor in complete silence. Two paces behind the watchers, able to hear their repulsive comments over the sick grunting of the third, he stopped and drew his blades.

Let it flow. ·

For once, he was in total agreement with his tormentor.

'I think you've seen enough,' he said.

The two *ulas* spun around, their mouths dropping open in almost comical synchronicity. One held out a hand in a placatory gesture. Takaar rammed a blade up through each chin, skewering their mouths shut. He left the swords where they were and walked between the *ulas*, who grasped at the hilts while blood trickled from their mouths, their voices silenced by desperate drowning gurgles.

The other *ula* was so focused on rape he hadn't even realised his friends were dying. Takaar reached forward and clamped a hand on the back of the his neck, dragging him off Pelyn and throwing him to sprawl over the bloodied, still moving bodies of the others.

He screamed and scrambled off them, tried to cover himself while backing away towards the door and an unlikely escape. Takaar checked Pelyn was breathing before he pounced on the rapist. He pushed the Tuali towards the centre of the room and pulled a dagger from its ankle sheath.

'This is how you choose to rebuild the strength of elves? By defiling my Pelyn?'

The *ula* frowned, confusion briefly replacing the fear in his eyes. Takaar whipped a cut into his chest, drawing a line of blood. He yelped.

'Do you know me, boy?' bellowed Takaar into his face. 'Do you know me?'

'You . . . ? I—'

Takaar danced around him. He sliced the skin across his back three times before the *ula* turned to face him. There were tears in his eyes and a dread fear caused his body to shake. He held out his hands, pleading.

'I am Takaar, and though my crimes cost the lives of so many, I never stooped so low as you have.'

'How—'

Takaar's blade flashed across the Tuali's abdomen. He cried out and tried to back away. Takaar capered about him, pushing him, cutting him.

Good, good.

'That you dared defile my Pelyn earns you an eternity of torment before Shorth. But your crimes are far worse than that. Who do you represent?'

'What?'

Takaar's dagger hand twitched and a cut appeared above the *ula*'s eye. Blood beaded, ready to drip. He whimpered and lost control of his bladder.

'I am unused to repeating myself.'

'The Tualis rule here. I am Tuali.'

Takaar opened another cut in the *ula*'s face, this time across his left cheek.

'And so is Pelyn, making her your property, I suppose.'

'She made her choice.'

'That is a lie.' Takaar laced three cuts into the Tuali's ribcage. 'Do you know what you have done here?'

'We have taken Katura for the Tuali. The other threads can't thwart us for long. Not without the Al-Arynaar.'

'You've taken it for the Tuali and made a gift of it for man!'

Takaar nodded, slashing the blade deep into the Tuali's forehead.

'Oh yes, they are coming. Where will your power be when the spells start to fall?'

He opened up the *ula*'s chin.

'You've told me what I need to know. Now you must answer to Shorth.'

Takaar drove his dagger blade through the *ula*'s eye and into his brain, killing him instantly. Takaar let the body fall. He looked at his hands and saw they were trembling. On the floor he saw what he had done to Pelyn's rapist with fresh eyes, and he felt sick at the sight.

You should be proud.

'Only that he is dead. This is not me. It can't be.'

Oh dear, reality bites you again.

Takaar cleaned the dagger on the *ula*'s ripped grey shirt and turned away. The other Tualis were dead, their blood soaking into a rug whose original pattern had already been wholly obscured by grime. Blood was pooling on the timbers and filling the gaps between them. Takaar bent over the bodies and pulled his blades clear. He moved

to the bed and cleaned them on the edge of the base sheet before
sheathing them.

Finally, he covered Pelyn's body with the greasy damp top sheet
and knelt by her head. She stank. There was mould on the threadbare
pillow and dried vomit in her tangled, long and prematurely greying
hair. The pillow, mattress and sheet were covered in sweat, blood
and vomit stains.

Pelyn displayed all the symptoms of an abiding addiction to the
worst of all elven narcotics. Crusted blood clung to her nostrils, and
frothy drool ran from the corner of her mouth. Veins in her reddened
ears pulsed and there was an intermittent twitch in the muscles of the
right side of her face.

Her breathing was terribly faint and her face was pale to the point
of whiteness, excluding the deep red and black smudges beneath her
eyes. Her skin was cold to the touch and slack against her body,
which was just so much skin and bone, so thin had she become.

Takaar sniffed and let his tears fall. His hand shook when he
placed it on her chest to confirm the febrile heartbeat, finding her
breast shrunk to nothing and her ribs far too prominent. He moved
his hand down over her stomach, drawing on the Il-Aryn to help him
discover the full extent of her physical degradation. Her vital organs
were swollen and barely functional.

'How did you fall so far?' he whispered.

That's what happens when those you love desert you.

'It isn't as simple as that and you know it.'

Strangely, I'm not solely blaming you. So many left her.

'She was never strong enough for this.'

Takaar's eyes came to rest on the table with its pipe and leather
bag. Edulis. The whole city was rife with it, and here, at the heart of
what should have been government, it held sway. A sweep of his
hand scattered dust and bag and sent the clay pipe flying to shatter
against a wall.

Takaar pushed himself to his feet, unable to sit and do nothing.
There was a jug and bowl on a stand across the bedroom. Takaar
filled the bowl, catching his reflection in the mirror above the stand.
The elf who stared back at him was pinched and drawn, close to
exhaustion. His eyes were wide to make sense of the dark and his
hair needed cropping back down to his scalp. But in that face he
could still see desire and belief.

Beautiful, aren't you?

'I've never been beautiful. But at least I'm still fighting.'

Yes, but fighting your inner demons doesn't count.

'That was almost funny.'

I do my best.

Takaar put a passably clean towel over his shoulder and brought the bowl over to the bedside table. He fed warmth into the water through his hands and let the steam invade his nostrils for a few moments before he dipped a corner of the towel into the water and began to clean her face.

'This is bringing you back to life,' he said. 'Back to me. The dirt will wash away and you will break from the prison of your addiction. Together we will find the new Il-Aryn adepts and so the race of elves will survive the plague of man.'

It's amazing what a little warm water can do, isn't it?

Takaar heard footsteps outside the room. The door opened and light spilled in from the landing. He did not turn, leaving whoever it was to take in the blood and bodies on the floor as well as the bedside scene. Takaar dipped the towel in the water again and cleaned Pelyn's mouth and nose.

'Take the dead and go,' said Takaar. 'Pelyn is mine once more.'

Takaar heard the hiss of a sword leaving its scabbard. He turned his head and looked over his right shoulder. Two elves stood there. More Tualis. They couldn't make up their minds whether to attack or run for help.

'You really do not want to do that,' said Takaar quietly.

The pair moved into the room a few paces.

'Who are you? What are you doing here?'

'I am Takaar. I am bathing Pelyn. Washing the Tuali filth from her.' He turned back to Pelyn, who had begun to shiver. She moaned and her eyes moved back and forth beneath their lids. 'Shhh, my love. It will pass. Morning will see you open your eyes to a new life.'

A floorboard creaked. Takaar had a jaqrui cocked to throw. They had advanced but there was no will to fight in them.

'Take the bodies or run for help. It makes no difference to me.'

'You cannot stand against us all.'

'I am not here to fight you.' Takaar waved a hand. 'Now leave me. You are intruding.'

Takaar rose to his feet and walked towards them, fighting to contain the anger that sought to control him.

'Pelyn needs rest and peace,' he hissed. 'She needs cleansing. She does not need you, nor the bodies of her rapists, here to remind her of her suffering while she was helpless to resist.'

The two elves took a pace back. Takaar stepped over the two he had killed first.

'Or perhaps you had come to join in . . . to take your turns? Why else would you come here?'

Takaar growled and his tormentor cackled. One of the elves shook his head and the other pointed at the blood-soaked floor.

'The blood,' he said. 'It was dripping through the ceiling.'

'You are right to be scared,' said Takaar. 'What you have done to Pelyn shall be revisited upon you tenfold when they arrive.'

'Who?'

'Man. Now leave. Let no one disturb us before dawn. Then I shall meet whoever it is who claims to lead you.'

'You are in no position to make such demands.'

Want to bet?

Takaar turned away and resumed bathing Pelyn. She had sweat covering her face and neck and the shivering had intensified. Her breathing had become shallow and gasping.

'I am sorry,' said Takaar softly. 'I should not have left you.'

Some who knew he was in the hall of the Al-Arynaar still had a spark of decency, and word of who he was had undoubtedly reached the ears of those who mattered. He was brought food, fresh hot water, clean towels and bedding and a long white shirt in which to dress Pelyn when he was done.

Takaar did not acknowledge any who entered the room. Whether they brought things in or took the bodies away they were all similarly ignored while he saw to his task. To thank them would have been pointless. It did not change what they wanted. Shows of generosity from enemies were only ever a means to a bloody end.

When he was done, he looked down on Pelyn. The marks of her addiction would never truly wash away. But at least she looked more like herself. And when she awoke to the sound of a lengthy deluge outside, he could at least bear to look at her.

Takaar could tell her eyes were slow in focusing. Several times she wiped shaking hands across her face. Eventually she recognised him. He smiled and sat down on the edge of the bed. The shutters were thrown open to admit light, air and water spray. The stench of filth and edulis was finally obscured by the fresh scent of rain.

'Pelyn, can you forgive me for my long absence?' he asked, his voice quiet, knowing her ears would be tremendously sensitive while the drug left her body.

Pelyn stared at him, those dark circles around her eyes giving her gaze a malevolent quality. She licked her dry lips and switched her gaze to the bedside table, which now held a bowl draped with towels. She shook her head and stared at Takaar again. Then she lunged at him. Takaar caught one of her wrists but her free hand slapped him across the face and she kicked at him, tried to bite and scratch him. She was weak, however, and he pushed her back onto the bed, holding her there while she bucked and twisted in fury.

'Where's my nectar!' she shrieked. 'What have you done with my nectar? Get it now. I paid for it. It's mine by right.'

'Pelyn, listen to me. Pelyn.'

'I. Need. It.'

'No, you don't. Not any more.'

She stopped struggling for a moment while his words sank in. Her eyes widened and she screamed so high that Takaar had to release her and cover his ears. She scrambled off the bed and ran to her dresser, dragging open drawers, pulling at doors, throwing the contents about the room while she searched for the edulis Takaar knew she would not find.

He stood in the centre of the room and watched her, hoping her anger would burn out. Her weakened body gave way first and she sagged to the floor next to the connecting door that led to her office. She began to weep, muttering her desire over and over.

Congratulations. You have found the only elf on Calaius further down the path to madness than you.

'Then it is up to me to bring her back.'

Yes, I'm sure she'd be delighted to achieve your level of sanity.

Takaar shrugged his shoulders as if that might dislodge his tormentor. He crouched by Pelyn but did not attempt to touch her. She was sitting with her back to the door, her legs stretched straight out and her eyes staring ahead. There were fresh beads of sweat on her brow and her whole face twitched as if beset by palsy.

'Let me help you,' said Takaar.

Pelyn barked out a bitter laugh and stared straight through him.

'Your *help*. Prayers, platitudes and promises. All empty. What I—' she drew in a shuddering breath '—*need*, you will not give me.'

'It is a testament to the strength of your spirit that you are not already dead from this poison.'

'Poison? Typical of the pious who have never tried the sweet nectar and lived the life of a mind without boundaries.'

'I've seen that life, Pelyn. I saw it last night. I wish I could show you how it looked.'

'Let me show you. I need more. Now.'

Pelyn was getting agitated again. She wiped her hands down her shirt and rubbed at her face. She wrinkled her nose.

'You need to come back to me. I want Pelyn back. I want the Arch of the Al-Arynaar.'

Pelyn's stare was so cold.

'I haven't seen you in a hundred and fifty years! Not you, and not Auum for fifty. The only one who stood by me was Methian, and even he has gone now. Where were you when it all began to unravel? Where were you when the thread gangs took over the streets and we were too few to turn back the tide?' Her voice became a whisper. 'Where were you when I had to sell myself to keep those loyal to me alive?

'You're too late, Takaar. Whatever you really want, you won't find it here. I won't help you. Not without more nectar.'

'I will not support your habit to get what I came for. I won't be complicit in your death.'

Pelyn leaned towards him and the breath that came from her was as rotten as the remaining teeth in her mouth. 'You already are.'

Oh dear. You really have nothing she wants, do you?

'Wrong,' said Takaar. He rose to his feet. Pelyn watched him, a half-smile on her face. 'How soon before the craving becomes unbearable, I wonder? How long will it take before you are begging me to give you what you need? Will you attack me again or just quiver away in a corner, waiting to prostitute yourself to whoever will supply you?'

Pelyn's head had dropped to her chest. Her hands were wringing together and she couldn't keep her legs still against the floor timbers.

'It'll be full dawn in an hour,' said Takaar. 'That's your first goal because no one is coming up here until then. They think they have me trapped, you see, and so they won't risk coming in when I specifically told them not to. And you think you have power over me too. If you say go, then I'll go, right?'

Pelyn raised her head. 'Go.'

'Yet here I remain. Think on this. I will find what I have come for, with or without you. My guess is that I have ten days or so to find it and remove it from the city. That means I have nine and a half days I can spend here with you, keeping you away from that nectar you so want and killing every elf that comes through your doors.'

Pelyn was staring at him again, this time like a cornered animal seeking escape. 'Why would you do that to me? I thought you loved me.'

'I do,' said Takaar and he chuckled at his tormentor's silence. 'So I will do whatever I must to free you of this curse. Not just for you, though. Perhaps in ten days you might be recovered enough to hold a blade and lead a defence. You'll need to be. All those people who rely on you, or thought they could, will need you. And you will be desperate to succeed.'

'Why?'

Takaar could see Pelyn gradually pushing herself upright against the dividing door.

'Because I'm being followed. I didn't want to believe it at first, but it's become obvious recently. Movements in the trails of magical force, that sort of thing.' Takaar waved a hand. 'Nothing I can do about it except take what I came for and try to leave you with some hope. So I need your help.'

Pelyn turned and grabbed the connecting door. She'd pulled it half open before Takaar kicked it shut again and grabbed both her arms at the shoulders, forcing her to face him.

'And I need that help now.'

'What? What!'

'This place is made up of ghettos now, right? You get to take me to the Ixii and Gyalan ghettos, the Orrans and Cefans too. After that I might just let the elf who supplies you live to see the destruction of everything he thought he was building here. Because when they get here, unless you stand against them, it really will be the end. No more Katura. No more edulis. Poor little Pelyn, what will she do then?'

'Who's coming? Who's following you here?'

'Thousands and thousands of men.'

Chapter 26

*The appetite for Calaian rainforest wood is insatiable. No one
of any means would consider the use of any other timber. The
bloody idiots would probably burn their own houses now if they
were fashioned of Greythorne oak.*

Reminiscences of an Old Soldier, *by Garan,*
sword master of Ysundeneth (retired)

Garan was sitting in his favourite chair in the western panoramic
room, giving him views over Ysundeneth. In decades gone by he'd
enjoyed watching the city landscape change; become less elven, more
human. Beauty was not something Ystormun appreciated; functionality was everything, and Garan defied anyone to find beauty in
Ystormun's version of functionality though the efficiency of his
redesigned Ysundeneth was certainly impressive.

The city was dominated by the imposing warehouse buildings
which housed the Sharps. Thousands were crammed into inadequate
spaces. That, combined with derisory latrine facilities, rations just
above starvation levels and elven herbs in quantities sufficient only to
cure mortal illnesses, was Ystormun's morale-sapping master plan.

It was most effective. The Sharps feared the withholding of food
as much as they did the draconian crushing punishments for stepping
out of line. The whole city was effectively a prison camp and a
storage and shipping facility of huge proportions taking resources
and wealth north to Balaia.

Sitting here, on a day that had begun with spectacular lightning
storms and torrential rain and was now steaming gently under a hot
sun, Garan started to wonder when his mind had begun to change.
The gods knew he had plenty of years to look across. He took a sip of
a honey drink designed to soothe the sores that ran the length of his
gullet.

He could dismiss the dimmer memories, like the day he heard he would never be going home or the day he knew he had become little more than an experiment. Not because they didn't hurt but because they were over a hundred and twenty years old. And he had to admit that watching everything unfold around him for the last century and a half was a significant compensation.

Garan's gradual grudging friendship with Takaar was certainly a factor. Though he couldn't recall much of their earlier conversations, Garan recognised that they had sown the seeds of a respect for the elven race. He'd always known they were far more than their portrayal as violent primitives.

What Takaar had taught him, in his often unhinged but always charming way, was that there was a depth of spirituality and, well, *humanity,* to the elves along with their skills, knowledge and strength, and that should be embraced not exterminated. It hadn't ever led Garan to believe the occupation of the rainforest by man was wrong, but he had slowly begun to think a feudal partnership might be more productive than occupation and enslavement, in the long term.

Garan sighed and shifted in his chair, trying to alleviate a pressure point in his backside that sent shooting pains into his right leg. What had it been, then, that one tipping point, if indeed there had been just one? Not Ystormun himself. Garan had developed some understanding of him in the last couple of decades, as he had mellowed as much as an ancient and basically evil bastard could.

He did respect Ystormun's pride in his achievements on Calaius and most recently his ultimately futile resistance to his cadre's desire to send the army out to exterminate the race of elves.

'Hmmm.' Garan took another sip of his drink. 'Of course it never is the how, it's the why.'

He had the answer now. Everything else was just skirting the issue. It had been some years ago now, perhaps fifteen, but they all blurred into one amorphous smear of pain and unpleasant smells these days. It had been the moment he learned that the work on Calaius would no longer be to the benefit of Triverne or, by extension, to magic in general.

Worse than that, further investigation had revealed exactly what all Calaius' wealth was being diverted to support. Garan loved Triverne, and he loved Balaia too, though he would see neither again. And what he knew was dreadful for both of them. The power he had dedicated his life to support would turn his country and his city to ash in its desire for dominion. Yet even though he was in possession of such knowledge, he had not thought he could affect what was to come.

But his mind had turned that day. And so it was that, years later, he was open to options when they were presented to him . . . and those options had led him inexorably to the action he was to sanction today. Now.

Garan had made sure that his people were at the door to the panoramic room and that his people were attending to his many needs. One slip now and the worst of deaths would be awaiting them all – all but Garan himself. He and his people had planned for this from the moment it had become obvious that Balaia and Triverne were facing war.

Footsteps approached his chair. A figure stepped in front of him. Garan smiled. It was exactly who he had hoped to see when the ship had docked late the preceding night. Still he was impressed that the man had arranged to be re-summoned by Ystormun eight years after his first visit.

Stein was a squat man, barrel-chested and broad of gut. His skull was covered in a thick mat of tight blond curls and his features were all slightly larger than seemed quite comfortable, especially when crammed together in an oval face topped by wild eyebrows and tailed by an impeccably trimmed beard.

'You got my message, then?' asked Garan.

'All of them,' said Stein. 'We don't have long. Ystormun wants to outline my duties.'

Garan gestured to a chair.

'You remain fantastically ugly,' he said.

Stein laughed and sat. 'Your saying that, when no mirror can survive your reflection, is a testament to your powers of self-delusion.'

Garan cleared his throat. 'I need to know that you understand the gravity of the proposition. Let's face it: I want to die. I'm equally sure that you don't.'

'Correct, and yet here I am. That should tell you all you need to know about the fear gripping any of us with half a brain in Balaia right now. It's much worse than you think.'

'How close?'

'Any day, literally. And the cadre really can win, despite the force that will be ranged against them when the day comes.'

'I'm not asking you to destroy your own,' said Garan. 'You know that. A show of force is all it should take.'

'How comforting.'

'But we're relying on the Sharps – the elves – to prevail out there in the forest. If they don't then we're already too late and this place will become a power base like no other.'

Stein nodded. 'And will they win?'

'The odds against them are ridiculous, but they are capable and the trio of generals in the field can't even spell the word "tactic" between them. It's all down to the mages.'

'It was ever so,' said Stein.

'Smug bastard. Look, assuming they do win, we won't have much time. I've got an ally in their midst but the others . . . they're dangerous. Really dangerous. Deliver what you say you can and they will eventually respect you.'

'I should think so,' said Stein. 'After all, we're here to help them. Sort of.'

'But don't step out of line.'

'Or what?'

Garan shrugged. 'They'll kill you.'

'Anything else?'

'Let me do the talking.'

'Or what?'

'Guess.'

With a lack of subtlety that was typical of the Tuali, Takaar heard them massing in the rooms below to attack. Pelyn had been very quiet for the last hour. She had taken occasional sips of water but refused any of the stale food that lay on the plate from the night before. She would not respond to his questions, choosing to sit in a threadbare chair and stare at a bookshelf from which no book had been removed for a very long time.

Stitched yourself into a nice little trap here, haven't you?

'Even for you, that was pathetic,' muttered Takaar.

He put his ear to the floor and heard orders being given. He was amazed it had taken them so long, and could only think his name still carried enough fear to encourage caution. The day was moving towards its zenith; rain had given way to blazing sunshine, and the hubbub from Katura's people outside offered a veneer of normality.

'The ideal time to get out and about,' said Takaar.

I'm sure they'll all stand aside and open the door for you too.

He whistled tunelessly while he cleaned his blades, checked the contents of his backpack and refilled his skin from the washing-water jug.

'Do you have to whistle?' snapped Pelyn.

'Ah, you can still speak.'

Pelyn's smile was nasty and triumphant. 'They're coming to get you. And the best thing about it is that then I'll get more nectar and I can forget you ever came back into my life.'

'What do they want with you?'

It was a question Takaar had asked her time and again.

'Stupid, aren't you? They want me because I am Tuali. Because I am the governor of this city and because I pass all the laws. Easy.'

But her laugh had a bitter edge to it and her eyes were brimful of sorrow – just for a moment, before the craving dominated her once again. Takaar nodded. He heard elves gathering at the bottom of the stairs. It wouldn't be long now.

'It's hard to believe the good people of this city, and I'm sure some still remain, would accept that shadow of control. You have no power here, but I can give it back to you.'

'There's only one thing I want.'

She's consistent, at least.

'Time to go,' said Takaar and his grin made her flinch.

'You're really going to try to take them all on?'

'Now that would be stupid, wouldn't it?' Takaar moved towards her. 'I didn't use the door on my way in and I will not be using it on my way out. So: conscious or unconscious?'

'What?'

The Tuali were coming up the stairs, making a poor effort at stealth.

'Never mind.'

Takaar's punch struck her on the temple, knocking her senseless. He caught her as she crumpled and threw her featherweight over his left shoulder. He ran to the connecting door to her office, across the dusty floor and out onto the open balcony. He leapt lightly onto the rail, dropped to hang briefly from his right hand and then fell the rest of the way to the ground.

The side street was quiet. Takaar headed away from the centre of Katura and ducked into an alley three turns from the hall of the Al-

Arynaar, hidden from the Tuali but still close enough to hear their rage when his escape was discovered.

Takaar cradled Pelyn's head and poured a little water over her face and into her mouth. She coughed and opened her eyes. For one glorious moment her smile lit her face up and the old Pelyn shone through, but it was gone the next instant and she pushed away from him and scrambled to her feet.

Still groggy, Pelyn had to steady herself against the side of a building. Takaar rose fluidly and pulled her round to face him, his hands clamped around her upper arms.

'The Ixii and Gyalans. Where are they?'

'Get me my nectar and perhaps I'll tell you,' said Pelyn.

'No time.' Takaar shook her. 'Tell me which way. Now.'

'Or what? You'll leave me for another hundred and fifty years?'

Oh she knows how to hurt you, doesn't she?

Takaar drove her back and up against the wall, holding her feet from the ground. She kicked at his chest but they were feeble blows.

'Don't become part of the problem.' Takaar stared into her eyes, holding her gaze until fear eclipsed craving like storm clouds moving across the sun. 'Dying alone in this place would be such a waste.'

Takaar dropped her and she crumpled into a hunched position on the ground, hugging herself, caught between her longing for edulis and her fear of him. His heart screamed at him to embrace her, but his mind, this time, was stronger.

'I have this one chance to save the elves from man; to build a new strength in our people. Help me begin to return what I took from us all.' Takaar shrugged. 'Or you'll have to die. I can't let anyone stand in my way. Not even you.'

She lifted her face to his. The sounds of the Tuali mob on the streets were echoing down the alley. They were closing quickly. If Takaar had expected the light of comprehension in her eyes, he was disappointed. There was nothing there but a base cunning.

'Swear to me you'll get me more nectar and I'll help you.'

It is the only thing you can offer her that she will take. Do it, Takaar.

Takaar opened his mouth and betrayed her again.

'Done,' he said, the lie slipping easily from his mouth. 'Now let's move.'

The centre of Katura was built in a series of concentric rings, in keeping with the aspect of the palm of Yniss. Industry was based there. The city administration rubbed shoulders with forges, bakeries, butchers, potters and all manner of other goods and services. Temples to every god had been built and, for a time, harmony had reigned.

Every elf was granted land to farm, or hunt or log or even to mine if that was their desire. The population began to grow and the city threw out shoots into the forest where those who preferred the old ways could live, bringing their goods to trade in the market which blossomed in the heart of the city.

It was impossible to pinpoint when the mood had begun to change, but the silence from the old cities and from those who had sworn to fight on and liberate the enslaved had began to gnaw at Katura's heart. Isolation grew and, alongside it, a sense of hopelessness, a knowledge that what they were building might be all they had left.

Their spirit began to fail. And where the spirit faltered, there were those willing to profit from weakness. Edulis was their weapon, and it was as powerful as it was destructive. Land changed hands and threads began to gather together. The descent had been terrifyingly quick, and while there were significant numbers who remained dedicated to their tasks, determined not to fail, the pressure of the thread gangs grew day by day.

Pelyn led Takaar out into the uneven sprawl of what had begun as attempts to build strong neighbourhoods but had become ghettos where a single wrong turn could be a fatal mistake. Takaar had seen enough to know that the Tualis were the dominant thread, but they did not desire to drive the others out, preferring to profit from their misery instead.

The streets beyond the central rings were tight and maze-like, as if mimicking the Warren district of old Ysundeneth. Most buildings were single-storey and all were of wood construction. Most were ill maintained but here and there pockets of smart houses rested within the dilapidated mass. Takaar shook his head. It was like walking back onto Hausolis before the Garonin came, before the War of Bloods took hold.

Pelyn stopped in the centre of a muddy street that twisted away ahead of them. Beyond the houses, the beauty of the falls, heights and forests that bordered Katura was undimmed. Down here, though, smoke mixed with foul odours; children grubbed about in the dirt, and the Ixii on the street bunched together, staring at the intruders.

'I thought you said you were still governor,' hissed Takaar.

'They haven't seen me in a while,' confessed Pelyn. 'I doubt they trust me these days anyway.'

Pelyn was shuddering from the exertion of the run. Her face was pale and covered in sweat and she was breathing hard. She looked at Takaar and spread her hands.

'Well, here we are, the Ixii ghetto,' she said. 'What now?'

A good question.

'Simply answered. Do they have a meeting place?'

'What for?' asked Pelyn. 'Katura wasn't built for segregation. That's just the way it's turned out.'

'This'll have to do then,' said Takaar. He began to walk towards the eight or so Ixii gathered in a doorway a few paces ahead of him. 'Please, I would speak with you. All of you. Every decent Ixii, and your Gyalan and Orran and Cefan friends too, in time. Will you listen?'

Parents beckoned their children towards them. The atmosphere cooled and suspicion reigned. No one moved to speak to Takaar. He raised his voice, using the Il-Aryn to aid him.

'I am Takaar and I bring you new hope,' he said, his voice echoing from the sides of buildings and running away into the side streets. 'Come outside. Hear me. Hear about the gift I can bestow upon you. The power to fight back against those who seek to control you. You, the Ixii, have it within you to become a new power among the elves.

'Please, hear me. I mean you no harm.'

A child began to cry. Voices were raised behind Takaar – Tualis who could not have helped but hear him. Doors opened along the street and curious elves looked out. Seeing others already gathered, they moved to join them, the pack mentality of the threatened thread strong within them.

Takaar had been counting on that. His ears twitched. The Tuali were close. He wondered if that would work to his advantage. He waited a little longer as the Ixii continued to gather. A hundred or more were moving in his direction or standing with their thread.

'Pelyn is here. Your governor endorses me. All I ask is that you listen.'

Takaar began to move towards them, Pelyn came with him, unwilling but compliant, her craving and his promise dominating her mind. The Ixii bunched together and moved back, but not through fear of him; Tualis were spilling into the street behind him.

They were well armed and drilled. Swords and bows were evident. Presumably, many of them had once been Al-Arynaar.

'Go back inside. This criminal is ours.'

Takaar's eyes fell on the *ula* who had spoken.

'What is his name?' he whispered to Pelyn.

'Calen,' said Pelyn, and there was admiration in her voice. 'Looks like I won't need you for my nectar after all.'

Takaar took Pelyn's hand. 'Stay a while.'

Well. If you wanted an audience, you've certainly found it. All this time I've been urging you to kill yourself. Silly me. All I needed to do was wait until your ego did the job for me.

Takaar smiled. He was so close to the Ixii that he guessed the Tuali would not use their bows. They were forty strong at least, but there were a couple of hundred Ixii behind him and more were hurrying to join them.

'Calen,' said Takaar. 'I've wanted to talk to you.'

Calen ignored him. He had a savage bearing. One ear was ripped and its tip hung out, broken. He wore dark clothes and a pale brown leather coat. His hands were latticed with scars and there was an ugly tear on his forehead.

'Pelyn,' he said. 'We were worried about you. What are you doing with this coward? He abandoned you long ago. You're with us now.'

Pelyn tensed to move and Takaar tightened his grip.

'She's fine right where she is. We have business with the Ixii, and then you and I must talk about the defence of Katura.'

Calen laughed. 'The Ixii are weak and hide in their hovels while those of us who remain strong keep them safe. You talk to no one unless I say so.'

Takaar glanced over his shoulder. The Ixii stared on, most not knowing what to think.

'Oh?' said Takaar. 'But Pelyn is governor of this city, is she not?'

A ripple of mirth ran through the Tualis. Takaar shook his head and turned to the Ixii.

'Let me tell you why I am here and why you must come with me.'

'There are ten bows trained on your back, Takaar,' said Calen. 'You will turn and respect me.'

'Shoot, Calen,' said Takaar, not turning. 'Will they all hit me? Or will some strike Pelyn or the Ixii you say you protect. Will you stand there when they rush you to avenge a murder? Shoot.'

Calen did not give the order. Instead he called on his people to advance. Takaar smiled, continuing to ignore the Tuali and to address the Ixii. He could sense the swirling potential of the Il-Aryn in them. He had to make them feel it for themselves.

'You will know nothing of the Il-Aryn. It is a power that runs through you, which you can harness to make you stronger. I have been studying it ever since man took our cities and I have teachers waiting to help you learn to use it. You have nothing to lose. There is a world of wonder awaiting you, should you free yourselves, and if nothing else, I am offering you a way out of the slow death you face here.'

The point of a sword pricked the back of Takaar's neck.

'Don't make this difficult,' said Calen. 'I had to force Lysael to leave and I will do the same to you. It is over.'

Takaar dropped to his haunches, spun and stood, one hand grabbing Calen's sword arm, the other placed over his face. Takaar fed the Il-Aryn along his arm, focusing it to a fine point and seeing, in his mind, a surging pale crescent that spun to a blur. He gave it freedom.

Fire encased Calen's head. The Tuali screamed and clawed at Takaar's hand, his strength already failing. The flames blackened his flesh in an instant and scored the hair from his head. His body juddered and twitched as the heat seared through his skull and into his brain. Steaming blood exploded from his eyes and mouth while his ears melted.

Takaar closed his hand, crushing Calen's skull into fragments. His body, smoking from the neck and what remained of his head, dropped to the ground. Takaar wiped his hand on his trousers and looked at the Ixii, who, like the Tualis and Pelyn, had backed away from him.

'Who wants to learn how to do that?'

Chapter 27

Our research on Garan has produced startling results. The magical renewal of vital organ tissue stimulates a certain level of skin regeneration. We can, without doubt, keep a human being alive indefinitely. We must now concern ourselves with age prevention methods to make our next leap forward.

From *On Immortality* by Ystormun, Lord of Calaius

Even at the speed of a TaiGethen, the run to Katura took five days. The humans would be there in no more than another ten. Auum had left two cells to harry the enemy, to try to slow them just by being seen, to pick off hunters and stragglers too, but it was no more than token action.

They had lost six in the disaster in the Scar while many others who ran with Auum were injured both in body and spirit. Without the two cells following the Ysundeneth army, and Corsaar with his two cells still presumably tracking the Shorthian force, Auum would reach Katura with only twelve cells. He gathered them to him in the last cover before the land opened up to reveal the palm of Yniss and its scarred beauty.

'We are hurt by our defeat but we are not beaten by it,' he said, putting an arm around Grafyrre's shoulders and pulling the warrior close. 'We are a family and the mistakes we made yesterday are understood and must be put aside. Today begins the final task. Should we fail, the elven race is finished. Should we succeed, and succeed we will, then the liberation of our people is at hand.'

Auum paused and looked into their faces.

'We have all heard the stories of what has happened in Katura. We all know the crimes committed against Lysael and we will avenge them. But not every soul in that place is evil. Strength and purpose are only obscured by a veil of despair and the lack of hope. Tear that veil aside and we will see the true spirit of elves once more.

'We must see it, because we cannot do this on our own.'

Auum released Grafyrre, kissing his forehead.

'Make no mistake. We are going to take control of Katura. There will be resistance and we must not hesitate to break it. Not one among us wishes to strike down another elf, but I can see no path before us where that will not happen. The vilest of criminals hides there and they will not meekly set their influence aside.

'Pray that the good and the wavering listen to us. Pray that the harmony is not torn beyond repair. Pray that those we love and have left for too long are still alive.

'Pray with me.'

Ystormun lay on his bed, his sweat soaking the sheets. The Communion was desperate and painful. He felt fear in the cadre's minds for the first time and it did him great physical harm.

'You have not acted fast enough,' accused Giriamun.

'How dare you,' replied Ystormun.

'Then how far from their goal are they?' asked Pamun.

'A maximum of twelve days. Less if the ground eases.'

A concerted howl erupted from the minds of the five and Ystormun shrieked with the pain that blistered his psyche.

'You delayed for too long before sending them out. Your love of the elves will be the undoing of us all.' Aramun's voice boomed around his skull. 'We *need* those men.'

'And you will have them,' said Ystormun. 'Surely your strength of arms is enough to hold off our enemies.'

'Idiot!' Pamun again. 'If it were, then we would not be wasting our energies on you.'

'Then I shall call off this attack and you shall have your precious men sooner. Unfortunately, that will mean handing Calaius back to the Sharps. Perhaps you consider that a small price to pay?'

'Calaius can never be lost to us,' said Weyamun.

'Then let me do my job as you do yours. You assume our troubles are caused by my failure. I contend that they are due to yours. Perhaps you need me to help you with your tactics?'

The noise was unbearable yet Ystormun found some small satisfaction within it.

'You gave me no choice,' he said. 'And now I am happy to return the favour. Do not trigger a conflict now. Direct your energies towards diplomacy for as long as you must.'

'Fool,' said Aramun. 'We are not the ones who seek conflict. Others do and we may be powerless to stop them.'

'Find a way,' said Ystormun. 'But if you fail, so be it. I will be the only one of us to survive, and I will remain strong here. I can live with that but can you die knowing it? This Communion is at an end.'

Ystormun broke the link before the battering could recommence. It was some hours before he began to worry that it had been so simple to do.

Auum led the TaiGethen into Katura as the afternoon began to wane. They spoke to no one, acknowledged no one and ran into the marketplace at Katura's heart before they stopped, a growing crowd following them. It had been over fifty years since any of their calling had entered the city.

The market day had already ended. Such stalls as there were, were either covered or dragged to the side of the circle. Auum took in the malevolent feel of the city. Two- and three-storey buildings and temples surrounded them. Cobbled roads led off in six directions. Domes, spires and steep-angled roofs dominated the skyline.

The TaiGethen had gathered on the Yniss stone in the market-place, the first laid in the new city and bordered by benches set among flower borders and blessed with messages from the priests of each god. But the flowers were dead and had not been replaced. The messages were covered with graffiti and had been defaced by weapons. The stone itself had been carved with the symbol of Tual.

Even the flagpole, which had once proudly displayed the symbols of every thread, was criss-crossed with insult and threat, promise and mindless muttering. It was bare of any flags and probably had been for decades.

During their run to the centre, Auum's heart had fallen. His worst imaginings about Katura had been exceeded. The place stank. Rubbish and faeces clogged alleys and gutters. Many houses and businesses had been boarded up, vandalised or reduced to skeletons, their timbers stolen for other purposes.

Addicts had stared at them from the open windows and doors of run-down dwellings as well as the streets, where they lay, all their possessions lost or bartered away. Elves of every thread walked with their heads down or glanced at them with haunted expressions before their curiosity overcame suspicion.

Boltha and Methian had painted too rosy a picture for him. There was no harmony here; Katura was as good as dead.

Word of the TaiGethen's arrival had fled through the streets and people were crowding in to see the spectacle. They filled all the spaces and pressed forward, eager to get a view of the elite warrior caste they had entrusted to keep them safe from man and to return them to their homes.

But a hundred and fifty years of waiting had lessened the awe in which the TaiGethen were held, and the first insult was followed by a barrage of others, the assembly emboldened by numbers and giving vent to their frustration.

'Faleen, take your Tai and get to the hall of the Al-Arynaar. I want Pelyn. Illast, take your Tai and go with her. This place is dangerous. Take no chances. Trust no one. The rest of you, form a perimeter around the flagpole. This is an opportunity too good to pass up.'

Auum climbed the flagpole, his agility hushing the crowd. He used the silence to begin speaking.

'People of Katura. My brothers and sisters. Hear me. I am Auum, Arch of the TaiGethen, and I need your help.'

The silence deepened. From his vantage point, Auum saw Faleen lead the way to the second ring, where the Al-Arynaar had built their hall, and he could see more elves hurrying to join the throng around him. He wondered who among them were the pure, and who were the fallen. They would announce themselves soon enough.

'You failed us!' shouted a voice.

Others took up the call. Auum waited for their anger to subside.

'If that is what you believe, then I shall not seek to persuade you otherwise. Nevertheless the TaiGethen have fought every day to free our country. Our blood has kept the humans at bay to give you the chance to rebuild. It seems to me you have spurned that chance. The reek of edulis is stronger than that of timber here. Perhaps we were wrong to fight on. Perhaps the elven race is not worth saving.

'But I have good news for you. For all those who believe the TaiGethen have failed them, I bring you the chance to show us how you could have done it better.'

Auum, his feet clamped around the flagpole and with one hand resting atop it, let his body swing around in a lazy circle. Every eye was on him, every ear waiting to hear what came next. A few insults rang out but were shushed.

'Two human armies are heading here. The first will arrive in ten days' time. Combined they field over four thousand soldiers and mages. Plenty enough they think to destroy this city and its entire people. Without the sixty TaiGethen, now reduced by a third, they would have arrived with almost two thousand more.'

Auum paused while the shock sank in. Katura should have been an eternal sanctuary. Those below Auum were the few who still worked for its good, or at least who had not succumbed to its drug-ridden underbelly. They had withstood a great deal while the city fell around them and now they faced losing everything.

'Ten days is ample time in which to run and hide in the rainforest. If that is your desire then go, because I do not want cowards standing by me when the enemy pounds on the gates.

'I am here to tell you to stand. To run would signal the end of elves. We would scatter ourselves through the forest to be picked off at their leisure. That is not how my story shall be written.

'I am here to tell you to stand and fight. To fortify this city, to arm yourselves and to join me in the battle that will decide the fate of elves across our land. How much do you want to return to the lives you led before the humans came? How much do you want to see the elves prosper once more without the malign hand of man controlling us?

'How much do you want to live?'

Auum watched while a furious babble broke out. Arguments rang back and forth, scuffles erupted. Some people pushed their way out of the crowd and hurried away to their houses, presumably to pack and run.

Auum waited, wondering if there would be any silence long enough for him to speak, to ask for what he wanted. Question upon question was being hurled at him. How had the humans found them? Did the TaiGethen lead them here? How could they defeat so great an army? Will the Apposans return? Is this why Takaar is here?

Auum started at the sound of that name. He scanned the crowd, searching for the one who had said it. In the sea of a thousand faces, it was an impossible task. He raised a hand, hoping for some quiet. He was granted enough for his purposes.

'We will answer all your questions; I know you have many. But please, time is short and every moment of every day counts. All of you who desire to live, I need you. I need metal workers, architects, weapon-smiths, fletchers. I need anyone who has training with a blade or bow. I need builders and I need your priests. All of you, come to the hall of the Al-Arynaar at sundown.

'Lastly, who spoke of Takaar?' A nervous-looking Gyalan *iad* near the front raised her hand. 'I would speak with you. Ulysan, see her inside the perimeter. The rest of you, please, stay in Katura to fight. We *can* win. No TaiGethen will leave here until the last elf has fallen. We believe. So must you. Go and pray for strength, and then bring me every skill and weapon you can.'

Auum shinned down the flagpole. The crowd moved forward on all sides, questions raining down on him. The TaiGethen shouted for them to disperse, reminding them all that there would be time enough at sundown. The *iad* was ushered into the ring and Auum sat with her on a bench while the crowd's bluster began to break up and they slowly started to disperse. Some, though, stayed firmly put, determined to see everything that unfolded.

'Thank you for speaking to me. I am Auum.'

The *iad* smiled. She was middle-aged. Lines of worry creased her forehead and grey flecked her hair. Her clothes were drab but clean and her face was proud.

'I am Nerille.'

'How long has Takaar been here?'

'For two days. His arrival caused trouble with the Tualis, and he killed Calen, head of the thread gang. For that we are thankful. Every dead supplier of edulis is a good one.'

Auum had to smile. Even in Takaar's madness, there remained a core that was good.

'Where is he now? With the Gyalans? Or perhaps the Ixii?'

Nerille raised her eyebrows. 'You know why he's here, then. He says it is for the good of all elves. I presume he's here to fight.'

'I wish that were true,' said Auum. 'But he wants to take those he seeks away to train them as mages when they should remain here and hold blades. How many has he convinced?'

'Quite a lot.' Nerille shrugged. 'Two hundred? I don't really know. He speaks to them several times a day, urging them to bring more to the next meeting. They are captivated by him.'

'Where does he speak?'

'In the temple of Ix.'

Nerille pointed across the circle to the garishly painted temple, its single spire twisting up to the heavens and its founding timbers carved to resemble the roots of trees.

'Thank you, Nerille, that is most helpful.'

She smiled. 'Can we beat them, the enemy? I have a family, *ulas* of fighting age, though two of the three seem to have become devotees of Takaar. I will not risk them in grand failure.'

'We will prevail,' said Auum. 'And if it makes you happier, I will stand by them and see them survive. We must save as many as we can. You are all that is left of the free elves.'

Nerille took his hands impulsively. 'We will stay. We will fight.'

Auum kissed her cheeks then drew back, another question on his mind.

'Is Pelyn still alive?'

Nerille sighed. 'Yes, after a fashion. She fell under Calen's spell and it is a spell not easily broken. She's with Takaar now, what's left of her.'

Auum stared at the temple. 'She's about to discover she has work to do.'

Chapter 28

There was a moment when some elves questioned their god-given right to own the rainforest and the survival of the entire race hung by a gossamer thread.

From *A Charting of Decline*, by Pelyn, Arch of the Al-Arynaar, Governor of Katura

As Auum marched into the temple of Ix, Pelyn was once again counting the time since her last smoke of nectar. Its absence burned through her mind and made mud of her bones. It shouted through every nerve and made each breath a quivering exertion of almost insurmountable magnitude.

Her nose could smell it, her teeth ground on its memory and her eyes fogged with images of it. She couldn't escape the memory of smoke writhing in the air, the glorious feeling of the spirit washing through her body, the escape over the waters to the retreat of her mind, the feeling of others around her, at one with her body and loving her flesh so much that they clung to her always.

'Need it,' she muttered.

'No, you don't,' whispered a voice.

Pelyn was startled. Takaar was in the middle of an oration. The temple was full of his acolytes hanging on his every word, devouring his promises and eager to taste the glory of the Il-Aryn. He was no better than Calen had been, busy peddling his own drug, his own promises. But Calen was dead and her route to edulis had gone because she was being chaperoned day and night. She'd only just remembered their names even though they were very old friends.

Pelyn hunched her shoulders and looked to the *ula* on her left. He was Tuali, strong and loyal, though if her memory served he hadn't always been that way.

'Tulan,' she said. 'You know I've broken the habit, don't you? So one more won't hurt. Just to say goodbye.'

'I'm afraid we need you clean,' said another voice, Ephram's.

Both were Al-Arynaar and both were wearing their cloaks once again.

'What happened to you?' she frowned, wondering why she cared. Neither of them seemed likely to supply her.

'When the purge came we hid in the ghetto, just as you told us to, waiting for our chance to return. As you said we should.'

'I said that?' Pelyn smiled. 'So I saved you. Are you grateful enough to find me some nectar? It really will be the last time.'

'I don't think so,' said Tulan. 'I—'

There was an *ula* walking down one of the aisles towards the dais from which Takaar was speaking. No one moved to stop him. No one dared.

'When did he get here?'

Pelyn had been aware of the odd snatch of noise from outside the temple but had thought it was just the normal business of a market day. A theatre group perhaps; there still was one in Katura. It seemed she had been wrong. She watched Auum. He moved with such poise. Eyes were drawn to him from across the temple and eventually even Takaar was forced to acknowledge him.

'Ah, a cloud has come to cover the sun,' he said, and the temperature in the temple seemed to cool. 'An ill voice comes to disrupt our harmony. Please, my elves of the new age, stay. I will return when Auum and I have spoken.'

'I have no intention of conducting this conversation in private,' said Auum, his tones providing a harsh counterpart to Takaar's gentle oration. 'This must stop.'

For a moment the craving left Pelyn while she watched the two most powerful elves on Calaius clash like panthers over hunting grounds.

'They will not listen to you, and why should they? These are free elves. Free of will and free of thought. And they have chosen the path for the new generation. The Il-Aryn courses through their bodies and I will give them control of it and so bring us the power we need to rid Calaius of man.'

'Going to do all that in ten days, are you?'

Auum's tone was contemptuous. He had continued walking until he stood a mere pace from Takaar. His whole body was a signature of the threat he posed. Takaar was quick but Auum was like lightning, and Pelyn could see Takaar knew it.

Takaar chuckled and waved a hand. 'With the TaiGethen among us, we need not fear man, surely?'

'You haven't told them, have you?' Auum pointed north. 'An army is coming. Following you. It will be here in ten days. The great Takaar forgot to mention it, didn't he? There is a time for magic but it is not now. Any of you who leave with him are nothing but cowards running from the fight.

'Look at you. All of you. Fit young *ulas* and *iads* whose minds are being tricked. What use is there in magic if there is no elven race left to save with it? You must stand with me and fight with blade, bow and fist. Standing together, we are strong enough. Leave and you weaken us all. When the battle is won, go with my blessing. But not now. I need you. The elven race needs you.'

'They do not need your blessing to become Il-Aryn.' Takaar's whole face was a sneer. 'But I tell you what: I will give them the choice you would deny them. Any of you who wish to fight, bleed and die with Auum, please move outside. Any who wish to stay and learn the greatest of lessons, remain seated.'

Not one of them left; they applauded and Auum stood humiliated. Pelyn feared what he might do, but there was not a twitch towards violence.

'You are a traitor to the elves, Takaar,' said Auum when the applause had died down.

Takaar did not appear to care. 'No, Auum, if anyone betrays us it is you and those who would deny the future of us all.'

'Very well. Take your people and go. But do it now. No other will be allowed to join you. Do not make a scene and do not make a fuss. I will not allow you to grandstand your miserable exit. And when you reach whatever hiding place you have in the forest, send me the Senserii. At least give me them. They are worth ten of each of your little gang.'

'I will not give up my loyal defenders,' said Takaar. 'But I will give you this.'

He unshouldered his backpack and proffered it to Auum with the reverence due a priceless religious token. Auum stared at it and then at Takaar, contempt making a mask of his features.

'For all that you are denying the elves of Calaius, you are giving me a sack in return? Insult me again and I will kill you and damn the consequences.'

Takaar raised a hand to quell the tension that had sprung up in the temple.

'Do not make your ignorance so public, Auum. Within this sack are those things I always worked upon and you always eschewed despite my urgent advice. But use arrows, not blowpipes. Pipes are too short range and I have perfected a viscosity that sits well upon an arrowhead.' He proffered it again and Auum took it. 'There's enough in there to kill two thousand, I'd say. Maybe a few more if you're careful with it. But don't touch it. Death on contact.'

Takaar smiled beatifically and Pelyn thought Auum would lay him out. The TaiGethen's left fist balled but then relaxed. He turned and stalked back down the aisle, daring any to speak to him. None did. At the door he stopped and turned and his eyes fixed on her.

'Pelyn, you are coming with me. That is not an option, Al-Arynaar, it is an order. You have a cloak. It is time you wore it once more.'

Auum simmered. Katura was in an appalling state. The TaiGethen had sought out those they felt could lead or add significant skills to their efforts and come back with an estimate that eighty per cent of the city lay in the hands of two suppliers of narcotics and luxury items – rare plants and herbs, spirits and fine cloth.

Much of it was sourced from the many villages still working, as they always had, through the long years of elven existence in the rainforest. But plainly they were under the control of the larger thread gangs, the Tualis and the Beethans. As for the edulis, which came at a staggering price in terms of land and goods, it was manufactured in the city.

'We should shut them down,' said Ulysan. 'Put an end to their influence here.'

The TaiGethen were beginning to assemble in the hall of the Al-Arynaar. The day was almost over and the evening chorus was sounding loud from the rainforest below the palm of Yniss. In the relative peace that had descended on the city now Takaar had departed, the sound of the falls, distant through the trees that lined the lowlands, was mesmeric.

'That is the Al-Arynaar's job,' said Auum. 'Or it should have been. We have neither the time nor the strength to clear them out. We have to win their support with word and action.'

'I think you're being naive,' said Elyss. 'We were out there while you were getting rid of Takaar. They won't speak to us. They just watch. They're dangerous and they have huge influence here.'

Auum shrugged. 'They have no courage. We are fighting for the survival of our race.'

'It's so simple for you, isn't it, Auum?'

It was Pelyn. She'd been asleep much of the late afternoon, Elyss sitting with her and guards positioned on her balconies. Tulan and Ephram, the two young Tuali Al-Arynaar, were organising the main hall for the evening's meeting, clearing the floor and setting up tables around the edges. Auum wasn't sure about them. Very quick to run, it seemed, and equally quick to return when the wind changed.

Pelyn still looked pale but there was some spark in her eyes again. Auum knew enough about edulis not to take that as a sure sign of recovery, but it was a start.

'It *is* simple,' said Auum. 'If we are defeated here, we are finished. If we win, we can cleanse our forest and resume the lives they stole from us.'

'But Auum, it's not in the drug gangs' interests to believe you,' said Pelyn.

'Really? Who will they sell their poison to if the elves are all dead?'

'You aren't listening. They won't relinquish their power. Their grip is so strong here.'

'And it should never have been allowed to become so,' said Auum, thrusting his face towards Pelyn. 'What happened to you? What happened to the Al-Arynaar? You were loved and respected and the city was growing so well. Yet the last Al-Arynaar I spoke to was Methian, and he'd been banished, his life threatened, just like Lysael.

'I trusted you, Pelyn. I believed in you. But you took the edulis. You failed yourself, the Al-Arynaar and the elves of Katura. When I walked in here I wondered why I was trying to save our country. Think on that and think on your own weakness.'

Auum's anger burned hot. He was standing over Pelyn, who had shrivelled before him. She was shaking and there were tears in her eyes.

'You weren't here,' said Pelyn, her voice tiny. 'You do not know.'

'I know that Nerille of Katura has raised a family in the midst of this chaos and violence and none of them are addicts, none of them fell. People who have no strength of arms but who have everything in here.' Auum placed a hand over his heart; his voice had dropped to a harsh whisper. 'And if we lose that, we lose everything.'

'Then why do you want me here? What use do you think I am?'

Auum stared into Pelyn's eyes. There he found confusion and loss and a terrible desperation – a longing that touched his soul.

'You are Pelyn, Arch of the Al-Arynaar. I know what you are capable of. I know the depth of your faith.' Auum took her hands. 'I hate what has happened to you and to this city, but that does not dim my love for you. But first you must admit your failings and make peace with Tual and Yniss.

'Only then can you replace your cloak and resume your rightful place. Can you do this?'

Pelyn did not hesitate. 'I will.'

Auum kissed her forehead. 'Then go to your temple to pray. Tomorrow, I need you to begin teaching those who have never held a sword how to survive a battle.'

Auum watched her go with Tulan and Ephram flanking her. Her bearing was proud but her left hand rubbed continuously at her right arm. He hoped Tual could give her the succour she needed.

'You were too hard on her,' said Elyss.

'Anyone who is not squarely behind us will drag us back. We cannot afford that.'

'So what about the drug gangs?' said Merrat.

The TaiGethen were all here now and Katurans were beginning to filter in.

'How many do they number?' asked Auum.

'In the hundreds,' said Faleen. 'And they may be able to bully more to join their cause, such as it is.'

'We can threaten people with death if they do not fight with us too, but it'll be death at the hands of man.' Auum thought briefly. 'We will not face them head on. Any resources they own, we will take. Any who oppose you with violence, strike down. Otherwise, they must be ignored. Let them make the moves, and so turn the population against them. Let them be the ones seen to risk all for their greed.'

The hall filled quickly while the night darkened. Torch- and lantern-light cast shadows high up into the vaulted timber roof. Nervous elves gathered in front of a line of tables behind which stood the TaiGethen. On the tables, paper and quills were ready to record names, skills, requirements and timescales.

Auum stood centre with Merrat and Grafyrre. He sampled the mood of the hall. Anxiety and determination dominated but there was still scepticism. With people still coming in through the open doors, Auum moved forward to speak.

'You are here because you believe in the hope of victory in the fight to come. For that I thank you, and for all the work that must be done to ensure this hope is not false. I am going to ask more of you than any of you can imagine. You may believe our task is insurmountable but it is not.

'I know what has happened in your city, but you can already see change is coming. The Al-Arynaar once again wear their cloaks with pride and purpose. They are few now but their numbers will grow quickly.'

Auum indicated the Al-Arynaar, thirty-four of them, who stood at the doors and ringed the walls.

'I know you have lived under the fist of the thread gangs. You no longer need fear them. Takaar has already cut the head from the Tuali beast's body. The Beethans have remained quiet, as the cowards they are.

'Their activities cease today. Help the addicts they have poisoned. Take back what they have stolen from you, not with a blade but with your will to turn this city around to face man and defeat him.'

A ripple of applause and a fledgling cheer rose up from the two hundred or so elves gathered in the hall only to be stilled by a commotion outside. Shouting, and the sound of swords being drawn, shivered through the hall, chilling the mood and giving Auum a taste of the task he faced to rebuild the Katurans' courage. TaiGethen began to move but Auum held his arms out for calm.

A large body of elves forced their way through the crowd, shoving people aside, snarling threats and insults on their way to the front of the hall. They were Beethans, with powerful frames as befitted those born to the god of tree, root and branch, and angular features with prominent cheekbones, arrowhead noses and narrow mouths.

An *iad* led them. She was dressed in fine cloth and carried a thin sharp blade. Seventy or eighty crowded around her, every one armed with a bow or sword. The ordinary people shied away. Some had already fled the hall but most filtered behind the Al-Arynaar, who had come forward into the centre of the hall to provide what little defence they could. The taunts from the Beethans were harsh and well directed, though, and Auum was not convinced he could rely on the Al-Arynaar to stand if it came to a fight.

The Beethan *iad* held up her hands for quiet and her mob bellowed for order. She glared at Auum across the table.

'You have a strength of arms that will give us all great heart when the humans attack,' said Auum. 'Welcome.'

'Save your breath, TaiGethen,' she said, her tone strident, her voice powerful and confident. 'I am Jysune and I thank you for ridding this hall of the Tuali and for removing Calen's head. But your assumption of command in this city is premature. Your every footstep is trespass on my territory. Your every word is spoken to an elf indebted to me.

'Your ruse is obvious and desperate; man has no knowledge of this place. There will be no battle here so I offer you this instead: defer to me in all matters relating to the city and I will let your people live. Offer your guidance on strengthening this city's defences against the attack that may come, one day, and I will sweep the streets clean of Tuali interference.

'With Calen gone, Katura is mine. The TaiGethen are great warriors but your numbers are too small to challenge us on our streets. This is not the rainforest and you would do well to remember that.'

Auum said nothing. He dived over the table, arms outstretched. His left hand clamped on Jysune's sword arm at the wrist and his right gripped her throat. He bore her to the ground, where she landed with a thud, her blade flying from her hand. Elyss and Ulysan landed either side of Auum, pushing the Beethans back.

'What say you I take your head too? What price your control then?'

Auum pushed his hand harder into her throat but Jysune could still force her words out.

'See for yourself,' she said. 'Arrow up.'

Immediately, every Beethan with a bow turned to train their weapon on the helpless Katurans. People screamed, some begged for mercy around him.

'Auum,' warned Ulysan.

'Release me,' said Jysune.

Auum dragged her upright and thrust her back into the arms of her mob. She laughed.

'*That* is power,' she said. 'That is control.'

Jysune stooped to pick up her sword. She motioned her archers to slacken their bows and signalled her people to leave.

'Talk all you like,' she said over her shoulder, turning when she reached the door. 'But nothing will happen in this city without my permission. You know where to find me.'

Jysune reserved a long and threatening stare for Auum, Elyss and Ulysan before stalking out into the night, leaving a momentary silence soon filled with a frightened babble. Auum bit his lip and jumped up onto the table, shouting for order and quiet.

'That's you being in charge, is it?' shouted someone.

'That is me making sure none of you die tonight,' said Auum. 'The *iad* has just picked a fight she cannot win. It was a desperate throw of the dice, the last twitch of a dying animal. The only way she can hope to win is to keep you afraid. Do not be afraid. She is the one who should be scared, because she knows she is losing control.'

Slowly, muttering and unsure, the Katurans gathered again to hear Auum's plans.

'There is so much we have to do and there is so little time. We have to look to our weapons, our food and water stores, our planning for injury and fire. We have to consider the rotas for duty and rest, we have to assign cooks, stretcher and water parties, quartermasters and field medics. But none of that will matter unless we can fortify this city against man's magic.

'We have an inexhaustible supply of wood, but wood will not do because man's magic, his fire and his ice, will simply destroy it. Instead, in ten days, people of Katura, I want to raise a barrier of iron and steel ten feet high stretching from the river to the east to the cliffs to the west.

'Fire the forges and never let them cool.'

Then the madness began in earnest.

Chapter 29

The light of Ix burns strongest and brightest in the bodies of the shortest lived.

The Aryn Hiil, later Calaian Writings

The arguments had gone on late into the night, and even when they were done the Katurans remained doubtful. Auum was exhausted. Being among so many people for so long left him fidgety and uncomfortable. He needed air and, with Ulysan and Elyss, he walked out into a drizzling night, heading for the marketplace. It was the largest open space in the city.

He ached as if he'd been running all day, climbing all night and fighting open handed between breaths, as the saying went. The fatigue clung to his mind and he felt unable to even speak until they had seated themselves on some of the benches around the flagpole.

'This battle cannot come soon enough. I hate cities.' Auum sampled the air, raising his face to let the drizzle dampen his skin. 'And this place is the worst kind. No parks, no trees and no space. It stinks of civilisation exterminating nature. It has no natural sound, like someone has shut out the whole forest. All I can hear are the cries of desperate addicts and the thuds of doors shut in their faces. We have such a short time to make such a long journey.'

Elyss was sitting by Auum. She put an arm about his shoulders.

'We'll do it.' She gestured behind her towards the hall. 'Your TaiGethen are there, talking with the thread priests. There is energy and desire alongside the doubters. And when they see the fires of the army, they'll double their efforts.'

'And what will the Beethans and Tualis do then, I wonder?' said Auum.

'Let's pray they sharpen their swords and stand on the walls alongside us,' said Ulysan. 'I'm more worried about what they will do tomorrow.'

Auum sighed. 'That's why I need Pelyn. She knows this city as none of us ever will, despite her fall, and the old Al-Arynaar will flock to her when she wears the cloak and calls for them. The gangs are hoarding critical resources. If we don't fortify sufficiently now, we're finished before we start. Has anyone calculated how much metal we need to get this wall up?'

Ulysan smiled. 'We just left the argument over how thick the plating needs to be and how many rivets or eyes and ties we need per foot.'

Now he tried, Auum could hear the search for raw materials already under way. The smiths' furnaces in the second circle were roaring, ready to smelt. The hammering and sawing he could hear would be the construction of plating moulds.

'Everything else is going to seem simple by comparison to that wall,' said Auum. 'What next?'

'Prayer and sleep,' said Elyss. She looked at Ulysan. 'Can you give us a moment? We'll join you at the temple.'

Ulysan smiled, nodded and trotted away to the temple of Yniss. It was a modest building, as they all were, free from desecration but also without a priest since the Tualis had driven Lysael away.

Auum looked at Elyss' face, smudged with dirt and damp with drizzle but still vibrant. She was shivering gently and Auum assumed she was cold in the rain and wrapped his arms round her.

'We should get inside, warm you up.'

'It's not the cold I feel,' she whispered. 'It's a new life.'

Auum felt the smile broadening on his face and the tears gathering in his eyes. He couldn't speak. He grabbed Elyss' hands and stared into her eyes. Tears were spilling down her cheeks and she was shaking all over. Auum's pulse was thudding in his neck. He placed a hand on her belly and imagined the life growing inside. Ynissul life. TaiGethen life. The future of the elves.

'We did it,' he whispered.

Elyss laughed, and the sound lit up the marketplace and echoed back from the blank dark buildings surrounding them. Auum glanced about him; it would have been an unexpected sound of joy in this place.

'You needn't sound so surprised,' she said. 'Just think of our future now. A TaiGethen child.'

'We've got to win first, both within and without our walls.'

'And can anything stop you now?'

Auum pulled her into an embrace he had no intention of releasing. 'Nothing.'

He kissed her cheek and the side of her neck. She pushed him back, her face taking on a serious expression.

'One thing. You mustn't worry about me and you mustn't try to stop me fighting. It's what I do. The greatest risk to our child is to have its parents worrying about each other and not concentrating on the enemy before them.'

Auum nodded. 'You sound like me.'

'Funny that, isn't it?'

Auum stood, feeling tall, powerful and replete with the blessings of Yniss. He held out a hand.

'Let's go and pray with Ulysan. He's part of this family.'

'All the TaiGethen are part of it.'

Elyss stood and froze, looking over Auum's shoulder. Auum saw her expression and nodded minutely.

'That's very touching, it really is,' said Jysune. 'Good news is always so wonderful to share, isn't it?'

Auum turned, staying close to Elyss. He faced Jysune even though three other Beethans, who had emerged from the quiet streets leading to the central circle, were now behind him. Jysune was flanked by two archers and had her sword in her hand.

'We are going to pray for the Katuran people and give thanks for their strength in the face of a powerful enemy,' said Auum. 'Join us.'

'You need to go a great deal further than the temple,' said Jysune. 'Go through the gates and back into the forest, where you can climb the trees with all your monkey friends. This city belongs to me. You are blind and deaf here, TaiGethen.' She spat on the ground. 'So much for your great skills. You didn't even hear us coming, did you?'

'A battle between us now will serve none of us when the humans arrive,' said Auum. He noted Elyss' hand gestures. Pairs of Beethans were moving up on either flank. They were surrounded. 'Sheathe your weapons and lower your bows. We are not here to take your city. We're here to save you. Help us.'

Jysune moved forward a pace. The archers either side of her tensed their bow strings.

'You're not listening to me, TaiGethen. I'm not fooled by your lies; the humans can never find us here. So you're leaving, right now. Both of you. Start walking or you—' she jabbed a finger at Auum '—will be leaving Katura alone.'

Auum stepped in front of Elyss and heard her hiss her displeasure.

'You will not threaten my people. Stand aside, Jysune. We will pray that it is not too late for you to see sense.'

'I will not tell you again,' said Jysune.

Elyss stepped out of Auum's shadow.

'We cannot leave,' she said. 'We cannot leave you alone to face what is coming.'

'Very well,' said Jysune.

She nodded. Bowstrings snapped and two arrows thudded deep into Elyss' chest, throwing her from her feet to slide across the ground until her head clipped the bench where she had just been sitting. Auum saw her come to rest and, groggy from the blow to her head, try to stem the blood flowing onto her shirt. He snapped his gaze back to Jysune. He moved.

Clarity. The blessings of Yniss must still have been surging within Auum because he saw the Beethans react as if they were wading thigh-deep through mud. Arrows passed behind him. He felt the change in the air and the hiss they made as they passed. He heard a cry of pain too – not from Elyss.

Auum crossed the space to Jysune before she could raise her sword. He leapt, kicked out with one foot and struck her on the chin, knocking her senseless. Before she hit the ground, he had both his blades in his hands. He landed between the archers and swept the swords left to right, feeling them bite deep into the first archer's gut and smash the bow from his hands.

Auum leaned his weight on his right foot and dragged the blades back right to left, higher this time tearing into the other's throat, slicing off an ear and part of his scalp. Auum was already moving left, a curving run. The first pair of flanking archers still had arrows nocked, though one also had a shaft sticking from his right thigh.

They brought their weapons to bear so slowly, to Auum's eyes. He could see their fingers begin to release. He leaned to his left, never breaking his stride, and the arrows whipped by his torso. Auum straightened. He increased his speed. Five paces from them he leapt, bringing his knees to his chest and cocking his left-hand blade high.

Auum smashed the blade into the top of his target's skull, releasing it in the same moment. He kicked out and down with both feet, feeling his soles drive the second archer's head down into his shoulders, compressing the vertebrae. He pushed against the falling body, gaining enough momentum to turn a roll in the air before landing and sprinting at the trio of archers he'd seen approaching from behind.

Auum watched them bring their bows into line and begin to draw. He pulled a jaqrui from his pouch and threw it. The crescent blade mourned away, sliced through bow and string and lodged in the central archer's mouth.

The remaining two released their arrows. Auum saw the flights so clearly. He angled his body right and let his head fall down onto his right shoulder. The shafts flew past him. The archers were fifteen paces away. Enough time to register their disbelief and begin to turn and run.

Auum swept his blade through the small of the first archer's back, took a single pace forward and cracked the heel of his left palm into the base of the other's skull, knocking him down. The Beethan's head crashed hard into a kerbstone. Blood began to flow while the body twitched its last.

Auum spun. The last pair of archers were already running for the side streets. Jysune was sitting up, her head in her hands, groggy. Auum ran at her. His feet whispered over the stones. At the last moment she looked up. Auum took his blade in both hands, crouched on his last pace and took her head from her shoulders.

The sword dropped from Auum's hands and he sprinted for Elyss. She was lying on her back, her breathing ragged. Her shirt was soaked with blood and bubbles were coming from her mouth. She coughed and cried out with the pain. Auum slid down beside her. He picked up her head in his hands, which were covered in the blood of her attackers, and cradled it in his lap.

'It's all right, Elyss,' he said. 'You're going to be all right.'

'Oh, Auum,' she said, her voice choked and desperate. 'I'm dying.'

'Ulysan! Ulysan!' roared Auum. 'No, you're not. Keep calm. We'll get you to a healer. We can fix you.'

'Liar,' she said, crying through the blood in her throat. 'Just don't leave me.'

'I'll never leave you,' said Auum. 'I love you. I love our child.'

Elyss sighed and closed her eyes. Auum swallowed hard. He prayed to Yniss to deliver her back to him. He prayed to Shorth to keep her from his embrace. She opened her eyes again.

'I will run with you again when the ancients call you, my love, my Auum,' said Elyss. 'Dream of our child. Never forget us.'

'Don't give up,' said Auum, but his voice was clogged with the sick certainty of her fate. 'Please, don't leave me here alone.'

Elyss' chest rose and then slumped. Blood came from her mouth and her chest, where the arrows must have punctured both her lungs. She stared at him and reached up a bloody hand to cup his cheek.

'A TaiGethen is never alone,' she whispered.

Her hand dropped away. A smile touched her face and her eyes closed. She sighed once more and her body relaxed. Her chest did not rise again. Auum leaned over her, the sobs shuddering through his body and the sounds of his anguish ripping from his throat however he tried to contain them.

It was all gone. The joy that had been so bright was now dark with the night. The future which had seemed so wonderful was nothing but bleached bones. The grief thundered in his head. The tears splashed on her perfect face every time he opened his eyes but hers did not flicker in response.

'Breathe,' he whispered. 'Please. Breathe.'

Auum recognised the touch of the hand on his shoulder. He rose swiftly and buried his face in Ulysan's chest, hugging the big Tai-Gethen hard. Ulysan's hands were on the back of his head and around his back. Auum heard him curse and then call the TaiGethen to muster.

Auum breathed although his lungs fought him all the way. He broke their embrace and looked up at Ulysan, seeing the fury in his face and the wobble in his chin. Ulysan glanced about the market-place and took in the scene under the flagpole.

'What happened?' he asked.

'They killed her,' said Auum. 'They shot her while she stood unarmed at my side.'

Footsteps were growing in volume with the approach of the TaiGethen.

'How—'

'All this came afterwards,' said Auum. 'They didn't give her a chance, so I did not give them one either.'

Auum knew what Ulysan was thinking. That a single TaiGethen could not bring down so many archers. Not spread out as they were, not unscathed. Auum didn't know what to say. He couldn't look at Elyss again. Not yet. Others had knelt to tend to her; to remove the arrows and clean her face and hands to make her ready.

'Beethans,' muttered Faleen.

Auum looked round. The TaiGethen were waiting for his order. But there was no more rage within him, no desire for revenge. He had already exacted that and he wondered how he had managed it. He felt a chill calm descend on him and it cleared his mind.

'No more killing,' said Auum. 'For now it is over. Tonight you need rest. We have so much to do in the days to come. Tomorrow, Pelyn and the Al-Arynaar will drive the Beethan and Tuali gangs into the forest, where they can do no more harm. And you will tear their lairs apart to find the metal we need to defend this city.

'To fail would be to shatter Elyss' dreams for our freedom, and I will not suffer that.'

'But first we will all accompany you and Elyss to the Hallows,' said Faleen. 'We are one TaiGethen.'

Auum shook his head. 'She was my light and my love. She is my burden alone as is our child sleeping within her.'

The sound of an addict crying for help echoed in the distance. The roar of furnaces and the glow of flames further broke the night. Yet the silence among the TaiGethen was abiding and, in it, Auum found his strength. He moved to Elyss and knelt by her, nodding his thanks to those who had cleaned her, and laid her arms across her stomach. He smiled; her hands were supporting their baby. So it would be as she travelled into Shorth's embrace.

Auum put one arm under her shoulders, the other under her knees and picked her up. Elyss' head fell back and her hair brushed the back of his hand. About him, the TaiGethen had knelt in prayer, each with one hand to the ground and the other open to the sky. It was a prayer of deliverance.

Auum turned a slow circle, showing Elyss to her brothers and sisters. Her family.

'You will never be alone,' he said.

He walked through the city and out into the forest.

Chapter 30

Without faith the outstretched hand seeks only to grasp at succour, never to offer it.

Auum, Arch of the TaiGethen

An hour after dawn, the whole city knew what had happened in the marketplace. Pelyn had awoken with her guts aching and her head screaming for edulis. Her bed sheets had been soaked with sweat and the stink of urine told that her bladder had failed her again as she slept.

She'd sat upright with the first light of dawn washing into her room on a wave of fresh, cool and damp air. Tulan had been there, standing by the window. He'd said nothing, just poured water into her washing bowl, indicated her clothes and her cloak and withdrawn.

Now she walked at the head of the Al-Arynaar, such as they were. They numbered thirty-seven including her. She felt sick and weak. Her leather armour and cloak were heavy, especially for her weakened body, and the sword in the scabbard at her waist had felt alien in her hand. She was not fit to be with them, let alone to lead them.

The Al-Arynaar were moving swiftly towards the Beethan ghetto. The eyes of many frightened Katurans watched them go. Away from the industry and energy palpable in the rings of the city there remained the taint of suspicion and, for Pelyn herself, a good deal of deserved contempt.

She instructed her people to offer no reaction to the taunts she would inevitably attract. With her head held high, Pelyn marched into the tight streets of the Beethan warren. The TaiGethen had reported little movement here in the small hours of the night and there was no doubt that fear of reprisals from the elven elite kept most behind their shuttered windows.

'Tuali whore!'

The shutter slammed before Pelyn could turn to look. Other shouts followed.

'Nectar hag!'

'Does the day hurt your eyes, slack face?'

'Keep marching,' said Pelyn. 'Let's face it. It's what I am.'

'What you were,' corrected Tulan.

'That is yet to be proved.' Pelyn took a deep breath. 'The craving will not die.'

Indeed it was particularly intense right now. She knew why. Edulis was manufactured here. So much nectar just within her grasp, so much of it stored behind the closed doors they walked past. She could smell it on the air, and the tip of her tongue burned with the remembered taste of it. Saliva flooded her mouth, her head beat painfully and her hands began to shake. Yet she kept walking.

The Al-Arynaar moved into the centre of the ghetto. Pelyn's vision had tunnelled and she was aware that she was beginning to gasp. Ephram cleared his throat.

'Orders, my Arch,' he whispered.

'Thank you,' said Pelyn. She called the halt. 'Put up the signs. Knock on each door. Force is sanctioned if there is any resistance. Archers to the rooftops. I want a clear path. No surprises. Not like last night.'

Pelyn had been taken aback by the TaiGethen's restraint. Though Auum had killed eight Beethans, including Jysune, no Tai had lifted a finger in further reprisal. In fact, Ulysan had been very particular when he ordered that clearing the ghettos should be carried out within the current laws of Katura. Pelyn had realised, belatedly, why it was being done this way. She signalled Tulan to make the proclamation. His was by far the loudest voice.

'By order of Pelyn, Governor of Katura, all those in breach of Article Thirteen of the laws relating to manufacture and supply of narcotics are to be removed from their homes. All possessions and land held by such parties are forfeit and to be returned to the people of Katura. All those in breach of Article Thirteen are forthwith exiled from the city and bounds of Katura. Any who return to the city will receive the death penalty.

'Let this order stand. Let it be carried out this day and all those in breach of it be taken beyond the city limits before nightfall. Any remaining within the city after the sunset must assume their lives forfeit. Any person harbouring those in breach must consider themselves in breach also, and so suffer the same penalties. That is all.'

There were a few cheers and a smattering of applause. Pelyn smiled briefly.

'Al-Arynaar!' she called. 'To work!'

The dwellings of all those accused had copies of the proclamation pinned to their front doors. Those doors not opened at the first knock were beaten down. Six Al-Arynaar worked to clear each house in sequence while the rest remained in support on the street.

There was little trouble. The archers who had escaped Auum's attack had taken the story of his speed and ferocity back to their people and none wished to suffer the same fate as their erstwhile leader. The occasional scuffle was quickly snuffed out with cudgels and the threat of blades.

It quickly became clear that many had already fled, most likely as dawn broke and the TaiGethen returned to the hall of the Al-Arynaar. Those who remained were herded into the centre of the ghetto, where they endured the abuse of those they had so recently controlled.

Pelyn let it happen. She looked at the faces of the gang. They were downcast, beaten now that Jysune had made her fatal mistake and left them pariahs, hated the most by the one group of elves they least wanted to antagonise. There was an old saying about the fate of any marked by the TaiGethen. Pelyn circled the humiliated gang, happy to remind them of it.

'*Sithiate, nun hannok thol, TaiGethen.*' *The marked shall die, never hearing the TaiGethen come.*

Ephram came to her when a hundred and seventy-eight Beethans stood within the ring of Al-Arynaar, all of them waiting for an excuse to exact revenge for Elyss' murder.

'That's the lot of them,' he said. 'And it gets better. There's so much metal here. Stills, stoves, pipework . . .'

'Good, although I'm afraid it will never be enough,' she said. 'Get them to the gates. With any luck you'll drive them onto the swords of the very humans they deny are coming. Perhaps they can take the odd one with them. Then send someone to get the collectors up here. We'll take a break, regroup, then hit the Tualis.'

'Think they'll still be waiting for us?'

'One or two will be. It's hard to leave all your power behind.'

'And how are you holding up?'

Pelyn rocked her hand from side to side. 'Up and down, you know. I could do with a rest and my head is killing me, but I'll survive. I owe it to Auum. I owe it to all of you. I've no idea why any of you are still standing by me.'

Tulan shrugged. 'Well I can't speak for the others, but as for Ephram and me, you know why, you must do. You gave us a second chance. We'll never forget that.'

Pelyn surprised herself by throwing her arms around his neck and pulling him close.

'Thank you,' she said. 'I am for ever in your debt.'

'The way I see it, we're even,' said Tulan. 'Ephram's over there. Let him take you back to the hall and I'll deal with all the Tualis. See you after lunch.'

'You won't find it hard to clear them? They're our thread, we three.'

Tulan shook his head. 'We must be able to cleanse our own or we cannot wear the Cloak. You taught me that. Now go, please.'

Ulysan, with Merrat and Grafyrre, had taken up a position from which they could see the wall of Katura. It was almost three quarters of a mile long with a single set of gates at the centre, a grand sculpted gatehouse surrounding them. All of it was made of wood, all of it vulnerable to man's magic.

The wall only stretched around the north and west sides of the city. The other two sides were open but nestled against the lake or river, which offered some protection. Ulysan was not concerned about them. The enemy had no boats since they had come inland and attack from those directions was extremely unlikely. It was possible for men to stand across the river and hurl spells into Katura, but it would be simple to evacuate everyone beyond their range. What concerned him more were the land sides.

The forest ended, barring a thin scattering of trees, some two hundred yards from the walls. And while they would line the outer edge of that open space with pits and traps, that would not hold back an army for long. Worse, to the west there was a mixture of forest, farmland and open ground in a strip three hundred yards wide which stretched all the way to the base of the western cliffs. It made them weak.

'Who's going to tell Auum there's not enough iron or steel on the whole of Calaius to do what he wants done?' said Merrat.

'I'm sure he already knows that,' said Ulysan.

'How is he?' asked Grafyrre.

Ulysan shrugged. 'I don't know. He's not returned from the Hallows. I will not rush him. We can handle things here until he gets back.'

Out here in the eaves of the forest the hammering of metal on metal was muted, through it echoed from the cliffs with enough volume to keep Tual's creatures silent.

'It doesn't matter how thin they make it, I can only see us patching the gate and a couple of hundred yards of wall either side. And that's the absolute maximum we'll manage.' Merrat shook his head.

'Stone,' said Grafyrre.

'What?'

'I know it was dismissed last night but we can't ignore it. It's stronger than wood and they have some cement here, though none of them are great masons. If we don't have the metal, we'll have to cement and dry-stone the gaps.' Grafyrre pointed at the open western edge. 'Particularly over there.'

'It won't withstand a barrage,' said Merrat. 'But at least it won't burn or freeze. Ulysan?'

Ulysan didn't respond at once but began to trot back towards the city.

'We'll have to take the trap detail for now, and perhaps some of the food gatherers too. With the quarry across the lake progress will be slow, but I don't think we have much choice.'

'I'll oversee it,' said Grafyrre.

'Thank you,' said Ulysan. He looked over his shoulder into the forest. 'Take your time, old friend.'

Auum had long since finished weeping over Elyss' body. He had prayed into the early hours of the morning before leaving the Hallows to let Tual's denizens begin the reclamation of the body. Elyss lay among those who had slain her, but Auum felt no anger. Her soul had departed to the embrace of Shorth with that of their child. Though their bodies lay near to hers, the Beethans' souls would travel a very different path.

'The soul continues; the body must return to that from which it came,' said Auum.

He had watched dawn break and had heard the city come alive to his orders. He took the opportunity to thank Yniss for the strength of the TaiGethen but he was not ready to return to the city just yet. He found a stream and washed himself and his clothes. Above, rain clouds gathered so he did not dress again; instead standing in a small clearing to let Gyal's tears bless his body.

Auum felt calm. He dressed in his wet clothes and put his back to a banyan, chewing on a root tuber and a sweet herb while he replayed, over and over, the events immediately after Elyss had been shot. He had assumed rage had driven him but he was wrong.

Something more basic than rage had aided him in those moments – and it had only been for moments. It was a survival instinct, a primal reaction to protect himself and his loved ones.

It had given him the utmost clarity of thought and tuned his senses more keenly than any other moment in his long life. It had given him greater speed of limb too, but the true difference had been in his reaction time. At any other time in his life he would have marvelled at what he had achieved. Today he could only regret the necessity.

But through the confusion of emotions Auum could accept one thing. In that state he was a powerful weapon, and he presumed every TaiGethen had the ability to reach it. Yet he had no idea how to bring it out, how to trigger it, how to control it or how to shut it off.

Auum looked into the heavens and held a hand up, palm open to the sky. He placed the other in the mud by the side of the stream.

'Yniss, hear your servant, Auum. You have shown me a great gift yet the price I have paid for it makes me wonder at its worth. If it is your will that I have my eyes opened to what I can become yet must continue to seek that ascension, then I accept it.

'But I am troubled, Yniss. The tasks you lay before me and before all elves are stern indeed. The gift of clarity . . . You have shown me the dance but have not taught me the steps. It could alter the battle and allow us to win against the forces that will range against us.

'All I ask, my Lord Yniss, is for a sign, a way towards under-standing how I might defeat our enemies and help the elves to glory in your name once more.

'I, Auum, ask this of you.'

Auum kept his head bowed and his eyes closed for a few moments. When he opened them, it was to see a pair of feet wrapped in tatty leather boots – TaiGethen boots. He let his gaze travel up the un-kempt clothing to the face and its wild eyes.

'I seriously doubt that you are any sort of sign for the good,' he said. 'Leave me.'

'I heard your pain and I heard your prayers. I know what you lost and I grieve with you. But I also know what you achieved, and I can help. Have you forgotten how fast I used to be? How easy I found it to best you when we fought on the way back to Ysundeneth?'

Auum stared at him and an icy shiver ran down his back, slow as a single drip of water.

'Then sit and speak to me. Unless this has to do with magic, in which case run back to your acolytes because I have no more use for you.'

Takaar sat.

Chapter 31

Question: Which is more deadly, a slighted ClawBound or a wronged TaiGethen? Answer: A yellow-backed tree frog.

Elven playground joke

This far from Ysundeneth Hynd needed other mages to lend him their strength to help maintain his focus. But none of them had to endure the dual sledgehammers of pain and extraordinary nausea during and after the Communion.

When he'd stopped being sick and drunk the contents of both his and Jeral's water skins, he looked reluctantly up at Ishtak, who was standing over him, that ridiculous sneer on his face.

'I said I'd come when I was sure I wouldn't puke on the high and mighty,' Hynd said.

'But he might still puke on you, Ishtak,' said Jeral. 'Which would do wonders for your body odour.'

It was dusk and the march had ceased for the day. They were only four days from the city. Mages, high above the canopy, had seen it in the distance, and the news that their goal was in sight had completely changed the army's mood.

Most of the humans were already feeling a little more relaxed, now it was evident that the TaiGethen had been driven away and had too little strength to attempt another ambush. Knowing the end of their march was in sight and there were a load of Sharps to take their frustrations out on had led to something akin to a party atmosphere.

Laughter and songs ran up and down the long line of the camp. Swords were cleaned and sharpened with renewed vigour and sparring had been reintroduced to sharpen reactions and remind them all of their drills, defence and attack. Bets were being laid about the length of the battle, the number of Sharps that would feel the edge of any given blade and the number of females the more repulsive soldiers could take on their first night of conquest.

The news had also been the signal for the generals to move back up to the head of the line, puffed up by the glory of their imminent victory and striding about with their heads high, safe beneath multiple shields.

It was exactly what Lockesh had predicted would happen. The moment the generals returned, Jeral and the rest of Dead Company had become the sacrificial lambs again and, time after time, were sent out to scout the paths ahead and any potential ambush points. Happily, Jeral's stock was high enough for mages from other companies to accompany them, providing the cover Dead Company so sorely lacked.

Most assumed that Loreb, in particular, wanted Jeral dead. Bets had been taken on that outcome too. The cheers that greeted Jeral's safe return were getting louder and Loreb's frown progressively deeper. Lockesh had warned him that there would be more direct action, and Jeral was getting very jumpy over the unfairness of it all. Hynd's news was about to put all of it in perspective.

'You will attend immediately,' snapped Ishtak.

'Or what? You'll have to fondle his balls for him?' Jeral was on his feet. 'Ystormun chose Hynd to receive the Communion. Hynd. That makes him more important than you. So you will *wait*.'

Hynd waved vaguely in Ishtak's direction and dragged himself to his feet.

'I'm ready as I'll ever be.'

'I'll come with you,' said Jeral.

'Your presence is—'

'Required.' said Jeral. 'This is my lead mage. Lead on, Ishy.'

'Stop calling me that, Captain, or I'll have you up on a charge.'

'The moment you stop being an utter wanker, I'll be happy to oblige.'

'Childish,' Hynd muttered as they began to weave the short distance through the line to the command post.

'One thing always bothered me,' said Jeral. 'Why did Ystormun pick you? No offence, but you're just a military mage.'

'Actually, Ystormun didn't pick me; Lockesh did.'

'Why?'

'Can you see Lockesh puking his guts up after every Communion? Bloody hell, Jeral, he's practically part of the cadre himself. If there's anything unpleasant like that he chooses a lackey for it. This time I got the poison dart in my arse.'

Jeral laughed, and even Ishtak had something approximating a smile on his face. All traces of it had gone by the time they reached the command post though. Ishtak waved Hynd on and stood in front of Jeral.

'Better let him have this one,' said Hynd. 'Tell you later.'

Hynd wandered over to Lockesh with a few choice words from Jeral speeding him on his way. Ordinarily Hynd would have been smiling, but the message he carried occasioned no humour. Seeing him, Lockesh snapped his fingers and beckoned him to hurry.

'You were summoned on the instant, not at your leisure,' said Lockesh.

'Forgive me my lord, Generals, but Communion over this distance leaves me temporarily incapacitated.'

Pindock waved a hand impatiently. 'Just give us your report.'

Hynd took a deep breath.

'Ystormun is under increasing pressure. He wants you to know that the cadre continue to demand this battle to be won quickly and with minimal casualties. Indeed their demands grow more urgent by the hour. The battle for Triverne is near. The cadre cannot hold back its enemies with diplomacy for much longer.

'The Sundering is almost upon us.'

Loreb took a long swallow from the bottle of wine in his hand. Pindock went even paler and sat heavily on a log, wiping at his face. Killith grumbled in his throat and pushed a hand through his greasy grey hair. Lockesh merely glared at Hynd.

'Is that all?'

'Yes, my Lord Lockesh. It was a short but pointed conversation.'

'What did you say to him?'

'Nothing but to assure him I would pass on his words exactly as I had received them, which I have done. I have left nothing out.'

Lockesh inclined his head a fraction.

'Your sacrifice is noted,' he said. 'You are certain he gave you no specific orders and mentioned no one by name?'

'Absolutely certain,' said Hynd, comfortable to pass on the whole truth.

'Remind us,' said Killith. 'What's the worst-case scenario for you mages if and when the Sundering occurs?'

Lockesh cast his gaze heavenwards.

'The Sundering is the once-theoretical-now-disastrously-probable shattering of the Triverne stone, the heart of magic on Balaia. You know that each mage uses mana which is channelled and focused through that stone. That's true wherever we are in the world, whenever we create a casting. So what do you think might happen if the stone shatters?'

Pindock spoke through trembling lips.

'It would be considerably harder to cast spells, I should imagine,' he said, plainly hoping that it would be a great deal less serious than that.

'No,' said Lockesh, stalking towards the career politician in soldier's clothing. 'Until another stone – another heart, if you like – was fashioned, it would prevent us from casting spells altogether. It would render us powerless.'

'We are inside a sound bubble right now, aren't we?' said Loreb. Lockesh simply sighed in his direction. 'Good. Because this news mustn't reach the army. That means you, Hynd, can't tell your pet a word of it. I will kill you, personally, should this news leak out. With your permission of course, Lord Lockesh.'

'Granted,' said Lockesh. 'Hynd, wait for me. Say nothing to anyone. Particularly, as the general says, to Captain Jeral. I will speak to you when we are done here.'

Hynd bowed and left the command post. He was shaking. During and after the Communion, the words had sounded like a death knell in his head but hadn't truly sunk in. Now they had, they terrified him. He kept sampling the mana flow to convince himself it was still there.

He couldn't begin to imagine what it would be like to be denied it, to reach for it only to find it absent. Like death, perhaps. It would be an unbearable loss, anyway. He hugged himself, head down, hands rubbing at his upper arms. A vague sense of nausea was building inside him. He sampled the mana flow again. Was it as strong and certain as before?

Hynd stopped abruptly, just a few paces from where Jeral waited impatiently, clearing his throat noisily. To build the shape for a spell and to cast it only for the mana flow to disperse without warning . . . Gods on a pyre, the effects would be disastrous, catastrophic even, and certainly explosive. Hynd shuddered and shook his head, trying to believe it wouldn't actually happen.

'Lost your way? I'm over here.'

Hynd looked up. Jeral was waving at him and had spoken as if he'd been hollering at him from a long distance.

'Something on my mind,' said Hynd, trying to relax.

'Well you look really jittery, if that helps,' said Jeral, walking over to him.

'Not in the least.' Hynd indicated they leave the column and he sat with his back to a tree, ignoring the dampness which spread through the seat of his trousers. Jeral squatted next to him. 'Funny, isn't it? When we started this march, I'd have cleared this whole space before sitting down and looked up until my neck hurt to make sure no snakes or spiders were going to drop on my head. Now look at me.'

'Yeah, you're a man the Sharps look up to now. But never mind that. Spill. What's the big news that's got you so twitchy?'

'I can't tell you.'

'Sure you can.'

'I've got orders.'

'Yes,' said Jeral. 'From me. So what did the old skeleton tell you? Whatever it was, those morons in charge must have reacted badly to it if you're anything to go by. Come on. I'm not your captain; I'm your friend. The one who clears up your vomit, remember?'

'I can't tell you,' said Hynd. He was fidgeting and couldn't stop himself. He nodded back towards the command post. 'Orders from a higher authority. He wants me to wait for him, so you might hear something from him.'

'Something major, though, right?'

'Right.'

They didn't have to wait long. With a stride that indicated his anger, Lockesh marched out of the command post, barking at soldiers to get out of his path. He beckoned Hynd and Jeral to him with a curt gesture and carried on walking, moving further from the column and out towards the pickets, whose firelight was bright in the deepening gloom.

'Those utter idiots,' he muttered. 'Right, Hynd. They think I am ordering you to try to commune with Ystormun again, to get clarification. Never mind that Ystormun chooses when to conduct Communion; their ignorance suits us for now. You and I will concoct a conversation over a bowl of whatever revolting broth is on the go.

'Jeral . . . You've told the good captain nothing, I presume?'

'No, he bloody hasn't said a thing,' said Jeral.

'Just as well.' Lockesh was silent for a moment. Hynd felt him constructing a spell shape and then casting with a circling of his right index finger in front of his face. 'Right. Jeral, I am going to entrust you with knowledge that, should it become public, will bring about your immediate, untimely and extremely painful death. Do you understand?'

'Yes, my lord.'

'Good. Ystormun has sent word that the Sundering might happen earlier than expected but given us no exact time for it. Suffice to say it could happen at any time and there is unlikely to be any warning that it is coming. You understand the difficulties that will cause, I take it?'

'Hynd has explained it to me before, my lord.'

'I'm sure he has,' said Lockesh. 'Sadly, whatever he told you was no idle speculation. As you can imagine, the prospect of losing all magical support has left our glorious leaders running in little circles of panic and bluster. It is also, already, leading them to make all sorts of rash decisions about our plan of attack that will be the death of us all.

'You've heard the mages' reports about the position of the city and its angles of approach. Soon you will have more information about its defensive capabilities. I need you to start developing tactics that can be effectively deployed assuming you have no magical resources at all on which to draw. And I also want plans for defending helpless mages from marauding TaiGethen. In fact, as far as I'm concerned, protecting me is far more important than invading any city.

'Work with Hynd on this. Develop plans which include very limited spell possibilities too . . . basic shields, walls and so on, perhaps – simple and quick castings. Just in case, you understand.'

Lockesh stopped and turned to face them both. Hynd should have been afraid but for some reason he felt a thrill that he shared with Jeral. From the certainty of failure had leapt the possibility of success, as long as his friend was in charge.

'The one piece of good news is that you, Jeral, are off their hit list for now. They need every capable soldier they can muster. Nonetheless, Hynd, you must not slacken in your efforts to keep him alive.

'The potential of a Sundering is going to make the generals rush in when they should wait and watch. They will attempt to seize victory in far too short a space of time and in doing so will make mistakes the enormity of which will be studied by students of war for generations to come. When those orders are given, you need to be ready to step in, Captain Jeral. If your stock is as high as I think it is, men will follow you rather than their orders, although that situation might not come about in an instant.' Lockesh licked his lips. 'And I will back you too, when the moment is right.'

Hynd flinched. That was something he had thought never to hear. He swapped glances with Jeral. For once there was no quick riposte waiting. Jeral understood the situation.

'Thank you, my lord,' he said.

'Trust no one. Tell no one,' said Lockesh. 'We risk much by doing this, should we have to, but we risk even more by not being prepared when the time comes. Do not fail me. I will not die here. Not for you and certainly not for our useless trio of quill-wavers.'

'I won't let you down.'

Lockesh nodded and his face relaxed. For the first time he displayed concern for those whose lives he risked alongside his.

'Look, Jeral. I'm asking a great deal of you, and even if we succeed here your future will be uncertain. I can protect you from some things but not from the machinations of the army. When we get home, they'll either promote you or they'll execute you.'

'Some choice, eh?' said Jeral and a smile touched his lips.

Lockesh nodded. 'Welcome to the world of Triverne politics.'

Chapter 32

There is nothing beyond the Claw.

Serrin of the ClawBound

Auum was gone for three days, and in that time, while he wouldn't say he came to understand Takaar, he did regain some small measure of respect for him.

Auum had watched Takaar go before returning to the city. Leaving the eaves of the forest, he saw and heard the work going on, and while he was lifted by the industry, he knew in his heart that it could never be enough. He saw Ulysan near the city gates and trotted past teams of elves digging pits on the open ground, past Pelyn drilling a fledgling militia in defensive sword moves and others practising with bows, spears, staves and pretty much any other weapon they could find.

Auum stepped aside to let carts carrying fruit, game, vegetables and herbs into the city, but his heart sank when he looked at the walls. The metal plating was fractured and thin. Stones, some cemented, some laid dry, had been hammered into place to augment the metal and protect the vulnerable wood. The covering, such as it was, only stretched across a third of the walls, and so far there was nothing to protect them from an attack across the open ground to the west.

Ulysan was directing another piece of riveted plate into position.

'Ulysan,' said Auum. 'Bless you for all you have done. I'm sorry I was gone so long. And thank you for checking on me.'

Ulysan enveloped him in a bear hug, eventually pushing him back to look into his face.

'A TaiGethen is never alone. You chose an unlikely partner for your prayers,' he said. 'Are you strong?'

Auum put a hand to his chest and felt his throat tighten. 'Elyss and our baby are safe here with me for now. Grief will have to wait. Tell me where we stand.'

'In all but one area, we are ahead of where we need to be. Unfortunately, that one area is the wall. We have neither the raw materials nor the skills to forge enough plate to cover the walls as you wanted. We have been to every building in the city and into the mines as well. Everything we have is waiting for the smiths' forges and hammers. They work day and night. There is no rest for anyone.

'We are ferrying stone from the quarry too, but it is a lengthy process and we will soon have to begin cutting more, unless we start digging up the foundations of the city. We are already taking up all the cobbled streets.'

'Stone will blow apart,' said Auum. 'Their ice can conquer cement.'

Ulysan shrugged. 'It is all we have and it is better than wood.'

'What about the western ground? It is an open wound. We have to block it somehow.'

Ulysan bit his lip. 'We have a plan, but it's a risky one.'

He pointed up to the head of the cliffs, hundreds of feet above the city. Auum could see elves moving up there and, now he focused, he could hear their grunts and shouts of effort.

'What's up there?'

'We've brought boulders over from the other side of the city near the quarry and got them up there with rope, pulley and muscle. Some of them are the size of twenty of you. Last count we had seven of them. Four more will be in place today, all ready to tip.'

Auum let his gaze travel down the cliff face and into the open ground below with its sporadic patches of forest, and on towards the western wall around Katura.

'The rain run-off will have eroded the cliff face over time. It looks loose all the way down.' Auum pointed while he spoke. Indeed the evidence of previous rockfalls lay all over the ground. 'Boulders of that size will start an avalanche, which could have enough momentum to sweep through the city walls. I don't know, Ulysan.'

'I said it was risky. The way we've positioned the boulders means the trees will limit the risk to the city. I've agonised over this, Merrat, Grafyrre and Faleen too. We don't think we can bring enough stone over in time to fortify the wall and felling trees to make a barricade only lessens our defensive advantage – and will be to no avail against their magic. We'd welcome another option.'

Auum imagined the avalanche and the sheer destructive power it represented was beguiling even though once started it would be completely beyond their control. Such a risk, but such potential too; and they were nothing if not desperate for anything that might give them an edge.

'When did you plan to release the boulders?'

'Today. We thought that if the worst happens, that gives us some time to rebuild, and to organise the rubble into a solid wall.'

Auum raised his eyebrows. 'I think that's too early – you're thinking too defensively. The enemy will see that ground as a weakness. They'll attack it, I'm sure. Let them come, let them fill that space. Then release your boulders. No magical shield is going to withstand such an avalanche. Remember, we have to win this fight, not just fend off defeat for as long as we can.'

Ulysan smiled. 'I'm glad you're back.'

'So am I.'

'Aren't you going to tell me, then?'

'Tell you what?'

'Whatever you and Takaar spoke about for three days on end.'

Auum thought for a moment, wondered if telling Ulysan would inspire him or undermine him. He banked on it being inspiring.

'There's another state of combat. Takaar discovered it while he was exiled and Elyss' murder cast me into it. It was extraordinary, Ulysan. I could see everything so clearly. My enemies were ponderous and I was so . . . precise. But it's a state that can't be taught. It must be found.

'When all this is over, we'll have the time to seek that part of our minds that gifts us this skill. To my great regret we cannot hope to learn it before the humans reach us. But for those of us that live through this, there is so much more for the TaiGethen to experience.'

'So don't die, all right?'

Ulysan regarded him for a moment. 'That was unexpected to say the least. You're going to have to tell me more.'

'Later. In private. Don't say anything to the others; it could be a distraction and Yniss knows we cannot afford that.'

'I'll find you,' said Ulysan.

'I'd be very disappointed if you didn't.'

The tracking cells had reached Katura bringing news that every soul already knew. The enemy campfires had been visible for a couple of nights now, and the sound of song and the thump of thousands of feet had echoed along the valleys since the day before. The enemy would reach them before nightfall.

Auum, along with the defenders and the population of Katura, had watched the mages fly overhead out of bowshot range. Sending abuse and threats skywards had eased the tension, and a sudden downpour had brought cheers when it sent the mages scurrying back to their camp.

Auum hoped they had seen enough to give them pause, and to hurry their decision to attack across the western space. He had stood on the gatehouse roof all day while final preparations and patches were made to the walls. Below him, the briefings and drills had become dress rehearsals for the battle to come.

Everyone knew their post. Everyone had their tasks to perform. The great question was whether the unskilled, utterly inexperienced elves would stand when the spells rained down and the enemy soldiers charged the city.

They had a pitiful number of skilled defenders. Just twelve full TaiGethen cells along with Auum and Ulysan, making thirty-eight warriors in all. Plus the hundred and eighteen Al-Arynaar who followed Pelyn. She hadn't the fitness for a day's fight and her eyes betrayed the depth of her enduring desire for edulis.

More than two thousand had been drilled as militia and some had proved themselves capable, but the raw fact was they were not soldiers. They were youngsters, or old *ulas* and *iads* . . . plus farmers, fishers and potters. Hardly a formidable force, and while some had the ability to command, Al-Arynaar were at the head of most. The rest of Katura's twenty-thousand-strong population would have to fight with tooth and nail if the time came.

Only the hunters gave Auum cheer. There were fifty of them, all with good skills with bow and spear. He had entrusted Takaar's tree frog poison to them, with a roving brief to shoot down as many of the enemy as they could, whenever they could get away a certain shot.

With the retreat of the enemy mages, he had advised everyone to rest. To gather together if they so desired, to eat and drink and tell stories. Or to visit a temple for quiet prayer, to walk the streets free of the threat of thread gangs or to simply spend time in the arms of those they loved and would die to protect.

Auum, though, was missing more than Elyss. He scanned the

forest to the north-east and the skies above it, watching for a sign he was beginning to lose hope would come. When Ulysan came to bring him to eat, he refused.

'Where is Corsaar?' he asked. 'Where is the Shorthian army?'

The following dawn he had part of his answer, and with it an end to any real hope. Mist hung over Katura as the sun came over the horizon, lifting sluggishly and only dispersed by a heavy downpour that in turn gave way to hot sunshine.

With the sky and horizon clear, Auum could see mages to the north-east and knew the second human army was only a day from their gates. Before them, emerging from the eaves of the forest to stand on the borders of the trap-strewn open ground, no more than two hundred yards away, was the Ysundeneth army.

Pelyn was standing on the gatehouse roof with Auum. So were Ulysan, Merrat and Grafyrre. The walkway behind the rampart was crowded with Katurans, as was every vantage point facing the forest.

The humans just kept coming, forming up in neat, professional ranks as they did. Mages flew overhead again, inviting the elves to look upon their death. Thousands of men all armed and armoured where, for the most part, the defenders wore everyday clothes and carried wooden clubs or farming implements.

Auum was taken back to that day on Hausolis when, standing on the Tul Kenerit ramparts, he had seen the Garonin horde emerge from the mists they had summoned to fog their approach. That day when Takaar's courage had failed.

'No wonder he left,' said Pelyn, mirroring his thoughts. 'How could he have faced this all over again?'

'He couldn't,' said Auum. 'But we need him nonetheless.'

A murmur swept along the rampart. The Katurans' courage was wavering and the enemy were still massing before them. Around two and a half thousand would have to emerge before they were done, and the sheer number was terrifying.

'We have to hold them,' said Auum.

The enemy were chanting and shouting, clashing their blades together and stamping their feet. It was an ugly sound, powerful and discomforting, and it was having the desired effect.

'Sing,' said Ulysan. ' "The Triumph of Verendii" maybe. Everyone knows that one.'

Auum nodded. 'Yes. Let's show these barbarians how beautiful the voice can really be.'

Those gathered on the gatehouse began to sing. Quickly, the words were taken up to either side of them, the tune one full of energy and pace. It was a song of victory.

'On ruined ground on shivered rock Verendii stood alone.
His enemies surrounded him, his courage was of stone.
Where blade did slice and arrow sing, Verendii walked so tall
He moved with such a grace and speed, he killed them one and all.
Verendii, o, of sword and bow, you stand as one alone
Verendii o, ne'er brought so low but died so far from home
Victory, great victory, the elven nation breathes
Victory, great victory, Verendii died for us.'

The song rolled out across the open ground and Auum watched the enemy fall silent. Few would have understood the words but their power remained undimmed. The last words echoed from the cliffs and the defenders roared a cheer.

'Well done, Ulysan,' said Auum.

Ulysan gripped his arm and pointed to the north-eastern edge of the open ground. Moving fast and low they came, spread wide to make harder targets for arrow or spell, haring up to the river and splashing through the shallows. Driving across the deeps they swam with measured strokes, heedless of any predator. Back onto dry land with no pause for breath, they charged for the gates.

'Corsaar,' Auum breathed and then he filled his lungs to shout. 'Come on, you old dog! Show them some speed!'

Quickly, the crowd on the ramparts joined in. Corsaar's name and those of his Tais were hollered out. Every shout demanded greater speed, to show their heels to the enemy or to howl an insult at the snail-like humans. They came across the open ground, leaping over traps and tripwires, skirting stakes and pits.

The response from the enemy was immediate. Mages in their wake, soldiers moved forward into the open ground but stopped short of the first run of traps.

'Corsaar!' roared Auum though his voice was surely lost. 'Casting! Casting behind you!'

Corsaar and his five ran on. Three hundred paces from the gates, they found the main trail and sprinted along it. Ulysan called for the gates to be opened. Auum stared out at the humans wondering why they hadn't—

Six, seven, eight bright blue orbs tracked across the sky, trailing smoke. They fizzed and crackled, white light like spears of lightning flashing within them. They travelled horribly fast, hunting down their quarry. Auum was standing dead in line with their path. He watched the orbs rush in, each one the size of a boulder. He could feel the heat begin to grow, even from his position on the gatehouse roof. The cheers along the ramparts trailed off. Elves pointed, shouting warnings. Corsaar looked over his shoulder.

Auum heard his desperate order.

'Split left! Split right!'

The orbs crashed into the ground in a flare of blue light and the explosions rattled the walls. Waves of fire consumed the ground, scorching grass and threatening some of the traps hidden with it. Smoke billowed and was blown away by the force of the blasts. Auum looked out to the scorched black and burning earth. Of Corsaar and his people, six priceless TaiGethen, there was no sign at all.

Katura fell silent.

The sound of cheering and celebration was deafening. Next to Jeral, Loreb was applauding heartily, and both Killith and Pindock were laughing. Lockesh had not even broken a smile.

'Good shooting,' said Jeral.

Loreb turned to him.

'Let's ram this victory home. We will suffer no delay. Captain Jeral, lead the advance to within spell range of those walls. The barrage is to begin as soon as you reach your positions. Concentrate on opening up that western corner. I want you leading an attack along the open side before midday.'

'With respect, General, I urge caution. Your plan is sound, but that is too simple a route to victory for the Sharps not to have planned for it. We should scout the open ground before marching in. Their ambush surely taught us that much could be hidden in there. Attacking will lead us into a trap. We should wait for the balance of the army to join us.'

'Are you questioning my order?' Loreb's face had turned red and his voice was rising in volume. 'Well, Captain?'

'I am offering an alternative.'

'There is no time for alternatives,' said Loreb, his words ground out between his teeth. 'The barrage must begin immediately. Order the advance.'

Hynd saw Jeral look up at Lockesh, whose expression was stoney.

'With the greatest respect,' said Jeral, 'I cannot risk my men like that.'

'How dare you,' grated Loreb. The three generals gathered like vultures over imminent carrion. 'You coward. Consider yourself relieved of your command and under arrest. Court martial at sundown and execution at midnight.'

Jeral's restraint was commendable. He unbuckled his sword belt and handed it to Loreb, who tossed it to the ground. Before walking away, the sneering Ishtak as his guard, he nodded to Hynd.

'Take care out there. Hang back.'

Loreb squared his shoulders.

'I think I'll do this myself,' he said.

He moved before the waiting ranks, opened his mouth and used his booming voice to considerable effect.

'Companies One through Six. Forward barrage positions! March.'

Company captains roared orders. Three ranks of soldiers moved forward with two ranks of mages behind them. Hynd moved off as well, behind Dead Company, urging them to fight for Jeral, for honour and for tomorrow. He began to prepare an orb casting, aiming to land it behind the walls and create whatever mayhem he could. He fought his fear that the flow might gutter and die on him as he cast. If it did, the backwash from his spell would incinerate him. And he envied the mages around him their ignorance of the risk they were taking with every casting.

Loreb was positioned in the midst of the front rank. Hynd could see him glorying in his decision, his men behind him and a massive blow about to be struck which would further his personal aspirations. He swaggered through the dense thigh-high grass, calling out the castings and marking the targets.

Hynd imagined rather than heard the crack of wood, but he quite clearly saw the branch that snapped up from the grass under Loreb's foot. It had a slice of tree trunk laid with spikes lashed to it, which struck Loreb square in the face, its momentum slamming the general's twitching body flat to the ground beneath it.

For a heartbeat there was no reaction. The soldiers continued to march on. Then there was a scream from the flank as men disappeared into a pit, their shrieks cut off by the spikes lining the bottom. Closer to him, three were caught when two tensioned branches snapped together, mowing the grass down in twin semi-circles before smashing their ankles to fragments.

Panic struck as the front rank halted but those behind them did not. The order to halt rang out, but not before more were pushed stumbling on to their deaths. Hynd glanced into a pit where three men lay impaled on spikes.

'Fall back! Fall back!'

Soldiers turned and ran back to the sanctuary of the army. Hynd walked more slowly, trying to retrace his footsteps, suddenly mistrustful of the ground and what lurked there. There were screams for help from the impaled and the broken, and word of Loreb's death swept through the army like a monsoon wind. Two and a half thousand men who had been so confident of victory a moment ago shuffled away from the grass in fear.

Pindock had disappeared. Killith stood gesturing hopelessly, his mouth open but silent. Only Lockesh retained any sense.

'Mages to me! Let's show our dim-brained soldiers the way ahead. Hynd, get yourself to the centre; you're in charge. Burn the grass. Burn it all to ash.'

Auum watched the fire eat away the grass, exposing and destroying the remaining traps. It was an effective and quick solution. Smoke billowed into the sky where clouds were gathering but would not douse the flames before they had burned themselves out. Yet it was still a victory of sorts, and Pelyn had been quick to make sure every defender knew it. One senior human had perished and the stamina of a good many mages was being exhausted with the fires.

It was good but they needed more, much more.

Well before midday the city approaches held no more secrets. Auum watched the army mass to advance once more, and this time there was little they could do but shelter and pray.

'Ulysan. Sound the general alarm. Clear the streets, clear the gate zone and the wall approaches. Ready the fire teams and stretcher parties. Who's taking the wall and gatehouse?'

Ulysan gestured below. Well over a hundred elves had been painted and garbed as TaiGethen. Auum smiled. They were a good imitations, good enough to fool the humans anyway.

'They are brave. It's going to be hard up here. Make sure they remember their cover positions.'

'Consider it done.'

'Then meet me at the western corner. We need to be ready.'

Ulysan gripped Auum's upper arms. 'This is it, my Arch. The battle that will determine our fate is here.'

Auum returned the gesture. 'And while we stand, while Elyss looks down on our beating hearts, there is still hope.'

Orders carried on the light breeze. Behind Auum, Katura braced itself. Doors and shutters were fastened. Buckets and butts were checked for the hundredth time. The streets emptied. Elves stood proud and tall along the walls. Auum climbed down into the gatehouse proper and looked across the scorched ground.

The enemy marched. Their mages prepared.

The battle of Katura had begun.

Chapter 33

Nothing compares to the joy of union unless it is the grief of parting. As Bound elves, we are blessed and cursed many times. The Ynissul are immortal. The lifespan of a Claw is terrifyingly brief.

Serrin of the ClawBound

Nerille fastened her shutters and hurried down the stairs. She was shaking. Her sons were gone, two with Takaar and one to the ramparts dressed as a TaiGethen. Ulysan had told them if they took cover when the castings hit they should be all right, but the wall seemed a flimsy barrier.

Nerille had been in Ysundeneth when man's magic had been unleashed for the first time. She would never forget the cries she had heard or the devastation she had witnessed that morning; and she was about to live through it all again.

She had done everything she could to help and was stationed with the quartermasters, handing out rations and keeping note of stock levels. Yesterday she'd seen the masses of food that had been brought in from the forest and the lake. She didn't think the battle would last long enough for them to consume it all.

She'd overheard TaiGethen talking to the Al-Arynaar: the humans were not interested in a siege. This fight could well be finished in a day.

Downstairs, in the gloom behind her shuttered windows and with the armoured city wall just across the street from her, she paused to listen. Not even an addict was crying out. Those poor souls had been removed to the lakeside to fend for themselves while the capable worked for the TaiGethen and the wonderful Auum, who had suffered so much.

Straining her ears, she could hear the approaching army and a smattering of conversation from the ramparts. But otherwise the city was silent. Thousands upon thousands waited for their chance to fight. They'd all do well to pray.

A glint from the plate set on the small table by the front door caught Nerille's eye. Her heart tumbled. It was her son's charm, a silver pendant of Gyal blessing the forest with rain.

'Jio, you idiot,' she muttered.

His courage would falter without it. She snatched it up and ran outside, heading for the gatehouse and access to the ramparts. The street behind the wall was completely deserted but the sound of her people up on the wall was loud enough for her to know she was not alone.

Nerille trotted to the main road and to the gatehouse door, pulling it open. She darted inside, and straight into Auum's arms. He caught her easily and looked at her, a moment's confusion clearing quickly.

'You can't be here,' he said, his face bright with tension. 'Head to the stores; you'll be safe there.'

'I have to give this to Jio,' said Nerille, holding out the pendant. 'He'll be lost without it.'

'Where is he?' asked Auum.

'On the rampart, dressed like one of you. He said he was going to be positioned towards the river.'

'I'll take it to him,' said Auum.

'No,' said Nerille. 'He is my son and this is my chance to help him. I need to do this. I need to look into his eyes and know he will live.'

Auum kissed her forehead. 'And it is your city. I understand. Go, but stay low and do not linger. Listen to the callers, and push hard into the wall if the alarm is given. Don't take any chances.'

'Bless you,' she said.

Auum let her go and she made for the ladder up to the first level. He spoke just before she disappeared from his view.

'Don't you dare get hurt,' he said. 'I'm doing this for you.'

She smiled at him and climbed the last few rungs. City folk and Al-Arynaar looked at her. Some protested, but most were only concerned with what was coming towards them and turned away.

'Jio,' she said. 'Where is Jio?'

An Al-Arynaar turned to her. It was Pelyn. Nerille caught herself before she gasped. Pelyn was sweating heavily, but not from the humid afternoon heat or from the weight of her cloak. Her eyes were sunken back into her head and her face was terribly pale. She looked fit to drop and was leaning on the gatehouse wall.

'He is halfway along towards the river, but you shouldn't risk going out there.'

'I have to,' she said.

Pelyn merely nodded. Nerille passed her on the way to the rampart and stopped to rest a hand on her arm.

'How many days has it been now?'

Pelyn managed a smile but it was brief. 'Eleven. It seems like a thousand years.'

'You will break it,' said Nerille. 'You have the strength, I know it.'

'Thank you,' Pelyn whispered.

Nerille hurried out onto the rampart. Her eye was drawn to the blackened field below her and her breath caught in her throat. There they were, thousands of men all bent on her destruction. They came on with such precision, the soldiers with bows and swords ready and the mages behind them.

They marched in three sections: one directly at the gates, the second to the west and the open ground they all feared would be their undoing, and the third going straight for Jio and his friends. Each section boasted hundreds of soldiers and more mages than she had ever seen gathered in one place, not even during the dark days of the fall of Ysundeneth.

They couldn't defeat this army. It was going to be a slaughter.

'You're not just going to stand there all day, are you?'

Nerille flinched and came back to herself. She looked round. Pelyn was at the gatehouse door.

'No, I—'

'Hurry,' she said. 'And then get to safety. There's not much time.'

Nerille nodded, sucked in a deep breath and hurried along the rampart, asking after Jio every pace of the way. The rampart was narrow and crowded and her progress was slow. Ladders leaning against it every thirty paces or so merely added to the hazards she faced. She had to pick her way past swords and stands of arrows, apologising with every breath.

Suddenly, there he was. Standing tall, playing the part of a mighty TaiGethen, showing no fear to the enemy below. On the field below them, an order brought the army to a halt.

'Jio!'

Her voice carried loud in the sudden silence. Dozens of heads turned to her and Jio's jaw dropped in surprise.

'Gyal's breath, Mother, what are you doing here?' he hissed, blushing scarlet and glancing at the smiles already cracking the faces of his friends despite the horror about to be unleashed on them.

'Leave the house without cleaning your teeth, did you, Jio?' said one.

'Or perhaps Mummy is bringing you some dry clothes,' said another.

'I know. You left your lunch on the kitchen table, didn't you?'

Raucous laughter, over-loud with nerves, rattled along the parapet.

Nerille ignored them and made her way to him and tried to hug him but he held her away.

'Jio—'

'The TaiGethen don't hug their mothers before battle.'

Nerille felt a great rush of pride for him. She stroked his cheek.

'Of course not, I'm sorry.' She pulled his pendant from her pocket. 'I brought you this. I didn't want you to miss it.'

Jio's hand went to the nape of his neck and his eyes widened.

'Dear Yniss preserve me, I forgot it.' Nerille placed it around his neck and gripped his hands. Jio's smile lit up both their faces. 'Thank you. Now I know I'll live to see this battle won.'

'Of course you will,' she said.

'Casting!'

The warning ran back and forth along the wall. Nerille looked out. The soldiers had all dropped to one knee. The mages were standing. Nerille felt a strange feeling come over her, like a wind that blew straight through her, warming her. The mages cast and Jio dragged her down, covering her with his body as they cowered behind the wall, praying it would hold.

The sound of castings froze her to her very core. A roaring and whistling sound, wrapped in endless rolls of thunder. The heat grew quickly and bright blue light cast them into a deep shadow behind the wall. The castings slammed into the gatehouse, the walls, and flew high overhead to land in the city.

Ten paces away, the top of the wall was blasted to rubble. Fire burst through, shattering the rampart and engulfing helpless defenders. Burning elves were hurled onto the street, thrashing and screaming as they fell. The wall shuddered under impact after impact and an ice casting landed right below them. She heard metal grind and protest and rivets pop. She heard stone blasted to dust.

Fire orbs detonated on the gatehouse roof. One flew straight through the opening where Pelyn had been standing and blasted through the open back of the gatehouse to splash against the main street. A second burst against the edge of the gatehouse wall, which held but the fire sprayed inside. She heard shrieks and saw elves slapping at themselves and diving off the platform, desperate to escape the flames that ate at their clothes and flesh.

Jio clung to her, all pretence at being TaiGethen gone. They watched fire orbs falling on their city. Harine the baker's house blew apart under a direct hit. An orb scorched across the rooftops of five houses in a tight knot in the Ixii ghetto, setting all to flame. A third dropped onto the Second Courthouse's balcony, splintering it and rolling inside, where the flames blew shutters open and scattered papers into the air to burn to ash in a heartbeat.

There was a moment's pause. Jio tried to stand but Nerille clung to him.

'Wait. There's more.'

The air chilled and the sky above them filled with blocks of ice the size of barrows. Spinning fast and freezing the air around them, they flew high and deep into the city, their momentum carrying them far further than any orb could travel.

'Tual's balls,' breathed Jio. 'Clear! Get clear!'

His shouts were useless. The ice began to fall right in the heart of the city. It smashed the spire from the temple of Ix. The temple of Yniss' roof collapsed under a trio of direct hits. Tens, hundreds of the ice boulders crashed down among thousands of Katurans who had thought they were far enough from the walls to be safe. One even landed on the steps of the makeshift stores. Nerille gasped. The quartermaster would have been standing there. He must have seen it coming all the way. She prayed he had found shelter in time.

The barrage lessened. Shouts for stretchers and fire teams echoed about the empty streets. Elves broke from their hiding places. The orbs had done terrible damage. Fire now leapt from house to house, business to business, the magical flames travelling with the speed of a jao deer.

Jio stood and Nerille stood with him. They looked down. Steel plate hung from broken fastenings. Stone was scattered about the base of the walls. The gatehouse was empty and on fire inside. There was no sign of Pelyn or the elves who had stood with her.

'Casting!'

They dropped from sight again. Jio was shivering, clutching at his pendant.

'How long can they keep this up?'

'Not long enough,' said Nerille. 'Have courage, Jio. The Tai-Gethen are with us. They fear nothing and each of them is worth a hundred humans. I have to get back to the stores and see what I can do.'

'No,' said Jio. 'You saw the strike on the steps. You could be killed.'

'I'm safer on the walls, am I?' Nerille smiled and kissed Jio's cheek. 'Worry about yourself. Don't take any chances.'

Nerille made for the nearest ladder and climbed down into the city. Overhead, the castings came in again. Fire and ice rained down on the city. She pressed herself against the walls, which suffered no fresh impacts. Mages clustered up in the sky, spotting fresh targets and directing the barrage. She cursed them and prayed to Gyal for rain and mist to give them some respite. But the day was hot and the clouds distant. Even Gyal was in hiding.

Nerille looked to her right. A body lay at the base of the gatehouse. It was moving, the cloak smouldering but not aflame. It was Pelyn, it had to be. Nerille hurried along the street, staying close to the wall. An orb seared the air overhead and plunged into a potter's work-shop, blowing timbers and splinters in all directions when it hit.

Nerille felt a splinter cut her cheek. She turned her head away and crouched, trying to protect herself while she moved. Pelyn pushed herself to her knees and used the gates to pull herself to her feet. Nerille reached her and offered a steadying hand. The elf's face was black with ash and red with burns, but the fire in her eyes was brighter than any fire orb.

'Good, you survived the first wave,' said Pelyn.

'You too. The centre of the city has been hit. They need help.'

Pelyn nodded. 'Let's go. Stay to the walls, use the cover. This bombardment isn't going to stop any time soon.'

The gatehouse blazed above them. Fire teams were speeding from cover, trying to douse the magical flames and risking death as they did. More spells soared overhead, spreading their destruction across Katura. Nerille and Pelyn headed inwards, where the city meant as a sanctuary had been turned to ash and ice.

Hynd stood by Lockesh, relaying his orders. The initial volleys had produced good results. Spotter mages reported considerable damage and panic in the city and it was clear the armour on the walls was weak in a number of places. All they had to do was hit the right spots and they'd destroy it.

Killith strode up and down the rear of the lines, urging greater effort. Soldiers itched to fight, sensing the Sharps' will already beginning to weaken. Fifteen hundred men and mages waited, ready to begin the assault across the western ground. Despite Jeral's concerns before he was arrested, Killith considered it to be the best approach in concert with an attempt to take the gates.

But for now the focus was on softening up the city. Nothing drained defenders' will more than seeing those they were tasked to protect being slaughtered while they stood helpless. And the Tai-Gethen on the walls were helpless. There were too few of them to mount a raid over the open ground and, for all their speed, they were still vulnerable to magic.

The late Loreb would, it seemed, get his swift victory.

Hynd sampled the mana flow once more while he watched the penultimate volley of spells cast by the first wave of mages arc over the walls and down into the city. It was as strong and sure as ever, but he knew that when he was asked to cast, his nerves would wreak havoc with his concentration.

'First wave! Prepare to withdraw and rest,' called Lockesh. Hynd relayed the order. 'Second wave stand ready!'

Killith marched over.

'We must push over the western ground now,' Killith demanded. 'Drive our advantage home and caution be damned. We are winning. I want my victory feast tonight and to sleep in an elven bed having taken my fill of elven whores.'

'Scout the ground first. The TaiGethen remain dangerous,' said Lockesh.

'The TaiGethen are all occupied, cowering on the walls,' said Killith, jabbing a finger towards the city. The first wave's final spells hissed away. 'I am the senior general here and I want victory before the su—'

'You are the only general here,' said Lockesh with a hiss to still his flapping tongue. Where is Pindock, exactly?'

'The order will be given. Your mages will support me.'

Lockesh stared blankly at Killith. 'As you wish, General.'

Killith stalked away, summoning his aides. Orders were barked out. The column began to move towards the west. Hynd watched them go.

'Your orders, my lord?' he asked.

'The second wave is to concentrate on the gates and that western corner. See if they can't land a few fire orbs on that wooden western wall too. The reserve is to clear the ground west. I don't want anything surprising us in the grass and I don't want a single tree left standing for the TaiGethen to hide behind.'

'You think they will be lying in wait there?' asked Hynd. He gestured to the walls. 'Surely—'

'There are rather a lot of them up there, don't you think? said Lockesh. 'I refuse to believe they are all the genuine article.'

'Yes, my lord.'

'Two more things, Hynd'

Hynd paused in the very act of turning. 'Yes, my lord?'

'Jeral shoud be released and brought to me. The charges against him died with Loreb and he should be seen watching Killith prove him right about that western ground. And secondly—' Lockesh pointed to the head of the cliffs overlooking the western ground '—I think we need a lookout or two up there. See to it. Four mages, two warriors.'

'At once,' said Hynd.

He stared up at the cliffs, which looked treacherous and uneven, then turned away to relay Lockesh's orders and to find some unwitting suspects to fly up and see the world from on high.

Auum watched the enemy's advance from the first of the trees that clustered before open farmland in the lee of the cliffs. He glanced up. There was a single TaiGethen up there along with forty Katurans, waiting for the signal to send down enough rock to sweep away half the city walls, should their momentum carry them that far.

A fresh wave of castings began to fall on the western corner of the city walls. The armour was thicker here and the stone cemented firmly into place. Ice boulders dashed themselves to pieces against the plating, making it ripple. Fire orbs deluged it with heat, the dramatic changes in temperature causing it to groan in protest. So far, it held.

All of the TaiGethen were with him along with twenty of the fifty hunters armed with poison arrows on the walls to his right, and thirty Al-Arynaar led by Tulan and Ephram. The warriors were hidden by the trees, and all knew what they had to achieve. Auum waited for the right moment, assessing the closing distance and speed.

'They will drop castings here,' he said. 'Be ready to fall back on my word. Get close to their swords and keep falling back to bring them beneath the avalanche zone. You know your markers. Don't lag because we cannot wait for anyone. Stand by.'

The enemy paused. Soldiers knelt while mages prepared.

'Hold,' said Auum. 'Cover!'

They all ducked behind the wide boles of the trees Beeth provided. Auum felt the heat of approaching castings. The ground vibrated with multiple impacts which scorched and ruined the farmland between the trees and the walls. Orbs were landing not twenty paces from them at the corner of the walls. Auum tensed.

'You have to get under their arcs,' said Auum. 'Don't give them the chance to adjust their aim.'

Satisfied with the destruction, the enemy moved forward again. Auum counted fifty paces before they stopped, bringing them to within a hundred yards of the walls and the edge of the burned ground. Spells ceased to fall on the walls for fear of striking their own.

'Stand by,' said Auum.

The human mages opened their hands to cast.

'Break!'

TaiGethen and Al-Arynaar stormed from cover, running hard across the still-burning ground, their feet kissing ember, ash and flame. Tulan led the Al-Arynaar down the centre. TaiGethen flanked them, meaning to break around the sword line and get at the mages if they could.

Auum held himself in check, keeping pace with Ulysan and Faleen's cell on one side and those of Merke and Quillar on the other. They moved to the enemy's right flank as spells roared overhead. Auum ducked, hearing a splintering impact among the trees. It was followed by dozens more.

He saw bows bristle behind the front line. No warning was necessary. Elven warriors broke formation, scattering wide, crouching low and angling their runs. A volley sped towards them. Auum ducked a shaft, and heard one thud home. An Al-Arynaar tumbled to the ground near him, clutching his thigh.

The enemy soldiers stood.

'Jaqrui!' called Auum. 'Away!'

Crescent blades wailed across the lessening space, bouncing harmlessly from magical shields, though they still made every soldier within the volley's arc throw his arms up to defend himself. Moments later, the elven line crashed against them.

Auum beat one blade into a soldier's gut and hacked his other down onto another's helm, knocking him cold. Ulysan and Faleen filled in around him. Ulysan's hands, quick as ever, flattened the nose of his target and tore out his throat. Faleen's feet swept the legs from under her enemy and her blade pierced his heart.

To Auum's left, the Al-Arynaar moved in. Moving with less speed and more power, they found a wall of capable swordsmen in front of them. Tulan called for the elves to hold firm and the Al-Arynaar closed ranks. Blows were exchanged. Human voices called orders and the enemy's flanks began to move in.

'Good,' said Auum. 'TaiGethen, flow!'

Merrat picked up his cry. The TaiGethen spread across the face of the army, each warrior looking only to himself. Ulysan shouldered into his target and drove a blade into his gut. Faleen jumped, kicked out left and right, landed and roundhoused a dazed human, sending him clattering sideways into his comrades.

Auum laced cuts into his opponent. The man was quick, fending off most, his body agile, weaving aside. Auum accorded him a mote of respect. He feinted to strike high but instead dropped to his haunches and drove in low. The man was too slow. Auum's blade slid into his groin and blood gushed from the wound.

Auum bounced back to his feet as a soldier unleashed a powerful overhead blow. Auum stepped left and sliced a cut deep into his neck. He dragged the sword clear, glanced left. The Al-Arynaar had stalled. He saw two fall as he watched.

'Lacking sharpness,' he muttered. 'Fall back three!'

Across the line elves pulled back, dropping three paces from the enemy, who surged after them. Auum fenced with a strong, lean man, his twin blades frustrating his opponent. Auum let him come on.

'Rolling back!' called Auum. 'Bring them on!'

Spells careered over their heads again, battering into the trees and splashing against the wooden walls, setting them aflame. Orders rang out across the enemy line and they pushed harder, their commander seeing victory in his strength of numbers.

Steadily, the elven fighters moved back. The corner of the city walls was thirty paces behind them. The human flanks pushed on and the poison archers stood ready. Arrows flashed across the open space . . . but not one pierced the magical shield.

Spells roared out in response, volley after volley hammering into the walls. The ranks of soldiers broke and reformed, pushing down hard on their right flank, coming closer and closer to the cliff. Auum smiled.

'Break!' he yelled.

He turned and ran for the blackened and burning trees, too fast to give the archers or mages a target. The humans chased after them. Auum glanced skywards in time to see two mage pairs fly high towards the head of the cliff, a warrior hanging between each pair.

'I hope you've seen them, Dimuund,' said Auum. 'Don't let me down.'

Auum turned again, seeing his people moving calmly back to cover, their retreat looking for all the world like a withdrawal to the city. He hurled a jaqrui at the enemy, trying to keep them on their guard, stop them from thinking too clearly. The TaiGethen followed suit.

'Eyes on me,' Auum called. 'We're nearly there.'

Chapter 34

Humans consider themselves superior yet they cannot distinguish between the approach of a jao deer and a ClawBound pair. They have no empathy with the world that surrounds them, making them inferior to the simplest of Tual's creatures.

Auum, Arch of the TaiGethen

Dimuund watched the battle from the crumbling cliff edge. He was afforded an unparalleled view of the battlefield and the city below and winced every time a casting wrecked another building, tore through a fire team or splashed flame across an open space. They were losing the battle.

Down in front of the city mages pounded the gates, which, with their thicker steel, were holding, but the walls to either side were beginning to give way. Stone had been blown out in patches twenty yards wide and behind them only wood remained.

Below, on the western ground, he saw Auum lead the TaiGethen in and watched the Arch's precision and the Al-Arynaar's power. The enemy mages continued to target the western wall. He saw the humans regroup exactly as Auum had predicted they would and move steadily towards his target zone.

'Get ready,' he said.

His forty Katurans picked up their hammers, iron staves and thick logs, ready to beat away the chock stones holding the boulders in place and then lever them over the edge. There had been no practice, there couldn't be. Dimuund had to trust the design would work because there would be no second chances.

A movement caught his eye. He glanced to his left. Enemies were heading their way. Mages carrying warriors were climbing fast in the shelter of the cliff a couple of hundred yards from him.

'Cover!' he called. 'Use the stones.'

Dimuund waved them all in, watching them scramble and slither over the flat stone that bordered the cliff before the forest took over once more. He doubted they could all reach adequate cover; there simply wasn't enough of it. And as soon as they reached the cliff top, the enemy would see what was going on.

Dimuund looked down over the edge. The attackers hadn't reached the trigger point yet. The TaiGethen and Al-Arynaar were still directly in the boulders' path and it would be a count of a hundred until they were clear. That was about seventy too many.

'Dammit,' he breathed.

He moved along the line of boulders, crouching by the last one, his right foot hanging over the edge of the cliff. The enemy mages crested the cliff sixty paces from him. They flew high, high enough to see their foe and the death they were set to unleash on the army below. Dimuund heard them shout to each other and they dropped towards the ground. Both warriors and three mages landed. The fourth flashed away back over the edge and down to give warning.

Dimuund cursed. He broke cover and ran towards the enemy.

'Prepare to drop them!' he called over his shoulder. 'Make it count.'

The warriors were twenty paces from him, the mages behind them preparing castings.

'Casting!' he shouted. 'Watch and cover!'

Dimuund drew a blade and a jaqrui. He threw the crescent blade at the right-hand mage. A warrior's blade sliced out and knocked it from its path. Two of the mages cast. One blue orb swept away to splash against the boulders, rocking them against their stays, and elves screamed around him. Dimuund closed his mind to their agony. The second mage thrust his hands directly at the TaiGethen and an invisible force struck him in the chest driving him back towards the cliff edge.

Dimuund's feet slithered on the ground, finding no purchase. He was moving fast. He glanced over his shoulder. Burning elven bodies lay thrashing on the ground. One of the boulders was alive with fire. Dimuund spun himself, using the magical force as a wall. He rolled across it, sprawling to the ground as he moved past its edge.

Both warriors and two mages were running towards the Katurans as Dimuund scrambled to his feet. A mage moved his arms left, meaning to batter Dimuund over the edge of the cliff. He leapt high, feeling the edge of the casting brush the soles of his feet, grabbed a jaqrui from his belt and threw it, seeing the blade chop into the mage's chest. The casting died.

Dimuund landed and ran. The human warriors had set about their attack. Dimuund saw an elf try to block a blow with his sledge-hammer only to lose both hands to a downward strike. Another was carved across the back as he ran for cover. A third threw a knife only to see it bounce from a magical shield.

Dimuund caught the mage following the warriors and swept his blade through the man's hamstrings. The mage collapsed forward and Dimuund drove a heel into the back of his neck and ran on. The remaining mage had seen him. He turned and cast. The orb flew straight, its heat incredible. Dimuund dived aside but the edge of the casting caught his trailing foot. He screamed, hit the ground and rolled.

The pain was extraordinary as unnatural flames wreathed his leg to the knee. Dimuund came to his feet with a grunt and ran on. The mage gaped. Dimuund dragged a hand across his throat and ripped his carotid open. Blood hissed onto the ground.

Dimuund howled, fighting unconsciousness. One of the warriors faced him but the Tai had no time to fight. He stumbled around the front edge of the boulders, the stink of his own burning flesh in his nostrils. Three boulders had been loosened and one was already rocking, ready to fall.

Dimuund seized a hammer and knocked away the stays holding a fourth boulder. He felt a terrible pain in his back and stumbled, turning and grabbing the stone for support. The human stood an arm's length away, his sword dripping with Dimuund's blood.

Dimuund's vision clouded. The warrior stepped in to finish him and Dimuund jumped back, whimpering and weakening. The warrior's strike missed, and he overbalanced, letting Dimuund grip his head and dash it against the boulder. The great stone rocked again; it just needed the slightest impetus. The warrior tumbled over the edge.

Dimuund lurched around the back of the boulder. Some of the Katurans had surrounded and killed the remaining warrior and others ran towards him, telling him he'd be all right. Dimuund wavered on his feet, clung on to his consciousness just a moment longer. He shook his head.

'You know what to do. Do it now.' He staggered towards the gently rocking boulder, timing his move as he dimly knew he must. 'But this one . . . this one is mine.'

Dimuund hit the boulder just as it reached the apex of its rock outwards. He felt it give a little, and then a little more. And at the very last, Dimuund was flying.

Auum saw the solitary mage flying down to the rear of the enemy lines. Moments later he heard the order sound to turn and run.

'I don't think so,' he said. 'TaiGethen, attack!'

They turned as one and flew back into the fight. Men, caught between a threat from above and the promise of victory ahead, swung back to press forward. Auum saw Faleen lead her Tai all the way down the right flank to keep the mages hemmed in. Quillar followed her.

Auum leapt and spear-kicked the same lean warrior he had fenced with before. He landed on the man's chest and drove a blade through his mouth then dropped to his haunches, a sword slicing by just over his head. He spun around, braced his hands on the dead soldier and kicked high into his attacker's chest. The man stumbled back a pace.

Auum jumped to his feet. He was pressed on three sides. He struck out right, his blade cutting deep into his enemy's thigh as he smacked the heel of his palm into the forehead of the man ahead of him . . . and the expected blow from behind never came.

'Mine,' said Ulysan.

The TaiGethen stood back to back, beckoning their enemy on. Behind the lines the flying mage was screaming at the humans to run. Some had broken, but the TaiGethen held most of them trapped in the fight. Arrows fell from the walls again, keeping the enemy tight to the cliff now the mages had turned to run, leaving them shield-less.

Auum heard a faint crack from above, then the duller noise of a massive weight of stone on the move.

'Break!' he yelled.

Auum landed a haymaker on an opponent's jaw, turned, grabbed Ulysan's shirt and hauled him away. The sky above them rippled with thunderous sound. Small rocks and pieces of debris began to rain down. The body of a lone warrior landed at the base of the cliff and panic engulfed the humans.

The sound of the boulders crashing into the side of the cliff was like nothing Auum had ever heard. They came in succession, and with each that fell the cliff screeched. Auum ran hard, Ulysan at his shoulder. To his left, Faleen and her Tai sprinted towards the burning walls of the city. Quillar was still behind them.

With a final shattering sound part of the cliff wall sheered away. The first boulder smashed to the ground amidst the enemy, driving twenty feet or more into the soft ground. The boulders fell like the hail of Shorth itself, obliterating enemies and sending elf and human alike sprawling in the dirt, such was the power that drove through the earth.

Auum picked himself up and ran on, the humans and elves behind him running together to escape the avalanche. The noise covered everything else. The wind blew down before it, carrying dust and vegetation. Countless tonnes of shale and rock slid and bounced down the cliff side, dragging yet more stone with it.

The speed of its descent was incredible. Auum dived behind the burned-out hulk of a tree and saw the cliff side tumble across the ground behind him. Powered by the thousands of tonnes still crashing down from above, the avalanche spilled towards the walls.

Hundreds of men were swept up and carried over the earth. Dust flooded the air in a choking fog with debris hurled in all directions. Auum hid behind his tree, feeling the impacts crack and split the dead wood, praying to Beeth that it would hold. The dust obscured everything, blowing through the remaining trees and hanging in the air.

Auum put his hand over his mouth. He rose to his feet, coughing and gagging. A man stumbled past him. Auum thought to strike, but saw the back of the man's head was already crushed. Auum looked for any of his people, but he could see no more than two paces in any direction.

The avalanche lost its power as quickly as it had been gained, and the noise began to subside. Auum's ears were ringing and his face and hands were covered in cuts from flying fragments of wood and stone. He didn't know if the walls had survived. He didn't know how many of his people he had lost. But he did know that the dangerous open ground had been shut off.

Any further attack would have to come straight at the front gates. Yelling for any who could hear him to muster at the rally point, he headed back towards the walls and the ropes back up into the city.

Killith sounded the retreat. Jeral watched the survivors return, the wounded helping the dying back from the scene of the avalanche. He took no satisfaction from witnessing the disaster, only from Lockesh, who stood at his side when he faced the dithering general.

'Pindock is still cowering from the noise and is more likely to shit himself than come to your aid,' said Jeral. 'And you, General Killith, and that useless drunk Loreb before you, have proved yourselves unfit to command this army. I have the company captains with me and the support of Lord Lockesh and the mages.

'I am taking command of this army and the battle immediately. Ystormun wants his soldiers to return to Balaia. I will see that done since you plainly cannot. While you are not under any sort of arrest, you will confine yourself and all of your aides to the rear camp positions. I expect you'll find Pindock and the Yellow Guard already there.'

'You have no authority to do this. This is mutiny. The cadre will hear of it and your life will be forfeit.' But there was no force in Killith's voice, his words sounding defeated and passionless.

'Maybe. But the cadre are a long way from here. Ystormun only speaks to Hynd, and Hynd reports to me.'

'Are you threatening me, Captain Jeral?'

'No, but I can if you want me to,' said Jeral. Lockesh hissed and Jeral grimaced. 'No, I'm not. I have no wish to spill your blood. After all, you have done yourself more damage than I could possibly have inflicted: the blood of the hundreds dead beneath that avalanche is on your hands. But you might want to consider your position and how the cadre will view your actions today.'

Killith sagged visibly. 'Good luck,' he muttered before turning and leaving the battlefield.

Word of the change in command spread like fire over tinder grass. Cheers rose across the army. Mages worked harder to heal the injured and ease the pain of the dying. Energy replaced the lethargy that had engulfed the army in the wake of the avalanche, while Jeral felt a frisson of anxiety. Beside him, Lockesh raised his eyebrows.

'Expectations,' he said, 'are interesting things. I hope you're up to the challenge.'

'We'll find out, won't we,' said Jeral, scanning the city, from the ramparts of which elves taunted their defeat. 'What's our casting capacity, Hynd?'

'Three companies: Eight, Nine and Ten,' said Hynd. 'It's enough to do the necessary damage until nightfall.'

'We need to strike a blow. Something to take their courage away, leave them vulnerable to us and leave them with the night to think it over. Only one thing to do really.'

Jeral stared at the city walls. They hadn't been tested severely and they'd withstood both fire and ice. The Sharps' industry in armouring the front face was impressive, but he could see plenty of potential to exploit weak points. There was a big one, right in the centre.

'Orders, commander,' said Hynd.

'Companies Eight to Ten to march within casting range. Concentrate everything on those gates. Knock them down and give me a way in.'

Hynd turned to relay the orders and Jeral heard them shouted across the army. Men got to their feet; company captains bellowed for discipline.

'You don't want to wait for Sinese and the Deneth Barine force any more?' asked Lockesh.

'No need when we can take the gates as we are. If you're right about the you-know-what, the sooner we get this done the better. Anyway, I rather like the thought of the elves seeing another two thousand marching into view at dawn tomorrow. If the gates come down today then we can have this finished by lunchtime tomorrow, whatever our offensive capacities might be.'

'Very good,' said Lockesh. He was smiling. 'You know, suddenly I feel I might actually survive this little expedition.'

'Stick by me and I'll see you all right,' said Jeral, just about stopping himself from clapping the mage lord on the shoulder.

'Quite,' said Lockesh.

The three companies formed up and Jeral gave the order to march. The sun was moving behind a heavy bank of cloud on its way towards dusk. There should be just enough time. He turned to Hynd.

'You know you should find yourself a replacement or you're just going to be remembered as an aide. Hardly worthy of your contribution.'

'I know just the candidate,' said Hynd.

'Good. In the meantime see the cook fires are lit. Hot food for everyone even if it's only that ghastly tuber stew the Sharps love so much. Then get hold of the other company captains. We should probably have a meeting or something.'

'We're not going in today?'

'I can think of no reason to. I have plans for the morning anyway. We have a whole lot more mages on their way, so if the Sharps think their city's a mess now then they've seen nothing yet.'

*

Quillar and his Tai were gone, buried beneath the avalanche. Dimuund was missing. Faleen had fractured an ankle and Hassek, her second, had broken both wrists deflecting debris from his head. Neither would fight again in this battle.

Yet Auum had to be satisfied. The day was on the wane and the humans had failed to take the city. He ran back to the gates, his TaiGethen with him, still fresh but mourning their lost ones. They looked so few: thirty able to fight and two under the care of the healers.

Reaching the gatehouse, he saw its burned-out hulk and feared for Pelyn. He called up to the ramparts. Tulan was there, Ephram with him, speaking of the victory and boosting spirits wherever they went.

'Where's Pelyn?'

Tulan pointed back into the city. 'Heading towards the stores the last time she was seen. They're moving further south, getting anything vital to the lakeside.'

'Good. And the walls?'

'Holding,' said Tulan. 'They launched most of their spells over the top. Killed over a hundred; it's a real mess back there.'

'So I've seen.'

Tulan was distracted from their conversation and glanced out towards the enemy. He blew his cheeks out.

'Here they come again.'

Auum raced up a ladder. Several hundred soldiers and mages were marching across the centre of the field, straddling the main trail. Every time they marched Auum wondered about going out to meet them and dismissed the notion. On open ground they would be taken apart by spells and arrows before they could ever close for a fight.

When the hand-to-hand battle began, it had to be inside the walls, where the streets were tight and the enemy formations would be broken. It was a paradox he was struggling with. He was desperate to keep them out of the city but was unable to cut down their numbers sufficiently on the field. To beat them, they had to face them on the very streets they were trying so hard to defend.

'What are they planning, I wonder?' asked Ephram.

'They need to get in,' said Auum. 'They probably feel they've softened us up enough inside, now they'll try to break the gates. Tulan, clear the ramparts around the gate. Keep the archers hidden in case they do breach the gates and attack. Ephram, I want more weight behind the gates; there are tonnes of timber in the streets.

Let's get it stacked there with bracing poles and strong elves to hold them. Go.'

Auum jumped back down to the waiting TaiGethen. 'Help get the timber and rubble to the gates. And somebody find Pelyn.'

Elves dropped from the ramparts to gather whatever they could to further strengthen the gates. Outside, Auum heard their attackers draw up. He and Ulysan carried a heavy timber and placed it on the top of the quickly growing pile.

'We need bracing timbers placed higher up,' he said. 'Any spell we make them use to take the gates down is a spell they can't use on our people.'

'I'll find something,' said Ulysan.'

'Casting!'

Word was passed along the rampart and back into the city. Every elf repeated the call. Fire orbs began to thud against the gates. Auum stood twenty yards behind them, watching the steel-clad wood rattle and shake. Around him, elves carried more and more timber to the base, shoring it up as best they could.

There were multiple impacts, landing one after another. Auum could see new fire spreading across the ruined gatehouse. There was a moment's pause followed by a terrified cry from the lookout.

'Ward!'

A massive detonation sounded and the top of the gates splintered. Glowing metal shards fizzed through the air. Right in front of Auum, one of the disguised Katurans was struck in the chest. The metal went straight through him, leaving an exit hole the size of his fist. The victim was flung backwards, slithering to a stop, dead, at Auum's feet.

'Clear the road!' shouted Auum. 'Bring the braces and shore up the top of those gates. Move!'

The top three feet of the gate had been bent inwards. Auum raced forward, seeing Ulysan and three others carrying the flagpole. He joined them and they planted the wide base in the mud where the cobbles had been dug out, and positioned the top against the seam about halfway up.

'It had been blown down,' said Ulysan. 'The top ten feet are missing.'

'Casting!' came the cry. 'Brace, brace!'

Ice boulders smashed against the breach in the gates. Orbs beat into the middle. Auum leaned hard against the pole along with seven others, his arms vibrating with every strike. Metal groaned, joints weakened and timbers split behind the armour. More of the gate failed, the top right-hand hinge was springing open, opening up a hole the size of an elf.

It was as relentless as it was inevitable. Another massive impact and the gates bowed inwards with the sound of screaming metal and the collapse of the shoring timbers, which slid lazily back. Auum saw the seam of the gates break. The heavy slide latches bent, ready to give. Wood was beginning to smoulder.

'Casting. Clear, clear, clear!'

Auum heard the note of panic and knew it was over. 'Run!'

He ran two paces and dived full length into the lee of the walls. He rolled onto his back and saw the third thundering impact rip a hole through the middle of the gates. The flagpole was shattered, pieces cartwheeling away. The gates rocked open, sweeping away the shoring timbers and slamming against their stays. Metal plates clattered to the ground. The tattered right-hand gate leaned out, hanging in space for a moment before falling.

More spells flew through the gap, doing little but knocking down already ruined buildings behind the gates. The smells of hot metal and burning wood mixed with smoke in the air. Katura was breached, and the ease with which it had been achieved made Auum wonder why their enemy hadn't done it hours earlier.

Auum walked towards the ruined gates and peered out onto the scorched field. He straightened in surprise and stood in full view of the enemy, watching them withdraw. Only one man stood there now and he raised a spear with a piece of grubby white cloth tied to it. Small groups of soldiers and mages stopped and turned before reaching their lines. The soldier waved his makeshift flag, took his sword from its scabbard and laid it on the ground.

'He wants to talk,' said Ulysan, coming to Auum's shoulder.

'I have nothing to say to a human,' said Auum.

'You have nothing to lose by hearing him out.'

'And nothing to gain,' said Auum. 'Clearly they feel the battle is won and he is seeking our surrender. He must know we won't agree.'

'Talk to him,' said Ulysan. 'Takaar always said knowing your enemy gives you an edge. He will give away more than you will. He's human, after all.'

'He assumes we respect some white flag? He's either very brave or very stupid.'

'He has mages ready to cast should he be struck down. He's not that stupid.'

Auum thought for a moment. 'It can do no harm, I suppose. I'll go.'

'You should guard yourself as he does.'

Auum shook his head. 'I am not afraid of them.'

He walked from the gates, keeping his eyes fixed on the human. To his credit, he showed no fear. He stood proud, the spear held in his left hand, its base on the ground and the flag hanging limp from its tip. Auum stopped when he was three paces away, the soldier shielding his body from the mages and close enough to kill his enemy with a single strike.

'I am Auum, Arch of the TaiGethen,' he said.

'I am Jeral, commander of this army,' replied the man in passable elvish.

'You? I don't think so. Three senior soldiers command your force. One we know is dead. Send one of the others.'

'There has been a change of command,' replied Jeral.

Auum nodded slowly. That explained the change in tactics, at least.

'What do you want?'

Jeral smiled. 'It's over, Auum. Your gates are gone. I can do the same to your walls tomorrow. I can flood your city with spells and send my soldiers in at the end to finish the rest. We know you have no strength of arms. We respect and fear the TaiGethen but you are terribly few. You have dressed your townsfolk up as soldiers, while I have an army of two thousand here and another two thousand will arrive overnight. We could defeat you without magic, such is our strength.

'Surrender.'

'To what end?' Auum knew the numbers, but to hear them from his enemy's mouth gave them greater force. 'We will not become your slaves.'

'I will give you until first light tomorrow. Any who wish to can leave through your broken gates and surrender to me without fear of death. I have no wish to spill more of your people's blood.'

'Liar. We know why you are here. To finish us. To end the elven race. And you may get your wish, but you will pay for it step after bloody step. Send your magic and your swords. We will kill ten of you for every one of us who perishes. You think we are beaten? You know nothing of the spirit of my people.

'Go back to your army, Jeral. Tell your soldiers that they must defeat the TaiGethen. This is our forest, our land, given to us by Yniss, and he will not turn his back on us. You will not prevail.'

Jeral nodded. 'So be it. Your words will chase you and your people to your grave.'

'I look forward to killing you,' said Auum.

'Not if I see you first.'

Jeral bowed, turned and walked away. Auum watched him for a moment before trotting back to the gates, where Ulysan was waiting with the TaiGethen.

'Well?' asked Ulysan.

'He does not fear us but some in his army doubt their victory is assured, which is why he seeks a bloodless end. I will not give it to him. We know his numbers and we know what he will do. Come, we have work to do before dawn.'

Chapter 35

Serrin granted me an audience some eighty years after he was called to the ClawBound. He showed me the tattoos of the Aryn Hiil text on his back and chest. This, he said, was the pure expression of a Silent Priest.

From *ClawBound and Silent* by Lysael, High Priest of Yniss

Jeral was enjoying a decent night's sleep in a hammock near a good roaring fire when the angry shouting disturbed him. He opened his eyes. It was full night. The argument was coming from his left, towards the forward pickets. He'd feared TaiGethen attack during the night and the wards were thick on the ground. Rested mages were ready to cast on anything that crossed the line.

He heaved himself to the ground and belted on his sword. He was joined by other curious soldiers as he walked towards the disturbance. This was high-level stuff. The raised voices were those of Lockesh and Sinese, commander of the second army. Their words were clear long before he saw their fire-lit silhouettes.

'. . . know what is best for those under my command. You have no authority over me, Lockesh. Back off.'

'We have cast all day. We have won the battle. Now your slack-lipped charges are here dripping poison into the ears of my mages.'

'They have a right to know,' Sinese spat.

His was a tall and broad silhouette. A career soldier, but one for whom the line between command and care was too often blurred.

'They have no *rights*,' Lockesh sneered. 'They are military mages. They do as they are ordered, the same as every soldier.'

'I am astonished by your complacency. This is not some trifling matter. Mages could start falling from the sky, or be engulfed by their own flame.'

'*If!* If the Sundering should happen. It has not, and while it has not your mages will join battle with mine. They *will* fight.'

'Gentlemen, gentlemen. The camp is awake and hanging on your every word,' said Jeral, nodding at Hynd, who was standing nearby looking, frankly, frightened. 'Can I help at all?'

Sinese looked at him as he might look at a smear of shit on his shoe. 'Who the hell are you?'

'I am Jeral, commander of the Ysundeneth army.'

Sinese tipped back his head and roared with laughter.

'Some good news at last. A real soldier, by the look of you.' His expression sobered. 'But no doubt you're also complicit in hiding the risk our brother mages face.'

'No, sir. I am anxious to see this battle won before that risk grows any further. What's happened?'

Lockesh waved a hand at Sinese. 'In his wisdom, the general relayed Ystormun's news to all under his command. His mages, he says, are now too scared to cast in case their spells consume them.'

'The information is clear,' said Sinese. 'This battle must be won by sword alone.'

'We heard different,' said Lockesh. 'We heard that the battle must be won at pace to avoid such risks. We have made great strides, but we must use our magical resources tomorrow.'

Jeral nodded. 'That's about the size of it, General.'

'Then put your own mages in the line of danger. Make them cast knowing every construct might bite them without warning.'

'Fair enough,' said Jeral. 'So long as your blades are the first through the gates.'

'That's not going to be so easy,' said Hynd quietly.

'What? Why?'

'My Lord Lockesh, if I may?' Lockesh nodded and Hynd continued: 'The damage is already done.'

'What damage?' demanded Jeral, suddenly feeling nervous. 'Talk to me, Hynd.'

'You have to understand how much of a mage's ability is based on confidence in the unbroken flow of mana, and how dangerous it is if that flow is interrupted. We've all experienced it in simulations, and not all of us have come through them unscathed.'

'But the flow isn't interrupted, is it?'

'Not right now,' said Hynd. 'But what about in the next moment, or the next? It eats away our confidence, and a mage worrying about the flow cannot make a solid construct.'

'But you have to risk it, right?' Jeral spread his hands. 'Every time I pick up my sword I'm gambling that the enemy I face isn't as good as me. Warfare is a gamble for every one of us. We need you.'

'I'm just being honest,' said Hynd. 'I've seen the look on many of our mages' faces. They feel betrayed that they weren't told, and they're scared of what might come next.'

'But you, Hynd,' said Jeral. 'If I asked you to fly, you would.'

Hynd held his gaze for a moment before letting it drop and shaking his head.

'I don't know, Jeral, I really don't.'

Jeral couldn't believe what he was hearing. 'All right, maybe flying's a bad choice. An orb, then. You'd do that, right?'

Hynd didn't answer.

'Gods on a pyre,' hissed Jeral. 'I've got to have spotters and I've got to have ground casting.'

'I cannot promise you much of either,' said Hynd.

Jeral jabbed a finger towards the city.

'That city is full of Sharps. Most of them aren't soldiers but every one of them is a dangerous fucker who's scared of nothing but our magic. We have to have an open field when we get inside. Right now they could hide around every corner and pick us off one by one. Without you we'll lose hundreds of men winning this thing.

'You have to help me. You have to clear the ground of cover so my soldiers, who have not turned into total cowards, can see who the fuck they are fighting.'

'It is not cowardice,' said Hynd.

'What would you call it, then?'

'I will cast,' said Lockesh.

Jeral started. 'My lord?'

'I will cast, like any common mage. I have not lost my . . . *confidence*.' He glared at Hynd. 'Let it be known. I will lead any mage with the courage to join me onto the field come the dawn.'

'Thank you, my lord,' said Jeral. 'Every soldier is indebted to you.'

'I merely wish to get this done and to be able to walk out of here alive.'

'Great,' said Jeral and he punched Hynd hard on the shoulder. 'Then we're done.'

'Not quite,' said Sinese, clearly raging at Lockesh's seizure of the moral high ground. 'I would speak with you, Jeral, about a proper chain of command.'

'Knock yourself out, but I'm not going to start reporting to you.'

*

Dawn arrived, and those few on the ramparts were afforded a view that would take the heart from many. With those first rays of sunshine pushing the shadows of night back into the forest, the enemy had emerged from the eaves of the forest to stand in ranks that stretched across the width of the blackened open ground.

Auum, with the bruised Pelyn beside him and a handful of TaiGethen spread along the ramparts to either side of the sundered gates, looked at the force ranged against them and could only pray for divine intervention.

Below Auum, the gates had been re-erected. Carpenters had patched the timber, and steel plates had been reattached, but it was no more than a token effort and the humans would know it.

'They'll come on hard and they won't stop until their work is done,' said Auum. 'Are your people ready?'

Pelyn nodded. She was rubbing at her arms and her voice shook but not from fear.

'A few have fled across the lake, looking for sanctuary in the heights above the quarry, but most have stayed. These are city people, proud people, and they know no other life. They'll stand and fight when they must.'

Auum had ordered the city evacuated behind a line to the rear of the hall of the Al-Arynaar. Katurans were hidden in the ghettos to the south of the city and scattered among the buildings in the outer circles. Only the TaiGethen prowled the areas nearer the gate, tasked to attack mages wherever they could once the invasion began. They had built many street barricades, but all of them were wooden and none would stand up to more than a couple of castings.

The archers were hidden on the roofs and upper floors of the tallest remaining buildings. There was no shortage of arrows and poison, but the mages and shields would have to be taken down before they could be effective.

'Here they come,' said Auum.

The human army began to march. Auum watched them until they stopped to prepare their barrage.

'Fall back. Let them use their spells. We can do nothing here but offer them targets.'

The defenders dropped from the ramparts and the Al-Arynaar dispersed into the depths of the city to stand with their nominated militia groups. The TaiGethen gathered to pray in the lee of the walls. When they were done, Auum faced them.

'Sell your lives at a high price if you have to sell them at all. Look to your brothers and sisters. May Yniss guide your every footfall. Marack, Illast, Acclan, Thrynn, take your cells to the west. Keep low, strike and run. Merrat, Grafyrre, Merke, Oryaal, Corinn your cells go to the east. Ulysan and I will free-run as decoys. If we can kill the magic then we can still win. Tais, we move.'

Auum took Ulysan and ran down the main street, past the gutted and shattered buildings of the Gyalan, Ixii and Tuali ghettos and up to the outer of the four circles. The main street ran directly into the marketplace, but within the circles the alleys and side streets provided good cover. Much of the first circle facing the gate still stood, but enough buildings had suffered significant damage to persuade Auum not to hide there for too long.

A whistling and roaring filled the air. Auum watched orbs and ice boulders soar high over the walls and come smashing down in the streets just beyond the gate. Only three mages flew in the sky. Castings smashed into the fragile gates and pounded the walls to either side.

From beneath an awning that hid them from the spotters, Auum and Ulysan saw the gates disintegrate and the remains of the gate-house rock on its foundations and tumble outwards, ripping holes the size of carts in the walls to either side. Orbs flew in again and again, melting the thin metal, popping lines of rivets and blasting stone to fragments.

Abruptly, the focus changed; the humans had seen something. The walls to the west of the gate were targeted hard. Other spells arced over the same section of the walls to land squarely in the Gyalan ghetto. Houses blew apart, timbers flew high into the air, spinning through clouds of splinters, clay and mud. The walls burst inwards, ice boulders crashing through them and flame orbs consuming the wood, between them creating a gash thirty feet wide.

Through the gap, Auum could see the humans begin their charge on two fronts.

'Ulysan, with me.'

The TaiGethen pair ran behind the barrier of the first circle. Castings were dropping all around them, rattling the ground beneath their feet, sending clouds of dust billowing along the tight streets and filling their noses with the smell of burning and the foul stink of magic.

'Take the next right,' said Auum.

An ice boulder drove into the building directly in front of them. Auum pushed Ulysan left and dived to the right as timbers exploded from the sides of the building. The boulder tore straight through, front to back, and cannoned into the building across the ring. The whole structure collapsed, sloughing into the road, covering everything for twenty yards around with thick freezing dust.

Auum wiped the blood away from a cut on his cheek and rubbed his hand on his trousers.

'Ulysan?'

Auum worked his way through the clogging dust. He saw a pile of debris shift and Ulysan emerged from it. Auum helped push away the wood and muck and dragged his friend back to his feet.

'All right?'

'You saved my life,' said Ulysan.

'You'll get plenty of chances to repay me, I'm sure. Let's get west.'

Auum raced down the next street and back towards the walls. He veered left, away from the main road. Castings were still falling but there were fewer now as the advance gathered momentum. He could see archers on the ramparts, firing down on the enemy. While he watched, two elves were hurled back, shafts jutting from chest and eye. The rest dispersed back to the second fire points.

They ran back into the Gyalan ghetto. Full of low houses, straight but narrow streets and a ceremonial fire pit at its heart. Auum heard elven voices. The ghetto had been flattened in a wide area stretching halfway to the western walls. Flames climbed high into the air and grey smoke pillared up into the sky. Turning a corner, he saw Acclan and Kepller kneeling to either side of a body.

Auum sprinted up, Ulysan in his footsteps. Acclan looked up, tears making tracks in the dirt of his face. Dysaart was dead. He'd been Acclan's second for three hundred years. A hero among the TaiGethen.

'He didn't even have the chance to fight,' said Acclan. 'Ice hit him in the back of the head. There is no honour in that.'

'Not for men, but there is for elves.' Auum reached out hands to the two survivors and brought them to their feet. 'We have all lost those we love. The enemy have breached the walls behind you. They attack us on two fronts now. Fight for him.'

The four of them moved off, Kepller limping heavily, favouring his right foot. Auum saw blood staining his left calf.

'It's nothing,' he said. 'I can fight.'

Three corners later he had to make good on his words. The ghetto was levelled beyond the breach. Spells flashed through it, creating space into which men were pushing. Archers breasted the broken timbers prepared to shoot. Auum kept his Tais just out of sight. Enemy soldiers boiled into the streets of Katura here and through the gates.

'Drop back to the next corner; I'll draw them on to you. We've got to take out those mages.'

Killith kicked the Sharp again. And again. The slave had long since stopped moving and had never once cried out. She'd stared at him just the once and even had the temerity to spit blood from her ruined mouth onto his boot, but that was all he'd got from her.

'Feeling better?' Pindock asked from his seat on a fallen log.

His ridiculously lavish personal security team was scattered among the trees just in case a spider got a bit aggressive.

Killith thought for a moment.

'No,' he said, giving the body another kick just to see it judder. 'At least, not yet. I've had all night to think about it followed by a good breakfast of slimy tuber soup, and my plan is to drink Loreb's stash of wines and spirits and then kick every Sharp I lay eyes on to death as my part in the war effort. Once I've done that, I'll figure out how to kill that fucking upstart Jeral.'

'Good luck with that. He's under Lockesh's wing now, isn't he?'

In the distance the sound of thousands running, fighting and dying and the detonations of spells carried through the forest. Closer to, they could hear bored soldiers pacing and what was presumably a heavy stumble over something hidden in the leaf litter, not an uncommon event in this ridiculous place.

'Poison does not respect the influence of mage lords.' Killith looked down at his boots. They were smeared with blood and dirt. He sat down, dragged them off and threw them at an aide. 'Clean them. Good to have a shine when you're taking revenge, I find.'

The aide stooped to pick up the boots, muttered a curse and dropped them again.

'Are you—' began Killith.

The aide wasn't looking at him; he was staring beyond him and a stain was spreading across his groin. Killith turned. Pindock was already whimpering and trying to scramble away though he must have known there was no escape. Somewhere nearby, a soldier was yelling for help.

'Stand with me, Pindock. At least pretend you are a man.'

Killith had never feared death, but then he'd never faced it all that closely before. And now the certainty of his was upon him, he felt relief at not having to face the questions of his masters back in Balaia. His one regret was that he didn't have his boots on.

So Killith faced them without flinching in his threadbare stockings and with his sword in his hand because he would not want to be found empty-handed. The elves had emerged with such poise that he even felt guilty for standing there. This was their forest, their land.

Killith watched them close in on him and the three men who had chosen to stand with him. Eight of the painted and tattooed elves, with their panthers in close attendance, stood in his arc of vision, and more were moving to encircle the larger encampment if the cries he heard were any guide.

Killith brought his sword to the ready, held in two hands and across his body. A panther leapt on him the next instant, its jaws clamping onto his shoulder and bearing him down into the leaf litter. The air was punched from his body and his sword sprang from his hands. He reached out for it and laid a hand on its hilt. It comforted him.

From where he lay, Killith saw the ClawBound running forward. Pindock screamed and begged for mercy. His wailing carried on and on, his life extended to voice the sum of his agony.

Killith fought to rise but a figure dropped onto his chest. The elf stared at him as if he were a museum exhibit, curious but unmoved by what he saw. He said nothing but brought his hands to Killith's face and slashed both his cheeks with his sharpened fingernails. Killith jerked and cried out, unable to stop himself.

The elf pushed his chin back, driving his head into the mud. The next fingernail sliced his forehead open. Killith shouted out for him to stop, that this was not what he deserved: to be a message, left like all the others, breathing but too hideous to look upon.

Only then did the elf pause to shake his head.

'Then you are fortunate,' he said in elvish plain enough for Killith to grasp, 'that you will not be breathing when they find you.'

Chapter 36

My suspicion is that elves have a natural affinity with mana that offers them great longevity, and replenishes and revitalises their bodies without the need for direct magical intervention. My forthcoming experiments will investigate how mana is channelled in an elven body. Happily, I have a large number of subjects available for my work.

From *On Immortality* by Ystormun, Lord of Calaius

Auum ran from cover into the sight of hundreds of his foe. His jaqrui bounced from a magical shield and then his blades were in his hands. He ducked an arrow and saw soldiers turning towards him while others ran on deeper into the ghetto. He sprinted on, leapt and spear-kicked a soldier who'd got ahead of his comrades. Auum dropped to the ground on his haunches.

Three blades came at him. One was moving left to right. Auum leapt above it and hacked down with his left hand, his blade splitting his target's shoulder. The second was a thrust to his chest. As he came back down, Auum buried a blade in his target's gut. Auum ducked a third flailing strike, jabbing up into groin and carving deep across the vital artery in the thigh.

Auum jumped straight up, turned a roll in the air and ran. An order was barked and a detachment of the enemy gave chase, bellowing promises of revenge against him and his mother. Too fast for them to catch, he tore around the corner to see his Tais standing with jaqruis cocked in either hand.

Auum jumped again, this time soaring over his Tais, turning a tuck in the air to land behind them and face the enemy. They spilled around the corner. Ulysan barked like a wild dog and six jaqruis howled across the space, downing the front runners, who fell into the feet of those behind them.

Ulysan led a charge into their midst. From an alleyway to their left,

Illast's Tai of Bylaan and Ashocc sprinted into the fray as well, driving into the invaders' flank. Illast buried a dagger in the face of his first target and heaved him back into the press. A blade in his other hand blocked a strike to his neck and Bylaan's kick drove the attacker back.

The enemy were maybe two hundred strong, ranks of soldiers defending mages in their midst. The street itself was tight but spells had widened the battle area. Some mages held shields in place while others cast fire and ice ahead and to the right. The noise was deafening, bouncing from the walls of the few buildings still standing. The thunder of spells taking down buildings, the roar of men's voices and the clash of steel all mixed with the dull thud of blade on leather and flesh.

Ashocc, less than a pace from his target, snapped a kick high into his face. The man toppled like a felled tree. Ashocc ran up his body and jumped high out over the enemy. His blades were at right angles to his body and he twirled them in his hands. He dropped right into the heart of the group of mages.

'Push!' yelled Auum.

Ulysan, Acclan and Kepller joined him. The four waded into the enemy. Ulysan knocked a man out with a single punch. Kepller stumbled on his injured leg and Acclan's blade blocked the blow intended to kill him. Auum knocked a sword blow high with his right blade and thudded his left into his opponent's chest. He could hear Illast calling Ashocc to clear; instead, Bylaan pushed towards him. Blood spurted high enough for Auum to see it. Mages were dying.

The line moved back as men turned to defend their mages while the men on the flanks continued to move up. Auum pushed back a pace and Ulysan had seen the danger too. He nodded to Auum and headed left. Auum went right, leaving the other two to keep the pressure on the centre.

Auum saw Ashocc's blade rise and fall and he heard the screech of elven pain too. Spells had stopped falling. He threw a jaqrui right but the blade bounced away. Auum swore; the shield was still intact. On the other side of the fight Illast's cries were getting desperate, while in the centre Acclan was parrying more than striking in an effort to keep Kepller alive. The injured Tai had abandoned all caution and was forcing his way deeper into the enemy.

Auum hit the right flank. Two soldiers faced him, swords defending their bodies. Auum opened his body and battered his right-hand blade towards the head of the soldier on the left. He spun with the momentum and rammed his left blade backwards into the gut of the other.

Still moving fast, he completed the turn and took off, his body horizontal and spinning up over the defensive line. He pulled his legs under him, reversed the grips on his blades and thudded down in the midst of the enemy. He jerked both blades back, feeling one slide into flesh while the other struck empty space.

Ashocc was in desperate trouble. Bodies of mages and soldiers lay around him but he was beset on all sides. He had cuts to his face and chest and one arm hung useless, the blood from the shoulder wound soaking his jerkin. Bylaan was still too far away to help him.

Auum switched his swords front and chopped overarm, one following the other. He took a soldier through the back, a mage across the face.

'Bylaan! Get clear!' Auum called. 'I'll get Ashocc.'

Bylaan had heard him. He spun, his blades ahead of him, blocking blows aimed at his head and chest. Ashocc drove out a front kick, knocking an enemy blade aside. His own sword crunched into a mage's side. Another soldier struck out. Ashocc jumped back but the blade nicked his stomach, biting deep. Blood flowed.

'Ashocc, turn!' ordered Auum.

Auum smashed his elbow into the face of an enemy coming up on his right. He powered on through the confused mess. His blades flicked out left, right, high and low, blocking and cutting, beating a path to his brother. Ashocc took another blow on his blade but tripped on a body behind him and fell.

Auum shouldered the last soldier out of his way, dashed a blade into a mage's ribs and leaned to seize the stricken TaiGethen. Blows came in from both sides and ahead. With his left hand, Auum grabbed Ashocc, trying to haul him upright. With his right, he fended away a strike to his flank. His left foot whipped out, tripping another attacker, balancing with his right. The stink of man and blood was filling his nostrils.

'Go!'

Ashocc's feet were back under him and the pair of them struck out. Auum could see Bylaan and Acclan fighting hard, trying to make space. Blows came in again. Auum swayed inside one, seeing the blade strike sparks from the ground. He parried another but a third got through and cut across Ashocc's face and neck.

Ashocc's legs gave way but Auum would not let him fall. He heaved the warrior through the enemy line and into a moment's space.

'TaiGethen, break and run,' he shouted.

Illast and Bylaan pushed back against the humans and took Ashocc from Auum. They sprinted away along the street, Ulysan, Acclan and Kepller with them, the latter dragging his leg badly and supported by the others. Arrows began to fly. Spells would soon follow.

Auum ran with Ulysan. Two blocks ahead, more men moved onto the street and closed in fast.

'Next left, on my mark.'

Arrows fell in front and behind. Auum saw them target those carrying the wounded. Kepller saw it too and pushed his helpers away. Ulysan grasped at him.

'Space,' shouted Kepller. 'I'll be fine.'

With his next pace, an arrow took him through the eye. He fell dead to the ground. Acclan spat out a curse and made to run to the attack. Ulysan caught him by the arm and dragged him down the left-hand turn. Above, a mage tracked them, too high to shoot down. From the right, poison arrows flew out, driving him higher. Ulysan ducked inside a house, shouldering the door in and running through to the back. He burst into the street and across it into another narrow way.

Castings struck the ground in their wake, sending waves of air across their bodies. One piled into the house, shattering its frame and causing a ripple collapse of others in the terrace.

'Ulysan, back to the fight,' said Auum.

He looked back over his shoulder. Illast and Bylaan had stopped to lay Ashocc on the ground. Illast closed Ashocc's eyes and kissed them before running on, fury in his eyes.

Ulysan led them down a wider street. Men surged past the intersection not thirty paces ahead of them, heading for the first circle, while a few spells flew past overhead. Abruptly, the enemy movement was disrupted. Voices were raised in alarm and weapons were raised high.

Auum saw a TaiGethen in the air, swords held out to either side. Thrynn. She landed in the centre of the enemy. Blood misted. Just like Ashocc only Auum wasn't going to let this brave elf die. Auum stormed into their right flank, chopping his way towards her.

Thrynn's blades were a blur. Men instinctively made a space around her, bringing them onto the blades of Illast, Bylaan, Acclan and Ulysan instead.

Auum butted the man directly in front of him, splitting his nose at the bridge. The man staggered back, raising his blade over his head only to bury the point in the skull of the soldier behind him. Auum slashed a cut across his throat and fell back, finding himself next to Illast.

Illast blocked a blow aside. A second sword point drew blood down his left arm. Bylaan took the pace from the strike and thumped a punch into the soldier's mouth. Auum glanced back and thrashed a sword across the chest of a man only half turned in his direction. He kicked another in the groin and followed up with a roundhouse to the temple, knocking him down. He heard Thrynn cry out and moved faster, Ulysan joining him.

Men were shouting warnings, calling for cover and screaming for more help. But there were eight TaiGethen among them and it was futile. Auum nearly reached Thrynn from one side and her Tai were almost there the other. Auum dragged a soldier back by his hair and stabbed him low in the back, letting him drop and climbing over his body.

A quick soldier laced a cut into Thrynn's thigh, unbalancing her. She began to fall and the soldier raised his blade to finish the job. Porrack of her Tai roared and burst through, blocking his blow. But he had left himself open and a sword took him across the stomach, spilling his entrails onto the ground.

Porrack screamed and collapsed. Thrynn roared his name and buried her blade in his killer's neck.

'Push!' called Auum. 'Straight through.'

He hacked down into an enemy's leg, shouldered a second aside and scooped Thrynn up with one arm. Auum put his head down and charged the line of soldiers ahead. They were already beset by Ataan, Thrynn's second, and Auum chopped out with his sword, not knowing what he was hitting. He heard Ulysan holler a war cry followed by the shriek of a dying man.

Auum burst through the line and carried on into a side street, back towards the main road in.

'Ataan, break and clear!'

The TaiGethen pounded away. Auum released Thrynn and looked back over his shoulder. All the rest were clear. But in front of them men were still streaming into the city and the spells continued to fall. Soon they would be among the city folk and Auum feared the slaughter that would follow.

Katura echoed to the sounds of falling buildings and the roars of men. Smoke billowed into the sky and blew through the ruined streets. The smell of burning wood tainted the air. The ground beneath Merrat vibrated with explosions and to the thundering of human feet as the invaders poured into the city.

He edged a fraction out of his hiding place to look down the street towards the gates. Ysset sprinted into view from the left, tearing down the largely undamaged centre of the Tuali ghetto. She slid to a halt and stepped into the alley, which lay in deep shadow.

'Corinn's Tai is coming. There are hundreds of soldiers, guarding a mage count of eighty or so, on her tail. Stiff odds.'

'Stiff odds for all of us,' said Merrat. He signalled across the street to where Grafyrre was similarly hidden. 'Remember: we hit the mages and get out. Lead them onto the next trap. Don't stop for the fallen. Tai, we pray.'

Merrat dropped his head but a whistle from Grafyrre interrupted his intended brief meditation. Grafyrre tipped his head up. A spotter mage flew the length of the street, above bowshot range, turned and flew back towards the gates. Merrat flattened himself against the side of a building.

As soon as he had passed Merrat leaned out again, just in time to see Corinn and her Tai of Arkiis and Perrar enter the street, the enemy force a few paces behind. The men's shouts and taunts, which had been muted, became loud and echoing. They were like beasts baying for blood, with no idea they were running headlong into a trap.

'Hold your nerve, Corinn,' whispered Merrat.

And so she did. A few arrows fell about her Tai but none really threatened them. Shafts which fell short bounced from the magical shield covering the enemy and were met with angry shouts. She was too close to the soldiers for mages to risk casting and had resisted the urge to up her pace to seek temporary sanctuary in the run of alleys where Merrat hid.

A movement above them caught Merrat's eye. The spotter mage had flown back and was hovering midway along the street, pointing out targets. Moments later, spells arced out from the main concentration of mages by the city gates, trailing smoke as they came.

Two clusters of blue-brown flame orbs, fizzing and spitting, plunged into houses either side of the road and about thirty yards behind Corinn's Tai as they continued their retreat.

Flame and burning timber exploded up and out. Burning debris was scattered across the street. Merrat heard at least one building collapse and a wave of heat and noise rolled past them, filling the air with the smells of fire once more. Merrat saw the spotter mage put his arms across his chest in an X-shape.

'Missed,' said Nyann.

'No, they didn't,' said Merrat, and he signalled Grafyrre to be ready. 'Corinn's in trouble.'

The air chilled so quickly that Merrat's next breath frosted in front of him. Freezing air blasted from both sides of the street across the burning buildings, flattening anything that remained upright and snuffing out the fire. Plumes of smoke and steam forged skywards. Merrat swore and gave the black howler monkey's guttural call.

'Tai, we move!'

Merrat led his Tai into the street. Grafyrre mirrored his move while overhead the spotter mage began signalling again. Corinn had turned at the sound of the flight call but had not otherwise responded.

'Corinn!' yelled Merrat. 'Run. Get back to us now!'

Like a dream running slowly, Merrat saw Corinn look at the blasted buildings behind her as if for the first time before beginning to run with her Tai. But at the same time, the first humans surged across the blackened, cold timbers and spilled onto the street, filling it quickly.

'Get among them!' shouted Merrat. 'Corinn needs a path.'

The chasing force roared and charged. Merrat led his Tai forward at a sprint. Elven arrows flashed across the space from high buildings on the outer circle. A few men were struck but all too soon the shafts were bouncing off a shield and spells began falling on the elven archer positions.

Merrat drew his twin blades and crashed into the attack, Nyann and Ysset at his sides; Grafyrre's Tai just to their right. Dozens of men had turned towards them leaving the rest to close the pincer on Corinn's Tai. Merrat could just see her, blood covering her sword, moving fast and keeping low and balanced, determined to take down as many as she could.

Merrat blocked a man's blade and chopped his free blade into his neck. Blood sprayed across the humans and the enemy collapsed to the side. Merrat moved up a pace, blades defending his body and head. He heard Ysset gasp, then the thud of her blade and her victim's scream. Nyann's blades weaved in Merrat's peripheral vision, one striking sparks off enemy steel, the other stabbing through a man's throat.

Merrat ducked a flailing strike and rammed both his swords into his enemy's gut. He stood, kicked the man aside and moved up, his Tai with him.

'Keep pushing,' he urged. 'We can break through.'

But on the flanks the enemy were beginning to understand the attack in the centre and were running round to box them in. Above, the spotter mage brought down fire and ice on buildings twenty yards behind Merrat and Corinn and her Tai were completely surrounded.

'Merrat!' It was Grafyrre. 'Too many. Break off, or we're trapped.'

Merrat smashed the hilt of a blade into his enemy's nose and with the other blocked a strike from another intended for Nyann. Nyann reacted quickly, disembowelling the man and swaying inside a thrust to his heart from his left. Ysset broke her attacker's knee with a straight kick before moving in half a pace, crushing his nose with her elbow and driving a blade through his heart.

'No! We can't leave them to die,' Merrat called back.

But he knew Grafyrre was right: the lines of men were thickening. A glance behind told him they were close to being cut off, and ahead an elven shriek followed by a roar of triumph told him that one of Corinn's Tai had perished. Merrat pushed back a pace, needing a moment to make a decision.

And then there she was: Corinn. She had leapt high above her enemies' heads, her legs brought up to her chest and her dripping red blades circling in her arms to strike down. Her clothing was drenched in gore and blood pulsed from wounds all over her body. Merrat took in her face. It was cut across the forehead and her cheeks and chin were smeared with blood. Her mouth was open in a cry of fury and her eyes burned with her hatred of man.

Eyes everywhere were drawn to her by the scream that burst from her lips. One of her blades hacked down into a man's neck, half-severing his head. Blood erupted from the wound and Corinn exulted. A blade was thrust up, skewering her through the gut as she began to descend. She faced her killer and drove her other blade into his chest. Both disappeared from view, into the midst of the enemy.

'No!' yelled Merrat and he made to move forward.

Ysset grabbed his arm and dragged him back. 'We have to go. Now.'

In the heartbeat before battle was joined again, Merrat's head cleared and he turned and ran, calling his Tai and seeing Grafyrre sprinting along beside him. His friend's face was grey and angry and the pain of defeat hurt more than the thrust of any blade. Behind them, men shouted and gave chase.

Merrat ran hard past the destruction wrought by magic. More spells bit into the street ahead of them, sending sheets of flame high into the air. More spells destroyed the buildings they ran past, revealing yet more men choking the city streets. The TaiGethen ran harder, Merrat moving them towards a narrow opening between two as-yet-undamaged houses.

Arrows hissed through the air, slamming into wood and dirt but sparing their targets further pain. Merrat slid to a halt at the opening and herded his charges inside.

'Keep running. Let's get to the central rally point.'

He took a last look at the invading humans, ducking back as a trio of arrows thudded into the timbers where his head had been. He ran after his people, feeling the first tears threatening. They lost the humans easily in the maze of alleys that linked the Tuali ghetto to that of the Ixii, and from there to the core of Katura.

Reaching the rally point, they paused and Grafyrre turned to stare at Merrat.

'How can we prevail against power like that?' he asked.

Merrat placed his hands on Grafyrre's shoulders and pushed back the despair that threatened to overwhelm him too. How easily they had been beaten. There was no defence against the might of magic.

'We fight on because it is all we have,' said Merrat. 'Until the last of us falls if that's what it takes.'

Beside him, Ysset wavered.

'Ysset?'

'It's all right, I'm—' A frown crossed Ysset's face and she dropped to her knees and then fell to her side. 'Merrat?'

Merrat crouched down beside her. Blood ran in a thin line from her mouth. Merrat looked quickly down her body. There was a spreading stain of blood from close to her left armpit.

'Oh no,' breathed Merrat.

'It's all right,' said Ysset, gasping her breaths. 'I knew it was bad.'

'You should have backed off, got help.'

'I will never desert my Tai.' Ysset smiled. 'I knew it was bad. No sense in seeking help.'

Ysset's smile faded and she sought and gripped Merrat's hand. Merrat stared into her eyes until she died. He felt a hand on his shoulder.

'Until the last of us falls,' said Grafyrre.

'Until the last of us,' said Merrat. 'Not long now.'

'Gods under water, I feel twenty-five again!' Lockesh shouted.

Hynd wondered whether to marvel more at his skill or at his joy, the like of which he had never witnessed before. The mage lord was soaked with sweat but his belief and confidence had brought over five hundred mages to the battlefield, where they were doing precisely what Jeral wanted.

They were inside the gates now, surrounded by a ring of soldiers four deep to protect them from attack. The TaiGethen had been beaten back and at least three of them had been killed. Jeral was leading the central thrust straight into the heart of the city. The elven archers could not penetrate the shields and there was no sign of the city folk at all now that they had been broken and scattered. Spells flashed out above the army and into the buildings ahead, ripping off roofs, destroying walls and burning everything to cinders. There would be no hiding places left. It was just a matter of time.

Hynd watched the spotter mages circling just in front of the three prongs of Jeral's trident attack. They were the brave ones. Despite all of Lockesh's entreaties, Hynd would never have taken wing to-day; only three mages had volunteered to. They had pinpointed the TaiGethen and archers effectively so far, and the advantage they brought was incalculable.

Lockesh released his spell. The blue orb with spectacular white lightning blazing inside it flew hard and fast into the buildings which surrounded Katura's central marketplace. Hynd watched it fly. It blew through a pair of shutters and detonated inside.

The force of the explosion rippled the roof so violently that it collapsed inwards and blew out shutters to either side. Timbers snapped inside the walls and the whole structure shifted to the right. The upper floor failed and dropped onto the floor below, the weight bringing the whole building down on itself. Dust billowed out and cheers rose clear over the sound of splintering wood.

The noise was so loud that Hynd didn't hear the shouts of warning the first time. Caught up in the moment, he was surprised by the sudden push behind him and almost fell into the mage in front of him.

'What the—' Hynd turned to shove the soldier back. 'Oh shit shit shit!'

A panther roared. Hynd saw its leap and its jaws, wide open and dripping saliva, clamp around a helpless soldier's skull. Tall painted elves strode behind them, their hands like rapiers, their teeth sharpened to rip the flesh from his bones. They and their panthers were everywhere. Swords rose; blood fountained into the air; men screamed. The defence pushed back against the elves, granting the mages a little space.

'Concentrate!' screamed Lockesh.

Hynd had never heard him sound scared before. He forgot the ClawBound and turned. Lockesh was focused on a mage right next to him. Hynd didn't know his name but he was sweating and rocking, plainly terrified, and he'd been about to cast when the attack began. Soldiers were pressing in on them from all sides, the mages trying to push them back, yelling for the space to cast.

'I can't . . .' he said, crying like a child.

'Yes, you can,' said Lockesh. 'Feel the shape and stabilise.'

Hynd let his mind fill with the mana spectrum and saw the shape of an orb in front of the young mage. It was tattered and, rather than spinning about its axis, was bowing into an oval, wobbling and juddering. Hynd swallowed hard. If the mage lost control of that construct it would spray lethal magical fire in all directions.

'Let it go!' said Hynd. 'Cast it!'

Hynd was struck from behind and had no chance to help himself. He pitched forward, shoving the mage ahead of him hard in the back with his hands as he did. Hynd hit the ground with a weight on top of him and a warm and wet sensation around his neck.

He rolled over, heaving himself half up to shift the weight. The soldier, his throat torn out, slid onto the ground. Hynd shouted and scrabbled away.

'Drag it back!' yelled Lockesh. 'Drag it back!'

Everything seemed to slow. Hynd stared up at the young mage through a crowd of legs and bodies, some trying to run forward, others trying to turn to face the ClawBound. A panther brushed past

him. He could see elven legs in among his people. And he saw the
mage lose his fight to contain the casting.

The young man's mouth opened to scream as the flesh began to
melt from his face. He put his hands to his cheeks and his eyes burst,
blood spurted from his nose and flames encased him. His hair
vaporised, his skin blackened and peeled away from his skull and
his lips swelled and ruptured.

He reached for Lockesh and the mage lord, still sampling the mana
spectrum, pushed him back.

'Run,' he shouted. 'Run!'

Lockesh tried to shove his way through but there was no escape.
The young mage erupted into a pillar of fire. Tongues of flame traced
the mana and buried themselves in other casting mages. Hynd was
flung back as if an invisible hand had punched him in the chest, and
Lockesh was picked up and hurled ten feet into the air, crashing
down onto soldiers six ranks ahead. His face had been burned away
to the bone.

Above them, two spotter mages had flown closer. Hynd saw one's
wings gutter and fail with the shock of what he saw, and the other
flew off, screeching and yelling.

'He's down! Lockesh is down!'

'Sundering! Sundering!'

Panic sped through the army like a gust of wind across the water.

'No, no, no!' gasped Hynd, but he had no breath in his body.
'There's no Sundering. Turn. You have to turn and fight.'

He pulled himself back to his feet. There was fire everywhere. He
couldn't count the dead through the smoke. He heard someone yell
for order, for a push back against the ClawBound, but there was no
way for the soldiers through the panicked mage lines.

Hynd stumbled again. Men were everywhere. Mages were fleeing
into the burning side streets. Panthers and elves ran after them,
brought them down like game in a hunt. Hynd almost sampled the
mana spectrum but feared what he would find. Lockesh was down.
All the shields were down.

Hynd didn't know what to do. He was surrounded by his own
people but felt so vulnerable. Still the ClawBound attacked and now
there was shouting from the army ahead.

'Here they come!' screamed a voice. 'Archers! Archers on the
rooftops. Get me shields. Hynd!'

It was Jeral, somewhere nearby, but Hynd couldn't think straight.

He heard a panther roar and jumped back, startled, only to find himself right next to Jeral. The captain hacked to the other side and Hynd heard an animal howl in pain.

'Cast,' said Jeral, backing away towards the centre of the army, fingers itching at the scars on his cheeks. 'You can do it.'

'I can't,' said Hynd. 'Lockesh is gone. I can't . . .'

Hynd felt a breeze pass by his left ear and saw an arrow slap into the mud. The next instant he felt an impact in his left shoulder. He grunted and stumbled.

'I'm hit,' he said. 'Jeral, I'm hit.'

Hynd's vision tunnelled. He tried to drag in a breath but it wouldn't come. He pawed at his throat but his fingers were numb. He felt his legs give way and he fell to his knees. A searing pain flashed down his body, encasing him. Every nerve screamed. Hynd scrabbled at his throat. The pressure grew and he tried to gasp but there was nothing. No air and his mouth wouldn't open.

'All right, Hynd, I've got you. You'll be all right,' said Jeral.

Hynd pitched forward onto his face, unable to turn his head or put out his hands to break his fall. His eyes were wide but he was blind. The pain reached a crescendo and he could not give it voice. The sound of battle faded and the last thing he heard was Jeral shouting for help.

Chapter 37

Garan seeks death at every turn. Does, then, the human spirit need to evolve to properly embrace immortality?

From *On Immortality* by Ystormun, Lord of Calaius

Pelyn saw it happen and knew their chance had come. A great wash of flame had erupted in the midst of the enemy and the castings had stopped. She had seen them panic and a human had been thrown into the air. The ClawBound must have lost many but their attack never faltered. She could only hope Auum had been watching too, wherever he was.

She roared the order to charge and led three hundred from the hall of the Al-Arynaar into the central ring, where the human advance had stalled. Archers surged up the sides of tottering buildings and began to shoot. Arrows finally found their targets; the magical shields were gone.

Pelyn had the Al-Arynaar in a single line leading the hastily trained Katuran militia. Elsewhere, ready to face other human forces, Tulan and Ephram had similar numbers. Every other Katuran had been ordered back to the lake and the falls, as far south as they could go before the blank rock faces stopped them.

The humans outnumbered her people by five to one, but without their magic Pelyn doubted their courage. She raced around the edge of the burning, collapsed courthouse and into the ring, where men panicked and elven temples burned.

Pelyn howled her fury and ran harder. The enemy saw her and, after a moment's shock, formed up on their commander's orders. Arrows flew from behind their front ranks and three of her Al-Arynaar fell. So did some Katurans who would never get to defend their city after all. The charge did not falter.

Pelyn and her front line crashed into the humans. Pelyn caught a sword on the hilt of her blade, turned it aside and thumped a punch into the man's face. She cut her sword back across his chest and kicked him hard in the ribs, sending him down among his fellows.

Two more came at her. She ducked a swipe at her head and whipped out her left fist, feeling it break teeth and split lips. Pelyn blocked a thrust to her midriff as she straightened then paced back, needing a breath. The soldier came at her again, overhead this time. She got her sword into position just in time and turned the blow aside. She kicked out straight, catching him in the stomach. He was fast, and his next strike cut her cheek while she tried to fend him away.

Next to her, an Al-Arynaar fell, his face bloodied and his skull split. A Katuran *ula* raced into the gap and delivered a massive blow with a shovel, slicing his enemy's face open from right eye to left cheek, breaking bones and knocking him from his feet. The human clattered into Pelyn's attacker and she seized her chance to bury her blade in his chest through his leather armour.

The shovel wielder was quickly cut down, but the Katurans kept coming. Another filled the gap, jabbing out with a long pitchfork, keeping his target well back. Pelyn moved into the space. She dropped to her haunches and swept her blade through her victim's knees, pushed upright and jabbed out, her blow glancing off an enemy blade and into her target's neck.

Pelyn breathed hard. Her heart was racing and the sweat was already pouring from her. Her arms ached and her legs were trembling. She needed water. She needed nectar. She would get neither. Promising herself as much of both as she could take when the battle was done, she shook her head to clear her vision and threw herself back into the fight.

Auum saw the last of the spotter mages fall, his shadow wings failing him. His poison archers were lords of the higher ground now and they wreaked havoc in the central ring. Auum brought his Tais with him into a side street leading into the marketplace. Men were breaking ranks and running towards him – mages seeking escape. Claws chased them down.

'Marack, get word to Graf and Merrat. They have to attack now. Then come back west to join Acclan. Acclan, go west with Oryaal and Illast. The Katurans must hit the enemy there too before their magic returns. Tais, we move.'

Auum raced towards the marketplace with Ulysan, Thrynn and

Ataan. Here the humans were attacked from in front and behind. Pelyn had redeemed herself at last and the ClawBound . . . Perhaps Auum's words, spoken an age ago in the depths of the rainforest, had reached Serrin after all. It hardly mattered. They were here now and they had changed the course of the battle.

They ran in, hurdling the bodies of dead mages and running beside panthers racing to rejoin their Bound elves once more. Entering the marketplace, Auum saw the extent of the chaos the ClawBound had caused. They were still on the attack at the northern end of the market by the part-collapsed temple of Yniss, holding their line at the end of the street to prevent flanking. Archers perched in the burned rafters fired over their heads into the enemy.

To the south Pelyn's Katurans and Al-Arynaar were holding against an organised defence, while in the centre mages with nothing but daggers were looking for soldiers to protect them. The cohesion of the army had gone completely and humans were scattered all over the central ring, most of them desperate to find a way out.

'Get forward and break the attack on Pelyn,' said Auum.

Human bowmen were firing into the rear of Pelyn's lines and up into the buildings on the edge of the ring, trying to dislodge his archers. Dead ahead, soldiers guarding the flank and the mages in their midst saw the TaiGethen charge and turned to face them.

'Jaqrui,' he called.

Without their shields to protect them, the humans suffered the full force of the crescent blades. Auum threw two, both of them finding their targets. He heard the mourning sound of more jaqrui and saw one slice the top from an enemy's skull, another chop away a mage's dagger hand.

Auum drew his twin blades and sprinted in at an angle calculated to take him towards Pelyn. The enemy readied but he had no time for them. Two paces in front of their line he jumped, turned a roll in the air and came down behind them in the midst of mages and bowmen.

A mage in front of him screamed; Auum slashed him through the shoulder and barged him aside. A bowman turned and shot; Auum saw the flight of the arrow and swayed his body to the right then lashed out his blade and split the bowman's skull. Auum thrust left and caught a mage's dagger. He turned his wrist, drove the weapon down and jabbed his blade into the man's face. Auum moved his right blade out, slicing deep into the side of another. He jumped above a clumsy hack. His feet licked out one after the other, smashing the soldier's nose and breaking his jaw.

Auum moved on, hearing his Tais driving into the fragile enemy flank. He glanced behind him, seeing the ClawBound beginning to fall back, their panthers tiring. They had done enough. Ahead, the humans had begun to make ground. Auum signalled archers on the wrecked courthouse to concentrate their fire on the enemy front line.

Three men ran at him, seeing him alone and thinking him vulnerable. Auum watched them come and saw the intent in each of them. They would reach him simultaneously but it would do them no good.

The first jumped in the air to hack his blade down two-handed. Auum simply stepped aside and reversed a sword into the man's back, skewering vital organs. The second had gone low, but Auum was already jumping above his swipe. He landed while the man was off balance and kicked his standing leg from under him. Auum thrust his right fist into the mouth of the third before he could deliver his intended strike. He finished the second off, stamping hard on the back of his neck and feeling it crack beneath his foot.

Auum paused. More came at him. Bowmen were also targeting him, but in the chaos he could crouch and run beneath their arcs of vision. With his own poison archers doing terrible damage to their ranks, he battered into the rear of the human lines, Ulysan once again at his shoulder.

Pelyn sensed the shift in the army behind the front lines and knew the TaiGethen had joined the attack. She was blowing hard and her blade speed had dropped. Most of the Al-Arynaar about her were dead, and the Katurans were beginning to waver before the humans' skilled blades.

'One more time!' she called, fending away a cut to her head and lashing a blow to a human's gut. 'We can break them.'

To her left, a Beethan *iad* screamed. Her meat cleaver went spinning from her hand, which had been partly severed by a savage blow. The soldier drew back his blade to finish the job but the *iad* leapt on him, her other hand ripping at his eyes and her teeth clamped on his lower jaw.

'That's it!' cried Pelyn. 'Hit them with everything you have. For Katura!'

Her words were taken up along the Katuran lines and they flew in once more. The enemy fell back a pace, regrouped and formed again,

blades working hard, doing dreadful damage to the poorly trained
city folk. The Katurans would not hold for long. Pelyn drew another
shuddering breath and pushed forward.

She faced a man with the mark of command on him. Pelyn dodged
back, avoiding his thrust to her stomach by a whisker. She bounced
forward, aiming a cut at his head which he blocked hard, sending a
painful vibration through her arm.

Katuran militia next to her lost their lives, their inadequate
weapons breaking in the face of keen steel. One lost her intestines
to a deep cut. Another's heart was pierced by a blow which sliced
straight through his unskilled defence. More took their places. Hope
remained, but Pelyn could feel it it faltering.

Pelyn's opponent advanced. He feinted right and struck left. She
deflected the blade but its edge sliced into her side. Pelyn gasped at
the sudden pain. She moved her blade left to right in riposte and the
man leapt back. Her sword point cut into the leather at his neck.

Pelyn heard shouts from behind and felt the Katurans press in
around her, their sudden move forcing the enemy back again. Her
enemy weaved his sword in front of her. As she tried to follow the
blade, nausea gripped her. She felt weak and her mouth was dry.
Pelyn took half a pace back and waved her blade in front of her
chest, trying to give herself a moment.

The enemy moved in. He butted her, his forehead smashing into
her nose before she could lift her blade. Pelyn staggered back, dazed.
Other humans moved to either side, driving her flanking militia back.
The man stepped in again and Pelyn struck out. Her thrust was
blocked and the next instant she felt a terrible cold pain in her chest.

The soldier put his hand out and pushed her away. His blade came
clear, its edges dragging against her ribs. Her mouth filled with
blood. Pelyn dropped her blade and fell, the pain gone to be replaced
by a roaring in her ears that grew and grew with each slow heartbeat.
She looked around and saw nothing but the gaping mouths and wide
eyes of dead Katurans.

Her head fell back against the ground. There were shapes in the
air, tumbling and rolling. Someone called her name but she didn't
have the strength to reply.

'Pelyn!' Auum landed astride her body, Ulysan a couple of paces to
his right. 'Fight! Fight for Pelyn! Fight for your lives!'

The Katurans had paused and some had lost their lives as a result.

Auum's arrival energised them once more, lent confidence to flagging spirits and turned them on their human foe one last time.

Ulysan led the charge, driving a wedge into the enemy lines that the Katurans filled. Jeral stood in front of Auum, his blade dripping with Pelyn's blood. He pointed at Auum.

'Kill him,' he said.

Four rushed in. Auum held one sword across his forehead and the other with its tip touching the ground. His body was forward and his legs straddled the breathing but dying Pelyn. He didn't wait for them to strike. Auum lashed his high blade across the face of the leftmost, his low blade up through the thigh of the rightmost. He balanced himself instantly, jumped straight up and kicked both feet into the chest of the third soldier. Auum landed on the unfortunate's chest and brought his blades across his body, batting aside the blade of the last with one and opening up his stomach with the other.

Auum walked over the soldier on which he stood, crushing his throat on his way to Jeral. The human commander stood alone. The human line wavered behind him, its flanks weak and its centre fatally pierced by Ulysan.

Jeral swept his sword left to right. Auum ducked under it and with his left blade blocked it down and aside. He took a pace forward and drove his right blade into Jeral's chest. The two locked eyes momentarily before Jeral's gaze began to fade. Auum dragged the blade clear with his next motion and cut as hard as he ever had across Jeral's exposed neck with his left.

Jeral's body teetered for a moment then crumpled sideways, his head rolling off his neck to fetch up at Auum's feet. The elf stared into the eyes of the men behind Jeral and fought for the word he needed in the clumsy human tongue.

'Flee,' he said.

They fled. Auum took Jeral's head by the hair and held it high.

'Their commander is dead!' he roared. 'Their magic is gone and their beast has no head. Fight, Katura! Break them.'

Katurans hanging back behind Auum roared their support and rushed past him. Auum watched them go. He flung the head towards the wavering enemy.

'Here, have him. I have no use for him.'

He saw the head bounce once in the mud and roll a couple of times before stopping, the eyes staring up and the mouth hanging open.

Auum turned to Pelyn and dropped to his knees by her side. She was almost gone but still she managed a faint smile when she saw him.

'You did it,' said Auum. 'You showed your true self. Shorth will welcome you and the ancients will honour your arrival among them.'

Pelyn tried to speak but her mouth was clogged with blood.

'Shhh,' said Auum. 'All is forgiven, Pelyn. They are broken. We have won. You have saved Katura and the elves.'

Pelyn gripped his hands and hauled her head from the ground. Blood flowed from her mouth and she coughed violently, spraying his face with a red mist.

'Always . . . believed in . . . you,' she said and fell back, her chest heaving and bubbles forming on her lips.

Auum nodded. He leaned over her and kissed her forehead and her eyes.

'Hero of Hausolis. Hero of Ysundeneth. Hero of Katura. Sleep. Your work is done. Yniss takes you for other tasks beyond death.'

Pelyn was dead. Auum smiled and rose back to his feet.

'Stretcher!' he called. 'Take Pelyn to the temple of Tual. See that she is comfortable.'

Auum looked to his people. The Katurans, with Ulysan in their midst, were driving the humans back across the marketplace. Thrynn and Ataan were fighting their way towards Ulysan through the tattered group of men. The ClawBound had re-entered the fray from the right and soldiers were scattering from their path.

Auum could see through the thinning smoke, down a street that led towards the eastern walls, that the enemy had been broken there too and was running with Katurans slaughtering any they caught. Auum strode through the marketplace. Here and there he found a human still breathing and sent them to the eternal torment of Shorth.

He stopped when he reached Jeral's head and spat on it.

'This is our forest. No man will ever conquer the elves.'

Chapter 38

Ystormun believes my spirit needs to evolve to enjoy the extra-ordinary pain I experience with every waking moment. That's what happens when you sell your soul to the demons, isn't it? Idiot.

Reminiscences of an Old Soldier, by Garan,
sword master of Ysundeneth (retired)

Don't let the whining get to you, will you? It's natural for some to complain even though you've saved them from certain death and are offering them power beyond their most fevered imaginings.

Takaar increased his pace towards the river and the boats ready to take the slowest and neediest back to Loshaaren. There he would leave his new recruits with their teachers while he concluded his business in Ysundeneth with the only human worthy of life. It was a paradox of the cruellest nature, given his final task there.

There were almost two hundred Il-Aryn-in-waiting: Gyalans, Ixii, Orrans and Cefans. A good number, and a challenging task for the Ynissul who would be trying to teach them under his and Onelle's guiding hands. But getting them to Loshaaren was proving a trial in itself.

Indeed. They're utterly helpless, aren't they? Did you see even the Senserii's expressions flicker? Just think what would happen if they deserted you. Who would hunt, gather and protect then?

Takaar scratched his chin, muttering. 'Soon to the river, soon to quick and calm travel. Let's not dally here or worry there. Can't help, only hinder and we don't need any more of that, now do we?'

'Takaar? Takaar!'

Drech, it was always Drech. He was the self-appointed speaker for every one of the elves traipsing moodily through the glory of the forest, whose spirits Takaar seemed unable to lift. He heard the young

Ynissul's footsteps through the easy undergrowth like thunderclaps in the heavens.

Turn and smile.

Takaar stopped and turned. He looked past Drech to the elves behind him, who had stopped. Again.

'What is it?'

What, no smile?

Takaar muttered under his breath. Drech raised his eyebrows and Takaar waved for him to speak.

'Many of your students are complaining of fatigue. There is much desire to rest until morning.'

Takaar looked up. The afternoon was just past its midpoint. There were four more hours of good walking left in the day.

'What do you say?' asked Drech.

Hmm. Tough one.

'Not tough at all. I'll tell you what I say.'

Takaar pushed past Drech and strode back down the deer trail. He scratched at his left arm where a fearsome itch had sprung into life. Blind, all of them, and stupid too. Did they really think—

'—that this is some sort of game, and you can decide to sit it out when your boots start to rub?'

The increasingly unhappy group was gathered among the trees surrounding a small pool where rainwater ran off the rock a few feet above. The delineation between them was clear. Those who had been forced to march to the palm of Yniss all those years ago and then build a city from nothing were on their feet, but they were few. Those who had been born and lived their lives within Katura's questionable security were seated. There were the majority, with the greatest potential.

'Do you think we are playing track and chase?'

Barely one of them would look at him. Some were still arriving and others sat with their backs to him. Takaar scratched harder at his arm through his shirt, where the itch was spreading. He jutted his chin in the direction of Katura.

'I snatched you from death at the hands of man. The TaiGethen are fighting there right now, giving you the time to escape. Is this how you choose to repay their sacrifice?' Takaar walked among them. 'Perhaps I was wrong to save you. Perhaps you are too weak to become Il-Aryn.'

Takaar dragged up the sleeve of his shirt and looked at the raw patch. He scratched harder, his nails raking at his skin.

'I do not have time for a stroll through the woods. I have work to do. There are things I must do and places I must go. You must not rest here. You may not. Dammit.'

Takaar stared at his arm again, seeing something move beneath the skin. He scraped harder, drawing blood. He hissed through his teeth.

'See? See? The reach of the human evil is long indeed. They send insects to crawl through my skin and steal the Il-Aryn from me. I will not let that happen. Not to me, or the elves are finished. All of us!'

Oh, wonderful. Your powers of motivation are undimmed.

Takaar stared once more at his bloodied forearm and fingers. Nothing moved there now.

As if anything ever had.

'Drech, Gilderon, to me.'

Takaar walked to the rainwater pool. Drech and the speaker of the Senserii joined him. He spoke loud enough for all to hear him.

'You know the way to the river and you know the safest paths to Loshaaren,' he said to Gilderon. 'Use the boats well. Make haste. Guard our people. They are weak and they must be made strong. Do not listen to complaints or excuses. Any who cannot keep up must be left where they fall.'

Takaar locked his gaze with Drech's.

'I will not lose any more time and you will not give succour to the feeble. I travel to Ysundeneth because I owe a debt to a human who is greater than all of those sitting and whining at my feet. Find Onelle and begin your studies to control the Il-Aryn. I will return as soon as I am able.'

Drech's face darkened. 'I will not leave any of these elves to die in the rainforest.'

'Then stay with them. It is your choice. Gilderon, you understand. You will lead.'

Gilderon inclined his head. 'Yes, my Arch Takaar. Three will run with you.'

'You can't spare them.' Takaar itched again. 'I have to go. They are seeking me.'

Without another glance at the elves he had beguiled into travelling to an uncertain future in the depths of the forest, Takaar turned and ran into the rainforest. It was ten days to Ysundeneth. He looked down at his arm. Tea tree oil would fix it and the warmth of the Il-Aryn would bind it.

'I'm coming, my friend. You will not die alone.'

Rain beat down on Katura. The falls swelled and the cascades sang in victory. Blood washed off the few remaining cobbles and into the drainage channels running along most of the streets. It pooled, diluted, in the churned mud of the battlegrounds.

As many as could had crammed onto what remained of the ramparts to see the remnants of the human army flee into the forest. Perhaps six hundred had survived the ferocity of the elves' revenge, just a tenth of those who had come to conduct their slaughter.

Fervour had overtaken the city in the wake of the rout. The Katurans had set about clearing their streets of the dead. Thousands of bodies lay witness to the intensity of the battle. Through the night, work continued. The elven dead were taken to the wrecked temples to be prepared for reclamation. The humans were piled on dozens of makeshift pyres out on the scorched open ground and burned, while the wind blew from the cliff tops and the smoke was taken north towards Ysundeneth.

At first light the following morning the work was still going on. Auum walked with the surviving TaiGethen towards the gates, where the ClawBound had gathered before leaving the city for the last time. Faleen and Hassek, both injured in the avalanche, were helped by others and the walk was necessarily slow.

Everywhere they went, Katurans paused to thank them, pray with them and bless them. Auum wished that more than fourteen Tais lived to witness their gratitude. Rebuilding the TaiGethen would be a long path which could not begin until their work was complete. More could still fall in the liberation of their cities.

In the marketplace the benches and gardens had been destroyed but a new flagpole had already been cut and erected. It was still bare but was a symbol of the city and a sign that healing had already begun. Auum saw Nerille talking to Tulan of the Al-Arynaar. He had a jagged cut down the left side of his face, which bore signs of grief for Pelyn's death, and for Ephram's.

'You're leaving, I take it?' asked Nerille.

'I made a promise to Koel in Ysundeneth and I intend to keep it.

Now the humans are broken, we have to cleanse our forest and our cities. Your son?'

Nerille smiled. 'Unhurt. It is a miracle. I'm sorry you lost so many.'

The TaiGethen acknowledged her words.

'Will you rebuild?' asked Ulysan.

Nerille blew out her cheeks. 'There is so much to do, but yes, I think so. I'm sure that in time, when we hear the cities are ours again, some will return to them. Not me. This is my home. My sweat helped to build Katura and I will be reclaimed here.'

'Good,' said Auum. 'Tulan, how many survived?'

'Thirty-five, though nearly all of us are are injured.'

'It's a start.' Auum paused, collecting his thoughts. 'We all made mistakes and they have cost us dear. The TaiGethen will never desert this city again, as long as one elf remains here. And to you falls the task of rebuilding the Al-Arynaar. Seek warriors from across Calaius and from every thread. We must never be so weak again and we must never forget we are one race against a common enemy.

'I name you Arch.'

Tulan's eyes widened. 'I accept . . . I am honoured. I will not fail you.'

'It is Pelyn's memory you must not fail, not me.' Auum turned to Nerille. 'Call on us whenever you need us. We are honoured to have fought beside your people.'

He and Nerille embraced.

'Thank you, Auum, for all you have done. Yniss bless you for what lies ahead. Perhaps you will find time to grieve.'

Auum's throat threatened to close. 'I pray for that day.'

He led the TaiGethen to the gates. The rain had not lessened, but the ClawBound, like every other survivor, were in the open, enjoying its cleansing powers. There were ten remaining pairs and all displayed battle scars. Claws and Bound elves stood when the TaiGethen approached. Serrin, his right arm covered in a healing balm, walked forward. Auum did the same, the two meeting between their peoples.

'You saved us,' said Auum. 'You turned the battle. Every living elf owes you a debt they cannot hope to repay.'

Serrin looked embarrassed. 'We remembered who we were, and that is all. You are the one who saved the race of elves.'

Serrin placed hand on Auum's shoulder and Auum returned the

gesture. The two old friends dragged each other into an embrace that released a century of pain and misunderstanding.

'I would have it as it used to be between our callings,' said Serrin. 'Back in the early years.'

'That is all I have ever wanted,' said Auum.

Serrin smiled. 'There is much for you to forgive.'

'It is forgiven.'

Around them, the panthers purred in contentment and their Bound elves held out their hands in new greeting. The TaiGethen crossed the space to welcome them and Ulysan's embrace with Sikaant was long and joyous.

'You're travelling to Ysundeneth?' asked Serrin

Auum nodded. 'If we can free the enslaved, we can overwhelm what defences men still have. And if we can reclaim Ysundeneth, the other cities will fall. Man has no courage without his magic.'

Serrin sniffed the air. 'Leave those in the forest to us. To hunt them will be joy undimmed.'

'Find Takaar,' said Auum. 'Tell him what has happened here.'

'Run fast, Auum.'

'Hunt well, Serrin.'

Auum watched the ClawBound flow across the open ground with its pyres and scorched earth and disappear into the eaves of the forest. One more task lay ahead.

'Faleen, Hassek. Stay here. Recover your strength and then head for Aryndeneth. We will find you there. Tais, we move.'

In the darkness of the panoramic room Ystormun tried to still his shaking hands. He had scanned the mana spectrum again and again. He had searched for the signatures of his Communion hosts over the endless miles of forest to the very borders of Katura and he had found nothing.

The silence shouted at him.

And out in the city the Sharps were singing.

Why were they singing? They could not know something he did not. But they could count the days and with each day that passed without word of men's victory, hope grew in their filthy elven hearts.

Ystormun walked to the windows and stared out over the rain-forest.

Soon the cadre would be inside his head again, and this time his assurances would not be accepted. He had nothing new to say to them. He had no information of any kind.

Ystormun took a long, shivering breath and realised that he was scared.

Chapter 39

A human with a hand outstretched in friendship holds a taipan's fangs in his palm.

TaiGethen saying

'Hello, old friend.'

Takaar had slipped silently into the fresh-scented bedchamber. Night was full but Garan was seated in his chair, the darkness close about him.

'You were expecting me,' said Takaar, moving towards the other chair. He raised his eyebrows. Garan was following him. 'You can see me?'

'Yes and yes,' said Garan. He sounded better than he had at any point in the last twenty years. 'I have friends who were looking for you, or rather for your aura, and those same friends have given me the benefit of temporary night sight.'

'You come closer to being an elf every day,' said Takaar.

'While you get no closer to being funny,' said Garan.

There was a prolonged silence between them borne entirely of acceptance. Takaar sat on the bed unable to look Garan in the eye for the moment.

'So are you going to tell me?'

'Tell you what?' asked Takaar.

Garan shook his head. 'Who won?'

Takaar stilled. Inside his head his tormentor was roaring with laughter. The ClawBound had found him less than a day from Ysundeneth and he should have realised: with mage communication gone, no one here would know.

String it out. Make him squirm.

'We did,' said Takaar. 'None will return.'

Pathetic.

Garan put his hands to his mouth, and when he finally spoke sounded more ancient than ever.

'I tried to warn him. And he only did this so he could send the army back to Balaia. He's weak now. Weaker than ever.'

'After all the trouble we've been to, I sincerely hope so.'

Garan chuckled, a reaction that quickly turned into a hacking cough.

'Not bad,' he conceded, then he sobered. 'A lot of wasted lives.'

'You were never invited here. It was always going to end this way.'

Garan inclined his head. 'But still you need help. Ystormun remains too powerful for you. There's someone I want you to meet. Now don't ov—'

Takaar heard the door to the washroom open. He pushed off the bed with his hands, turned a quick backward somersault and landed. He pivoted on his left hip and jammed his right foot under the jaw of the man who had emerged. The man cursed and Takaar pushed his foot in, threatening to choke him.

'Relax, Takaar. He's a friend of mine,' said Garan. 'Stein, I did tell you to wait until I called you. I told you he was dangerous.'

Takaar stared at the odd-looking human for a moment before removing his foot.

'What are you?' he demanded in the language of man.

'He is Stein,' said Garan. 'He leads a team of twenty-five mages. They, Takaar, are my gift to you.'

Takaar turned to face Garan. 'How?'

'I don't know how many of your TaiGethen are coming here, but they won't be enough, not without magic. Stein and his men believe as I do. Calaius must be rid of Ystormun because the power this territory grants him and his cadre is too great. There's a war coming in our country, Takaar. Ystormun and his ilk must not win it. If we weaken him here, it will give us a chance.'

Takaar walked towards Garan. He heard Stein follow him.

'What will you do?' Takaar asked.

'Whatever we can to keep Ystormun and his men at bay,' said Stein.

'We'll need the wards removed from the slave pens, the gates and the piazza temple walls,' said Takaar. 'And you'll have to stay clear when the elves are released. Many humans will die.'

'You'll trust me?' asked Stein.

'Garan trusts you. I trust Garan.'

'Thank you, Takaar.' Garan nodded. 'And now, Stein, you have to leave. You know why. I'm tired, and Takaar has a promise to keep.'

'You're sure?' asked Stein.

'I've had a century to mull it over,' said Garan.

Stein shook Garan's hand. 'You've done the right thing.'

'Eventually,' said Garan.

Stein looked at Takaar. 'I'll be outside. We must speak, lay plans.'

'I'll find you,' Takaar replied.

Stein closed the door behind him and Takaar knelt in front of Garan. Garan put a clammy hand on his cheek.

'At last,' he said. 'Don't get all emotional on me.'

'You will be a legend among elves when our history is written.'

'I seriously doubt that,' said Garan. 'I want to thank you, Takaar.'

'For what?'

'For talking to an old man, for keeping him at least partly sane. My loneliest and most painful hours have been eased by the thought of your conversation.'

'You showed mercy when I carried Katyett from here,' said Takaar. 'That is something I could never ignore or forget.'

'You have a chance now,' said Garan. 'Stein is talented and his men are loyal. Don't fuck this up. My ghost will be watching you.'

'You don't believe that.'

'No, but it makes a good legend, doesn't it?'

Takaar smiled. 'It does at that. How shall it be?'

'Quick,' said Garan.

'I can promise you that.'

'Good. Then see it done, my friend.'

'Goodbye, Garan.'

'Goodbye, Takaar.'

Takaar's dagger pierced Garan's temple, and he watched the one good human die.

That was well done. Now don't get all emotional about it. Oh. Too late.

It had been a bittersweet run back to Ysundeneth. Auum's route took him past the Haliath Vale on his way to the Ix and the humans' barges, there to discover the Apposans' fate. They had taken a fearful battering. Two out of three were either dead or badly wounded.

Both Boltha and Methian had survived, but memories of the Scar haunted their faces and Auum cursed that two such old and brave elves should have had to witness such times.

Auum's arrival with the TaiGethen had been greeted with joy, but while Boltha asserted that the sacrifice of the Apposans had been worthwhile, his people's faces belied his words.

Knowing their passage downriver to the city would be swift, Auum had invited Boltha and all who would travel with him to come to assist in the liberation of Ysundeneth. Fifty volunteered, Boltha among them, but Methian refused. He chose to return to Katura to help Tulan rebuild their city and the Al-Arynaar.

The barge the elves took passed sites of conflict along much of the length of the Ix. Body parts and bones were scattered along the banks, animals taking what little still remained. The forest bore the scars of human magic, but the river itself was quiet, almost reverential.

Auum landed a half-day from Ysundeneth, well out of sight of any who might be watching. He led his people along the river bank on the easy ground, trampled flat by men's boots. With every step he considered his options, and every one led back to the same scrap of knowledge: without magic they would never be able to enter the city.

Takaar had said he would be waiting for him, but it was still a surprise when Auum saw the wild-looking elf emerge from the treeline two hours south of the city. Auum shook his head. He called a halt to rest.

Takaar spread his arms wide and had that ridiculous beatific expression on his face. Auum went cold at the sight of it.

'What have you done, Takaar?'

Grafyrre, Merrat and Ulysan were with Auum.

Takaar raised his eyebrows. 'You make my arrangements for our victory sound like a crime.'

Auum exchanged glances with Ulysan.

'Where are all your followers?' asked Ulysan.

Takaar waved a hand to the east. 'Safe in Loshaaren by now, I hope, and perhaps even beginning their training. Leaving me to show you into Ysundeneth and the gift Garan gave me.'

Auum tensed. 'There is nothing a human could give you that would be to our benefit.'

'No? Not even if it was the power to dismiss the wards about the gates, to clear the slave pen fences of alarms and to cow the strength of Ystormun himself?'

'You have got to be joking,' snapped Auum. 'He's given you mages? *Human* mages? I can't believe this. I can't believe that even you would be so . . . so *naive*.'

Takaar's face clouded with anger. 'These mages are with us. They are twenty-five-strong and they want him gone as much as we do.'

'And why do you think that is?' shouted Auum, grabbing Takaar's collar and pulling him nose to nose. 'So they can lord over us afterwards! You are repeating Llyron's mistakes. You're as arrogant as Sildaan and I will not let you do this to us.'

Auum threw Takaar back. He did not stumble but came forward again, his eyes locking with Auum's and his expression clear and complete, without a hint of his madness.

'Without them we cannot hope to drive Ystormun away. We can't defeat his magic without having some of our own.' Takaar spread his hands. 'Auum, you must believe me. You must trust me. Look at how few you are and remember what Ystormun did to Katyett. Without magic to aid us, he can do the same to all of us and will be free to continue his domination. For Katyett's memory, for Pelyn and Elyss, you must trust me. I am not a traitor.'

Auum hated it right into the depths of his soul but he knew Takaar was right. He'd known they would need help all along but he'd managed to persuade himself that the Il-Aryn would somehow be strong enough in time.

'Yniss forgive me,' he said. 'All right. You have your wish. Just keep them away from me and tell them that if one of them so much as twitches the wrong way, the TaiGethen will slaughter them in a heartbeat. You tell them that.'

'They already know,' said Takaar.

Auum turned to his people.

'Let's go,' he said. 'This ends tonight.'

The gates of Ysundeneth were shut. A trio of guards stood atop them, staring out into the night and the din of the rainforest. Theirs was the simplest of duties; any trouble visited upon them would be preceded by trouble on the Ultan bridge. But the mages on the bridge belonged to Stein and they had undone every ward protecting it, and the bridge guards had never known what hit them.

Auum moved silently beneath the gates. He motioned Ulysan to his left and Merrat to his right. They climbed fast and silent. Above them the guards talked and laughed and their fire crackled away happily.

Auum signalled. Three TaiGethen hands reached up, three throats were slit and three bodies dumped to the ground in front of the gates.

Auum dropped into the city. The singing he had heard a few hours before had subsided and the slaves were quiet, sleeping if they could. Ulysan and Merrat unbolted the gates and edged them open a crack to allow the TaiGethen and the Apposans into the city. Behind them came Takaar with five human mages.

'The wards are gone at the pens?' he asked Takaar.

'Yes, and Stein's mages have gone too. Any you find there are enemies.'

Auum looked at the mages with Takaar.

'Your friends are all going to die,' he said.

'They are not our friends,' said one.

'A pity,' said Auum. 'Tais, to the boatyards. Boltha, bring your people too. I have a promise to keep.'

Auum didn't trust the human mages and he kept the advance into the city slow, quiet and careful. Patrols were few and weak, just pairs or trios of soldiers with no idea what was stalking through the streets they thought their own. None of them would live once they found out.

Takaar directed them through the yards to the perimeter of the compound holding Koel and thousands of other prisoners. Auum breathed the fetid air and for the first time it tasted of victory and of freedom. He sent a prayer to Elyss and his child in the arms of Shorth and waved his Tais forward.

Six guards stood by the gates, all oblivious to their peril. Takaar came to Auum's shoulder.

'Are the wards gone?' asked Auum.

'Every single one. I told you to trust me.'

'Not until Ystormun is dead,' said Auum. 'Merrat, Graf, Merke, take the three on the left. Ulysan, Marack, with me. Tais, we move.'

Koel was afraid. He lay wedged on the floor between two others for his time of rest but could not sleep. They had sung loud and fervent tonight, and the messages their songs carried had been relayed to every pen in the city. Koel had long prayed for the elves to prevail, and there had come a moment a couple of days earlier when he was certain his wish had been granted.

The doors to their warehouse had been shut and barred, the elves crammed inside with only the food and water they already had. To

Koel, that meant the TaiGethen had won and were coming to liberate their peoplem, but now, on this third night, with hunger and thirst threatening to take the weak to Shorth, he had begun to doubt.

He knew human workers had been arriving. Perhaps there were many more than they had feared and their imprisonment would continue until the human army returned. That evening Koel had decided that they must try and break out themselves, and so he was afraid.

He must have slipped into sleep because he saw a shape above him and he heard Auum's voice.

'I said you would be the first, my friend, and so it has proved to be. Come, stand with me, Koel, hero of Ysundeneth. You and your people are free.'

In truth, most of Auum's words were lost in the explosion of noise all around him as the elves woke to the fact that the TaiGethen were among them. They screamed and shrieked and surged for the doors, threatening to sweep Koel away, but the TaiGethen held him firmly and the liberated elves flowed around them and away into the night.

'The mob will do what it must. Our role is to open all the pens and come to the temple piazza,' shouted Auum.

'I'll lead,' said Koel. 'Enough will follow me.'

'You have friends outside,' said Auum. 'Boltha is here.'

Koel burst into tears and hugged Auum hard.

'That old dog,' he sobbed. 'Will he never die? Thank you, Auum. Thank you.'

'Let's see this done,' said Auum. 'Beware of Ystormun and his guard; they are still dangerous.'

He and Koel walked from the pen together and through the gates to freedom. Koel was shaking and his legs gave way beneath him when he caught sight of Boltha. Auum left them together and rejoined the TaiGethen. The streets of Ysundeneth were alive with the sounds of elves. Their cries of joy mixed with howls of fury. In there somewhere were the screams of dying men.

'Five thousand will become thirty thousand,' said Auum to the TaiGethen. 'And they will sweep this place clean of men's filth. Come, the piazza awaits.'

'We should direct them,' said Ulysan. 'Keep them from danger.'

Auum shook his head. 'This is their night, not ours. The mob has its own mind and will find its way.'

The TaiGethen moved swiftly towards the piazza amid the sounds of the city coming alive to a riot. Fresh roars signalled the release of more slaves. They saw the arcs of spells, but they were desultory and never cast from the same place twice. The mob did indeed have a mind of its own and it was circling the city, heading to the barracks area on its way to the piazza to face its greatest tormentor.

Auum saw soldiers and mages retreating to the piazza, trying to regroup in the only place of power left to them. Soon Stein's mages would have to prove their mettle. It was the only worry left to Auum, but he found to his surprise that he trusted Takaar . . . So make that two concerns, because of the mad elf himself there was no sign.

Auum brought the TaiGethen around to the west of the piazza, where wards had once clung to the sides of temples in dense clusters and had covered the alleys like mould on damp walls. He stopped behind the temple of Orra, and motioned the TaiGethen away.

'It's time to see if Takaar was right,' he said, and before they could protest, he slapped his hand against the wood and began to climb. No fire reached out to scorch his flesh. 'Looks like he was. Follow me.'

The TaiGethen hid among the carvings and plinths that adorned the Orran temple and looked down on the piazza. The desecration that man had visited on the temples was awful. Graffiti covered every wall, carvings were missing, the spire of the Ixii was gone and the temple of Yniss had been completely destroyed.

Auum tried to concentrate on the ground. Soldiers covered the approach from the Path of Yniss ten deep and thirty across. At least forty archers stood behind them and a third formation was made up of dozens of mages. A group of them had already cast what were presumably shields and the rest were preparing a barrage.

'We've got to time this just right,' he whispered, though no one on the ground could hope to hear them, such was the approaching din. 'Ystormun is still waiting for his moment, and we need to keep the castings and the arrows off the crowd. We've got friends down there, remember.'

Auum watched the freed elves approach. Fires were burning all over the city though not one of the elves carried a torch towards the piazza; only the human constructions were being destroyed. The elves were running, the old and sick among them too, all rushing up the Path of Yniss with more and more joining from the side streets.

Some held the limbs and heads of men aloft, taunting the defenders

of the piazza, who were shifting nervously now. The baying howls of
the elves were drawn from their ancient bestial side, and the violence
they would inflict would be truly ferocious.

They advanced quickly, with no time for fear and with their desire
for vengeance driving them on. Fifty yards, forty . . .

An order flashed around the piazza. Castings were readied, arrows
held in drawn bows.

'For the enslaved,' said Auum.

The TaiGethen leapt from the roof of the temple of Orra. The
noise dimmed for Auum. He streaked towards the mages, feeling his
feet barely kissing the piazza stones. He threw a jaqrui and saw it
chop into a mage's side. The man looked round, gaping at what he
saw and opening his mouth to shout a warning.

Auum saw faces turn and mouths open to curse. He drew his
blades, sprinted three more paces and jumped. Auum soared over the
first group, his body horizontal and his arms spread like wings. He
gathered his legs beneath him and landed in among them hacking left
and right, his blades slicing into flesh and skewering organs, grinding
against bone.

Castings arced away towards the onrushing mob, but they were
few and would not be repeated. Auum kicked a mage in the face and
followed with an uppercut that chopped right through his chin and
tore off his nose. He heard the thud of arrows and pushed through
the dwindling number of mages to see TaiGethen ducking and rolling
into the attack.

And the mob . . . the mob burst over the terrified soldiers in a
seething wave of vengeance. The repressed fury of a hundred and
fifty years of slavery, cruelty, evil and humiliation was visited on the
humans tenfold. Auum saw hands rip at faces and teeth tear into
necks and shoulders.

A hundred slaves grabbed at every human and each was torn to
pieces, engulfed in hatred and sent to Shorth for eternal damnation.
With every rent limb raised above a head there came a howl of
triumph. For every head ripped from its shoulders by a dozen clawing,
grasping hands there was recompense for the torture, the executions
and misery untold.

Auum had to turn away. He faced the temple of Shorth and there
he was; standing alone on the roof above the main doors.

'*Cascarg*,' muttered Auum, then shouted, 'Cover! Break, break!'

The TaiGethen scattered towards the temples, but for the mob of freed slaves there was nowhere to go.

'Get back to your pens!' roared Ystormun. His voice was unnaturally loud and echoed from the temple walls. It stilled the mob in an instant. 'I am the ruler here.'

Ystormun raised his hands and forks of black light sped out, seeking souls. Auum ducked into the doorway of Orra. Black fingers ripped at the timbers and felt along the cracks. A network of black lines chased over the piazza and buried themselves in elven bodies.

Those so recently freed screamed as their flesh scorched and their skin was flayed from their faces and hands. The stench of burning meat filled the piazza. Ystormun laughed and the lightning was shut off.

'Go back to your pens. There is no victory for you here. No elf can defeat me.'

'No,' said an equally voice loud. 'But we can.'

Other figures appeared across the roof. Ystormun's head swept round, his skeletal face thick with anger and his robes swirling about his bones.

'*You*,' he spat.

Ystormun raised his arms and the black lightning speared out again. Stein and his mages were ready. Their casting flared and bucked beneath the force of Ystormun's magic but it held. They steadied under his barrage and began to move forward, driving Ystormun's black light back towards him. Ystormun tried to push back but they were too strong for him, just. They held him, they had him.

'It is over, Ystormun,' said Stein, his voice echoing out over the total silence of the piazza. 'Your rule is over.'

'You cannot kill me,' sneered Ystormun. 'If you were three times your number you would not have half the power you need.'

'No, but we can diminish you.'

'And I will return, with the one thought of feeding your soul to the demons.'

'So be it,' said Stein. 'Begin.'

His mages ran to encircle Ystormun, whose black light was losing its force. He dismissed it and put his hands together. Auum saw a ball of deepest blue growing within them.

'Pressure!' called Stein.

His mages spread their arms and Ystormun screamed. The ball in his hands guttered once and blinked out.

'No,' he said. 'You will not do this.'

Auum could see him staring hard at one of the mages.

'No!' shouted Stein. 'Do not catch his eye. Look away!'

Too late. The mage's eyes began to smoulder. Fire engulfed his head, black and roaring. He clasped at his face and it crumbled beneath his fingers. He fell.

'One,' intoned Ystormun.

'Harder!' cried Stein.

Ystormun screamed again. He thought to stare another down, but his head was forced back and his eyes could only glare up to the clouds gathering in the heavens for a downpour that would cleanse Calaius of the stink of man. Ystormun struggled within his invisible prison as the walls pushed against him. His arms were forced down to his sides. Auum heard bones snap as he resisted, and Ystormun gave an agonised shriek.

Stein called for another effort. The twenty-four mages pushed again and Ystormun wailed. His body collapsed, his ribs folding on his heart and his brain exploding from the top of his skull as it was crushed. Robes and blood and bone hung in the air for a moment before Stein dismissed the spell and Ystormun's remains dropped to the roof.

For a moment there was silence, and Auum thought he heard a shriek echoing away into the night sky.

Then the crowd found its voice again. The explosion of sound was like the falling of a mountain or the breaking of the ocean over the whole of the land. Every temple shook with it and the ground rippled with it. It went on and on, passing through the massive gathering until every elf knew that Ystormun was gone.

Auum put his head in his hands and wept as the sound rolled around him. He felt hands dragging him upright and Ulysan giving him his trademark bear hug.

'It is over!' he was shouting. 'It's over!'

The mob began to move. People ran for their temples to pray or broke off into the night, looking for food, drink and humans to kill. A large number had their eyes on Shorth, the temple that had become the symbol of their oppression. They surged forward.

'Block the doors!' ordered Auum, already racing across the piazza. 'Keep them back.'

The TaiGethen flowed after him and Auum ran inside.

'Close the doors. Hold the line outside and talk sense to them. Those mages must be allowed to leave unharmed.'

Auum sprinted through the temple, hearing the doors clang shut behind him, muting the sound of the mob. He raced up the stairs and to the ladders up to the roof. Stein and his mages were waiting there. So was Takaar.

'I wondered where you'd got to,' said Auum.

'One should never miss an opportunity to learn,' he said.

'Well, you'll have to teach yourself anything else you need to know. No man may remain on Calaius.'

Stein walked towards Auum. He held out his hand.

'We have never met but I thank you for your trust in us. A great blow has been struck for freedom on Balaia.'

'I don't care about your motives,' said Auum. 'I only care that man is defeated. My people are free and you are trespassing where you are no longer welcome.'

He did not take Stein's hand, though something on the man's palm caught Auum's attention. Stein held up both his hands to quieten the displeasure of his mages.

'I remind you that we were not expecting any thanks,' he said to them. 'But a word of understanding would not go amiss.'

'Really?' said Auum. 'I understand that humans kept my people as slaves and treated them like animals for a hundred and fifty years. I understand that your magic gives you power but it does not give you courage. I understand that the elves will never again be enslaved by men.'

'But you should also understand that we are linked. The war that is coming in Balaia will touch every corner of our land, and it will reach yours in time. If Ystormun's cadre are the victors, then one day they will grow strong enough to look to your shores, and you will need to defend yourselves.'

'Ystormun is dead,' said Auum.

Stein shook his head. 'No. He is diminished. We do not have the power to kill him. Only his cadre can do that. His soul is with the . . . you call them the Arakhe . . . and he will return. He will not forget, Auum, and he will never forgive. And one day we may call upon the elves to fight with us to keep him and his like from dominion.

'You must answer that call, when it comes, for the good of both elves and men.'

Auum's hand snapped out and he grabbed Stein's wrist, turning it over to reveal his palm. A birthmark stained it, in a shape not unlike a tree.

'You have proved that you can keep your word and for that I grant you respect,' said Auum. 'But until four generations of your kin are grown and one holds this mark again, no man will be welcome here. No man will survive coming here. That is my promise and, unlike you, I will be alive to keep it.'

'So be it,' said Stein. 'We'll take word to the other cities. Without Ystormun, they will fall to you like leaves in autumn.'

'Thank you,' said Auum. 'We will bring an army to Tolt Anoor and to Deneth Barine. Any humans we find will suffer the same fate as those here. Tell them that too.'

Stein gave a command, and in a few moments all his men had shadow wings on their backs.

'I hope that, one day, elf and man will greet each other like brothers,' said Stein.

'As Garan would say,' said Takaar. 'Don't push your luck.'

Stein smiled. 'Goodbye.'

Auum watched him and his mages fly high into the sky and head out towards a ship anchored in the deep water beyond the harbour. He walked to the edge of the roof, feeling the splintered bones and blood of Ystormun beneath his feet.

'That one's for you, Katyett,' he said.

'And for every elf who died by human hand,' said Takaar.

They stood and looked out over Ysundeneth. The hoots and calls of the mob were mingled with songs that rose in ten thousand throats. Across the city fires were burning and elves prayed in every desecrated temple, thanking their gods for their deliverance.

Auum looked directly down. The TaiGethen still stood in front of the doors though the crowd in front of them was beginning to disperse. Ulysan sensed him and looked up. He put his hands together and smiled. As one the TaiGethen began to sing a hymn of remembrance for their fallen.

Auum sighed. Tears for Elyss and his child were in his eyes. Beside him Takaar was staring towards the forest and the clarity was gone from him. He twitched with the desire to leave. Auum didn't blame him.

'Bloody hell, Takaar, but we've got some work to do now,' he said.

Takaar looked at him, and the ghost of a smile played over his lips. 'Four generations isn't very long in human terms.'

'Can you have some Il-Aryn ready by then?'

'I think so.'

'Good,' said Auum. 'Then you'd best get to it.'

Auum jumped from the temple roof to join the TaiGethen in song.

Acknowledgements:

Thank you to Gillian Redfearn for fantastic insights, friendship and support; to Robert Kirby who works so hard on my behalf; to all my friends and fans who have stayed the journey over the past thirteen years and are still hungry for more; and to all at Gollancz who help make every book we publish together better than the last.

And thank you most of all to Simon Spanton. You've been a rock in my life as an author ever since 1999, as well as a truly great friend, and though we aren't working together right now, I'll never forget all you have done for me. I aspire to be a man with as much heart and soul as you.